THE THREAT OF THE HUNT

"A YA *Mad Max*—thrilling and deep, with richly drawn characters and spot-on pacing. [...] Dyer's Untamed series is a must-read for dystopian fans."
T.A. Maclagan, author of *They Call Me Alexandra Gastone*

"Fascinating and intriguing."
A Drop of Ink Reviews

"Dyer is as much a poet as a dystopian scribe."
Marissa Kennerson, author of *The Family*

"Strong writing and well-rounded characters."
Heidi Sinnett, author and librarian

"Dyer provides all the elements you're looking for in an action-packed dystopian adventure."
Kimberly Sabatini, author of *Touching the Surface*

"A kick-butt story with amazing characters and outstanding world building."
Readcommendations

"Highly recommended."
Dr. Jessie Voigts, *WanderingEducators.com*

"Dyer writes with an urgency and a rhythm that compels you to turn the page."
Sue Wyshynski, author of The Butterfly Code series

"Readers who enjoy dystopian novels would enjoy this book."
The Story Sanctuary

"An intriguing saga."
Tracy Clark, author of The Light Key Trilogy & *Mirage*

BOOKS AVAILABLE FROM MADELINE DYER

THE UNTAMED SERIES

Untamed
Fragmented
Divided
Destroyed
The Dangerous Ones: A Dangerous Game
The Dangerous Ones: This Vicious Way
The Dangerous Ones: The Threat of the Hunt

THE SPIRIT OF FIRE SERIES

Spirit of Fire
Blood of the Phoenix

THE ROSEHEART BALLET ACADEMY SERIES

The Rhythm of My Soul
Swans in the Dark
Phantoms Under the Lake

THE CALLY HARPER SERIES

Cally Harper and the Graveside Murder

THE ACES IN LOVE SERIES
(WRITTEN AS ELIN ANNALISE)

In My Dreams
My Heart to Find
It's Always Been You

STANDALONE NOVELS

Girl, Vanishing
Forever is Now (written as Elin Annalise)

STANDALONE NOVELLAS

The Curse of the Winged Wight
Inside the Night
When We Were Young (written as Elin Annalise)

ANTHOLOGIES (EDITED BY MADELINE DYER)

Unbound
Being Ace
Being Aro
These Bodies Ain't Broken

POETRY

Captive: A Poetry Collection on OCD,
Psychosis, and Brain Inflammation

THE DANGEROUS ONES
BOOK THREE

MADELINE DYER

INEJA PRESS

The Threat of the Hunt
Copyright © 2022 Madeline Dyer
All rights reserved.

Madeline Dyer asserts the moral right to be identified as the author of this work.

This second edition published September 2025 by Ineja Press

Edited by Michelle Dunbar
Cover and Interior Design/Formatting by We Got You Covered Book Design

Paperback ISBN: 978-1-912369-07-2
eBook ISBN: 978-1-912369-06-5

The author can be contacted via email at Madeline@MadelineDyer.co.uk
or through her website www.MadelineDyer.co.uk

For Michael

BLOOD POOLS AROUND MY FEET. So much of it, lapping over my toes. It stings as it covers the cuts on my feet.

"Now," Ysabelle shouts from behind me, and I try to turn, try to look behind, but the ropes hold me fast against the trunk. I grunt as the bindings get tighter, dig into my ribs, commanded by the power of the spirits and the Overlord Seer.

"No, please…" I cry, pain wracking through me. My head throbs, and there are dark spots in my vision.

A figure appears in front of me, her arms and legs all jutting angles as she crouches in front of my bound feet. It's Iralda, with her small skull and the devil in her eyes and too many teeth crowded in her mouth. She still wears the red-dyed clothes to mark the celebration of her sixteenth year, clothes she's had on for four days now, even though she stinks.

Iralda has the bowl of blood, and she watches me, almost goadingly. I don't rise to the devil in her. I just wait.

A moment passes, then she splashes the blood over my ankles again. It's too warm, too fresh. I can still hear the screams of the bison they took it from maybe an hour ago. A young female calf, barely four months old. The Overlord Seer said that the creature's age and sex were important, and his word is law here. The hunters didn't even wait until the bison's soul had left her body; they just slashed her neck to get the liquid they needed.

And all because I am, apparently, bad.

It's on my face, too, the bison's blood. The saltiness of it burns my tongue, and I taste it at the back of my throat. It makes me want to cough. But I know the rules of cleansings by now. I've seen enough of them. If I make any movement, they'll see it as a sign of the Beast inside me. The one they say has possessed me. The one they say will hurt them if they do not hurt it first.

Then again, if I don't move, they'll still hurt me. The swaying body of my friend Jaqueline is proof of that. She hangs to my right. All the cleansings I've seen before today have just been done with a knife, but after Jaqueline's first stabbing, she begged for a gunshot—a quick death. The Overlord Seer said that was proof of the Beast fighting back, because the Beast wanted a modern weapon. They hanged her instead, said they needed to make a point to the Beast.

This Untamed group don't use modern weapons. Not like we did at D'Elinous. This Untamed group believe modern weapons and technology are all that is wrong with the world. Technological advancement is what feeds the Beast, just as it marks the Enhanced Ones for what they are: soulless.

Ysabelle said Jaqueline had been possessed from birth—my friend had known her whole life that on the second full moon of her twelfth year, she'd be cleansed. And likely die.

I was twelve when I joined Ysabelle's people, yearning for a new group after the destruction at D'Elinous. Last month, Ysabelle told me she'd seen the Beast in me right away, but she never told me at the time, and I didn't have a clue. Unlike Jaqueline, I'd grown up without that impending doom. And I still wonder why Ysabelle and the Overlord Seer never told me, why Ysabelle waited two years. Jaqueline suggested that me knowing the coming horrors might've bound us together even more, made our Beasts stronger. But that didn't make sense. Jaqueline knew the younger children with Beasts, too. All I can think is my Beast wasn't spotted before, or it's not there at all, whatever *it* is, and the clansmen are just using this as an excuse to get rid of me. For what, I don't know.

No. I grit my teeth. I will not die. I don't have to die. If I survive the cleansing, I get to live. Ysabelle will banish me, but I'll be alive. I won't be welcome at any of the Untamed groups in this region. Not when the Overlord Seer will gouge the mark of the Beast into my skin. But I'll have air in my lungs and a beat in my heart. Which is more than Jaqueline has now.

I have never seen anyone survive a cleansing—but I'm sure the Overlord Seer mentioned a boy who did. He told a story of it maybe a year ago, but last month, after I learned I'd have a cleansing straight after Jaqueline's, I asked him again. Begged for more details as my head pounded. The Overlord Seer refused to speak directly to me though. Screamed about me not being worthy of his conversation.

Iralda unfolds her frame, standing in front of me. I shouldn't want to smirk because I recognize the irritation on her face—even bound to the tree, I'm still taller than she is. I'm taller than everyone here. Iralda's nostrils flare once, twice, as she dips her fingers slowly into the bison's blood. I hear the heaviness of her breaths—she's both proud and nervous, now she's officially her mother's second-in-command.

"I told you that you'd pay." Her voice is low, her words laced with the same accent of Ysabelle, her mother.

I didn't do it. But I bite back the words. No point giving her the satisfaction of hearing me beg. I just stare at her. And I didn't do it anyway—I didn't take her precious doll two weeks ago, something that she's certain I did because she's never liked me. When her doll—a prized possession from her grandmother—went missing, she just assumed it would be down to me, the person newly announced to have a Beast inside them. Ysabelle had agreed with Iralda; "We know what you're like now," Ysabelle had said—but she didn't seem to realize that that didn't fall in line with her earlier insistence that she'd *always* known of my Beast. And if my Beast likes to steal, I'd have been stealing all this time. Not just since my Beast was made public knowledge.

The bison's blood drips from Iralda's fingers as she lifts them to my face. She digs her nails into my skin, hard, as she paints the required circles and lines across my nose and my cheekbones. Her eyes hold the sharp edge of a knife in their glints, and she is happy about this. Two years separate us—and soon she thinks worlds will too.

But I'm not leaving this world, or my body, or anything that's beating and alive.

"We ask the Mighty Divine Ones, the ancient Gods and Goddesses, to help us in this cleansing." Ysabelle's voice—rich, dark, velvety—booms from behind me, mingling with the tinkling of her Amber-bead necklace. The sounds cling to me like a second lot of binding. "For we cannot have contaminated people among our village. We are protectors and worshippers of the Seventh One, and we will not introduce evil."

I can't see Ysabelle, but that doesn't make her presence any smaller. She's always had that effect—unlike Iralda, whose presence seems to diminish the moment she's out of sight, the visual absence of Ysabelle only makes her more foreboding. Predators need to be kept within sight.

"Kassandra Kachler has the Evil Eye of the Great Beast inside her, and her soul is calling to those also touched by the Beast, and we will not let such evilness succeed."

I want to claw Ysabelle's words off my skin because

her speech is no longer an invisible rope tying me to doom—each word is an insect with too many feet. They're crawling all over me, greedy, trying to devour me.

Iralda bows in front of me, makes the signs of the Cleansing Gods and Goddesses, and retreats to the right quickly, to where the huts are. A cold wind wraps around me. The ropes binding my ankles seem to get hotter. No, it's the blood. The Overlord Seer infused it with his magic as he took it from the calf, and I look around for him now.

There. I see him, standing by the huts. A lone figure. Pasty white face, red hair—just like Ysabelle's and Iralda's. All their family have that hair color. They say it proves their power, proves they're supposed to be the ones in charge.

More pain closes in on me. I become aware of a humming in the air. I clench my fingers into fists—it is the only movement I can make that doesn't cause me more suffering.

My vision blurs. The work of evil spirits. I look around for them but cannot see them. But I know the Overlord Seer keeps them in carved wooden boxes ready for the cleansings. Because Ysabelle's group always has cleansings. Too many people in this area are tainted by the Beast, and the Beast needs containing. That's what she says, else the Beast will spread beyond our section and into the section where the Savior Seer is. We mustn't let the Beast contaminate the one Seer who can save us all in the War of Humanity. And it's Ysabelle's duty, as leader, to protect us all.

The humming turns to chants. My vision blurs again, a watercolor painting just like what Jaqueline used to paint, and then the other clansmen are coming out of their huts, flocking around the Overlord Seer.

Sweat drips down my forehead, and I search them for someone who might help me. But it's a futile thought. A desperate one. Selma—the only other one who was on my side, my friend, and a friend to Jaqueline, too—was instructed to go hunting this morning. No one here will help.

"And now we are ready." Ysabelle's voice croaks as she speaks.

About time, I want to mutter.

Finally, Ysabelle slinks in front of me, revealing herself. She wears no mask, and her eyes are burning amber, brighter somehow than her hair, and she makes the signs of the Gods and Goddesses, just as Iralda did. She's even shorter than Iralda.

"This knife will get the evil out of you," Ysabelle says, looking up at me. She holds up a hunting knife. Her eyes burn, make her face look even more lined, like she's older than her sixty years. "The Beast is still glowing inside you."

My aunt, Caia-Lu Kachler—the most powerful Seer I know—always said you can tell a lot by someone's eyes. Not just if they're Untamed or Enhanced, but you can tell their intentions. Whether they're honest or not. If they're dangerous. A month ago, Ysabelle said she could see the Beast inside my eyes, but whenever I've looked since then, I just see my brown eyes.

There's no Beast.

But—

I grit my teeth. There's *no* Beast.

"Yes, it's here all right," Ysabelle says, touching the tip of the knife to my chest.

"There's *no* Beast in me."

"But there is, Kassandra. The evil Beast is sitting right here."

My heart pounds. And even though I know what's coming—I saw them torture and hang Jaqueline—I want to scream that my name isn't Kassandra. I go by Kacey. Everyone calls me Kacey. *Kassandra* shouldn't be coming from these people's mouths. They've never called me it before, and I don't know why a spirit would tell them of it.

But I don't say anything, because I know if I do, I'll start fighting. Earlier, Selma told me and Jaqueline not to fight. "If you fight, it's the parasite fighting. You have to remain still in the cleansing," she said.

If I'm going to die either way—because there's no way a person can survive being stabbed that many times, or hanged—then I'm putting up a fight. I will not go down easily. And, really, isn't this what they'd expect from someone who has the Beast?

I strain against the bindings around my body, screaming at Ysabelle. My saliva lands on her face, and she recoils. But it's only ignited more of the fire in her eyes. I hate her eyes—Jaqueline once said they were too Untamed, too much was visible. You look at Ysabelle and you know exactly how much she hates you.

I fight my bindings.

Ysabelle stabs me.

Pain, my side. Raw, pulsing. I scream, and it doesn't sound like me screaming—but it is. My head's splintering, and I can't see and—

More pain. Hot, white flashes in front of my eyes. Iralda's shouting, and so is the Overlord Seer.

"Get it out of her!" someone yells.

Pain in my leg. I scream again.

There's no Beast. There's no Beast. There's no Beast.

Another slash of the blade.

My blood, mingling with the bison's and—

"Don't look down!" Ysabelle shrieks, necklace clanging, tinkling, making so much noise. "The Beast is strong in you, Kassandra. I think we need another knife."

No sooner has she said the words, when a clansman's in front of me. It's Dev, the hunter who taught me how to refine my spear-throwing. He holds a bigger knife.

"Her throat," Ysabelle says. "The Beast has moved to her throat!"

Dev lifts the blade to my neck. His eyes are glowing purple—the Overlord Seer must be controlling him.

Ysabelle's knife wriggles in my side. And I feel it—the darkness. It's stirring.

Something is stirring inside me. Fury and fear.

"Stop! I'm not possessed!"

There's no Beast. There's no Beast. There's no Beast.

"Stop, please!" With every word, I feel the other knife tickling my throat. Dev's not applying any pressure yet, waiting for Ysabelle's command.

"Aw, the Beast is begging," Ysabelle says, and behind her, I see the moon, a hazy halo around her flaming hair. "The Beast thinks it can outwit us and—"

And something moves inside me. Sharp pain and—

It's in my chest, rising into my throat.

No—what the hell?

What the—

My throat burns as *it* erupts from me. A wave of power and light and sound—and Iralda shrieks and Ysabelle shouts and the Overlord Seer races toward me. The Beast gets them. Fries them. The stench of rotting flesh fills the air as they fall, as more power floods from me. More and more—until it's all out.

All the darkness, the badness, the Beast. I slump forward as far as the bindings will let me.

"There is a Beast," I whisper, as I see the bodies of the clansmen. All of them. "I am the Beast."

And then my eyes are too heavy, and the pool of red at my feet is too big, and somewhere there's a baby crying, but I see no more.

THE TRUCK RUMBLES OVER UNEVEN ground, and for what has to be the hundredth time, my head crashes against the inside wall. Smack.

"Look at her—she can't even stay awake. I don't understand why my mother likes her so much." Celena doesn't even try and hide the disdain in her voice.

I yawn, rub my shoulder, and pretend I can breathe without being choked by Celena's ridiculous perfume. It's way too strong; she may as well have bathed in it. "Maybe I can't stay awake because I'm the only one who actually did any work." I give her my best glare. "And sleeping when we know we can is smart." Because now is a time we can rest—as much as we ever can. And rest is what we need. Especially when tomorrow is the big day.

"Oh, for the love of the Gods." Celena rolls her eyes then adjusts the sling that her left arm is in. She sprained it two weeks ago, and it should be better now, but she insists it isn't. Though it *was* interesting that she was dancing and flinging that arm about at the Moon Worship with apparently no problem. "Do you ever not sound like a walking-talking-instruction-guide?"

"Better to know how to lead than pretend." My words are dry.

Between us in the back of the cab, Shweta flashes a nervous smile in my direction. She's quiet, beautiful, and usually has a calming influence. She doesn't speak to either of us, doesn't side with one or the other. She's our group's Seer, and she's only just started accompanying us on raids again. For the last four months, grief has blocked her powers—grief for her girlfriend Hana who was killed. Grief that ripped her apart. I didn't realize at first that her grief was so intense, intense in a way that she couldn't cope with. I've never really grieved for anyone… not someone close to me, because I don't remember my parents, and then when the D'Elinous ambush took everyone, I didn't really see any deaths. I was concentrating on escaping, on surviving. I had no time to explore it, no time to even remember Jaqueline or Selma. I just pushed all the clansmen out of my mind.

But Shweta had time. Time when she couldn't do anything. Time when she said she was turning inside out as she tried to use her Seer powers to find who Hana had been reincarnated as, until her powers wouldn't work anymore. Shweta became obsessive for a while, insisting that we had to travel around. She had to find Hana, again. She had to feel her soul once more.

She ran away twice, taking nothing with her. No food, no water, no weapons. We sent search parties after her, finding her both times, collapsed from dehydration, feeble, barely stirring in the earth, like she'd tried to bury herself but had given up.

Some people started to say she was crazy, recounting how they'd seen her talking to thin air, convinced Hana was still there. That she was collecting two meals at a time instead of one, to make sure Hana had food.

Maggot and Evor were very worried about her. Evor tried to consult with the Gods and Goddesses. He talked with Shweta. And slowly, slowly, she began to get better, act more like we'd expect, like she used to, after those intense weeks. Now, she's almost back to normal—or, rather her new normal where she's quieter, subdued, more contemplative. Her powers are emerging again too now—and just in time. We're going to need her tomorrow.

Tomorrow.

My heart pounds a little faster, adrenaline filling me. I'm excited by the plan, of course I am, but that doesn't mean I'm not apprehensive. And it's not just the gravity of the situation, of what we're planning to do. It's more than that—it's the effect it'll have on me. What it will unleash inside me again. Because I've kept the Beast contained since that day with the clansmen. And I vowed to the Gods and Goddesses never to let it out again. Never to kill.

And we're going to have to kill, if this plan is going to work.

But, before I can think more about the plan—and my worries—Celena launches a verbal attack on me, one all about how she's got *leader blood* and I'm *just a stray*. It's the usual spiel.

"Cut it out, you two," Evor snaps from the front. He's driving—always the designated driver as he's got ridiculously good skills. Kazem is in the front with him, riding shotgun, but only because he gets travelsick if he sits in the back. He's also not that great at driving, and it's something I tease him about constantly.

"Oh, Evor, I'm sorry," Celena says, and she leans forward and, with her good arm, pats him on the shoulder. He squirms and leans away a little, but Celena doesn't let that deter her. She stretches forward even more, the back of her shirt riding up, exposing her lower back—and what's sticking out of the back pocket of her jeans.

A pregnancy test.

Wow.

Shweta sees it, too, if her sharp inhale is anything to go by.

"What?" Celena turns to her.

Shweta shrinks back into the seat. Her hands are clenched. Shweta is a bit scared of Celena—and it's no surprise, given that Celena's the type of person who thinks she can throw her weight about, due to the status she was born with, as the daughter of Maggot, our leader. But because Shweta's a Seer, her status is actually higher than Celena's, higher than all of ours because a Seer is always top dog, that's what Maggot says. But Shweta's not the type of person to enforce that, and Celena's definitely the type of person to challenge everyone else's status constantly.

"Pregnancy," I say, leaning forward. Celena's gaze crosses onto me, and Shweta sinks back, like she's trying to melt into the sticky leather seat. I point at Celena's pregnancy test. "Really? That's what you went to the pharmacy for?"

"Where else would I have got it?" Her tone has a goading edge to it.

Kazem's looking around now from the front. His dark eyes are wide, peeking out from under his shock of hair. The flash of blue hair-dye that he added for a joke a couple of months ago has faded now, makes his black bangs look slightly iridescent. Now, I'm sure he's thinking what I am—because Kazem and I are in tune, in sync, whatever you want to call it. And Celena is stupid. And with what we're planning, too. That was the rule for everyone who moved here from the Muskoxen group—no children. Anyone who's under Maggot's leadership and can get pregnant cannot be having sex. Not when we all volunteered for this, put ourselves forward for this job. We need runners, fighters, and soldiers here. Not mothers.

Just last year, two women became pregnant and made the journey back to the Muskoxen group. Maggot didn't want us to rely on them when they wouldn't be here during *the moment*. Which is set to be tomorrow. And now Celena's choosing this day to reveal it—because if she really wanted it to be a secret, she'd not have stashed that test in her pocket like that.

Celena's eyes narrow on me. "I'm not pregnant."

"Just as well with the amount you drank yesterday at the Moon Worship," Evor mutters.

I want to laugh, but there was is something about the tone in which Celena spoke with—hurt—that is twisting around me, and I remember the miscarriages she had when we lived at the Muskoxen site. How her marriage fell apart due to the losses. How she agreed to come with Maggot when some of us relocated, as *the Goddess of Fertility clearly isn't blessing me and maybe me being a mother isn't meant to be*. But before I can voice anything that might be sympathetic—even though by definition she's broken our no-sex rule—she pulls the test-stick out of her pocket and throws it at me. It lands on my lap, and I stare at it, my hands frozen in mid-air.

"Ewww, that's been in your urine. And now it's touching me." I indicate my jean-clad thighs. "Like, disgusting." And with those last two words, I mimic Celena's own high-pitched voice.

Kazem's lips quirk into a smile.

Celena glares at me.

"Kindly take back your property," I say.

"If you call me by my chosen name, I will."

I laugh. Not even a urine-dipped test-stick is going to have me calling her *Flesh*—she wants to sound edgy, with a name akin to Maggot's—so I flick the stick toward her with one finger. The jump the test does is short though, and it lands on Shweta's lap. Shweta doesn't move, just stares at it, her eyes all glassy. Bags hang under her eyes, making her tawny skin look sallow. It's the same look she always gets after she's used her powers. She used them earlier—mainly, her power to compel—as we'd got intel that New Bere, a town three-hours away, was having a refurb done on a weapons store. It was too good an opportunity to miss, and what we did doesn't even count as stealing *weapons*. The Enhanced call it *sports gear*. Much better.

Of course, Shweta's powers are why she's vital

tomorrow, and it makes me feel better knowing she'll be with us. Like, maybe, there'll be no need for me personally to cause any bloodshed, with her powers backing us up.

But I know that's wishful thinking. Maggot's put Shweta in a different team. We're not unleashing our Seer on the Enhanced until our runners have secured the perimeter of the town. Until it's safe for her. We can't have our Seer murdered—or converted—by them. That means I'm most likely going to have to kill—and control the Beast.

"I said cut it out," Evor mutters. "I know you're nervous about tomorrow—all of you—but don't wind each other up."

Twenty minutes later, Evor parks the truck as close to our base as we can, which isn't that close, and we trek through the grassy lands. It's almost dark now, low light levels kissing us, and we keep radio contact with Maggot and the rest of the group as we lug back our new weapons. I keep an eye on Shweta. She didn't have to keep the compulsion power going for long, but it takes a lot out of her. It's also the reason why we will use her in a time-limited fashion tomorrow, to persuade all the Enhanced in one go. Shweta's power is limited by time rather than by numbers. Compelling one person uses the same amount of energy as a hundred. Tomorrow, the thousands of Enhanced we're up against won't be the problem. Keeping them immobilized for an hour before her role *will* be.

Evor and Shweta walk at the front of our group. Kazem and I are next, and Celena's trailing behind. I keep my eye on her. Last time she walked behind me and I wasn't paying her enough attention, she kicked me in the back of my left knee. Sure, that was right after Maggot made me her second and publicly humiliated Celena, but I learnt my lesson then.

And a leopard never changes their spots.

"Who do you think she's sleeping with?" I ask Kazem. The usual balled-up carrier bags he always has on him are rustling from his pockets. I used to hate that sound, but now I'm used to it. It's part of Kazem, and the bags are always handy if we're out raiding or gathering.

He shrugs. "Someone who's confident they won't get found out." His answer is kind of blunt, just as it always is when I bring up sex in any way. I don't mind talking about it, but he does. "Anyway, won't matter after tomorrow."

After tomorrow. The time that we've all dreamt about. The time that many of us have been uncertain would ever come. But it's going to. We've gone over this plan so many times, and we know exactly what we're doing. We've got solutions planned and rehearsed for all possible outcomes. And then we'll be…free. We'll have buildings and safety and food. We'll be where we're supposed to be.

We'll be setting the example, proving that the impossible can be done.

Just as we're almost at the entranceway, Celena overtakes us all, spins around, and holds her good hand up in a stop-signal. "Don't say a word about that test to anyone." Her voice is low, and she glances at each of us in turn. Shweta and Evor first, because she knows they won't be the issue here. Neither's Kazem really. It's me.

She doesn't trust me, and rightly so. If she's broken the rules, then Maggot should know. We have rules for a reason. Knowing she's broken them means I can keep an eye on her, even if I don't tell Maggot—but I need to know who the other participant is.

"Sure, if you tell me who's been doing it with you," I say.

Her eyes narrow. "What is your weird obsession with sex?"

I snort-laugh. "My weird obsession? I haven't got one." But I notice how Kazem's eyes get all shifty and he looks toward me quickly. I don't look at him, though I feel his burning gaze on my face. If I look, it makes it more obvious. Not that there is anything to be made obvious. Not in the way that anyone here would find interesting. We've never broken the rules. We have no intention of it.

"Yeah," Celena says. "You're always prying, always trying to catch people out."

I'm not. It's just that as second-in-command, I have to uphold Maggot's rules. And…and there's something more too. I'm kind of fascinated by the idea of sex, because I've never done it or felt like I *want* to. It's this thing that I just don't understand, and I'm curious, I guess.

Kazem's gaze is still burning a hole in me. I know what he's thinking: how I should just be quiet, not talk about sex at all. I turn my head farther away from him. "I won't report you," I tell Celena. "Or ask any more questions about who the other person is. If you do something for me."

Her eyes narrow, and her brows furrow. "What?"

I beckon her closer and then step away from Kazem. Evor and Shweta exchange looks then Evor says we should all keep walking again. So, we do, but I make Celena hang back a bit, giving her a look.

"What?" she asks again.

"Tell Maggot that you want Clive on your team tomorrow."

Celena laughs abruptly, then stops when she apparently realizes I'm serious. Another waft of her perfume drifts over to me. "Really? You don't want Clive?"

"No," I say.

It's not so much Clive himself, but what he makes me remember. He's ten years old, and he's the youngest of the Griffin children here. The others are older teenagers, some just a few years younger than me, but Clive's different. He reminds me of the clansmen children I massacred. I've always found it difficult around children—and that's part of the reason why, when we were part of the Muskoxen group, I jumped at the chance to work with Maggot in what I thought would be an adult-only group. Then I discovered that the Griffin children were all coming with their parents. Like Evor, the Griffin couple are doctors, and Kate and Markus insisted that their five children came with them. The children are in-training. And Maggot agreed in the end. Although Evor's Maggot's half-brother and a perfectly good doctor, she didn't want just one doctor. She wanted three. You never know when one of them could be killed.

"Why?" Celena raises her left eyebrow. She has a small scar across it, where her hair doesn't grow. Maggot told her it's less noticeable than it actually is. She got the scar when she walked into a thorny tree branch, a few years ago. "What's wrong with Clive?"

"Nothing," I say.

"There must be something."

"There must be someone you've been sleeping with."

She smirks a little then wipes sweat from her forehead. "Fine."

I flash a smile at her. All this time, I'd been stealing myself, telling myself I'd just have to work with Clive tomorrow and hope that it's not one of the times my flashbacks arise, but this solves it perfectly.

Celena nods, and I nod. Then we join up again with Kazem, Evor, and Shweta. Kazem brushes his hand against mine, and I smile up at him.

"What was that about?" he asks.

I shake my head. "Nothing. All's good."

His sharp look tells me he doesn't quite believe that, but then the entrance to our base—a limestone mouth peeking out from the grassland—is in sight. We inhabit the caves and tunnels that extend down and across, below New Zeralzi, an Enhanced town, and a couple of figures are milling about in the tunnel entrance. Our guards, as we call them.

"You're just in time for practice," Tammy says, greeting us. She's a couple years older than me and an excellent fighter. "Maggot wants another session for the free-running teams. That includes you, Celena. Without your sling."

Celena groans. "I'm tired!"

"Bet you wish you got some sleep on the journey back now," I say.

She gives me the finger.

I ignore her. "I'll get my running shoes on."

"Good." Tammy nods. "Maggot's meeting all the runners out here in fifteen."

I GRUNT, TUCK MY HEAD in as I roll through the night air, then land on the balls of my feet. My momentum pushes me forward, and I cartwheel twice, get to the other side of the courtyard. I look up. Wait. My breaths are short, calculated, careful. The buildings rise around me, and I listen, hear the thrum of electricity. And his footsteps.

Good. He's coming.

A grin stretches across my face, and I turn, sprint across the courtyard. The building ahead is red brick, with scaffolding starting from the second story. I hurtle forward, kicking off from the concrete slabs, and use the momentum to propel myself upward. One step. Two. Three. I stretch up, grab the metal bar above. *Yes*.

Adrenaline pounds through me. I always love running up walls. I swing myself upward and tuck my head in as I launch myself through a gap in the scaffolding. My knees land on the wooden board of the scaffolding's floor, and I roll to the side, dissipating some of the energy, before jumping back up. Scaffolding makes everything so much easier. Maggot graded this building as a level five before the

Enhanced decided it needed repairing. The scaffolding makes it an easy level two. I roll my eyes. I almost want it to be harder. More challenging. I have this constant need to prove myself. Maggot says that's my flaw. But I think it's good to be ambitious. And Bhavesh agrees. His lessons are all about that.

Never get comfortable with your abilities, that's when you mess up. Rule number one of free-running.

A swift glance down shows me Kazem is on the other side of the courtyard. His mirror eyes flash and send a direct, burning beam into my gaze as he sees me. He runs for me. Silent, of course. We're always silent.

Go!

I have a ten-second lead on him, but Kazem's faster at climbing than me. I know that.

I climb as quickly as I can, using the scaffolding. My heart pounds. Got to get to the top. If I can get to the top before Kazem's hand lands on my shoulder, I'm good.

My lungs burn as I climb and climb. Energy floods through me, pounds deliciously through my body. The electricity hums louder up here—it always does— and I pull myself up, past a window. A lone green light winks from somewhere inside that room—but it's okay, no Enhanced will be in there now. The green light just shows their alarms are set. And then the window's gone, far below me, and I'm here. The roof. Four stories up. I smile as I race forward, using my arms to adjust my center of gravity according to the angle of the roof. My shoes barely make a sound on the gray slate tiles.

Run quick and light on the balls of your feet.

Kazem is behind me, his steps soft. I picture his mirror eyes flashing in the darkness, and it makes me smile. Because every time I see him like this, he's danger and familiarity, and it sends a new kind of warmth through my body.

No. Can't get distracted.

I've got to jump now. I smile as the cold, night air wraps around me, lifts the few tendrils of hair that have escaped my ponytail. They weave around my face like moths. No, like snakes. Ghostly snakes.

Kazem may be faster at climbing, but I'm better at jumping.

I glance back, grinning at him. He's ten feet away. Then I inhale and run, plowing toward the end of the roof. The night expels me as I jump. I soar through the air, downward and across, tuck my head in, my arms circling my knees.

Tuck tighter. I can hear Bhavesh's voice. One of my early lessons.

I tuck tighter—I've got a habit of not tucking my legs enough as I roll through the air and—

Dust flies up as I land, and energy pounds through my shoulder. I roll over and over, disbanding the energy.

And I feel *alive*. So alive as I stand, grinning.

I turn and look up. Kazem's on the edge of the roof. There's nothing like being chased through an Enhanced Ones' town to make you feel alive.

I smile, and he gives me a thumbs up. Passed the test. Of course I did.

"Watch out!"

The shout comes from my right. Maggot's sharp tone. I flick my head, see our leader. She's watching Clive—her directive was issued at him, not me. Because he's about to be grabbed by a mirror man.

Clive yelps and twists, tries to jump, but of course the mirror man grabs him. It's too dark for me to tell which of the men it is. Winston, Bhavesh, and SJ all have similar builds, and we're all dressed in the same loose, dark clothes. Kazem only stands out more in these conditions because he's so tall.

Clive curses, earning a reprimand from Maggot and whichever man is holding onto him. I think it's probably Winston, though I didn't catch the exact tone.

Kazem jumps from the building—his body tucks in mid-air, a bullet plowing to the ground. He lands silently. His dent in the dust isn't as far out as mine. I'm better at leaping than him, and I often remind him of this. Usually, when we're play-arguing.

"Good job," Kazem says, and I stare up into his mirrors. See myself reflected in him.

My face is sharp angles, and I immediately look at my eyes in his—as if I need to prove to myself that I'm still Untamed, that we're winning. It's too dark to see the details of my eyes—a shame, I like my eyes—but I can see they're not mirrors. And that's enough for now.

Kazem wraps his arms around me, and I lean into him. My head tucks neatly under his chin, and I feel his heartbeat.

"Did well," he says, smiling.

I look up at him, want to kiss him. But that can wait. I don't like kissing him when he's got his mirrors in anyway.

He squeezes me once, then we pull apart.

We're all congregating here now. All seventeen free-runners that our group has—half of us still posing as mirror men—plus our guards and leader. Maggot tucks her pistol into her belt as she walks over to me. Behind her are the Griffin siblings, two of them with mirrors in. We've just completed a relatively basic practice, something that wouldn't risk great injury. We're all free-running tomorrow, divided into many teams.

Everyone's breathing hard, and Maggot says something to one of our guards, before he nods and walks to the edge of our group. He'll be watching for the enemy. The *real* enemy.

"I think we'll be all right," Maggot says. She has a scar below her left eye, and it looks more ragged, the skin puckering. "On the 'ole." Her gaze crosses to Clive, the youngest of the Griffin siblings. He looks both annoyed and like he's going to cry.

But Maggot knows what she's doing. She's the best leader, ever. Her name isn't really Maggot—it's Margot—but I've only ever known her as Maggot. She said the word was used as an insult when Enhanced Ones caught her thirty years ago. They underestimated her, and she kicked their butts. She got away before they converted her. She was twenty-four years old, and she killed twelve Enhanced Ones. Since then, she's used the name *Maggot* as a badge of honor. I think she likes the squeamish factor it gives her, how it makes the little children at the Muskoxen group more scared of her on the occasions when we go back for the Night Celebrations, every six months. It keeps her revered.

And we're going to win this war, because of her. I just know it. I mean, sure there's an augury about someone else who will save us, an augury that says, *The Seventh One, born of Light, holds the strongest Seer powers. Her side will win the War of Humanity. The rest will be destroyed, and Death will call the Seventh One back to him at the end of the war.* It's an augury that has apparently been delivered to some Seers—but not all. No one at D'Elinous spoke of her, but so many of the Untamed groups, Maggot's and the clansmen included, believe in this augury, though I've never had any proof that this Seventh Seer is real. What I do know is the Untamed have Maggot. She's the leader we need. She's real.

"I won't be far from you, tomorrow," the mirror man who caught Clive says. Now we're closer, I can see it is Winston. Clive's the youngest of the Griffin family, and he's the only one who's not pale like the rest of them. Instead, he's got Winston's dark skin and the two look *very* similar. And Winston's always been good friends with Kate, the mother of the Griffin children. No guessing who Clive's biological dad is, even if no one ever outright acknowledges it.

Winston gives Clive a squeeze, before grabbing his bag from one of the guards. He opens the pouch on the front, then removes one of his mirror eyes.

"Not out 'ere." Maggot shakes her head at him. "We've still got to get back. An' we don't want to lose 'em."

"Don't want to lose my sight either," Winston says, pulling out the container for the lenses. He's still got one mirror eye. "Especially not ahead of tomorrow."

"The lenses *are* irritating." Kazem grunts, rolling his shoulder.

I've only worn them a couple times. When we practice our free-running and parkour, we usually do it as Untamed—under the cover of darkness, of course. We're not stupid. And we've got systems in place to alert us if the Enhanced come over here. But we choose to do it in the regions of New Zeralzi that they lock up at night. Their labs. The council buildings. The locker rooms near the sports fields.

When we began putting this plan in place, Maggot decided we'd best get used to the feeling of being chased by the Enhanced—chances are it's going to happen on the day. Tammy got hold of the mirror lenses.

"Fall back," Maggot says. She starts to turn. She's wearing a Cami top that reveals the upper part of the tattoo that fills her back—it's a tiger. A crude, badly drawn one, its face distorted and lopsided. But Maggot loves it. "We'll discuss final arrangements inside."

The entrance to the tunnels isn't far. Our guards are wearing the mirror lenses too, and they station themselves around us, in case the real Enhanced come out. Then they can pretend they're Enhanced and have caught us. At least long enough to get us all out of there. Most of us aren't afraid of shooting.

We walk for ten minutes across the flat, grassy plain, climbing up a few steps and moving several loose limestone blocks in the wall so we can climb through the barrier that marks the edge of the city. We replace the blocks after the last of us is through, then keep going through the steppe until we reach the entrance to our underground network: giant layers of limestone rise from the rocky grassy ground at a slight angle, giving birth to the narrow entrance of a cave. Tammy's still on guard, sitting cross-legged by the entrance, in the grasses and wild hollyhock, but now she's been joined by her older brother, Mal. They've got the whistles. If any Enhanced Ones come along and find the entrance, Tammy and Mal can disband them with the guns or alert us with a shrill sound if the former option isn't possible or doesn't work.

Not that the Enhanced come out here much. This is the spirits' territory. It's not just the Turnings that bring them out, but the spirits lurk about a fair amount of time anyway. Most of the spirits leave us alone though, so long as we avoid looking at them and go underground as soon as they arrive. But the Enhanced Ones hate the spirits. That's why they generally don't build many towns out here, and why they constructed high walls around this one. Huh. As if a thirty-foot wall and domed roof can keep the spirits out. They could smash through that in seconds if they wanted to.

Tammy and Mal nod at us.

We slither on our bellies through the entranceway to our network, then descend into the earth, into a larger space that we can stand in. Kazem's just behind me. These tunnels have been our home for the last two years, ever since we split from the Muskoxen group. Underground, there's a whole network of the tunnels, and they spread right under the Enhanced Ones' buildings. There is one small exit from our tunnels that leads into the town directly, but we keep that one blocked up; from the town's side, it just looks like another rocky outcrop, of which there are a lot in New Zeralzi.

We walk to our main chamber—the largest 'room' in the network. The rest of our group is waiting here.

"We're all set then," Maggot says, sitting on the edge of the desk at the side of the room. She swings her thighs. She's the biggest woman here—muscularly built and tall—and her physique outranks several of the men, too.

When we first moved in here, we didn't have any furniture. Hard to carry stuff like that out of New Zeralzi without the Enhanced noticing, even harder to get it through the perimeter wall. But the Muskoxen group sent us some. Assembling that desk though, in the meagre lighting in here, wasn't easy. Involved a lot of swearing on Maggot's part.

"Tomorrow it is," she continues. "We're goin' with the first plan, 'kay? So, the runners will go out first, lead all the Enhanced toward the center. That's where our guards will be. We'll contain 'em in the rink. Patrol teams will round up anyone else. We've got their guns. They're not goin' to fight us."

Because violence is bad.

"But what if the reports from the Muskoxen are true?" Rohan asks. He's one of the oldest men in our tunnel-dwelling group. When we split from the Muskoxen group and came here with the intention of eventually taking New Zeralzi for ourselves, Maggot and the council decided we could only take people who could fight. They wanted the upper age limit to be sixty. Rohan's sixty-three now. But he's the best shot out of everyone. We'd have been stupid to leave him behind. He's going to be important tomorrow.

"The reports can't be true," Maggot says. "The Enhanced despise violence."

Kazem looks across at me, but I don't say anything. We've all heard the rumors, that some of the Enhanced are resorting to violence, that their weapons aren't just for sport, but that they are going against their core beliefs—the ones they convert us in the name of. We heard the new preference for violence originated in New Kimearo, a town in Section Three, under the orders of Raleigh, an Enhanced man who is apparently growing in popularity there. The Muskoxen group hacked into some of the communication channels— that's where we get our info from. Traci and the others at the Muskoxen settlement give us regular updates on the Enhanced Ones' plans in the war, across our Untamed channel.

And New Kimearo is where most of the violent Enhanced are. This inclination toward violence may be spreading, according to what we've heard, but we're nowhere near New Kimearo. We're in the middle of Section Five, and New Kimearo is in Section Three, south-west of our section. If this Raleigh guy is using violence and it *has* become the norm in Section Three, it hasn't reached Section Five yet. We're safe until the Enhanced here start backing that plan.

Maggot goes through a few other details about tomorrow's plan, but it's not new stuff. We've been going over this for months.

"Get some rest," she says finally, "because we're about to have the biggest ol' day of our lives. We'll meet here in the mornin' for the final prep."

THREE

WITH MAGGOT'S DISMISSAL, WE HEAD back to our rooms. But we're smiling. All of us, not just the free-running crew. We've got more guards—those with good aims—and a communications team. Our engineers made the radios for us and rigged up a sound system across the city. Bhavesh and the older Griffin siblings got the speakers in place at various points around New Zeralzi last week. We'll be using them tomorrow, ordering all the Enhanced Ones to the rink who haven't already been lured out with our parkour display.

I smile. I know I shouldn't think of it as a display. It could be life and death—well, death in the sense of conversion. And conversion is worse than death.

For hundreds of years, the Enhanced Ones have been hunting us down, converting us into them. They believe all emotions need to be controlled so that they can only feel positive things, because negative emotions are the source of all things bad in the world. They take augmenters, the highly addictive chemicals that were created to only allow people to feel good things. Augmenters also give you mirror eyes. Evor says he heard an Enhanced man spout off a load of crap about the eyes being the doorway to the soul or something and how that needs to be guarded, so they made their augmenters simultaneously create mirrors. But at least that means it's easy to see who is Untamed. Who is resisting. Who is still *wild* and *bad* and *evil*.

Who still has their humanity.

Kazem and I reach our sleeping place. Most of the 'bedrooms' are on one side of our underground network, where several large spaces have been divided by an amalgamation of wooden planks, tree branches, grass-woven mats, the occasional bit of discarded building materials salvaged from New Zeralzi, and leathery drapes made from Saiga antelope hides. Our room is at the edge of one of the divided cavernous spaces, and dry-stone walling holds back the surrounding earth. Most of the network consists of manmade tunnels leading from the cave. Shweta reckons the network is from *before*. Before the first augmenters were created and before the first Untamed turned themselves into the Enhanced. Before the War of Humanity.

When we first found these tunnels, guided by a Seer from the Muskoxen group who'd had a prophetic dream, they were full of cobwebs and rodents. There were bones of steppe marmots, gerbils, and the skull of what looked like a corsac fox. Maggot thought she could smell a bear in there, even though brown bears are rare in this part of the steppe lands, but sure enough, there were signs of recent bear habitation. We were skeptical about going inside at first, but no bears came. Every tunnel smelled damp and cold, and it took a while to make it all habitable.

"I can't believe we're doing this tomorrow," I say, as Kazem and I get changed.

"I know," he says. "Mad, isn't it?"

I nod, and we climb under the covers together. His arms are sturdy, strong around me, and we hold each other close in a way the others don't understand. They think we only don't have sex because of the rules here, but neither of us feels that way—not to anyone—but we're still together. We don't need sex to make a relationship. We're happy as we are.

Of course, the others here are looking forward to being situated in a town so they can start sleeping with each other. They've made comments to me and Kazem about how we can *finally make our relationship proper.* They say we've *only half been living.*

I didn't like the way those words made me feel. It has worried me a little, I must admit, the thought of being in New Zeralzi properly. Because what I feel for Kazem may even be love, and here, the two of us are certain about each other, and we're close. But out there, things could be different. What if he decides he wants to do more than just hold and kiss me? What if it *is* the rules that are keeping us 'sexless' here and he doesn't actually feel the same way as me? I mean, would I try out sex even though I've never felt sexual attraction? I'm curious, sure, but my curiosity is more about the *idea* of sex. When I hear other women gossiping about it, I want to listen and find out more. But as soon as *I'm* part of the equation, I just don't want to do anything.

Kazem has assured me that out there, he'll still feel the same as he does in here—he says we're soulmates because we both feel the same way and the Gods and Goddesses must've guided us together. He's even said he's glad for the no-sex rule here because it means he doesn't stand out. But even if he doesn't actually *want* to do it, what if he feels the need to do it to fit in when we're out there, when these tight restrictions have been smashed to pieces?

I guess I'm just worried about things changing. About us being different, about losing him.

Kazem tightens his grip on me, and I rest my head against his chest, listen to his heart. Our legs entwine, and I breathe deeply, easily, happily.

"I can't wait for a shower tomorrow," he says. "In one of their powerful jet showers or whatever they are.

Gods, it will be like cleansing my whole soul in that."

Cleansing. I shudder as I think of the stabbing that revealed the Beast. That was the first time he ever came out, took control. Ysabelle should've been more careful really—if you suspect there's a dangerous animal, you don't stab it for fun. You stab to kill.

That was the first and only time I unleashed the power inside me—the Beast. The dark thing in me. And it's still here now. I assumed that everyone would see it—that its eruption had marked me—but after the clansmen were all dead, apart from one baby who somehow survived, and the Beast returned to my core, and I awoke to find myself bleeding but somehow free of the bindings, I traveled. On my third day, I found the body of my friend Selma. Apparently, my Beast had reached her, too. She was lying broken on the woodland floor, her arms at unnatural angles. An animal had ripped into her leg, pulling chunks of flesh and muscle away, and flies were buzzing round her.

But finding Selma's body wasn't the worst of it. I left the baby behind, Dev's daughter—left her there to die. The Beast may have killed the clan, but by leaving, I killed the baby, and it's something that still haunts me. I can never forget what I did. That baby could've lived.

After the massacre, I found a hunting party from the Muskoxen group on the seventy-ninth day. They were in the middle of a month-long hunt, aiming for their annual muskoxen kill, but they welcomed me: Traci, with her warm hugs, and Maggot with her blunt voice, Celena with her friendly smile—she had not yet realized how I'd usurp her—and Kazem with his curious, kind soul. I joined their hunt and three days later, we made a sacred muskoxen kill. It was another week or so before we got back to their settlement, driving a bit of a round-about route, and there were so many Untamed there, but not one person thought I was bad. They were kind. None of them mentioned the Beast inside me, so I figured either they couldn't see it like the clansmen could or that I'd squashed it deep.

For six years, until I was twenty, I lived among the Muskoxen Untamed. Then we found the tunnels under New Zeralzi and realized the advantage it gave us. We believe we're the biggest surviving group of Untamed, since the Muskoxen group absorbed what was left of the Marriballii tribe the year before I joined them—the biggest group in Section Five, definitely, as we're only aware of a small group of reindeer hunters farther north, and we're possibly even the biggest group out of the whole world—and now a good number of us is ideally placed to take over a town. When we succeed, we'll bring the remainder of the Muskoxen group here. And sure, word will get out among the Enhanced that we've beaten them in one place, but that means other Untamed will hear it about, too. They'll either come to join us and we'll grow in numbers or they'll take over more towns themselves. And that's what Maggot reckons we need—bases to operate from when the mysterious Seventh One of Light wins the war.

It still surprises me, really, how everyone here—and among the clansmen—is so sure that this Seventh One exists. That she *will* win the war for us. Ultimately, I know it's just a nice story. Something people in this area—and others, too—tell themselves to make them feel better. When I lived at D'Elinous, long before I joined Ysabelle's group, I'd never heard of this Seer. No one had. I doubt she's even real, outside of people's minds and hopes. The thought of her is just a comfort, and I'm sure, deep down, everyone knows this. Otherwise why would any Untamed go on killing-sprees among the Enhanced, when supposedly the Savior Seer's going to handle it all?

No. It's just a story. We have to face reality. If we're going to win, we have to do it ourselves. And that means killing.

I swallow hard and try to stop the Beast stirring inside me. He's hungry, ravenous, starved for so long. He wants me to kill. But those screams—the clansmen massacre that *I* did. That's exactly why I can't. Why I haven't killed since.

Why I won't.

Why a small part of me—the most unrealistic part of me—wants to believe this Seventh Seer exists, that the augury will hold true. Because I don't want to kill.

But, practically, I know I'm going to have to.

We're going to get this town back. We've been working hard. We've worked it out to the tee.

Anything goes wrong, and we've got a plan for it. We have thought of every possible thing that could happen. And whatever does, we'll be victorious. Because it all involves killing. And tomorrow I'm going to have to break the promise I made to myself, eight years ago, when I vowed never to unleash the Beast again.

FOUR

I WAIT UNTIL THE EARLY hours, when Kazem's deep in sleep and even Winston's gone to bed and has stopped pottering around and I can escape from the tunnels unseen, unknown, except for Mal who's still guarding the entrance. I can feel it inside me—the Beast. When I am free-running, it disappears. It's just me then. The energy and the excitement and the adrenaline squashes it down. But as the hours creep by, it wheedles its way back.

The night air is cool on my face as I step outside. I hug my jacket to me, tighter. My arms are goose-fleshing under my sleeves, and I breathe deeply, stare at the moon. Of course, we looked at it during the Moon Worship, the night before we raided New Bere. We had a whole party for it, praying to the lunar body. But it always feels more special when I'm looking at the moon when I'm on my own.

I remember looking at the moon at D'Elinous. It's my only clear memory of my aunt, Caia-Lu—well, of any of my family. I have no memories whatsoever of my parents, and it kills me now that I don't even know their names, what they looked like, what their voices sounded like. I have no idea if I ever met them properly, or if they died when I was a baby, or maybe when I was a few years old. All I remember is Caia-Lu, Dad's sister. She'd sit out with me in the warm evenings, our toes bare and sinking into the soft sand. We'd sit close, shoulders touching, and stare up at the moon.

"Remember, Kacey, neshama sheli, remember this: there's great energy in lunar power," Caia-Lu said once. We were sharing a blanket, and I could smell her wondrous, spicy perfume amid her many shawls and layers of patterned fabrics.

I was only little so I didn't ask her more about the moon, about lunar energy. And when Caia-Lu began telling me of the lunar energy, I didn't really think much about what she was saying. I just wanted her to tell a story. I loved her stories. My aunt was the greatest storyteller of all time, even better than Bea— and I'd heard the amazing tales Bea would tell her siblings—but Caia-Lu's stories were only for me. They ran in our family, she told me, and so I always wanted them. I wanted the connections. I wanted to feel like I belonged.

I still want to feel like I belong.

But now I think of the moon a lot. The energy. Lunar power. I wish I'd asked my aunt when I'd had the chance—because as an adult, the power of the night interests me more than stupid stories about fairies. I think of Caia-Lu's lost knowledge every time I see the moon.

And the Beast is stronger under the soft moonlight.

I try to keep my breathing even. I don't want to get agitated. I need to stay calm.

Maybe Caia-Lu felt the Beast in me. Maybe she'd been testing me, seeing if I was aware of it by telling me about the lunar power. But what had she been going to say? Something to help me get rid of it?

But the moon can't do that. The moon isn't powerful in that way. And thinking it can do impossible things is just a hope, wishful thinking. There's only one way to get the Beast out of me and let me live freely, a method that won't put me in danger—or at least I don't think it would, not like Ysabelle and the clansmen did.

"Please, Gods and Goddesses and ancient spirits." I gaze up at the sky—the whole night sky with the Milky Way and the stars and the moon—as if by concentrating hard enough I'll suddenly see the Divine Ones I pray to. I've no idea what Gods and Goddesses look like. I only know one person who claimed they saw a God, and that was the Overlord Seer of the clansmen. But he'd never tell me what the God looked like. Said that if I was supposed to know, I'd see one myself.

And I'm obviously not. Not when I can feel the Beast inside me.

"Please, evict *this thing* from me." My voice cracks. I'm showing too much desperation, too much emotion, and something tells me it's a bad thing. I crack a wry smile as I realize that's what the Enhanced Ones would say: negative emotions are bad.

But it's hard to stay upbeat and positive all the time, with this thing inside me. No one here knows about it. Maggot's never said a word. Kazem's never said a word. No one has, and if they knew, they'd tell me. And I'm not going to tell them, give them a reason to hurt me, like Ysabelle did.

So, I pretend around them all. The free-running is amazing because it quietens the Beast, makes it easier to pretend I am normal.

Normal.

I hate that word.

It's exhausting, being *energetic and fun and confident* around Kazem and the others—too happy and forcing down the darkness inside me. But out here, at night, when I ask the Gods and Goddesses and spirits to evict my Beast, the darkness does rise up. My mood drops. It's one extreme or the other.

Maybe that's because I'm dealing in powers I don't know—and asking the Divine Ones to remove my

Beast would be a big thing. Especially if it meant entering into an agreement, a deal, even with a spirit. I've heard about people who do that—*stupid people,* Maggot calls them. Spirits are powerful, and they're usually on the Untamed side when we're fighting the Enhanced. But that doesn't mean they're on our side other times. Spirits are dangerous. They kill people. They eat people. And no one should make a deal with them. A deal means certain death.

I take a deep breath. If today my prayers can be answered and the Beast is removed—if some majestic otherworldly force can just do that for me, do it out of kindness and pity for my desperation—then I can help Maggot and everyone else with the plan. Maybe I would be able to kill the Enhanced who try to stop us, without my Beast exploding and taking down all life. All of us, Untamed included.

You should've told Maggot about this.

But I couldn't. It's vain of me, I know, but I love my position as Maggot's second. I like them all looking up at me. If they knew my secret, I could be an outcast. Just the thought of Celena's satisfied grin makes my resolve harden. If I don't have to kill, then I can control the Beast. Maybe I can manage today without killing— but if the Beast is removed, it's less of a risk overall.

"Please…" I guess I should be asking for their help today, for all of us, as well. For their prayers and good wishes and for the Gods and Goddesses to be blessing us, watching us, keeping us safe. But it seems greedy to ask for that as well as the Beast's eviction—even if they have never given the eviction before.

But I can't bring myself to ask for more, because what if this is the time when they do grant my wish? And we don't need their help to get this town—I'm confident of that. We've put in too much work to have to rely on ethereal help.

But *I* need their help. I need the Beast gone.

"Please, please do it," I whisper, and my voice shakes and—

"Kachler?"

I turn, my heart pounding at the voice.

A figure stands in the gloom. My mouth dries. Is *this* it? A Goddess has heard me? Or…or an apparition? The Seventh One?

No, it can't be… It…

My head suddenly feels too light, and I don't know what to say as the Goddess, the person, moves toward me, as—

It's Celena. Brilliant.

My mood darkens, and irritation pulls through me—and I know I can't be irritated when praying to the Gods and Goddesses, so, there's no way they'll grant my wish now. All because of her.

"What the fuck are you doing out here?" Celena demands, her tongue sharp as ever as she steps right up to me, gets into my personal space.

I don't step away, just look down at her. I'm slightly taller, but she's broader. She has the same build as her mother. But that's where the similarities with Maggot end. Celena's skin is paler and her hair blond. And she's stuck up. Maggot earned her respect from everyone, but Celena thinks she's entitled to respect, like it's her birth-right.

"What are *you* doing?" I counter. "Sneaking out to meet this secret lover of yours?"

Her eyes flash. "You know nothing."

I roll my eyes—mainly because her interruption stopped me talking to the Gods and Goddesses, and not because of what she's saying.

"Don't roll your eyes at me," Celena hisses.

Yes—it's that easy to annoy her. There's no way she's leader material. "Celena, just go away." I fight to keep my tone even.

She folds her arms. "No." Her eyes narrow, and she moves closer to me, silently. "What are you doing out here?"

"None of your business." I clench my jaw.

"It is my business if you're going to sabotage us."

"Sabotage? *Me*?" I snort. "Why would I do that? That seems more like *your* forte than mine."

She scowls, and I know my words have hit their mark. But she has cost us missions on numerous occasions. Mainly due to her lack of foresight. Lack of planning. Lack of common sense. She's never intentionally messed things up for us—that I know of—but it just proves she's nothing like her mother.

"What *are* you doing out here?" I try to keep the anger and frustration out of my voice. I need to stay calm, else the Beast is going to get stronger. I can feel him stirring still. Like he's laughing, because he's still here. Of *course* he's still here.

Celena's eyes narrow. "*You* don't get to ask me questions." Even her voice is annoying. Whiny and shrill—reminds me a bit of Iralda's voice, and that's never a good association to have. "You've got to be careful. You need to learn to respect me."

I snort again. "Is that supposed to be a threat?"

She holds my gaze, steady. "I'll be your superior soon and—"

"Yeah, right," I mutter.

If something *does* happen to Maggot, I'm the next leader. Sure, Celena could try and take over, but no one here is going to back her as leader. She's too toxic-natured, not to mention petty. This grudge she's held against me ever since Maggot began training me just proves what kind of person she is. She's not a leader. Whereas I am. I'm well-liked, supported, here. Some of the Griffin children are even scared of Celena—and not in the way they're scared of Maggot. No, the children revere Maggot, but they hate Celena because she's a rat, really. Despite Celena's desperation to be a mother, she mocks them, and when she doesn't get her own way with them, she lies to their parents. Says they've done shit that they haven't. Celena thinks this makes her revered too—but it doesn't.

She's just annoying and half the time I wish something would happen to her. I don't mean death or anything, but something that means she'd go back to the Muskoxen group. Something that means I wouldn't have to see her day-in, day-out. I know Kazem wishes it, too. He had to do training with her for a few months, and I swear, after each session he was even more antagonized than before. Maybe if she does get pregnant, it would fix all the problems. I know she's desperate for a baby. She prays every week to the Goddess of Fertility, and now I think about it, maybe I should pray for Celena to become a mother, too. We could both get what we want if she has to leave.

Mind you, that won't apply after tomorrow. Not when we have got the town and the Muskoxen group are joining us there. Still, there's more space in the town. I could avoid her.

"You haven't answered my question," she says.

"Neither have you. And I don't answer to you."

Her top lip twitches slightly, and then she tilts her head up, so her nose is higher in the air. The action just makes her look haughty. "I'm watching you," she says, her words slow.

I scoff. "Wow, I'm really scared."

"You want to be careful, Kachler," she says. "You want to be nicer to me. You need to be nicer to me."

"I don't need to be anything toward you." I shift my weight a little, so I'm more grounded as I stare at her.

"Oh, you do," she says. "If you want to live."

"What the hell is that supposed to mean?" I nearly laugh. Is she threatening me?

The angles of Celena's face seem to get sharper. "I know we need you for the siege tomorrow. That we apparently can't do it without you. But once we've got the town, you're going to lose status, Kachler. Mark my words. We won't need you. I won't need you. No one will; you're not even some important person. It's not like you're the Seventh Seer—and she is going to come and rescue us once we've got this town, and you won't be needed. You won't even need to be alive once we've got the town."

"So, you admit this won't succeed without me." I let a sly grin take over my face.

She doesn't do anything—doesn't even blink. "Accidents *do* happen, unfortunately. Especially after people have achieved great things. They get…careless. Think they're invincible, then bang—they have a bad accident."

The Beast rises. I lunge at her, grab her by the neck. My fingers squeeze slightly, and she makes a sort-of choking sound. "You really think you can threaten me?"

"My mother's not going to be happy to have your fingerprints around my neck." Her voice is a little strained.

I tighten my grip until her eyes bulge. "Maggot's not going to be happy to know what you're planning. Even if it's all talk. I mean, Celena, really? Stay in your lane."

"My name is *Flesh*," she gasps.

I snort. "It's almost admirable that you think you could do it—kill me. We both know who's more powerful here."

I keep my hold on her neck until she starts to tremble—until the Beast is *really* interested in her— then I throw her to the ground. She falls, spluttering, choking, and when she eventually looks up, wiping saliva from her mouth as she gasps and gasps, I see it in her eyes: burning hatred.

"You'll pay for this," she mutters.

"Whatever."

I leave her on the ground and head to the mouth of the tunnels, nod again at Mal who nods back, then crawl through the gap, down into the network. I head back toward the room I share with Kazem, but of course it's just my luck to find another person in the tunnels. Shweta.

My shoulders sag. I'm tired now. I need to sleep. Shweta's not bad or anything—but she's different now, since she's been grieving. She's just…here, a lot, wandering about. I seem to see her everywhere. I'm always bumping into her, and each time I feel this duty to check on her.

However, it's Shweta who speaks first this time.

"Are you…" She looks at me quizzically.

I tilt my head to the side, waiting for the rest of her question.

Her face flushes. "I keep sensing that you know, but…"

"Know what?" I frown and yawn, then rub my eye.

"Nothing. Sorry," she says.

She nods at me—and that seems to be it. I nod back at her, a little confused.

"Are you okay?" I ask.

Another nod, and she scurries off. I watch her for a moment, until she's out of sight. That wasn't like before, when she got obsessive about Hana being reincarnated. But there's something about this interaction that strikes me as odd. What did she mean by *I keep sensing that you know*? I turn it over and over in my mind, but I can't make sense of it. I'm too tired.

A few minutes later, I slip back into mine and Kazem's room, and into the bed. He's breathing deeply and doesn't stir. But I can't sleep. I'm too riled up, and the Beast is active.

I curse Celena. I need my sleep. Why did she have to follow me out there and annoy me?

If anything goes wrong tomorrow, it's her fault.

I AM RUNNING THROUGH WOODS, *and my skin is glowing red—and I don't know why. The moonlight is broken and in stripes, and the thing inside me is rising, growing and growing. I can feel it trying to burst out.*

"Soon, you won't be able to hide it away," a voice says, and I turn, trying to see who spoke.

But there's no one here. It's just me and the woods, the trees illuminated by my skin. And I'm still glowing, and I don't know what it means—and this isn't like a normal dream, and my arms shouldn't be glowing!

It's the Beast—he's making me glow. He's marking me!

My breaths come in huge gasps that make me shudder and choke. My mouth is too dry, and coughing makes my eyes smart, slows my pace until I'm barely moving. The sharp pain of a stitch dives into my left side, just under my ribcage, and I pant and pant. And now that I've stopped, the glowing's getting brighter. My skin is luminous.

Fear pulls through me,

"Run!" Caia-Lu's voice. My aunt. "Boy! Run!"

Boy? I jolt, and I'm shouting for her, looking between the tree trunks and turning, trying to see her. Her rounded figure, her kind eyes, her graying hair.

But I can't.

'Where are you?" I cry, and the darkness around the trees seems to get darker and darker, and I think of all the monsters, the bad things that it's hiding.

"Get as far away from here as you can!" Caia-Lu's voice sounds scared, and, still, I cannot see her. "You're not trapped yet—but it's coming. It will be balagan when it does! She thinks it'll only be for Kacey, but it's going to extend to all of you, so you have to get away. You can't get trapped as well! You have to break it!"

"Who? Break what?" I shout, but my voice is not mine. It's low and rich and dark. A man's voice. "What's happened to Kacey?"

What's happened to *me*? Um, what?

I lift my arm to shield my eyes—and I don't know why I'm doing it when it brings my glowing red hand closer to my eyes, makes everything have that crimson glow. Crimson…like the blood that soaked the clansmen after my Beast got them.

"Run, boy! Run now!"

"But I don't understand! What's happening?" *I speak again with this deep voice that is not mine.*

"Don't get trapped by it!"

A whoosh of energy shoves me forward, and I fall. Thorns scratch my hands and knees, and then something wet and sticky is on my face. I try to claw it off, gulping in huge lungfuls of air that taste bad. And the trees are moving above me. Their branches are closing in on me.

I scream as cold, wet twigs wrap around my arms, my legs, pressing my body to the ground. And then there are vines—so many vines, growing over me, tumbling round and round my chest, my stomach, my thighs. My thighs that are more muscular than they should be.

This…

"Don't get trapped!" Caia-Lu shrieks as the forest claims me. "Don't let her trap you!"

SIX

I WAKE, BREATHING HARD, PART of me convinced I'm still being held down by vines.

But I'm not. I'm just tangled in the covers. What a strange nightmare. And Caia-Lu, my dead aunt, calling me *boy*? That doesn't make sense at all. Although I know Caia-Lu often called everyone boy or girl, regardless of age, it makes no sense that she'd call *me* boy in that dream. Even if my voice was so…manly.

I sit up, careful not to disturb Kazem. He's still asleep—a deep sleeper. Always has been.

I make my way to the toileting area—a large, wide space at the back of the network. The area is empty, bar Rohan. He's emptying the toileting pots, replacing them with new ones. The old lantern that hangs from a hook on the ceiling sways a little.

"Be the last time I'm doing this," he says.

I nod and smile. "Tomorrow, we'll wake up in actual beds, and everything will be different. Better."

He gives a tight-lipped smile, then he's leaving.

I go to the toilet, then wash my hands. We've got a system rigged up for this, using minimal water. Showers aren't possible here. We head out to the big river for those, about twenty miles away. We all go once a month or so. And it's been a while since I've been. I sniff under my arms. There's no question about it that I stink, no matter how I use a cloth to wash—but at least it's the same for all of us.

I grab the deodorant can and spray it liberally and—

A jarring sensation fills my head and—

"No, please, no! I don't need that—"

"You do. A level three conversion."

"I'm fine! I'm not Untamed!"

"Even Chosen Ones need re-converting from time to time."

"I said I'm fine!"

"But you're not! If you were fine, you wouldn't have allowed that woman to go Untamed for so long. And she wouldn't be dead now, nor would we have had to use up valuable resources restarting your heart."

I gasp—the man screaming he's fine, begging not to have a conversion, is the same man whose voice I spoke with in that dream with Caia-Lu. I splutter, but there's a sudden pain in my head. So much of it. My heart pounds, and I look around—but there's no one else here. It's just me. Yet the voices... two men... I heard them and—

No, their voices weren't normal. Didn't sound normal.

Were their voices in my mind? I frown. It felt a little like an echo, a memory. A memory that's not mine. Was that dream his too, this man's? Just what the hell is going on?

I blink several times, holding my breath. The deodorant can is on the floor, on its side. I dropped it? I scrunch my eyes for a few seconds, then open them, expecting for everything to make sense. Only it doesn't.

I... I don't know what just happened.

My chest aches, and, in the shard of mirror, under the weak lantern light, I see my eyes widen. See how small my pupils are. I step nearer to the mirror, frowning.

I blink again, then rub my forehead. My eyes return to normal a moment later. I watch them, and it should be reassuring, I know that. Only it's… it's not. And I can't shake the crawling sensation that's slipping down my spine.

Those two men—I heard them. And they were *Enhanced*.

Why have I got the memory of an Enhanced man?

"You okay?" a voice says.

I jump and turn. But it's just Shweta. She looks even smaller this morning than she did in the tunnels in the early hours. Her eyes look different—huge bags under them. And her skin's kind of lined now. She's still beautiful, yes, but she's also…older? I frown.

"Kacey? What is it?" Her words are soft.

"Uh, no. I'm fine… I just… something weird happened. Or I thought it did—but it can't have done."

She steps nearer, nearer, until she's right in front of me. Her face is thinner too, skin hanging off her skull. And her hair—are those gray strands in it? Or have I just never noticed those before? Her breathing rasps a little. "Are you in the cycle, too?"

"The cycle?"

"Yes, with it happening again," she says. "Kacey, you can tell me."

My eyes narrow. I take a step back. The cycle? "I don't know what you mean." None of this makes sense.

"You do know." She nods.

"I really don't."

She clasps her hands together. "Talk to me, Kacey." Her voice is different, a bit lighter, but there's something else there, too. Concern? "Look, it happens to me, too."

"What does?"

"Remembering things no one else can."

Like an Enhanced man's memories? I swallow hard, my throat suddenly feeling like sandpaper, then I cough. But I shouldn't have those memories. If Maggot finds out, she'll think there's a connection between me and the Enhanced. That I'm a liability.

No. I'm *fine*.

But I'm not on my own. "You remember things no one else does?" I look at Shweta. "Like what?"

She shakes her head, waving her hand a little. "Just trust me with this," she says. "Tell me what's going on. I won't judge you or question you. I'll believe you straight away."

"I..." I say, and maybe it can be okay—she's a Seer. She's respected here. Maybe this is a Seer power that I'm getting? But, before I can say anything, the Beast stirs. I feel him rising, and I inhale sharply. What if the Beast, all this time, has been the soul of an Enhanced man trapped inside me? What if these are *his* memories? And, somehow, he knows Caia-Lu too? But the Beast is stirring now and stirring a lot.

Don't say anything. It's like he's trying to say that. And of course I can't risk saying anything, because if I tell Shweta there's a soul of the enemy inside me, and it turns out she's talking about a completely different thing for her, I'll be kicked out the group.

And anyway, the Beast can't actually be an Enhanced One, can he? No. I'm tired, sleep-deprived. My mind's playing tricks on me because I'm *normal*. That's what happens to normal people who are kept awake at ungodly hours. Hell, even Celena had a hand in that.

"I'm fine," I say again. "Really, I am." I flash a smile and stand straighter.

She nods and hovers in front of me for a moment or two longer, before walking past me to the toileting area.

I breathe deeply for several moments, aware that Shweta may well be looking over her shoulder at me. I take one of the longer ways back to my room. All the tunnels are interconnected, and there are numerous options for the journey back. My chosen path is a route that takes me past Maggot's quarters, the ones she shares with Evor and Celena. That vicious rat. There's movement from inside there. People moving about. Can't hear any voices though.

I leave. Don't want Maggot being suspicious of me if I'm hanging outside their area.

Ten minutes later, I'm back in my room. Kazem is up now, dressed in navy joggers and a black T-shirt, and sorting through his bag. He turns and embraces me.

"Your hands are going to bleed at the slightest thing." His dark hair falls over his eyes as he bows his head and inspects my palms and fingers in the candlelight of our room.

It's early morning. The day of the attack. The day of the new beginning, a new future. We can hear the others: low voices, murmurings, last-minute reassurances.

I look down at my hands, encased in his. "It's just from the gravel out there."

You'd think my hands would've toughened up with years of parkour and mountain climbing. But nope. My skin is always cracked and callused and splitting at inappropriate moments.

I take several deep breaths. Fatigue hovers over me. I curse myself. I need to be in top form for today. Can't be hallucinating voices, for the Gods' sakes!

"I think you should wear your gloves." Kazem lets go of my hands and gently touches my shoulders. I look up into his face, and I'm overtaken with that sphere of warmth I get every time I look at him.

"I can't get as good a grip with gloves." Especially when I'll be climbing different textures and surfaces. Bare hands really are best. Plus, I always feel more confident without my gloves. Like I can connect and mold with the surface I'm using. Really become one with it, and then evolve further—become something else. I *love* running bare foot, even more so when I'm just running on the steppes. I said that once to Bhavesh. He laughed. I didn't tell anyone after that how connected I feel to the earth.

"If you're sure." Kazem pulls me close. His body is warm, and there's something about pressing myself against him that grounds me so much more than anything else does. He's strength and stability and stone.

I look up at him, at the way his dark eyes hold so much life. At his beautiful dark hair, his golden skin that's unblemished except for a small scar below his left eye. And I look at his soul—because when I look at him, I *see* his soul. And I feel relaxed. I feel happy. I can't help but smile and feel lighter—like I haven't got a Beast inside me—when I'm with him.

"This time tomorrow we'll be waking up in our own town," I say. Because we're going to do this. We're going to win. Of course we are. So far, all Kazem and I have known is danger and we're still this much in love. I can't even imagine how much more relaxed we'll be when we've got safety and security. When we'll have all the time we want. Being in Kazem's arms is the best feeling ever, and I won't lie—I'm very much looking forward to endless lie-ins with him, snuggled against him, kissing, his fingers curling around my hipbone. So long as he still wants things to be as they are between us now…

Kazem nods slowly, and I feel his stubble grazing my forehead.

We hold each other tightly for a moment, then we hear the gong.

"It's time." My words are breathy.

"I know," he says. "But I wish I didn't have to let you go. I want to hold you forever. And I know I shouldn't say this, but I've got a bad feeling, Kace. I'm scared I won't see you again."

"Hey." I press my hand against his face. His eyes are pools of glossy, dark liquid, and they drink me up. "It'll be okay. We're the best runners."

"I'd feel better if we were running the same routes."

"So, you can help me if I get caught?" I give him a haughty look. "I'm *not* going to get caught. I'm one of the best runners."

"I know. It's nothing. Pretend I didn't say anything." He looks over my shoulder for a moment, then pulls away from me. As he does so, he winces.

"What is it?" My voice is sharp.

"Nothing." He gives me a smile, but it doesn't reach the corners of his eyes.

"Kazem? Are you hurt?"

He exhales a long breath. "Just a bit stiff."

"Where?"

He points to his right side, just underneath his arm. "It's nothing."

My eyes narrow. "That jump. The landing—was it that? Is it painful? We have to tell Maggot."

"We can't." Kazem shakes his head. "And it's nothing anyway."

"But you want us to run together—so *I* can have your back?"

Kazem presses his lips together for a moment. "I didn't actually say that."

Of course he wouldn't. Kazem rarely asks for help. "That's what you meant though." It's obvious—he knows I don't need help, but he does. "We have to tell Maggot you're injured."

"I'm not. I'm fine. It's nothing. The gong's already gone, anyway. It's time. We can't change the plan now."

My mind whirs. There are seventeen free-runners in total. Our plan utilizes everyone—in fact, all the plans we came up with do. Seventeen free runners are required for *every* option. And there isn't anyone who can take Kazem's place. "But what if something happens? Something could go wrong. We have to tell her."

Kazem shakes his head. "I'll be fine. I'm worrying about nothing. You know what I'm like. Come on." He takes my hand, pulls me along. "We're going to be late. Maggot won't be happy."

"Hey, forget about Maggot's happiness. It'll be worse if you get caught… Maybe I can swap with… Sian. Yeah? That would put me behind you. I can be your backup." And I wouldn't be in the same team as Clive then, too. Because it seems like Celena's not doing a thing about that.

"No." Kazem shakes his head. "You've got the most

dangerous job, Kace. You and Bhavesh. Sian would be no good for that. She can't jump like you can, and she and Bhavesh don't get on. Come on. Forget I said anything."

He pulls me along, and I bite my lip, try to work out a way around it. I glance at Kazem as we walk, then rub his shoulder. He tells me again that he's all right.

"Load up at the station." Tammy greets us with a quick nod at the main chamber then directs us to the weapons station. Our runners don't normally get weapons—hard to do parkour, not to mention dangerous, with them. But we can't take risks today. We all need every ounce of protection we can.

I pick up an unloaded pistol and a round of ammo. Slide them both into my belt. Separately. Can't have a gun going off if I've got to tuck and role. Just have to hope that if I need to use it, I'm quick enough to load it before the Enhanced get me.

Kazem grabs his gun and ammunition too.

"All guards are to take survival kits," Tammy says. "Yeah, Shweta, you're a guard for this with team B?"

Team B. That's Kazem's running team. I glance across at Shweta.

She nods. "*Of course* I'm a guard again." Her tone is almost bored, and I don't understand it. Is she trying to goad me, or someone else, into saying something, picking a fight with her about how she's not taking this seriously? I don't understand her behavior—and before too. This is not her at all. This is more what I'd expect from Celena. Could it be Shweta's grief again, messing with her?

Maggot glances in her direction, and Shweta immediately stands up a little straighter.

"I'm ready," Shweta says, her voice brighter. I wait for her to say something else, maybe a mutter or something linked to what she said earlier, but she doesn't.

I look around for the others in Kazem's team—but they must already be on the way up. It's only Shweta here, nodding as Tammy goes through the usual safety rules for the guns. As if we haven't heard it hundreds of times before.

I wait until Tammy's finished talking before I make my way over to Shweta. It's not ideal, having to ask her.

"Uh, Shweta," I say, trying to assess her.

Her eyes lock onto mine. "Yes?"

"Can…can you keep an eye on Kazem?" I pray that this is okay to ask of her. I'm not overloading her, am I?

"I'm keeping an eye on everyone." Her voice has a strange challenge in it, like she's daring me to question her abilities. "Like I *always* do. Every bloody time."

Woah. "Uh…" I let out a small laugh, because I've never heard her swear before. Is it the pressure of today getting to her? Something more? I make a mental note to mention this to Evor after this mission. "Uh, no. I mean…" I lean closer, make sure no one else hears. I promised Kazem I wouldn't tell Maggot, but I didn't promise not to tell someone else. "Kazem's a bit sore from—"

"—yesterday's jump," Shweta finishes for me.

"Oh, you know?"

She rolls her eyes. "What isn't there to know after all these days? This is always the starting point."

"Uh, *what?*"

Shweta just blinks. She… she looks so different to yesterday, in the truck and just as I'm about to ask if she really is okay, if something happened last night when she was wandering the tunnels, Maggot calls, "Hurry up, everyone!"

I focus back on Shweta. "Look, uh, I just wanted to say about Kaz. He says he's fine, but I think he's injured. I'm just giving you a heads up that he might need extra backup. And I, uh, hope you're okay." Because now isn't the time to get into a deep conversation about her emotional space, right?

She nods.

"Okay." Maggot's booming voice cuts me off. "Slight change of plan. Clive's running on Team B now."

Everyone's in here now, and I find Celena's face. She nods once at me, then looks pointedly away.

"He'll follow your lead, Kazem," Maggot says. "Winston, Bhav, and Kace—you'll work together as a three. Got it?"

I nod, but Winston doesn't look very pleased that he's no longer on the same team as Clive.

"We ready?" Maggot says. "Then let's go and kick some Enhanced Ones' butts."

It's the most unlike-Maggot-thing she's ever said, and we all laugh—but Kazem catches my eye, just as I'm looking toward the other runners he's paired with. He shakes his head at me, his eyes widening a little. A second later, he mouths, *I'm okay.*

I purse my lips for a moment. I have to trust him. If Kazem wasn't up to this, he'd tell Maggot. He wouldn't put everyone's lives in danger. I'm worrying about nothing. Like I always do.

WHEN I'M NERVOUS ABOUT SOMETHING, I distract myself. And so, as I march to my position, I keep thinking about the new army boots on my feet and how there's a layer of rubber between me and the earth, and how much more connected and in tune I'd feel if I was bare foot. And the whole thing about needing a distraction *now* is ridiculous, since this is it: the moment we've waited years for. Bhavesh is behind me, and I've got the radio, currently turned to silent, in my belt. I should be concentrating on all of this, should be as alert as possible.

The sun is just rising.

Bhavesh and I skirt quickly and lightly around the pharmacy buildings, and then head down a backroad that has long shadows.

I used to be scared of shadows. Jaqueline and I both were. We'd play this game when we were with the clansmen, where we had to get from the hut we shared with her family to the food hut without letting any shadows touch us. We thought we'd get burnt. It was a game, but it was also our fear—that's what made it all the more real. Now, as we merge with the shadows, the adrenaline pulsing through my veins is comforting, it's one of my favorite feelings in the world. The shadows are my friends. They protect me. And they make me feel close to Jaqueline—my best friend. The girl I didn't save. Could I have, if I'd tried? If I'd unleashed the Beast sooner? But the Beast only saved me and the baby, the baby who I then abandoned, and I can't help but feel guilty about all of it, even though I know it's not a productive feeling. Feeling guilty won't change the past. It won't bring Jaqueline back. It won't bring the baby back. He'd be nearly nine years old now.

I swallow hard. I need to focus on the task at hand.

I glance at the sky, see a narrow strip of it above, in the space between the two large buildings either side of us. I can't see the moon. Or any stars. Too much light pollution. Not like at D'Elinous.

Bhavesh and I make it out to the other side of the alleyway. We scale an eight-foot fence, dropping lightly to our feet on the other side. I bounce on the balls of my feet, saving the energy. Letting it dissipate is silly, especially when I'm going to need to run. And climb.

We have the most dangerous job—scaling the tower. It's the Enhanced Ones' headquarters, and so far only Maggot's been inside. She scaled the tower to the third floor and managed to get enough of a reccy to make some rough floor plans when she got back to our tunnels.

"It has to be on the top floor," she'd said, talking of the Enhanced Ones' communication hub, their network that allows them to talk with the nearby towns.

And that's what Bhavesh and I need to disable before the siege on New Zeralzi fully begins. Can't have them calling for backup. We've worked out how we can neutralize the population here—but if more arrive, we'd be doomed.

The tower is in sight now, and seeing it—all twelve floors of it—fills me with energy and excitement, awe and wonder. It's massive—and it doesn't matter how many times I see the tower, I always have this reaction.

I rub my hands a little as I walk, keep an eye on the surroundings. No movements in the shadows. Good. But I pat the pistol and ammo in my belt, check it's all there, all the same.

Maggot's instructed Bhavesh and me to climb the tower from opposite sides. East and west. It's still dark enough that we shouldn't be seen, but if one of us somehow is—by an Enhanced One looking out of their dorm window or something—then only one of us should be spotted. Likely, a commotion will occur and the Enhanced will put their effort into catching whichever one of us they've seen, leaving the other free to continue.

And we're both quick. Chances are if one of us is spotted when we're a few stories up, we'll still be able to get higher—possibly to the top and disable their comms—before the Enhanced drag us down.

I rub my hands together and smile. Although Kazem's faster at climbing than me, I'm less likely to make mistakes under pressure. And they're not going to catch me.

But if they do, you can just kill them. It's the voice of the Beast, and I squash it—or him, because I am thinking of him as gendered now—down quickly. The Beast is not supposed to be able to speak, not when this much adrenaline's flooding me!

He's not part of me, he's not me, and soon I'm going to find out a way to get rid of him.

"*Shit.*" Bhavesh's voice.

I turn to look at him, and then I follow his gaze to the…the mirror men.

They're not our guards. These mirror men are real. And they're coming for us, but they're unarmed.

Bhavesh pulls his pistol from his belt.

I widen my eyes at him with a shake of my head. A gunshot will alert the other Enhanced—and we've planned everything down to the very last second, including when we fire the first shot. Because when that happens, we all have to be in position. Most Enhanced should be sleeping right now in the dormitory blocks. We've got runners covering their entrances, barricading the Enhanced in. There's only so long the augmenter supplies in their rooms will last. Meanwhile, Maggot and her team will be at the factory, smashing the augmenters, destroying them all. Ada's team and Kazem's team will kill any who try and hurt us.

And only then—when we've got all the Enhanced Ones locked up—can we fire any bullets. And that's just if we discover a lone Enhanced out and about.

Like these ones. Shit.

"Don't come any closer," I say to the mirror men. My heart speeds up. We need to keep them talking long enough for the clock to strike the hour—that's the point at which we can fire gunshots. Assuming everyone safely makes it to their places. But that's— what? Three minutes away? More? And one of us still has to disable the communications hub.

"Stay back!" I yell, my voice a little louder. I pull my pistol from my belt, load it, hold it threateningly toward them. Safety's on. I give Bhavesh a glance and he nods, the movement small.

"We'll shoot if we have to," he growls at them.

"You need to put your weapons down," one of the mirror men says. His voice is horrible and grating.

"Fat chance of that." I grit my teeth, look around. There are only four of them. If Bhavesh and I take two each, and disarm them—hell, even kill them as silently as we can—then we've still got a chance to complete the plan. We can't be the ones to let everyone down.

"We know what you're planning," the man shouts. "You're not going to win, you can't take over a whole town! You're all going to get crushed if you don't join us willingly. Tell the others to step down."

They *know*?

No, they can't. They're bluffing.

"We know you're trying to take over. We have all

the details. It's not going to end well—and we'd rather have you join us alive than be shot dead when we're defending our town."

Bhavesh sends a glance at me.

"You'd hurt us?" I snort at the Enhanced. "Even though you hate violence?" My heart pounds.

Just kill them! The others will be in place by now! the Beast begs.

"I know *you*, Kacey. We all know you," the mirror man says.

I jolt. "How?" I don't like the way he says my name—he shouldn't even know my name—and the hairs on the back of my neck rise.

"Because we know *all* of you. We know that at least one of your group isn't as polluted by the Untamed parasite as you might think. They came to their senses and told us."

A *traitor*. My eyes widen.

"Someone told you?" Bhavesh's voice is low. "One of us?"

"I also know your boyfriend is injured," one of the men says, his face turned toward me. "An injury, in an operation such as the one you're planning to carry out, will only lead to unnecessary deaths."

My breathing quickens, and my chest tightens. Shweta is the only one I told about Kazem's injury, and she was acting odd last night and this morning. There was something off about her. And she looked different, older. Have they taken the real Shweta and put an imposter in her place? I've heard their appearance-altering augmenters can work wonders.

"Join us willingly, and there needn't be any deaths," the Enhanced say.

"No!" I yell.

The Enhanced men step toward me. Then their hands go to their belts in unison, and at the same time, each of them produces a gun. My heart hammers. Adrenaline courses through me. They have weapons?

"Kacey?" Bhavesh's voice is sharp.

"Fire!" It takes everything in me to utter the word, and as I do, I line my gun up, flick the safety off, and pull the trigger. It's a fluid movement, and the Beast is happy, and my bullet gets the man and—

Another gunshot.

I flinch, duck, and the movement judders my teeth together. Energy thrums through me. Bhavesh is shooting, and a mirror-eyed man falls.

"You can't take over the whole town!" another Enhanced man shouts. "This is our town. It doesn't belong to people like you. We're prepared; we've got people waiting at the points where your people are going. Call it off now, Kacey, and save the lives of your people."

I fire my gun at them in quick succession, somehow managing to get them all. The gunshots seem so loud, and part of me flinches—but the other part of me, the part that's home to the Beast, doesn't startle at all.

I look around for Bhavesh—but he's gone. Just… gone. But more Enhanced will be coming here now.

I run and grab my radio, hold it to my mouth. "Abort, the enemy knows what we're doing." My breaths come in short, sharp bursts and it's all I can hear in my ears. "I repeat—abort the mission! The enemy know the plan. Do you copy?"

I listen for someone to acknowledge receipt, but the line's fuzzy, crackly, and I'm breathing too hard, too fast, anyway. Can't hear any words, any voices. Just static. I don't know if my message got through. Or if it was in time.

The clock hasn't struck the hour yet, but I can't think. Would I even hear it from here? I look around. I'm in the lowest part of town. Worst for radio signal—I know that. Some sort of shadow being cast by the nearby rocks. But am I too far away from the clock tower?

My head pounds. An old, barely-used entrance to our tunnels is nearby. I need to get the abort message out, and I can boost the signal when in our base, thanks to Mal's tech.

Sweat covers me like a second skin as I run. Adrenaline pounds through me. Shweta told them. Oh Gods. I knew she was acting weirdly this morning. I should've said something to Maggot. Should've realized that the Shweta I spoke to most likely wasn't her. Maggot and I could've evacuated the tunnels completely. Because taking over this town—that's out of the question now. I can feel it in my gut: there's going to be blood spilled because of this. A lot of blood.

The Beast smiles.

I find the entrance, though I struggle on my own to remove the large stones blocking it. But I do manage it, and I try to replace them as best as I can.

Cursing, I find part of the roof has collapsed just behind this entrance, and I only just about manage to get through, scraping my arms and face in the process. It's a lot of work, but I eventually make it.

I run through the tunnels, my feet pounding, my heart pounding, my head pounding. Everything pounding.

"They know the plan!" I yell into my radio, trying it again. It crackles and buzzes.

No one answers.

I run farther, getting nearer to the amplification port. It should be automatic, as soon as I'm in range. I try again, shouting the words. My fingers are slippery with sweat, and I nearly drop the radio, and I'm fumbling with it just as it buzzes.

"Copy that," a voice says—Celena's, on the radio. "Everyone, fall back to the tunnels!"

Oh, thank the Gods. Never before have I been so pleased to hear her voice. She got the message. Someone heard me. Someone—

"Ah!" I scream as a hand lands on my shoulder, and I whirl around to face mirror eyes.

They're in *here*.

"Nice to meet you, Kacey," he says. A broad-shouldered Enhanced man. Dark hair. Pale skin.

He lines up his gun—and somehow it all happens

in slow motion.

He pulls the trigger, and he's smiling, and I see myself reflected in his eyes. See the way my mouth falls open a fraction of a second before I feel the pain like a hot ember in my chest, an ember that grows and grows.

And then I feel nothing.

"NO, PLEASE, NO! I DON'T *need*—"

"You do," Abdi snarls, his face right in front of mine. "A level three conversion."

Level three? No. I can't have that. Can't.

The bindings hold me tighter. I still can't believe they've tied me to this chair. I thrash against the ropes. "I'm fine!" I yell as loudly as I can, even though the door's shut and I know these rooms are soundproof. I also know I shouldn't be yelling, not with so much emotion and fear—because I need to show them that I'm calm, even when I'm running lean. "I'm not Untamed!"

"Even Chosen Ones need re-converting from time to time."

Abdi laughs, his eyes flashing. In them, I see myself. And I look like my mother—the desperation's etched into my face, into my fading-mirror eyes. It hits me like a dead weight to my chest. My mother was an addict. Not to augmenters— but I am addicted to those.

No. Addiction's the wrong thing to call it. This is right. This is good. I am a Chosen One.

"I said I'm fine!"

"But you're not." Abdi moves like a panther stalking around the room. He's wearing a pristine suit, and it's well-

pressed. It's identical to the suit that hangs in my apartment. Because we have the same uniform. We are equals.

Or we were.

Abdi shakes his head. I see sympathy in the way his skin crinkles around his eyes, in how he tilts his whole head to the side. "If you were fine, you wouldn't have allowed that woman to go Untamed for so long." His voice is softer now. "And she wouldn't be dead now, nor would we have had to use up valuable resources restarting your heart."

I flinch and lean forward, trying the ropes again. They don't give. "I was bringing her here—she was right here! You saw here. And so many others from that village too!"

"They weren't here because of you!" Abdi's tone hardens. "You didn't do that. They were taking the Seventh Seer back. And because of you, your careless actions and the medical attention you needed, we were distracted. They got away."

"No." I shake my head. "Raleigh let her go because the Gods hadn't made her a Seer then. So don't twist this and pretend it's something else. I am fine. I do not need re-conversion."

I gulp, my heart pounding. Because I remember the first time. After D'Elinous. The attacks there. When I tried to get away, with the other Untamed, and when they caught me. I shouldn't remember my fear—and I'm only remembering it now because I am running lean—but I remember it. The pain. The pain of the conversion.

"I just need augmenters," I say. "I am fine."

"Sorry," Abdi says. "These are boss's orders. And it's what's best for us all. Don't fight this."

I OPEN ONE EYE AND stare up at whiteness. A ceiling. My breaths are shallow, low. There's pain in my head and my arm, and the ceiling looks too white, too bright. But I can still see that man's face there, the imprint of it. Abdi.

Wait. Who the hell is Abdi? I don't know anyone called that. And I've never been in a conversion room before and—

Oh my God. I was him again. My Beast. The Enhanced man. That was his memory—from when he was alive, before his soul somehow ended up in me. Has to be.

"Where are the augmenters?" a voice asks, and I jolt, look around, but can't see anyone. Just the white ceiling. I—I can't move my head.

"We need more over here. We've only saved a fraction of this group." The voice is low, but frantic, and immediately I know where I am: in their compound, in their *conversion* chamber.

It's about to happen. Oh Gods. I try to move my arms, my legs, but I can't. Am I bound? I can't move my head or neck to check. Lying flat. Panic rises inside me, and my throat feels too raw.

"Those damn Untamed got to our supplies." The voice doesn't sound like Abdi or the Beast. Someone else? Sweat breaks out across the backs of my arms and legs. Too sticky, plastering me to the bed or platform—whatever it is I'm strapped to.

"They shouldn't have! We had warning, for the Gods' sake."

"Well they have! That bitch smashed a lot of augmenters."

I try to listen to more, but something's whining inside my head, and that whining sound is annoying, too high-pitched, and it's blocking out their voices.

And then maybe I lose consciousness or something, because the next thing I know, I'm opening my eyes and the ceiling isn't white. It's yellow. A buttercup yellow.

I bolt up—and nearly faint as pain lassoes around me.

Then I realize I'm not bound now, if I even was before. My hands fly to my eyes, as if by pressing my palms against them so my eyeballs sting and water I can tell if they're mirrors. I blink, lowering my hands. They feel normal. I feel normal—apart from the pain around my chest and shoulder and hips.

Pain. A negative thing. The Enhanced Ones hate pain. So, this means I'm Untamed, still, right? If they've converted me, I wouldn't be feeling this— would I?

Deep breaths, Kace.

I swallow hard as I get off the bed. The mattress is soft. There's a door straight ahead, so of course I run for it, find my gait is slow and labored. I try the handle. Locked.

No window in it. Just solid wood.

I take a deep breath, looking around. It's warm in here, and I can feel the early whispers of perspiration forming on the back of my neck. I take more deep breaths.

There's nothing else in the room. Just the bed. Mattress.

I touch the duvet—it's lumpy, sort of all bunched up on one side. I was lying on top of it. Not in it. I look at the creases on the bedding. That seems important. If they'd converted me, they'd make me sleep in the bed properly, right?

But I know I'm just guessing.

Still, I assume my state of worry means I am Untamed. If augmenters were in my system, I'd not be worrying. A couple years ago, I saw five Untamed get taken by the Enhanced. Saw augmenters rammed down their throats. Saw the mirrors slide across their eyes and the loopy smiles of artificiality glaze over their faces. I can still hear their voices—not their words, for I can't remember them exactly, but their tones. The drugged way they had of stumbling over their words as they tried to tell us how wonderful being Enhanced was—because that's what I imagine them saying whenever I re-enact it in my mind.

Right. If I'm still Untamed, the clock's ticking against me. There's no window in here—just the light from the fluorescent strips above—so I've no way of knowing how long I've been here. Except my bladder's not twinging at all. I can comfortably go four hours without any awareness from it. So, it's still the day of the siege?

The siege that Shweta betrayed us on. No, not Shweta. The imposter. They'd already taken Shweta, and we should've realized.

Everything inside me tightens, and somehow the pain in my body gets stronger. I flex my fingers. My joints crack. I try the door handle again. I can't just do nothing.

Maybe I should shout…

I breathe deeply. Is shouting going to be a bad idea? Would it bring the Enhanced here to convert me next? Maybe I'm in a queue or something—especially if they got a lot of us. My gut clenches as I think of the Griffin children here.

And Kazem? Is he here, too? He could be in the

conversion room right now…

I swallow hard. No. I can't worry over stuff I don't know is happening. And Kazem's strong. He'll have got away. I know he will.

Maintain a level head, Kace. Come on.

I pace the room. Pacing often helps me think—or it did in the tunnels or beneath the skies when I was asking the Gods and Goddesses to get the Beast out of me—hell, why didn't they do it? Why did they literally let me have the soul of an Enhanced man inside me all this time? But pacing's not so much helping here though…

Unless…

My heart lifts a little. The Beast. Can he help? Can he get me out of here? I swallow deeply. I don't even know how to summon the Beast so he physically takes over my body—not since I killed Ysabelle and the clansmen. Ever since then, I've fought with all my vigor to keep him under wraps. After I killed fifty people in the blink of an eye, I vowed to never use him.

But I have to get out of here.

Yet Kazem and the others *could* be in rooms adjacent to me. If I let the Beast out and that energy wave decimates everything around me again, I'd be killing them.

Death is better than being Enhanced.

And being Enhanced is what's going to happen to me if I don't do anything.

I head to the wall on my left, and then knock on it. Three quick taps. If anyone's next door, they either don't hear me or ignore me. I try the wall on my right. Then the wall behind the bed's headboard. Nothing happens.

"Hello? Is anyone there?" But I daren't speak too loudly. "Kaz?"

Do it now, Kace.

I have got to get out of here.

I clench my jaws as mild nausea rises. This *is* the best thing to do, isn't it?

I breathe deeply and focus on the Beast inside. He feels warm—a ball of kinetic energy that tumbles and tumbles inside my soul. I feel the way he stretches and rolls, feel the layers to his body, feel how he is connected to every part of my being.

And I coax him out. It's different, this time. I was scared before, under direct attack, blood pouring from the gashes and stab wounds. And this time, this time I'm scared still, but it's a different kind of scared. The danger is anticipated, lurking, but not present right now. I coax him out. He slides smoothly from my core, and—

Something clicks.

My head whips up, my eyes on the door. The handle turns, and the door opens.

I throw the Beast forward—a blinding flash of light and—

The wave hits the Enhanced man, but then it stops, because he's holding his hands up. And at first, I can't process what's going on. All the lights—lights from his hand, another Beast?

"I wouldn't do that if I were you," a low voice says, and my heart sinks—but the Beast gets stronger. The Beast is singing, and I know what that means. I want to shrink away.

I'm going to have to kill.

Another massacre.

One that includes my people here. More Untamed deaths.

"DID YOU HEAR ME?" THE Enhanced man asks. Mirror eyes. A shock of jet-black hair and a Beast. I feel it—feel it calling to the one in me. He has a *Beast* too.

With Jaqueline, I never sensed her Beast, doubted they existed until Ysabelle awakened me to my own. But with this man, I can both sense his and see his and feel his. But it's more than just the Beast. There's something familiar about him, this man—

I inhale sharply. I saw this man reflected in Abdi's eyes in that strange dream. He looked different then. His skin was sallow and drenched in sweat, and his eye-mirrors had faded. But it was *this* man. This man whose memory I just saw—he is the Beast. The man whose soul I've got—he's not dead. He's alive. So I can't have his soul…unless the Enhanced don't have souls?

But I've got his memories. And he knows Caia-Lu, too.

"You remember me, Kacey, don't you? No, don't do that," he says, just as I'm about to lunge forward. He's left the door open, and I need to get out of here, whether I know him or not. He's *Enhanced*. "You wouldn't get far. And my power overrides yours.

Really, that wave was pathetic."

He thinks his Beast is a *power*? Huh.

"Come on, Kacey. Don't mess things up. I'm on your side."

"You're Enhanced." I snort.

"No," he says. "I'm Untamed. It's me—Red. From D'Elinous."

"Red?" I blink at him. D'Elinous was the village I was born in, but I was ten when I left there. Left with Aahna, an elderly woman who survived the ambush. And I traveled with her for a couple of years, until we joined the clansmen. Aahna died shortly after we joined, even though she seemed healthy. I didn't think much of it at the time, as Iralda said elderly people do just suddenly die, but after my cleansing, when I was traveling alone with the guilt of the massacre, I wondered if Aahna's death was Ysabelle's or the Overlord Seer's doing. Because I needed something to be angry about that wasn't my fault.

"You've forgotten me?" The Enhanced man lets out a short laugh. "We used to play together. You and me and Keelie. Sometimes Elf and Inga, too."

Keelie, Elf, Inga—names I haven't thought of in so long. My original group, where I lived with Caia-Lu. And this is Red? That annoying boy who followed Keelie everywhere? But it can't be him. He was killed at the D'Elinous ambush, the attack that ended the group. I start to laugh, but he's not laughing. He's looking at me all sincerely, but he has bloody eye mirrors. Unless they're fakes, like what we used.

He smiles. "Listen, I need you to trust what I'm saying, okay?"

"Don't come closer." I manage to get the words out even though everything is spinning.

"Kacey. You're still Untamed, and I'm on your side. I'm going to get you out of here."

I take a step back. My heart hammers. My eyes narrow. I saw Red's eleven-year-old dead body. I saw him lying in a pool of blood. I heard Keelie screaming because of it. Yet he was alive? And now he looks like he's Enhanced. Even if he says he'll help me.

Could he be telling the truth? That he is really Untamed? I have his memories in me. He's connected to my Beast, somehow. And I'm Untamed. So does that mean he has to be too? But I don't know enough about Beasts and what they actually are. All I know is they're bad, dangerous, evil—and I know they kill.

"I need you to go along with what I'm saying, okay?" he says.

My guard gets higher. "How many others are here?" My voice cracks. "My people?"

"They've converted twelve already." He says the words so matter-of-factly. No emotion at all. "I could only get one of you out and into this room—and I chose you. They'll be converting the rest now. But you're safe—it's okay. I've got you."

He *chose* me? A strange warmth filters through my body, starting at the top of my spine and travelling down. He chose me because he can feel this connection we have? The Beasts, the shared memory thing? Wait—can he access my memories, like I can his? If that *is* what is even going on here…

Then I jolt as I realize what he said. *They'll be converting the rest now.* My stomach roils. "Who are they converting?"

"I don't know their names."

"But I need to know!" My voice is frantic. I picture Kazem with mirrors, real this time. Or Maggot. Bhavesh. Winston. Tammy. The Griffin siblings. My chest hitches. I reach out for something to grab to steady me, but my hand bats at thin air. And somehow that makes it worse, hits me like a punch to the gut: my people—those I swore to protect—are gone. Enhanced. Or dead.

"Why?" I stare at him, my emotions welling up inside me like an angry tide. A vicious storm. "How could you let them be converted?" I shake my head, nausea getting stronger. "Where are they? We have to go now. They could still be Untamed. We can still save them."

"Kacey, we can't help them," the man says.

"Then that's proof." I fold my arms. "You're not one of us. You're Enhanced." My gaze hardens—and I *feel* it hardening, like there's a film over each eyeball solidifying. Oh Gods—are these mirrors? I twist around, trying to find something to see my reflection in, but all there is are his eyes. And I see myself in them. Still Untamed.

He takes a small step closer to me. He's tall and broad-shouldered, taller than most of the Untamed men I know. He's wearing a white dress-shirt with the sleeves pushed back to the elbows, revealing taut muscles and tattoos. "I'm not," he says, his voice low, like it's a warning. "I'm *undercover*."

I nearly laugh. "No undercover Untamed would let other Untamed be converted without trying to do something." My head spins. I need to think—and fast. I need to get out of here. My Beast stirs again.

"They would," he says. "We have to, else we get caught—and then where would we be? But I saved you, Kacey. That should be proof enough of who I am and whose moral code I follow."

Moral code? I snort. Like the Enhanced even *have* a moral code.

"Proof would be you trying to save every Untamed. Not just me."

"I can't."

"Then I guess we know who is more Untamed out of the two of us." Every muscle in my body tightens. "Where are they?"

And I'm trying not to think of Kazem—of him with mirrors that are real this time, stuck to his eyes, mirrors that *are* his eyes. But, of course, as soon as I try not to think of him, I do. And I see him—because the Beast is rising in me, and he feeds on my imagination.

"No," Kazem screams, and he's thrashing and thrashing at the bindings that tie him to the bed. "No, let me go!"

But Enhanced Ones advance on him, grinning grins

that get wider and wider, revealing too many perfect teeth. Row upon row, and these aren't normal Enhanced because they're gliding across the floor. They're robots. They're holding scalpels and augmenters with needles in. Sickly pink ones. Too bright. Too wrong.

"Let's gouge the Untamed parasite out of you," one of them says.

Kazem shouts and shouts some more. He pulls on the bindings, but his arms and legs don't budge an inch.

"You'll feel better soon," another Enhanced says, their voice all fake and curling, like the words are old and left over, and they're trying to reuse them.

The augmenter gets closer. The scalpel gets closer.

Kazem screams as they bite his skin. Anguish. Pain. Fury.

I can almost *hear* his screams—that's how powerful the Beast is. I gulp. Is it the truth? Can the Beast not only show me Red's memories but also what's going on with others? No. Kazem can't be Enhanced! He can't.

I try to calm myself. I think about the visions, how that one of Kazem was different. I *was* Red in his memories, but I was an observer of Kazem's situation.

I take in a shuddering breath that has me panting even deeper. Kazem will be fine. He has to be.

"Kacey, we cannot go and help the Untamed," the man claiming to be Red says.

"We have to try," I bite back. "We always try. We *always* go for our people."

"We do when it's safe."

"So, find out if it's safe," I counter, tapping my foot. "See what's happening. See how many Enhanced are with them. There were sixty of us in the tunnels. You said twelve have been converted already?"

His eyes narrow, but he nods. It's a small movement.

"Who are they?"

"I do not know their names."

"Was one a man with black hair? Brown skin? He's tall and—"

"Kacey, I don't know."

I let out a frustrated sound. "How many conversion

rooms are there? Because there must be Untamed queuing or something, being made to wait, tied up and whatnot. So, we can overpower whatever guards are there and—"

"It's too late, Kacey," the man says. "It's too late."

Not if only twelve were converted in the time I was unconscious. And more are being done now. I grit my teeth, and I want to cover my ears with my hands because the Beast is making me hear Kazem's screams again as he's converted, as he's injected with augmenter after augmenter. "Prove it. Prove to me it's too late."

And I want to say it's never too late—except it could be if they've been given augmenters. One taste is enough. One taste is always enough. Instant addiction that can never be broken. And when that's combined with brainwashing and torture techniques of varying degrees, well… I grew up with all the warning stories, and while I'm not sure just how many of the torture devices are actually used, I can't discount it. Because torture is powerful. And when it's layered on a background of brainwashing and addiction, it's impossible to break.

Once you're Enhanced, you're never the same person again. You're gone. Lost.

Kazem.

My heart squeezes.

"Kacey, this isn't necessary. This is just drawing out the pain," the man says.

"Prove it!" My whole body is trembling. Any moment now, I'm going to break.

With a dramatic sigh, he pulls a radio from his belt and presses a few buttons. He holds the device close to his ear, so close that all I can hear is the mumble of static and sound, not individual words. Then he tucks the radio back into his belt.

"It's too late," he says, looking at me.

"I don't believe you."

He laughs but it's not a nice laugh. "Should've known you'd be like this. You always were stubborn.

Just like—" He cuts himself off and presses his hands together.

"Just like what?" I glare at him.

"You know, you should be grateful," he snaps. "I didn't have to save you. I didn't have to do anything. We're undercover, Kacey, and I risked everything— my position, my job, the work of my whole group— for you, and you've done nothing but complain and moan and be angry. Well, you need to be grateful. You've got a chance the others haven't."

A metallic taste fills my mouth, but I don't trust myself to speak. My head is still spinning, and I feel like I'm not quite here, not quite taking in everything.

And I look at him. This man who claims to be Untamed but looks like an Enhanced One. The man who says he is *Red*? What are the chances of this happening, realistically? D'Elinous is nowhere near New Zeralzi.

"Why did you choose me to save?"

"Because I recognized you." He rolls his eyes—but the gesture doesn't look like Red, not the little boy that I remember. And Red being here, really and truly here and Untamed, is just too good to be true.

"No, I don't believe you," I say, even though my Beast recognized him. Because this *is* too much of a coincidence. What is it, some kind of ploy where the Enhanced try to win your trust through lies before they take you to the conversion room? Is it better for them if we agree willingly, filled up with their lies?

He folds his muscular arms. Tattoos twitch. "You really want to waste time assessing my validity?"

"Look, if you're going to convince me you're not Enhanced, that this undercover stuff is real, then I need more details." The Beast is still very much awake, and I try to coax him out a little, get him to feel out this man.

"We haven't got time for this. I need to get you out of here—and I can, if you do everything I say."

"Then give me a reason to trust that you are who you say you are." My Beast stretches against me. It wants more freedom than I'm granting at the moment. The Beast wants to burst through the seams and edges of my body. The Beast wants to wrap around this man like a Cobra, squeezing and squeezing him. The Beast wants the man's last dying breath and the Beastly part of him, too.

The Beast wants to see itself, to be with its own kind.

So many different things inside me, inside the Beast, fighting for attention.

The man rolls his eyes again; I don't like it when he does this, and my own eyes narrow. "At D'Elinous, you had this stuffed toy that you loved. It was a rat. With spectacles knitted on."

"Anyone could know that."

He lets out an exasperated sigh. "I'm *Untamed*."

"Your eyes say otherwise."

"They're contacts. You just have to trust me, okay? I understand it's difficult. I get it, I do. But I'm going to get you out of here. In the meantime, wear these." He takes a small vial out of his pocket.

For half a second, I think it's an augmenter—but then I see it's a contact lens case.

"You have to wear these if I'm going to get you out," he says.

"You're getting me out now?"

"Later today." His voice is crisp, curt. I find myself looking at him properly now. He's filled out a lot. I suppose he's like the conventional attractive man— muscles and a sharp jaw. Not that it does anything for me. There's only one man I am attracted to, but it is attraction that's aesthetic and romantic, not sexual.

Kazem. Kazem who could very well be Enhanced— or dead—now.

"They're really careful about the town borders. So, I can't get you *out* out until later. But I can get you to my apartment—away from the conversion compound. Put the lenses in, and we'll go."

I breathe deeply. Seems like the best option.

I take the lenses and insert them as quickly as

I can. I always hate wearing them. I blink several times. My right eye starts watering. Mirror lenses are much bigger than normal contact lenses, the type that Maggot once told me they had in the olden days. Mirror lenses cover the whole of your eyeball, not just the iris and pupil.

The man—Red, if he really can be trusted—hands me a tissue from his pocket. I wipe under my eye, hating how it must look like I'm crying.

"We'll go now," he says. "Give me your hand."

"What?"

"Just do it. And don't even think about getting away or using that power of yours again. Don't make things difficult for me. Not when I'm helping you. Be grateful, Kacey. I could've picked anyone to save. But I chose you."

A thousand thoughts swim in my head, thoughts that I need to sort out, but I can't do that now. I have to stay alert—not let myself get distracted inside my own mind.

The man—I still can't bring myself to think of him as Red because Red was Untamed and this man might not be—takes hold of my hand. His grip is warm and firm. Then he marches me forward.

"Match my pace," he says. "You're not my prisoner."

"Then why are you pulling me along? Holding my hand?"

"We are lovers."

Lovers. I nearly snort but stop myself just in time.

The Beast inside me shifts a little, mellowing. I feel him getting smaller, but I know the Beast and he's not disappearing. He's still awake. He's just trying to lull me into a false sense of security. Then he'll pounce. And if Red's Beast does the same… well, two Beasts working together? Who knows what will happen?

We march through corridor after corridor. I'm still wearing my clothes—Untamed clothes—and I realize with a jolt that my army boots are scuffed. That annoys me.

"The Beasts—what are they?" I ask once we're outside in a sort of courtyard and the man's indicated that we're going to the right.

"The Beasts?" He's frowning.

"The things inside us."

"The energy. Ah, you don't know?" He looks surprised.

"We got it from D'Elinous. Well, I assume so. It's a *power*, not a Beast. All of us who were there, I think we all have it. Though it is elsewhere, too. Specific energy. I could always feel it in me, and sense it in others, but only recently has it become stronger." He swallows visibly and his Adam's apple bobs. "It awoke truly in me, a few weeks ago. I never could have imagined its full potential, how powerful it could be. Now I feel its surges stronger than ever, and it's easier to control." He smiles.

Control? He can control his? It's not a wrestle? "Wait, you said we *all* have it? You've seen others from D'Elinous?"

"Keelie." He says her name quickly, like it burns him.

My eyes widen. "You've seen Keelie?" Keelie's alive? My heart thuds.

"Yes. I've seen Keelie."

"And?" I prompt.

"And what?"

"She has this power, too? What about the others?" I list names from D'Elinous—names I haven't thought of in years, names I'm not even sure are correct—but he just nods at each one.

"We're special, Kacey. All of us. Though you and I have the most energy inside us. It's barely detectable in some of them. Or it was—that might've changed. I don't know. I haven't heard. We've all been given this energy for a reason."

"What reason?" I ask.

"To make us more powerful, stronger. So we will be invincible."

Invincible. Huh. But this man knows about this

energy, this Beast inside me. He knows more than I do, and I need to know what he knows. I need to get rid of my Beast. And something tells me that Red knows the answer.

ELEVEN

RED TAKES ME TO HIS apartment. Number 18. The rooms are bright and airy, with minimalistic-style décor. Lots of sleek surfaces, and everything is either black or white. A large mirror hangs in the living room, above a black leather sofa, and I startle when I see myself reflected. See my mirror eyes in it. I look like I'm Enhanced. And what's to say that my eyes really are Untamed under the contacts?

"Just make yourself at home," Red says, heading into the kitchen. "I'll get us some drinks. You like coffee?"

"Yeah," I say, even though I have never had it, but I'm not concentrating on that. I slip behind the sofa, so my face is inches from the mirror, and I peer at my eyes. Carefully, I pinch the contact lens on my left eye. Pinch it a little too hard, and I flinch, but the film comes away, revealing my very Untamed eye. The sight of my brown iris and slightly off-white sclera fills me with more relief than anything.

A silly grin stretches across my face. It makes my reflection look a little demonic or something, given I still have one lens in.

"You should wash your hands before taking the

contacts out," Red says, walking back into the room. "Don't want you getting an eye infection. That would be hard to get treated here without them discovering what you really are."

"It's fine," I say. I mean, it's not like we had access to a lot of clean water and soap in the tunnels, yet few of us got eye infections despite regular use of lenses.

"Kettle's just boiling," Red says. "Be a minute or so."

I nod. I can't hear the kettle though. But before I can question it, Red asks me to take my shoes off.

"I'm very house proud." He's already taken his off.

I kick my boots off, watch them bounce a few feet away. His carpet is soft under my feet. My left sock has a huge hole across the toes, and sudden shame fills me.

"So, the Beasts inside us—the powers," I correct quickly when I see his sharp look. "How do we get rid of them?"

"Get rid of them?" He laughs but stops short when he appears to realize I'm serious. "Why would you want to do that?"

"Because it's dangerous. Unnatural."

"How can it be unnatural? We were born with the seeds of the energy in us. The power is part of us."

"I don't want it," I say. Darkness curls at the edge of my soul. "It's too dangerous, Red. You don't understand. I killed a whole village."

"An Untamed village?"

I nod.

His quick intake of breath is sharp. "Where?"

"Far to the west, months' travel away from here." I take a few steps toward him. "It just got out, this power. I couldn't control it. And I can't have that happening again."

"Of course not—but, Kacey, I can't sense any unpredictability in it now. Were you young when this happened?"

"I was fourteen. Is that young?"

"Yes." He chews on his bottom lip for a moment. "You're in control of it now, though, Kacey. I can sense that."

"But I want it gone. Look, I could've killed you with it—an undercover Untamed." Because him being that has to be the truth. "It's too risky."

"But it's a gift." He laughs. "And the Untamed are going to need all the gifts they can get. You know, I'm in an optimal position here, and the Chosen Ones—sorry, the *Enhanced*. I have to call them by *their* name all the time here. But the Enhanced Ones' technology is phenomenal. We have to keep all the advantages we can. Now, will you be all right here? I need to check in with the others."

"The others?"

"The other undercover Untamed." He gives me a casual smile.

"Then I'm coming, too," I say. There are more of them than just him and Keelie? I need to meet them.

He gives me a look. "No, not yet."

"But—"

"No buts." He gives me a sterner look, then rolls his sleeves up. The movement reveals tattoos. The kind of tattoos that I know many women say are attractive. "Maybe in a few days, Kacey. We can't suddenly have you walking freely around the town like we do. The Enhanced would notice you. We've all got IDs here, and specific jobs, too. And security is tightening up. I'll get an ID sorted for you, see if I can get you an official job with the Enhanced. After that, you can join our rebellion. Just lie low for now."

I smile. "Okay."

Red's brows furrow a little, like he expected me to put up more of a fight. "Well, I'll see you later then. Make your coffee, yeah? You'll know how you like it. Coffee jar's on the counter, milk's in the fridge, sugar's over there. Make yourself at home."

And with that, he leaves.

And this is…

This is *weird*.

Quickly, I check the whole apartment—for what, I

don't know. But it's common sense to check for any overt danger. But there's nothing. There's not really anything in here. Just furniture. There's no character. Even the laptop in the bedroom looks devoid of personality. It's pristine and perfect, no stickers stuck to it, no fancy case with it. Nothing.

The Beast inside me stirs.

I tense. Then an idea comes to me. Red didn't say that it *wasn't* possible to get rid of the Beast inside me. He just said I should want to keep the Beast because having it gives me an advantage. But that means that it should be possible to get rid of the Beast. And Red has to know how.

I grab his laptop and sit on the bed. The duvet cover is scratchy, and the springs of the mattress protest a little. I've seen laptops before, usually in use at cafes that I've walked by, but Bhavesh stole one once. We crowded around him as he used it, clocking how the battery was running out, knowing we had limited opportunity to learn. We have to be clever, quick to adapt. I open the laptop. The screen asks for a password.

I groan and look around. No books here, so no book titles stand out. There are no pets. No nothing.

My heart speeds up a little. What does Red like more than anything?

Keelie?

The two of them were inseparable before, and he said she's undercover, too. I type in her name—and oh Gods, it *works*.

I'm in. A wicked grin slides over my lips.

He must have some info on the power or the Beast or whatever it is, and so I begin searching his files for it. Red seems like a methodical man now.

But I can't find anything. There's no folder labelled for it. Hell, there's not even anything I can find about his undercover work. But he wouldn't be silly enough to do that. An undercover officer wouldn't have a folder labeled *Undercover Work*.

I try to find records of Untamed conversions instead.

Any spreadsheets or anything that I can search. See if Kazem's name is there. But I can't find any files for that either.

I search through more and more folders, and then I find a folder called *Nbutai*. I frown. The name sounds vaguely familiar to me—I'm sure I remember Lìxúe, Keelie's mother, talking about that group when we were at D'Elinous. It was led by a man she knew. Ah, what was his name? Jahn?

I click on the folder and find it's full of photos. I open the first photo. It shows several huts on a desert land. And people. Untamed. My heart beats faster.

An Asian woman who looks quite like Lìxúe—curvy, with long hair and a wicked smile—is shouting something, her arms full of energy. But, actually, she doesn't quite look like Lìxúe. She's younger, and her face a little softer and her build skinnier, and behind her is a child who looks abound ten or eleven. A child with the glossiest black hair and a wide face. It's Keelie, and is that *Mila*? All grown up. Seeing what Keelie looks like now makes me feel weird. Like this image should just replace what I remember her as—the scrappy eleven-year-old. But now Mila's that age. Mila who was only a baby when D'Elinous was destroyed.

I flick to the next photo. A dark-skinned middle-aged woman is sitting with Keelie. Both of them are looking at something stretched across their lap. But it's dark in the picture, and I can't tell what it is.

The next photo is Mila playing football—and Elf! I see him, Keelie's twin. It's got to be him. He's tall, and he looks like their mother again. Not so much Owen, their father, though. Elf's build is skinner. He looks happy. Behind them, in the background, are smaller figures. Another woman who's—oh my God, it's Bea! It has to be. She's a spitting image of Lìxúe, but she's got Owen's slightly stockier build too. There are two men as well, in this photo, Untamed. One has white skin and one dark skin.

A smile breaks across my face. Keelie and Elf and Bea and Mila all got away. They found these Untamed—the Nbutai group? I flick through more and more photos, see more Untamed. More and more.

And then—

"Woah." Heat floods me as I see a photo of Red and Keelie together. They're kissing, and the camera's quite a way away. They look confident, happy. I click to the next, and the next—more and more of them kissing. Then clothes are coming off.

Oh, Gods. I hurry past those photos, feeling like a trespasser, and breathe a sigh of relief when we're back among the huts and the other Untamed. Keelie's in one of these again, but this time she looks annoyed. She's arguing with Elf.

Then there are ones of her crying, of people patting her on the shoulder. Of a bloke staring at her—and another of her kissing this bloke who definitely isn't Red. My eyes widen, and I feel even more like an intruder, like I'm watching all this unfold before me, but I can't look away. It's addictive.

Another shot of the middle-aged woman with the dark skin is next. She's got a pendant around her neck. She's the Seer of the group?

I shift a little on the bed. The mattress creaks again. Then I'm looking at photos of a motorcycle. A woman's riding it—and at first, I think it's Keelie, but then there's a close up of her face, and I think it's the older sister, Bea—and then she's speeding down a steep mountainside, sand billowing behind her. It's followed by a shot of Keelie and Elf apparently arguing again. Both look animated, annoyed, angry.

And a photo of a calendar—I don't understand its significance. There's nothing written on it, from what I can see, though the photo's not that clear.

I frown, click through more and more photos. People and food and tools being made.

And then it's dark, so dark in this batch of photos. Nighttime. A truck at the edge of the village. People climbing out. Hundreds and hundreds of snaps of them, that almost make a stop-motion film. Six people are climbing out of the truck. Elf is one of them, and there's a pale-skinned woman with short, cropped dark hair. And a man who has the same thicker build. A dark-skinned girl who looks about sixteen, seventeen. And a man in his thirties, I'd say, with red hair.

Elf's in a lot of the next photos, looking more and more serious—and in all of these ones, he's wearing the same clothes, hasn't moved much from each photo, like they were all taken in quick succession. Then a dark-skinned young woman in her twenties is putting her arms around him, and he's resting his head on her shoulder. He's crying.

Keelie isn't in any more of the photos, and a dark feeling spreads through me.

My heart feels heavier, and I don't want to keep looking—but I do. What story are these photos telling?

The next snap is a closeup of Elf's face. Tear-stained. The next has him covering his face with his hands. I click to the next—people crying. More and more Untamed.

My heart pounds faster, heavier. I start to feel sick. What are these photos?

I click to the next and—

My heart drops away and nausea grabs me. It's…

"No," I mutter, as I see the Enhanced in the photos. Enhanced men rising up and—

It's an ambush—just like at D'Elinous. A choke strangles in my throat, and I'm helpless as my fingers keep clicking, keep showing me the next photos.

An Untamed man lying in blood on the desert floor. Two dogs jumping up at an Enhanced.

That dark-skinned Untamed girl who's sixteen or seventeen, being led away by an Enhanced man. Then a young man pointing a gun at that Enhanced man, trying to save the girl?

Tears slide down my face as I watch the action unfold. More and more bodies. A large Untamed woman lying on the ground. A truck with headlights—Untamed getting into it?

I frown, peering closer.

Did some get away?

I click to the next photo—only it's not a photo. It's a video.

I click play. Sound blares out—loud and bone-drilling, and it takes me a moment to realize it's a man screaming. The image is dark and grainy at first, and I adjust the brightness of the laptop, trying to see more clearly and—

"You let my daughter get away," an Enhanced man shouts.

He steps into the camera frame.

I recognize him. It's Owen. From D'Elinous. Keelie and Elf and Bea and Mila's father. And he's here—with…with Red, because suddenly the lighting changes—a light flicked on—and I see Red is in the video too.

Red's slumped on the floor, his mirrors in. And he's barely moving.

I frown. So, Owen's here too? He survived D'Elinous as well? Why wasn't he in the earlier photos with his children? My head spins—so many of us survived, and Aahna and I had thought we were the only ones.

My heart rate rises, but I feel wrong too. I can't work out what's happening. Wait—that screaming I heard at the start? That was Red? I go back to the start, then let the video play all the way through.

Red screams.

"You let my daughter get away!" Owen shouts.

"I did my best, I already told you — we can find Bea."

"Well then where the fuck is she? Why haven't you found her already? Come on — you're healed now after Keelie shot you, so why haven't you found my daughter?"

My eyes widen. Keelie *shot* Red?

"You're not fit for this — something's gone wrong with your brain, you're not behaving like we should."

"It's grief!" Red shouts. "My soulmate is dead. And how can you not care? You thought Keelie was your daughter —

you raised her—and you don't even care she's dead."

"She was never my daughter," Owen says. "I've only got two, and now only Bea is alive. And you're being too soft, too weak. You're letting the Untamed win."

I frown and lean back a little. Well of course he'd let the Untamed win. *Because he is Untamed,* I think.

But then Red's getting up. He's shaking. "I messed up, okay? I got too into it all, this pretending. I thought I was doing the right thing—but I can see now I wasn't. And I will find Bea. I will."

"Good," Owen says. "Because I want my only surviving child with me. I want her converted. I want her saved."

Bea, converted? Saved?

That's when I realize it: They're not talking like they're undercover Untamed.

They're talking like they're both Enhanced.

And Keelie shot Red? Did she work out he wasn't really as undercover as the rest of them were? Or maybe she wasn't either—because there was never any photo of her with the mirror lenses. But she's dead now…

And what if there are no Untamed who are undercover? What if there never were?

My heart pounds faster.

The video finishes abruptly, just as Owen and Red are shouting more, but I miss their words because of the rushing of blood in my ears. But then the next video pops up. I click play before I can think.

"No, please, no! I don't need that—" Red shouts.

"You do," an Enhanced man shouts, his head right in front of Red's. *"A level three conversion."*

I freeze. Those words—I know this. The Beast showed me this memory—to warn me. The Beast is looking out for me?

"I'm fine!" Red yells, and his face twists. *"I'm not Untamed!"*

"Even Chosen Ones need re-converting from time to time."

"I said I'm fine!"

"But you're not! If you were fine, you wouldn't have allowed that woman to go Untamed for so long. And she

wouldn't be dead now, nor would we have had to use up valuable resources restarting your heart."

Red flinches.

My head spins and spins, and I feel numb as it keeps playing. It's a different scene now. Different room. Different camera angle.

Red is strapped to a chair. Thick bindings wind around his arms and legs.

"Try the next level," a smooth voice says. I can't see the speaker. "We need to make sure he really is amenable to our way of life. Can't have him taking liberties again, even if he thinks leaving them Untamed for longer will be beneficial in the end-game. That's not how we work. We convert all the Untamed upon their immediate extraction and return to our villages."

The camera shakes, and then Red's screaming, and it all goes dark.

My breaths come in short, sharp bursts.

I don't know what the hell is going on. I don't know how I got sent part of Red's memory before, but I need to get out of here. I need to find my people and get the hell out of here.

TWELVE

I SHOVE THE LAPTOP TO the side and stand. My legs suddenly feel too weak, too insubstantial—and hell, this is stupid. I'm a free-runner, a freaking acrobat of the land. I swallow hard. But how could I have been so stupid, trusting Red?

Yet he didn't convert me... Just like he didn't convert everyone when he found the Nbutai group and Keelie? My head pounds.

I run back to the living room and grab my shoes, nearly trip as I pull them on. My heart pounds, and any second, I expect the door to fly open. For Red and other Enhanced Ones to rush in, grab me.

But they don't.

I get to the door.

It's not even locked. It opens easily.

I inhale sharply. I'm in a block of apartments. I'm going to bump into other Enhanced—and I've only got one contact lens in.

I hurry back to the mirror. Find the discarded lens on the floor and try to wipe off the little hairs that cling to it before forcing it back in. My eye waters and stings. But it's in, and I don't waste time.

I run.

My shoes slap on the marble floor of the corridor, and I take the stairs down to the bottom of the block, wiping at my streaming eye.

And I walk out of the block, and I pass Enhanced Ones and they don't even bat an eyelid at me.

Keep breathing, Kace. Now, where's the conversion compound?

It takes me a moment to orientate myself, and then I'm breathing hard and walking purposefully. The conversion compound isn't far.

It takes me ten minutes. And there are Enhanced Ones right outside. Shit.

But of course there would be. Because this is the most likely place that Untamed are going to try and break into to rescue their people.

And just how many of my people are in there?

Tears burn my vision, and I blink them back quickly. Need to appear strong and confident, not like I'm an emotional wreck.

I head inside. Again, surprisingly easy. There's no one in here.

I ball my hands into fists. This… this isn't right.

My steps are light on the floor, and my heart beats faster, faster, faster. Where is everyone? Where—

"Kacey?" a voice whispers.

I turn back. For a second, I can't see a soul. But then I see there's a door open to my right. A door into a cluttered store cupboard, and a small figure crouches there.

"Clive?" My voice wobbles. He whimpers when he sees me, his eyes widening. Oh my God. It's *Clive*. The kid.

"Are you…" His voice is frantic, scared, and he gulps. "Enhanced?"

"It's okay. Lenses." I move quickly to the cupboard and look around. Then I head into the cupboard. Clive recoils, and there's not much space. I pull the door to, so only a little light gets in, and we're bathed in shadows.

"No, please," he whimpers. "Don't convert me!"

I remove a contact—just for a second before I let it cling again to my eyeball—and he breathes a loud sigh of relief.

"They've got them all," he whispers. There's a large cut on the side of his face, and his clothes are ripped.

"Them *all*?" I ask. My heart sinks. *Kazem.*

For a second, I feel like I'm sinking. Everything in my body is turning to stone and falling. My Kazem… an Enhanced One?

No. Maybe Clive's wrong.

"Kacey, I didn't know what to do."

"It's okay." But annoyance flutters through me. I look down at Clive. I'm going to have to look after him, aren't I? I breathe hard. This is payback. Payback for leaving the baby behind with the clansmen. Has to be. I've lost Kazem all because some divine force wants to punish me.

Clive looks like he's going to cry.

"We'll get out of here," I try to reassure him. I do not want him crying on me. "How did you avoid conversion?"

"I tripped and hit my head." He wipes a string of snot from his nose onto the flapping end of his gray scarf. The wool's started to unravel. "They must've thought I was dead. I came around and they were restraining the others. I played dead until they took the last person away—it was Winston." Tears fill his eyes. "I didn't do anything to help him. Or any of them. My…my own family."

"It's okay," I say again, even though this is clearly not an okay situation. "Don't think of that. Just… stay here." I reach for the door—I need to see if there is anyone else who can be saved—but Clive grabs my hand. His touch is sticky, hot.

"Don't leave me!"

I try to keep my voice soft, remind myself he's scared witless and that I need to be kind. "I've got to see if the others are still Untamed." Got to find Kazem.

"They won't be. I heard their screams, Kacey. All of their screams until they…changed. They asked for more… more augmenters. Kacey, there's no one left." His bottom lips wobbles again. Please, just get me out of here."

Hell no, I am *not* dealing with a crying ten-year-old. No way.

I do not like children. I mean, that's a general rule with me—if I can avoid interaction with children, all the better. Sure, some are okay, but mostly they're… not. It's not that I hate them or anything, it's that they're liabilities. They're not as experienced. And they remind me of the baby I left behind. The baby I killed. And Clive—well, he annoys me the most. He's the smallest and youngest of our group, and he often plays the baby. Turns on the waterworks easily. I've heard the other women call him 'endearing' and 'cute', but he's just annoying to me.

It's just typical that the one person who's still here and Untamed is not only a child but the one who irritates me the most.

"Okay." My heart pounds. I swallow hard. I'll get Clive out, and I'll do a quick check at the same time, looking for our people. Anyone who can still be saved. *Kazem.* "Have you got your mirrors on you?"

He shakes his head and sniffs loudly. "They fell out my pocket."

Of course they did. I pat my pocket—but of course my original pair has gone. Taken by Red, perhaps? Red, who then gave me extra…

"Okay, you'll have mine. You're going to walk straight out of here, okay?" I peel out my contacts and hand them to him.

"We shouldn't swap lenses," Clive says. "Maggot warns about eye infections."

"What choice do we have?" My tone is blunt.

Clive looks startled, but he puts the lenses in—really struggling with one of them in particular, and it seems to take an age—and then I scoot him toward the door.

"You're going to have to be confident, okay?" I say.

"What about you?" His brows furrow, and he shakes his head. "Aren't you coming with me?" He reaches for my hand, but I don't let him take it. "I can't go on my own."

"You can," I say, and I try to keep an ear out for sounds outside of this cupboard. Are any Enhanced Ones going to come here?

"I really don't think—"

"You have to. You're going to walk straight out. I will be coming as well—but we have to be strategic." I'm more likely to get caught if glimpsed by the enemy, so we need to take different routes. We can't have both of us being apprehended. And besides, I need to take a different route because I need to check all of the conversion rooms. Check to see if anyone else is hiding, like Clive has been. And I need to see Kazem. If he's converted, I need to see it with my own eyes. I focus back on Clive. "But you're going to be brave."

Brave. And Clive's got it easy. *I'm* the one who's going to have to be stealthy. The ultimate challenge to see how good I am at free-running. Because if I run quickly enough through the town, the Enhanced won't be able to stop me even if they do see that I'm Untamed. And they wouldn't think that an Untamed would be stupid enough to free-run and show off in their town in broad daylight right after a mass conversion of their own people—right?

"We're doing this, okay?" I look into Clive's eyes. I'm not sure, but I think he's got one of the contact lenses inside out. It doesn't look quite right, but it'll do. It has to do. He found them hard enough to put in. "It'll work, I promise. But I need you to do this. Just walk out there. Be confident. Embody the confidence of an Enhanced One. I'll be keeping an eye on you, I promise. You won't see me, but I'll have your back. And I'll meet you at Dawn's Rock."

THIRTEEN

THE ROOFTOPS ARE THE EASIEST route out of New Zeralzi, so I make my way to the top of the conversion compound while checking every room I come across. Each is either locked or empty. It's too quiet. No sign of anyone else. But the rooms have been used recently, I can see that. There are signs of struggles. Some augmenters are smashed, and I wonder if that means at least one of our people got away. Hope rises in me, but no one calls my name.

I try to work out which room Kazem might've been in, and then I tell myself that he will have escaped, because he's Kazem. He's my wonderful Kazem. We're not going to get separated.

"We'll be together," I mutter, over and over. Kazem's probably outside, back at the tunnels, waiting for me. Yes, that'll be it.

Bar Clive, whom I glimpse walking far below from the window of a deserted conversion room when I do a quick check on his progress, I don't see anyone at all. Not even Enhanced Ones. I don't know whether to be glad about this or not. How would I react to seeing the enemy marching away one of our people, a freshly converted Untamed with real mirrors? Would I freeze? Fight? And what if Clive is wrong and they haven't *all* been converted? He might've just thought they had…

Part of me wants to stay here and look *properly* for them all now, not give up on Kazem, but the other part knows I have to go. I'd be stupid to stay in *case* there are Untamed here who need my help when I know that Clive is out there, still Untamed, and in need of my assistance. Because let's face it, he has no chance surviving on his own. I'm going to need to teach him, train him. And my own chances of survival will improve dramatically with another capable person. *If* I can make him capable.

And maybe, just maybe, some of our people already got away… like Kazem.

I breathe hard as I let myself onto the roof through a roof-top door at the top of the conversion compound. Cool air wraps around me. My thighs burn with anticipation as I creep closer to the edge of the roof.

Roof-to-roof jumping—not my favorite, not when I consider just how far I would fall should I miss—is my best option. And I can do this. I grit my teeth. I *have* to do this. Clive needs me. This is my chance for redemption.

From the roof's edge, I work out my route. The gap to the next building—a block containing labs—isn't big. I can jump that easily once I give myself a run up. From there, it'll be another easy jump across the roofs to an old apartment block. I know from experience that that roof can be slippery on the far side though, so I'll have to be careful. Then, it'll be a case of getting enough momentum going. There are grab-rails on the next building after that which I can use, and the compound that follows is huge, has roofs of different levels, but no jumps between buildings for a few minutes. I can't see farther than that building from here, but my memory is good, and I know that after that, the blocks get farther apart the farther out of the town center you get. That'll be trickier, if I decide to stay on the rooftops out there.

Would require bigger jumps.

But I can do this. I know I can. And I haven't got any more time to ponder this or plan. Clive will be waiting for me soon, by Dawn's Rock, and I can't be late. He'd probably crap himself or something if he thinks I've been caught.

The familiar adrenaline fills me, and my steps are light as I head backward to give myself a run-up to this roof's edge. I smile, relish the way my heart pounds.

Let's do this.

I run, propelling myself forward. My adrenaline fuels me—and it's like a drug, addictive. This is what I live for. Being able to do this.

I make the jump across to the next roof with ease, landing in a slight crouch before veering forward, using the energy to fuel me. Energy's fluid, that's what Bhavesh always says. Energy can be absorbed, but if you can preserve the energy, redirect it, then you'll do better. Use less overall.

Bhavesh—who's now dead or Enhanced.

My chest tightens, and my breathing quickens. *No.* I can't think like that. He'll have escaped. He has to have.

I plough on, hear my blood rushing in my ears, feel more and more adrenaline as I jump from roof to roof. My breaths are even, short, sharp, and I feel superhuman as I make the next jump. The wind carries me though the air. I am weightless, invincible, and I almost wish there were loads of Enhanced Ones about to see this. I want them to witness how good I am, how confident, how I'm escaping and there's nothing they can do about it.

I want Red—wherever he is—to look up and see me. Maybe glance out of a window and see me soaring past, see me flying. To know that his story hasn't fooled me. To know that a few lies can't hold me prisoner.

I want—

I wince as I land awkwardly. Pain in my ankle.

Shit. Wasn't concentrating. I right myself, slowing my pace slightly as I test my ankle. No, I'm fine. I can keep doing. That was just a warning to me not to get too cocky.

Right.

I center myself—can't let that misstep and tiny error throw me off. Every jump is a new jump. And I can do this.

Now.

I run, jumping into a high arc as I soar over the gap between the next roofs. I land perfectly.

There. My heart pounds. I can do this. Yes.

I run and run, count the roofs as they disappear under me. I'm getting close to the edge of the town now, and there's still no one about. I look ahead. Can see the rock where Clive's going to be waiting for me. Can't see him yet, but I don't look properly. Got to concentrate on this, on the—

I jump and—

I know the moment my feet leave the solid surface, that I've jumped wrongly. Got the angle incorrect. Know it instantly. And it's not like before, when I made that small error. This is bigger.

Shit.

My heart pounds, and I throw my body forward, through the air, trying to propel myself and—

But my jump is short.

I know my jump is short.

Shit. Shit. Shit!

And there's nothing I can do to fix it.

Six stories up.

And I'm plummeting to my death.

"IT'S KACEY," A VOICE SAYS, and I look up.

And it's Jaqueline—Jaqueline from the clansmen, my friend! My friend with her tawny skin and her kind eyes, and her body still twelve-years-old. My friend exactly as she looked. My friend whom I didn't save. My friend whom I let die, when I could've unleashed my Beast sooner.

I could've saved her—and it's something I try not to think about. Not after I had all those nightmares for years. Why didn't I just save her?

Why did I kill every one of the clansmen? And the baby... The only baby there—whom I left behind.

"You're here?" I stare at Jaqueline, and she's in front of me, and... and I don't understand.

Where am I? I try to look around, but then I see her eyes. Her beautiful dark eyes are glazing over. Like watercolor's been painted over them, but the watercolor's drying, becoming metallic. Mirrors.

I inhale sharply, and I'm trying to recoil, trying to get away. But my body—I can't move it. I look down at my arms, and hands, and my neck clicks, and then my fingers are breaking off. Like I'm a porcelain person, and I'm fractured and broken.

"No!" I cry, and my lips are breaking, crumbling.

"It's all right. We'll save you. We always save everyone," Jaqueline says, and she's smiling, and her teeth are changing as I stare at them. No longer crooked, getting straighter, whiter, bigger. "And you will be easy to save, when you're already connected so well with him."

Her teeth are still growing. They're so big until they are all I can see, and there are cracks across my vision. Hairline cracks that grow and grow.

"We can fix anyone who's broken," Jaqueline says. Her voice booms around me, too loud, and it almost feels abrasive against my skin. Rough, like sandpaper. "It was so nice of Shweta to tell us where you were."

I am trying to shout and trying to move—only I can't.

She gets out an augmenter. Neon pink. I've seen it before, but I can't think what it is, what it does. My thoughts are muddled and—

"Drink up and then you'll feel better."

Suddenly, it is close.

Suddenly, my mouth is open.

Suddenly, the augmenter is syrup on my tongue.

I gag, but I'm choking, and some goes down my throat, slips so easily.

No!

I am screaming.

"It's all right, Kacey," Jaqueline says, and she's the last person I see as the world dims and squeezes life out of me. "You're one of us now."

"KACEY? ARE YOU... OH GODS... Please... Wake up, Kacey... Kacey?"

The voice is insistent, fighting through the fog shrouding me. The voice is wobbling. It's a wobbly rope, and I can see the rope, and I don't understand... My head, it doesn't feel... Ah, what's the word?

Right.

It doesn't feel right.

Nothing feels right.

I open my eyes—and I struggle to do it. My eyelids are too heavy, like they're made of concrete. And the pain in my eyeballs—it's...

"Fuck," I mutter.

No, not just my eyeballs. It's everywhere...and I feel...spongey. My body... It's not... I don't feel substantial. I don't feel like I'm here... I....

I *fell*.

Fell *six stories*.

I inhale sharply, and it wracks pain through my body. Then I'm aware of colors. They're moving and merging into each other, turning everything a horrible murky shade until the colors separate again. Red and blue and green.

"Kacey?"

The colors swirl around me until they stop dancing and mixing, and instead sit next to each other nicely. Patches of orange and olive and white and pink and green. More and more patches, making a collage of Clive's face. He's hovering over me, and there's blood on his face, and there's dirt and stuff caught in the congealing blood. And he's got mirrors.

I recoil, breaths squeezing out of me. "Are...are they still... lenses?" I ask—only my words are barely audible. I'm wheezing, and it seems to have taken everything out of me just to speak.

He nods, and I need to ask him to prove it—but I can't. Just forming words is...

The floaty feeling in my head is back.

"Kacey, oh sparkling Gods! Can you move?" Clive looks around, and there must be something wrong with my head, with my vision, because one of his eyes gets left behind and it's floating next to his head. It reminds me of a painting that Maggot hung up in her quarters. She said it was a famous one, had been passed down the generations of her family.

Clive is speaking. Suddenly, it's like the volume's been turned up, and his words are deafening. They hurt my head.

"We have to get out of here. Come on." He pulls on my arm, and the movement kills.

I scream, and Clive presses his shaking hand over my mouth.

"You can't scream, Kacey. They'll hear us. You've got to be quiet. Here." He pulls off his scarf then wraps it around my head, sliding part of it in between my teeth. "Bite on that. It's what Mum always does for us if we get hurt. Remember when Sian broke her arm in the tunnels?"

Yes, I nod. That was... that was last year... Sian was screaming and screaming and that seemed loud enough, but Maggot said she'd be even louder when

Evor reset her arm. So Sian had to bite on fabric. We can't be too loud in the tunnels. Not when they're under the town. Our own secret maze…

Only it's not a secret any longer.

It's not a safe place.

It's *over*.

But—but I'm *alive*. The realization suddenly grabs me.

I fell six stories, and I'm *alive*.

"I'm alive," I say. I focus on his eyes again. The mirrors. One of them's a bit duller than the other, but I can see myself in them fine. One side of my face is red. I touch it, and my fingers come away sticky.

I try to wipe them on my jacket, and then I start to think I'm focusing on the wrong thing. Because we're still in New Zeralzi. An Enhanced town. We need to move. But I can't make my body work as it should. Everything's too foggy, like I'm still dreaming… and that dream… Jaqueline… Was it a dream, a nightmare? I look around for her, but I can't see anyone. Only Clive.

"I thought you were dead," Clive says, and I focus on the gap between his two front teeth. "But I'm so glad you're not," he adds quickly, then he looks around, and his movement reminds me of a meerkat I once saw. "Come on."

Clive slides his thin arm under my shoulders, and he hauls me up and—

I scream into the scarf.

My leg. I can't put weight on my leg. Shit.

My vision darkens, and my heart pounds. Dizziness pours over me, and somehow it feels worse than my pain and—

"Use your other leg," Clive says, and he's small, only ten years old, but he's taking most of my weight. His voice is strained, and I feel his muscles trembling. "It's all right. We'll get you out of here."

But I can't see how I'm going to get out of here. Is my leg broken? And Clive's just a child, and I'm an adult. I'm a tall adult. He can't carry me, and something tells me that I'm not even feeling the full extent of the pain—but that I will soon. It will crash over me like the darkest sea, and then I'll drown.

But Clive's taking charge now, and my head's foggy, and yeah, we have to try and get away. Get away before the Enhanced see us... How haven't they seen us? How... And where's Red? Only it won't be Red who sees us... We'll become Enhanced and...

"A gun," I say. "Have you got your gun?" My voice is weak, croaky, and I can't really hear my words. I'm not entirely sure I've spoken them out loud at all, until Clive answers.

"Yes."

Thank the Gods. "If they're going to get us, shoot me," I say. "Because I won't be able to get away. And I don't want to be one of them."

He nods, his baby face becoming sincere. He scratches the side of his face, where all that blood is, and I watch as he winces. "And I'll do me, too." His mouth sets into a thin line.

I want to tell him no, that he needs to live, but I know he'd not get away. Not on his own. It's just luck that he's alive right now. And being dead is better than being Enhanced.

Somehow, I start moving. Everything sways, and it's hard to breathe, and the pain in my head is like thunder. My own personal storm. My breaths are labored, and my skull is too heavy. It's weighing me down, adding more and more weight for Clive to take. His breathing's loud too, kind of raspy, and I feel my body slumping over his more and more as we walk.

But we walk out of the town.

Right out. We just walk, and no one tries to stop us.

I look around, because Clive's not. He's not aware of our surroundings. He's just staring forward with every step, so I have to look. I have to be our eyes. But there's no one

And no one stops us.

SIXTEEN

MY HEAD THREATENS TO TURN inside out as we walk, farther and farther from New Zeralzi. My stomach keeps twisting savagely, and bile rises. I taste it, sharp and acrid on my tongue. I try to spit it out, but I'm not sure if I manage it because there's more in my mouth. It's pooling, flooding me. My heart pounds, too heavy, too fast. I expect to see it burst from my body any moment now, a ragged mess of pulsing flesh and pink stuff erupting from my chest.

My vision darkens, and it's too hot. The sun's high, and it beats down on the back of my neck with hot and sticky fingers. I'm sweating—every part of me. And I can't feel my left leg. There's a strange numbness. My foot's dragging behind me. Clive must be half-carrying me now, but there's something wrong with my neck because I can't really look down or across at him to see him.

Think, Kacey.

Yes, I need to think. I should be thinking, planning what we're going to do. There was something about…

I grimace, and the words are gone. The thoughts are gone. Only me and how unwell I am. I want to shut my eyes, see if that helps my spinning head, but I can't… I know I can't. I shouldn't. And we're walking away, and it's still too easy.

It's too easy.

Clive tries to make conversation, but I can't really follow his words and on the rare occasion when I try to think of an answer, it gets stuck in my head. My brain is a maze, the walls are too high, and I'm not clever enough to work out the way out for it to escape.

I end up mumbling. My tongue is too big, the roof of my mouth furry. My eyes are too heavy, still, and I want to lie down. I need to lie down.

"I don't think your leg's broken," Clive says, and we're stopping. I feel the ground rising up around me, and something hard is under the back of my head. The sky is blue, but then the sky is his face. He's peering into my eyes. "But your pupils are too dilated. I think you're concussed."

Concussed.

I see the word flying toward me, then the word grows arms. Spindly little arms. And its arms are holding a hammer, lots of hammers, and the word is angry and it's coming at me. *Concussed* soars toward me, and I duck, try to get out the way. Only I don't manage to duck—I'm not in control of my body. Can't move. Shit!

The hammer hits my skull. Pain reverberates through me. Nausea.

"Ah!" I cry as more bile rises, and I choke.

Everything blurs and then the word's gone, and, for a moment, I see Jaqueline. With her mirror eyes.

I retch again, spew up actual vomit—so much of it. It clings to the side of my face as I roll in the dirt. It's slippery and thick, viscous. I feel hands lifting me up, propping me against something, and I stare at my vomit on the ground, how specks of dirt and dust are sticking to it. How some of the vomit's thinner, watery, and it's running away, making a wet trail down a slight slope.

A cough hacks through me, and I'm only distantly aware of Clive trying to talk to me, trying to calm me down. His voice is worried, and I start to sink down again. The ground's too soft and—

"Kacey?" a voice hisses. "Clive?"

I startle, turn, and then slide away from Clive. The left side of my head is too heavy. I feel like there's a magnet in it, and the magnet's pulling me to the ground. Something hot rises in my throat, and I burp.

"Kacey? Kacey? What happened?" A voice. Insistent. Urgent. A voice that I know, but I can't think... can't...

"Maggot!" Clive shouts. "Help me! Kacey fell off a roof."

Maggot's alive? I blink and try to move my head. If Maggot's here, then Kazem will be, too. He has to be.

"What?" Maggot's voice says. "Oh Gods." And then I see a figure. Her figure. She's here. Somehow she's here, and she's moving closer to me. "Is it just you two?"

"Yes," Clive says. "I'm sorry, I couldn't—"

"Not your fault."

"No... it's the traitor... the traitor's fault," I mumble. "There was a traitor... Maggot... a traitor... and—" I trip over my words as they blossom from me like the darkest flower. But the traitor... I can't think who... who did this? "And where's Kazem?"

"Kacey's really hurt," Clive says. "I didn't know what to do. Her eyes aren't right, and she's been sick."

"Yes, I can see that." Maggot's voice is brisk. "Okay. It's good you're here. We didn't know if any more of us were coming out."

"More?" I ask, looking around, but everything's in shades of gray. But there's no one else in sight...but I can't see much. And why is it so cold?

"The others are back there." Maggot jerks her chin behind her, and I follow the direction, but it's suddenly even darker, like nighttime has fallen. Nighttime must have fallen.

"The others? Who?" Clive asks. "Is it my mum?"

"Let's just get Kacey there," Maggot says. "Evor

might be able to help her."

"Evor," I mumble. Who the hell is Evor? The name has no meaning. It's empty, no figure attached to it. Maybe I misheard. I must've done, because Maggot must've said Kazem's name.

"We have to go now," Maggot says. "We have to get to the Muskoxen group before the Enhanced find us out here. That's if Muskoxen's still intact. We don't know how much the Enhanced know about our group."

Hands try to lift me by the armpits, and I squeal and curse. Clive recoils into the darkness, but it doesn't deter Maggot. She hoists me up, and my arms flail around her shoulders, and… my chest… my heart, it's trying to get out. It's doing it. It's a fleshy pink thing climbing out of my body.

"My heart!" I mumble, but my tongue's still too big, and I can't see… and I can't speak…

"Clive, take her other arm. Shit, she's heavier than she looks."

I can't speak, and I can't think and…

My eyes are shut. Why are my eyes shut? Am I asleep?

Yes, asleep is what I should be.

Maggot and Clive are talking, but then I realize Clive's not here. I don't know. Even though my eyes are shut, I sort of see him as he melts away. There's so much darkness around me. It's a thick, fluffy coat. But the darkness is here. The darkness is inside me.

It's the Beast. And he's stirring. Power ripples through me.

He's hungry. He wants to kill.

"No! Not these people!" I think I manage to shout the words, but they're slurred. I sound like I'm underwater, and I open my eyes, but there's loads of pressure like I *am* under water. "Kill the Enhanced," I mumble, "if you have to kill…"

Did I see the Enhanced earlier? I can't think. Everything's too mixed up, too… But I was in Red's apartment.

Red.

"No!" I shout, and the word is a bullet. It slices through everything. It pushes everything away, all the fogginess and strangeness, until all that remains is sharp and focused. And I can *see*. "Stop!"

"What is it?" Maggot asks, her voice gruff.

I spy trees ahead, and rocks. Dawn's Rock. Clive is to my left with his mirror eyes flashing the sun at me, and Maggot is on my right—and wow, she's been punched. Her right eye is blackened, bruised. Her face has swollen up. Her flesh is like a cushion, and her skin's stretched so tight it looks shiny.

"I..." I say and then I think I'm going to be sick. I make a choking noise but that's all that happens. *And I was in Red's apartment. And Red let me go.* "Maggot... I think I'm being tracked by them... the Enhanced. It's the only explanation," I pant, tasting blood at the back of my mouth. "They let me go, Untamed, so it has to... has to be for a reason." I look around, because I expect to see them rising from the shadows—the enemy. And... and didn't Owen say something about Red not converting Keelie straight away... that video... what was it? Something about how it would lead to a better outcome... like the whole of Nbutai being ambushed.

But the air is still. And it's just Maggot and I here in the night. Clive's gone. What the hell? I whip my head to the left, looking for him, but it's just the night. Was he ever here? I rub my forehead. My skin is tacky. My fingers come away stained. I frown.

"Then let's check you for a tracker." Maggot runs her hands lightly over me. Her touch is quick, efficient. "Can't feel anything."

"But they could've injected it deep or something." I shove my sleeves up, trying to see some sort of mark on my skin, but my jacket's in the way, and my vision does that thing again where I can't see.

Maggot tells me again that I'm okay. I don't know if she's repeating the words over and over, or if it's a sign of something really being wrong with my brain, because I hear the phrase repeated again and again. *You're okay. You're okay. You're okay.* But I let her lead me farther on. Maggot's breaths are hard and raspy, and I hear her breaths at the exact same times as I hear her words. Maybe her breaths just sound like those words. I don't know. I don't really care.

I'm not sure how far we walk, whether I start to zone out or something, but it feels even later, and then ahead, figures loom. Two of them. Untamed. Neither is Kazem. My heart sinks.

No.

No.

No!

I look at them, hatred burning through me because they're not him. He should be there! Kazem should be there.

Then I realize who *is* there.

My mouth dries. Fury—this hot, vapid thing that hisses and hisses—fills me. It's *her*.

"It was you," I shout, and my voice is angry, and I am angry and the Beast inside is angry. He's rising, and he's so fucking angry, and he fills me and he lets me move. I am him, and he is me.

"Kacey Kachler!" Maggot yells, her voice a warning.

But I'm not listening. I'm glaring at Shweta—who obviously isn't Shweta, because she's still got that stupid disguise where she's too old to actually look like her. She tosses her glossy hair over her shoulder. She has the audacity to look hurt even though she's taken away the most important person from me. Because Kazem isn't here.

He's back in there. In the town. Either dead or converted.

I've lost him. My soul mate—but those words don't even do justice to the connection we had, because soul mates sounds like some clichéd crap. But Kazem and I—he is *everything*.

Poison fills my veins as I stare at the Shweta-imposter. "Maggot, she's Enhanced!" I yell and my voice sounds strong, then I focus on her. The fucking imposter. "You're going to pay for this."

Before anyone can stop me, the Beast takes over. I lunge at her.

She is going to die.

SEVENTEEN

MAGGOT AND EVOR PULL ME off the imposter—after I've got three good punches in thanks to the Beast's power, so maybe he's good for something. But the moment they yank me away from the conniving woman, the Beast shrinks, and I'm filled with pain. It is intense, head-pounding, ribs-constricting, vision-darkening pain. It curls through me, expanding, forcing itself into every muscle and sinew of my body.

I fall back, twisting around. My arms flail out—my fists still clenched—and I hit someone, my punch connecting with muscle. Is it that woman? I can't tell. I'm on the ground, grit in my mouth as I taste blood. I kick out, trying to see where the imposter is, screaming so hard something inside me feels close to breaking.

"Get a fuckin' grip on yourself," Maggot snarls. Her swollen face looks shinier. It's like a pin cushion that Sian has, and I want to get a needle, push it into Maggot's face. See if it's all soft and squishy inside or whether it will deflate like a popped balloon.

I blink a bit, surprised. Then I focus on the important stuff. "It was her!" My breath is ragged. "Maggot, she's not the real Shweta... That's an Enhanced! They got the real Shweta! That's not her!" My words ring out, seeming to echo, but there's something about the echo that's not right. I can't tell if I'm actually saying the words over and over. I blink, trying to see Maggot or someone, but there's just murkiness in front of me. Something wet slides down the side of my face, and then I'm struggling to stand. "Look at her hair, her skin! That's not her!" I shout and I'm trying to point at where that woman is, but I can't even tell which way I'm facing. Everything is just blurry.

But if they're not going to sort this, then I will.

I have to.

My hands are on the damp ground, and I try to shove myself upward. My right foot is under me, and I push down on that leg, feeling hands on my shoulders again, and—

Red-hot rods of pain slide through my head, like lasers burning through flesh, muscle. A jarring sensation that twists and twists. I scream, and my left shoulder hits something hard. More dampness. I can't see a fucking thing, and that makes it worse. There's a screeching sound—a sound that I think comes from within me, but I can't tell.

But something is very wrong with me, and it's enough to distract me from the Shweta imposter.

"Kacey?" The word echoes over and over, and it's metallic. The word *tastes* metallic. My name is metal. It is hard and brutal. It can be wielded as a weapon. It can do so much damage.

Me and the Beast, together, we can do so much damage.

"Just breathe, Kace."

I don't like how the person says *Kace*, because that's what Kazem often shortens my name to. That's *his* name for me. And he's not here.

I scream, but I don't know if I make any sound.

Someone tells me to breathe with them—in and out and in and out—and my gulps are ragged. Hands help me sit up. How long was I lying down again for?

Something cool touches my face, and I try to move

closer to it.

"Why can't I see anything?" I ask, and my voice wobbles.

Are my eyes shut? I reach up to them, fingers shaking. I prod at them, but I feel disconnected. Shouldn't they hurt when I press my fingers into them? Or maybe they are hurting—maybe I've reached the limit with the amount of pain I can feel. Because my body is writhing with it.

Oh, Gods. How injured am I? I know about concussions. How dangerous they are. And head injuries, brain bleeds… *Fuck.* "Am I going to die?"

"It's all right," a voice says. I think it's Evor. Yes. I know who Evor is now. "Just relax if you can."

I detect movement around me—I'm not sure how, because none of my senses seem to be working as they should. But then things are happening. Things are—

I vomit, sudden and hard. The force of it makes me dizzier, and I start to slump, but they're holding me up. They're looking after me—and I don't like being looked after, needing to be cared for. But it is what it is.

And gradually, gradually, my vision lightens. The darkness lifts. Shapes and people emerge around me. Clive and Evor and Maggot and *Shweta*.

I stare at her, and she stares at me. She's crouching in front of me, and I can see where I punched her face. Red marks are blossoming, and she's got a hand clamped to her jaw.

"I did nothing." Her eyes brim with fire, and she glances at Evor—for backup?

I scoff as I turn to look up at Maggot. The movement is jarring. "The Enhanced knew we were going to attack… One of the men said…" Damn. Why can't I speak properly? "They were told… told about our plans… and you—" I point to the imposter, and wow, it takes so much effort to even do that. "You're one of them!"

She rolls her eyes and snorts. Actually rolls her eyes and snorts! If I was uninjured right now, I'd be killing her, I know that. But all I can do is stare at her smarmy little face.

"Kacey, this is a huge allegation," Maggot says. "This is Shweta Basu—the *real* one. Ha, as if there's any other! You're concussed, Kacey, but you can't just say this stuff."

"She's hallucinating," Clive says. He still has his mirrors in, and they throw light everywhere like pebbles. "Must be. Like I said, she fell from the roof. She's not making sense."

"Hold on." Evor's voice is sharp. "How high up was she?"

"It was the pharmacy building," Clive says, just as a new wave of nausea takes over me.

"Shit," the imposter says.

I growl at her. "You don't get to talk, *traitor*." The strength and confidence I try to conjure is ruined by me emptying my guts up next to us again.

"If Shweta had betrayed us, she wouldn't have escaped with us," Evor says. He's moving toward me, and then he's kneeling at my side, and his gentle hands are on the back of my head, my neck, going down my spine. He's asking me if I've got pain there, but I can't concentrate on that.

"She would escape… with us…." I say, trying to spit more vomit out, but it's clinging to my teeth. I wipe the back of my hand across my mouth and try to focus. "If she knew some of us had got away… she wants to round us up… have us ready… ready to deliver us to them later."

That's exactly what Red did with Keelie, isn't it? Yes… my memories are returning. He didn't deliver her to the Enhanced because he was waiting to get the *whole* village.

"Kacey, you're not seein' things straight," Maggot says, sounding exasperated. She crouches, wincing. "Evor, can you do anything?"

Anything apart from prodding my spine?

"But it was her!" I shout, wincing.

"I didn't do anything," the imposter says in a small

voice—and hell, that voice actually sounds like Shweta now. Our enemy's stronger than we think.

"Then why were you saying all that weird shit… before?" I challenge. "I remember that… and that wasn't you. And you're different… you look different. You don't have gray hair or wrinkles like that." I turn to Maggot, and the movement nearly winds me. "Look at her!"

Maggot frowns. "That *is* Shweta."

"Hallucinations," Clive says.

"No!" I scream, my breaths ragged as I glare back at the imposter. "Why are you here? Tell me what's going on… else I'll… I'll kill you!"

Yes, the Beast thinks, and I feel his interest like a coil unwinding as he perks up.

"Like you'd believe me if I told you," the imposter says. There is fire in her eyes and it's burning sharper and faster and harder. "You never do."

What the hell does that mean? I blink.

"Shweta?" Maggot asks.

But the imposter laughs, lifting her arms, as she looks right at me. I don't like it—the way her gaze bores into me. I want to get away. I want to run. But I also want to kill her. The Beast is watching her through my eyes. I can feel him.

"If there's one thing that you are, Kacey, it's consistent," the imposter says. "Even if this fall *is* new. What happened? You got too cocky this time? Well, I suppose it had to happen eventually. Don't worry, by tomorrow this won't have even happened."

"What?" I press a hand to my forehead, but doing so sends numbness into my shoulder.

"Time resets," the imposter says, rolling her eyes. She throws her arms out. Then she pulls them in quickly to her sides, as if she didn't do the gesture at all. "All of this. It's happened before, Kacey. A time loop. I've been stuck in it for months—years, even. I don't know anymore. It's taking a toll on me—that's why I look so different."

"A time loop?" I snort and spit at the ground. "You actually think we'll…. believe that?" I turn to Maggot, waiting for her reaction, but she just runs a hand through her hair, looking bewildered. "Look, either she's a fucking traitor… or she's fucked in the head." My head pounds. "We should just kill her. Safer for us."

"Will you just *shut up*?" the imposter shouts suddenly. "Look, it's always the same! I'm the only one who remembers it. We've done this day over and over, and oh dear Gods, I am so freaking fed up of this. I'm the only one who ever bloody remembers this."

"Maggot, are you hearing this? She's crazy… she's actually crazy! This Enhanced Ones is crazy." *Crazy, crazy, crazy.* The word grows bigger in front of me, and there's something high-pitched and whining, buried in the layers in my head.

But Maggot isn't looking at the imposter. She and Evor and Clive are talking. Evor's no longer touching my spine, and I don't know when he stopped, when he moved over to the right. When all of them stood up and backed away a little, leaving me and the imposter. I blink.

"I haven't got any of my concoctions," Evor is saying. "Nothing. And Kacey could have brain damage. A Seer's the best bet to heal her." He looks at Shweta.

"I haven't got my powers now," she says, looking over her shoulder at him. "Side effect."

Of course she hasn't bloody got her powers, I want to scream, because it's *not* her.

"We need to find a Seer with healing abilities," Evor says.

"Oh my Gods," I say, and then my voice cracks, and I remember all over again that I've lost Kazem. I scream, and I turn on Maggot and Evor. "Are you not listening to this woman? How are you not concerned with what she *is* saying? This time-loop shit? That… that proves she's Enhanced! She's panicking and… trying to make stuff up!" My tongue feels like it's swelling and there's so little room in my mouth.

"Yeah, because I'm crazy, remember?" the imposter

says. "I may as well say weird shit." And with that, she rises, turns on her heel and heads off.

I try to see where she's going, but the land's sort of shimmery, and I blink because it hurts my head.

Clive looks at me, then Evor. "Should I go after Shweta?"

"Yeah," Evor says, waving his hand a little dismissively. "Maggot, do I fully check over Kacey while we're here? Or do we get farther away first?"

"Check her now, quickly. Do what you can. Her leg ain't lookin' good though."

"I haven't got anything to strap it up with. I'll do what I can though."

After the most stupid examination ever, Evor says I'm definitely concussed and he can't tell the extent of the damage to my brain. My head and my leg are his main worries. What a surprise. He's literally given me no new information.

"I'll be fine," I mutter. My eyes are already trying to close again, and I'm welcoming it. I don't want to be in this place. "I just need to sleep."

"Not yet," he says. "I need you to stay awake. And Maggot wants to get moving now. And the other thing: I know you're in pain, but you've got to be nicer to Shweta."

"Nicer?" I snort.

"Yes." Evor nods. "What you said to Shweta was hurtful, Kacey."

"Hurtful?" I snort again. And it seems like all I can do is repeat his words. "But she betrayed us. Hell, that isn't even her."

"You don't talk about her mental state like that. It's not acceptable, whatever she supposedly has or hasn't done. She's still suffering. You're going to apologize to her. I don't care if it's the concussion talking. You don't get a free run just because you're hurt."

Apologize to that imposter? My eyebrows shoot up. "You can't expect me to—"

"I do," Maggot says, and then she's here, right beside me, and I recoil. How did she get here? Where had she gone? I can't think.

I shoot a glance at Maggot, but I know which battles to avoid.

"Fine," I say. "I'll apologize later. But you better watch your backs. I'm telling you that woman is the problem here. She is an Enhanced, an imposter, and I don't know why the hell you can't see that."

But they will, I think. Sooner or later, they're going to realize I was right. And I'm going to have to stick with them, and the imposter, to make sure they don't end up dead, too.

I look toward the imposter now. The Beast lifts his head inside me.

I'm watching you, I mouth at her.

The imposter doesn't react.

We walk for six hours before Maggot tells us to stop for a rest in the heart of the night. None of us have ever walked to the Muskoxen group before. Whenever we had to see them, we'd use the radios in the tunnels under New Zeralzi to contact them. They needed two days' notice to send a truck to our meeting point which was only a two-hour walk from the tunnels, but still a long, long way from their base. We passed that meeting point long ago.

Well, I didn't walk. I can't walk. Not really. Not anymore. Evor ended up carrying me for a while. I protested at first, and then I cried about Kazem, and then I think I slept because now I feel hazy, and I can't remember much of the journey.

No Enhanced Ones appear to have followed us though, and none of it makes any sense.

Red left the door unlocked. He made it easy for me to escape, and no Enhanced tried to find me as I walked through their town. No Enhanced were there when I fell. And if Red's going to track me so he can get to the remainder of my people, there *has* to be some sort of tracking device on me. Unless he's relying on the imposter.

Now, Evor is making a fire. Maggot scouts the area, and tells Clive to keep an eye on me, and then helpfully reminds me to apologize to Shweta.

Anger curls through me. Fine. I will apologize—not that I'll mean it, it'll just be for show—but first I need to make sure there really is no tracking device on me.

I check my skin, inch-by-agonizing-inch, then my clothes, my hair. I look under my broken nails—now filled with dirt and blood—and I dig my sharpest nails into the cushiony parts of my upper arms. That's where a tracker would most likely be implanted, right?

But I have no clue, and I can't find anything.

"There's probably no tracer," the imposter says to me, and her voice is sickly sweet. "I mean, there hasn't been so far. And although your fall is new, I doubt things have changed that much in this timeline."

I don't even want to grace her with an answer to that, but I hiss at her, "Tell Maggot and Evor that I apologized to you. If they ask."

"But you haven't."

"Just do it. Okay?" I grit my teeth. I'm in too much pain to have such a pointless conversation.

I turn my back on her and lie down in dampness. My head feels fuzzy. Like there's a layer of fur between my skull and my skin, and it's irritating me. My fingers buzz to claw the fur away, and I scratch at my face. The movement makes me groan. And then, somehow, it reminds me of a time when I pulled a muscle in my leg, and Kazem was looking after me. His kind eyes, his soft touch, the way he held me.

Tears fill my eyes, and I wipe them away and find the imposter is hovering over me uncertainly.

"Go away," I snap.

"I'll get Evor," she says.

"I just want to sleep!" I yell angrily after her.

She disappears. Just like everyone disappears from this world. It's just me.

And Kazem's gone.

He's really, truly *gone*.

I gulp.

He's gone.

My Kazem.

Gone.

I'M SITTING AT A TABLE in a cluttered hut. Cluttered with porcelain plates and bowls. The table has a red Tartan tablecloth on it, and my chair has a cushion. I notice all these details, and they seem important.

There's a creak behind me, and I turn as the door opens fully. A woman with long gray hair and a smile that stretches from one side to the other greets me. "Kacey!"

My body jolts. It's me, this time? Not one of Red's memories.

"Aunt Caia-Lu?" I stare at her, feel my breaths melt away.

Caia-Lu steps closer. Her face is thinner than I remember, hollows hanging beneath her eyes, around her cheeks. Her hair is nearly fully gray too. No black strands, but her eyebrows are dark. And her eyes are the same—powerful, glistening, mesmerizing.

"It's so wonderful to see you again, neshama sheli," my aunt who is dead says.

Dead.

I'm dead?

I look around. Is this the New World?

"But we haven't got long, girl." She sits next to me— suddenly there's another chair in here. Was it there before? I can't remember, and I blink. But my head's not hurting *now. Of course not. I'm dead.* "I need to talk to you."

"Talk to me?"

"You have the energy," she says.

"No!" I cry. "That's what Red said—and that was just him. I'm not..." *But I don't know what I'm trying to say. My thoughts are still muddled, confused.*

"It's Rijikarii," my aunt says. "And you must learn how to control it, Kacey. It's my fault Rijikarii is in the world, and I should've realized that the largest amount of it would gravitate to you, for you have my blood and my soul. So, you have to wield control over it. It's not as bad as I thought. For so long I was convinced it was the end—but I can see the way now. But we have to get there. You have to learn before it's too late, and you have to find others with it, else I fear none of this will happen."

"Too late?" *I stare at her.* "For what?"

"They're going to come after you, Kacey, and you need to make sure that when they do, you can control the power, the Rijikarii."

Who's coming after me? "The Enhanced?" *I inhale sharply.* "The Enhanced are coming after me?"

And where am I now? Because I'm not actually in this hut with her... Am I?

I breathe deeply.

"Learn its ways and master it, Kacey," Caia-Lu says. "Embrace who you are before it's too late."

And then she stands, and her chair disappears. Something hisses, and as I'm staring at her, she disappears.

And then everything's a whirlwind of movement, objects being whipped away by some invisible hand, until there's nothing left.

Until I'm not here.

Nothing is.

Just emptiness.

NINETEEN

I JOLT AWAKE, CHOKING. FEEL sick and—

"It's all right," Evor says, and he helps me sit up—just in time for me to vomit all over him.

My stomach twists and turns, and there's pain in my chest when I breathe. A tickling sort of pain—or at least it is at first. But with every new breath I take, it gets stronger, like it's the sharp end of a quill digging deeper and deeper.

I try to move back, away from the vomit that seems to splatter everything. The smell is putrid and curls around me.

"You'll be okay," Evor says. His arm is around me. In the dark, I can't see his eyes—but I detect the worry in his voice, in that statement, in that *lie*.

How will I ever be okay? Kazem's gone. Doesn't he realize that?

My Kazem.

I gulp, and tears slide down my face. I'm never going to see him again. Never going to—

"Just try and stay calm," Evor says. "This isn't going to help your head." He leans back a little, and I think he's staring into my eyes.

But there's moonlight. I concentrate on that. On the moon. I like the moon, don't I? But as I stare at it, my stomach twisting, feeling rubbery and stretchy, I can't remember why I even like the moon. What it means to me.

Without Kazem, I'm not even me. I'm just floating. I'm nothing, I'm—I don't even know. My head... There's something really wrong with me. Is this what grief feels like? Is this—

"Enhanced!" Shweta's scream cuts the night.

No—not Shweta. The imposter. The correction seems important, and then I jolt.

The Enhanced. *They're going to come after you, Kacey.*

My eyes widen. *Shit.* I jump up. Pain lassoes around my leg, and I feel foggy. There's movement to my right. Maggot and Clive and—mirrors, behind them. So suddenly here. And it's him, leading the pack: it's Red, smiling that gallantly smug smile of his. Because he thinks he's got me. Got all of us. And his Beast thinks it, too.

But he's wrong. He's so bloody wrong.

"Surrender to us willingly," Red calls, his voice as clear and sharp as glass, and I have this moment where I think I must still be dreaming. There's not enough detail here. Things are happening too quickly.

"Surrender," Red shouts, "and we will—"

"Get back," Maggot shouts. "We're armed. We will shoot you."

Armed? But I look around, and I see no weapons. No nothing. We have nothing.

More mirrors shine in the rich, velvety dark, shining like stars, and I turn, see more Enhanced Ones to my left. My feet keep moving, more pain in my left leg. They're behind me too, and to my right. I hear Clive gulp, remarkably loudly.

"We're surrounded," Evor says in a low hum.

"I said *get back!*" Maggot shouts louder.

But the Enhanced don't get back. Red leads his men closer and closer, the circle tightening. I spin, shifting my weight from foot to foot.

"We have to run," I hiss at Maggot, then Evor. "There are gaps between the Enhanced. We can get out." They're not big gaps, but they are gaps nonetheless. Gaps that are getting smaller as they close in. "We have to run now!"

I surge forward, but my head spins. The land tilts toward me, and everything's off kilter for a second, two seconds. An arm grabs me, and I think it's Clive until I see the mirror eyes and—

A flash of a gun. Moonlight glinting on metal. We have guns?

No. They're *theirs*.

"Obey!" an Enhanced shouts, pointing the gun at the imposter.

Wait, why would they point it at her? Or is it really Shweta?

But before I can think, before I can do anything, Clive screams.

I spin toward him, see an Enhanced One grab him. See colorful vials—so many—and they reflect the mirror eyes. So many of them, too. A whole galaxy in the dark.

We're outnumbered.

Red grins.

We all know we can't get away from this.

No! We have to try, we—

My Beast lifts up inside me—and maybe I'm summoning him, or maybe I'm not. Maybe he's in control or maybe we both are. Maybe we're working together, because he's rising now, and I'm not scared. I am raw and I am rage, and I've got people to protect. I *want* to kill.

I want it. I want it. I want it.

So I do.

I scream as the power surges in me. Scream and scream, and Maggot's shouting, but then she's not. I can't see her, all I can see is me, my power. My Beast. Crimson energy burning, spreading from me in a wave.

It incinerates the Enhanced Ones.

It incinerates Red.

Clive cries and I turn, see him in the corner of my eye as my Beast reaches him.

"No!" I yell, and my Beast obeys, pulls back.

Evor's mouth has dropped open.

Another wave of Enhanced Ones looms, drawing closer and closer, like they're magnetized to me and my Beast. And my Beast keeps taking and taking and taking. Screams and splatters of blood and labored breaths and hushed pleas for life…until it's over.

Until it's done.

My head pounds. Stars dance in front of my eyes, and my legs weaken. I stumble as I look around.

My Beast killed *all* the Enhanced out here. All of them. They're just lying there, dead. Fallen.

Only us left. Me and Maggot and Shweta and—

The Beast didn't kill Shweta. Her eyes are wide, her breathing heavy. Her hands are clenched to her chest, her shoulders curled. Her dark hair is a mess, and the injuries on her face—where I hit her—look worse now.

She locks her eyes on me. "That's new, too." Her voice is strangely breathy. "Maybe this pathway's the one."

But I haven't got time to mull over her words because Maggot grabs me.

"What the fuck was that?" she screams. "You a Seer? All this time? You can kill them?"

"No, I'm not a Seer." My throat burns and I swallow hastily, feeling like I'm going to choke for a second or so. "I didn't foresee this—"

Except…except I did. I didn't *foresee* it, but I was warned. Caia-Lu warned me that Enhanced Ones were coming. But that wasn't a Dream Land warning. Was it? My gaze crosses to Shweta. I don't think she's Enhanced now. I think she *is* the real one, because all the Enhanced have been killed. By me. My Beast. It's just us. Just Untamed.

Shweta just stares at me. Then she makes a startled gargling sound, and I see her gaze fix on something behind me and a little to my right.

I turn and—

"Oh Gods." Maggot's words are low. She doesn't move. Just stares.

We're all staring.

It's Evor.

He's lying on his side, blood pooled around his head. His eyes look strange, glassy, and his skin tacky, sticky. I look at his chest. Look for the rise and fall.

There is no rise and fall.

I take a sudden step back. I touch my head, feel the lump there, under my hair. Evor's *dead*?

"It was the Enhanced," Clive says to me. "They shot him. It wasn't you."

I breathe out slowly. It wasn't me. Not another Untamed death on my hands.

Maggot is stone-still, just staring at her brother. Shweta snaps out of her stupor and rushes to Evor. She kneels beside him, placing her fingers against his neck. Then she shakes her head and rolls him onto his back.

We all watch as she starts chest compressions. I want to go forward, I want to help—there's a part of me that wants to. But there's a bigger part of me that's numb and unfeeling, watching as Shweta tries to save a man who I know is already dead.

We all know that.

"His death won't be in vain," Maggot says.

I look at her, see the hardness in her steel eyes. Her fists are clenched so tight her knuckles are like pearly white pebbles that seem too bright in the night. And I *know*.

I know what's going to happen now.

That's what I'm here for, the Beast says. His voice is silk stirring in my stomach.

Maggot knows what I can do. Maggot is angry. But Maggot is our leader. Maggot always puts her people first. And I know she is going to use me to protect her people.

I'm going to have to keep killing now. I'm going to

be doing exactly what the Beast has wanted me to do for all of these years.

And the worst thing is how I feel about it now—because I don't feel fear or repulsion. I feel nothing. Absolutely nothing at all.

TWENTY

ALL MY LIFE, SINCE THE clansmen, I've hidden this power. Refused to kill. Didn't want to. But with Kazem gone, I don't care. Maybe my will has weakened and my thoughts are really the Beast's now. So maybe this isn't me. But I *don't care*. Everything that was soft inside me, everything that was beautiful and blooming with life, everything that cared, has gone. All that is left is red and raging and raw, and my insides sting and burn as I stare at Evor's body.

"Okay," Maggot says. "Okay, okay, okay."

"We need to send his body off," Clive whispers. "Else the bad spirits will come for us."

I can't concentrate. There's too much going on inside me. Too much lava bubbling in time with the Beast's heartbeats. But under my burning, I am empty. A gray husk. A wasteland with no pulse, no nothing. I am either the Beast or I do not exist at all, and I don't know which is more frightening.

Evor's eyes seem to be looking at me. Because he knows he's dead because of me. I have this power, and I used it too late. I didn't save him.

"We have to send his body off *now*," Clive says, his

voice becoming a whine. His face is streaked with tears, looks blotchy, even in the moonlight.

Maggot grunts. She scoops up Evor's body. He looks so small now, so...flat and deflated, like a deer carcass after we've gutted it, now the life within him has gone.

In one fast movement, Maggot slings his body across her shoulders as if he's not heavy at all. As if he isn't her brother—just a sack of bricks or something she doesn't have an emotional attachment to. Her whole frame shudders, yes, but it's because of the weight, clearly. Maggot knows how to turn her emotions off when needed. That's something I value a lot about her.

Clive takes in huge gulps of air, and Shweta puts her arm around him.

"Where's the water?" Maggot asks, her voice brisk.

I look around, try to get my bearings, but the land looks different. I know we can't be that far from New Zeralzi, but I don't recognize anything. It's like my eyes are inside out or upside down.

"I think it's that way," Shweta says, pointing.

We follow her lead, Maggot at the back. Part of me thinks I should offer to help carry Evor, especially when his death is my fault, but the rest of me is just numb, just wants to do nothing because the Beast is the other part of me and he wants to consume everything. I am either all or I am nothing.

My head pounds as we walk. My leg's not as bad though. I'm only limping, not dragging it. My vision blurs in and out of focus. I rub my right eye. That whole side of my face seems more tender now.

"You okay?" Maggot grunts at me. I've fallen to the back of the group, with her.

I nod.

"Good to have you," she says, but not in the way she normally says it, to me as her second. This is...*more*. Because she knows I have the Beast inside me, and she believes it's good. Suddenly, I can read her emotions so easily. Too easily. Frighteningly easily.

She's going to take me around the Enhanced towns and cities, get me to kill them all. Suddenly, I know that with clarity. Shweta and Clive are going to come with us, because they've got nowhere else to go.

But I can't have anyone with me. They could get killed so easily. Like Evor. Or by me.

And…and Caia-Lu told me the Enhanced were coming for me. There's a tracker on me or something. There has to be. The Enhanced will *always* find me because they're in control of the hunt. They are the hunters.

And more blood will be shed, can only be shed.

The solution is simple: I have to leave them. Maggot and Clive and Shweta will be safer without me about. I can go out, go off to cities on my own—or draw the Enhanced to me so my Beast can kill them—and the last of my group will be safe.

I will not kill any more Untamed.

I grit my teeth. I have to go. Maggot would never let me go alone, she's all about safety in numbers, so I have to sneak off. Now? I look around. There's just more barren land. Not easy to walk away undetected when we're such a small group. And of course Maggot's keeping an eye on me. I breathe out hard. The pain behind my eyes gets stronger, but the Beast is keeping most of it at bay as we walk and walk and walk.

"The land's different." Shweta points ahead, her other hand now a shield for her eyes from the emerging sun.

I blink, a little surprised that this much time has passed.

"There should be water there," Shweta continues. "The lake. Remember?"

I nod, but I cannot remember. The land looks different, but I think any land I see would look different now. My eyes, my vision, it's *all* different. I am different, different again.

"How can it have changed?" Maggot grunts. Her face is red, sweaty. The swollen, shiny bit is a mash of bruising. Evor is still over her shoulders.

"More's changing this time," Shweta says.

More? I frown and—

"Oh Gods," Clive shrieks.

I spin toward him, getting ready to push the Beast to my forefront, to fight the Enhanced. Only there aren't any. It's just Clive. Clive reaching down and picking something up from the ground.

It's a small object, and he turns it over in his hands.

"It's a Watcher Doll." My voice is breathy. "It's a Seer's."

Caia-Lu had one. All Seers need something to stop them getting stuck in the Dream Land. The object changes depending on which group you're with. The D'Elinous group used Watcher Dolls. The Overlord Seer of the clansmen used one, along with his mask for double protection. Shweta has a Seer pendant, which seems to be common for the Seers around this region.

"There's another Seer here?" Shweta looks around. "More Untamed?"

"The Enhanced have Seers, too," I say. "But they don't get warnings from the Dream Land. If a Seer's converted, they won't need their protection. Could be why the Watcher Doll's been discarded."

"We should hang onto it," Maggot says. "In case it belongs to an Untamed. We might find them. They might need it."

The thought of someone else around here doesn't make me feel good. Another Enhanced? Or Untamed? And before I know what I'm doing, I'm letting the Beast take over again. That hot and raging vicious thing inside me, rearing up, looking out of my eyes, scanning the area. Searching, searching, searching.

Yes, the Beast thinks. *Untamed*. He licks his lips, looking far to the right.

"They're that way," I say, pointing to the right where the lake should be, according to Shweta, but is not. "They're Untamed."

Maggot nods at me, then turns to Shweta for clarification.

"It could be Mum," Clive says, his voice hopeful. He blinks several times. I want to snap at him that it won't be. Kate's gone, just as Kazem is gone. But none of us actually point out to Clive that it won't be his mother, or that this Watcher Doll must belong to Untamed who are not from these lands, Untamed who perhaps originate from other Sections, like me.

"You should go that way," I say to Maggot. "Find those Untamed. Safety is in numbers." And I will go a different way. Lead the Enhanced away from them.

Maggot grunts at me.

"Let's just send Evor off first," Shweta says. Her eyes are on me, and I don't like the way she's watching me. It's like she knows something. Something that she is not too happy about.

It's almost dark when we find water. A whole day has passed, and all we have is the half dried-up remains of a stream. The land is squashy, squelchy beneath our feet, and Maggot lowers her brother into the six-inches of shallow water. Muddy water splashes up. It smells rotten.

It's the only water we have found, the only choice we have. We've walked so long, weakness and hunger and pain invading our bodies. We found some berries on the way that Maggot thought were safe to eat. I only had a few, because they were so strong and made me feel sick. My stomach's queasy, feels kind of hollow as I stare at the water. I don't think it will be enough to send Evor on his way to the New World, to make sure he doesn't get trapped here, but I don't say anything. We are all silent, but I'm sure we are all thinking it.

Shweta says the Spirit Releasing Words. Maggot's eyes are a steely gray. Clive clutches the Watcher Doll to his chest. I think about Kazem. If he is dead, those words won't have been said. He won't make it to the New World.

We move away after Evor's body has been released. It feels weird, leaving him. But we have to.

We walk for some time more, and then we stop. Need to rest.

It's dark now. Night has fully crept in, and the others have settled down. I volunteered to be the Night Watch first, but Maggot didn't think I was up to it. She told me to rest, that I shouldn't overdo things with the concussion, that she'd do it, but I cannot sleep. I stare at the dark sky above, and just as I'm listening to a little rodent or something digging in the long, damp grass, the Beast whispers to me.

Now. It's time. Time to go.

So I do. I glance at Maggot. She's a little way away. Hard to see her in the dark, but I can tell she's not looking at me. She's sort of slumped. Maybe she's asleep.

Go now.

It's strange, the way I am when the Beast takes over. The way I just seem to melt away. The way I do what he wants. The way I don't even think.

And I am exactly thirty-five steps away, when a voice in the darkness says, "Where do you think you're going?"

TWENTY-ONE

IT'S MAGGOT, FIERCE EYES BURNING, voice thick like she needs to cough. "You're just sneaking off?"

"I have to go." My voice cracks, and the Beast has backed down. Typical man, leaving me to deal with the fallout. "It's because of me that they found us, the Enhanced." Caia-Lu told me they can find me. "Evor died because of me. I led the enemy to us. And I should've realized, should've been able to save him. But I didn't, and its's only going to get worse. And you want me to kill them, I know that, and it makes sense. So I'll go on my own. Go around all the towns alone."

And I will look forward to killing them all. Eradicating the world of Enhanced Ones. The Beast will make sure I enjoy it. The Beast will turn me into a weapon.

No, this isn't you, a voice inside me says, a voice that isn't the Beast. *The Beast isn't you.*

But I push it away. The Beast is me now. He's been in me all along. I've been fighting him, but he's here for a reason. Right?

"Kacey, we have to stick together," Maggot says.

"No. I'm putting us all in danger. The Enhanced let

me go for a reason. They're tracking me. My aunt told me. They can find me."

Maggot does a quick look to the left, then right, behind, then in front, even though neither of us can see much in the dark. "What aunt? When?"

"Caia-Lu. She died in the D'Elinous attack. I had a dream—look I know how this sounds." I hold my hands up in the surrender gesture. "It wasn't the Dream Land, but just hear me out, okay? It was real, this warning from Caia-Lu. She told me that Red's tracking me."

"Red? What's Red?"

"A man," I say. Another man whom I've killed. "He's Enhanced. He used to live in my village, too. At D'Elinous. But he's Enhanced now, pretending to be Untamed to lure me in or something. He was the one who let me go, when I was caught at New Zeralzi. But this doesn't matter now—the Enhanced will always be able to find me, whether Red's alive or not." I run my hand through my hair. My fingers snag on a tangle and it sends a bolt of pain across my scalp—a bolt that then dives deeper inside, swirling round and round. "That's what Caia-Lu told me in this dream. It's me—they're tracking *me*." And saying this is difficult, because it forces me to acknowledge head-on that it *is* me. I'm putting the group in danger, not Shweta.

"Wait? You had a warning dream about this? About the Enhanced attacking us?" Maggot frowns. "It's not just this power you have? You're a Seer, then?"

Exasperation runs through me. I thought Maggot was clever. "No—I'm not a Seer. I didn't see the bison or whatever it is in the Dream Land—I didn't see that. And I don't think it could've been the Dream Land. Just my aunt. She was a Seer, so maybe in the New World she can still contact me. But that doesn't matter—none of the details do."

"It does if the Dream Land is evolving."

"It's not evolving." Heat wraps around me. "Look, we were lucky this time. With the Enhanced. Next time, we won't be. So, I have to go. I can't put you all in danger."

"Kacey, if you're a Seer, we need you to stay." Maggot glances back at the sleeping forms of Clive and Shweta. "We need an active Seer with access to powers."

Why is she not getting this? "No. I'm not a Seer. Trust me. I have to go. I'm leaving now, okay?" I look around, and part of me wants to gather up bags and make a big display of leaving. But I have nothing. Our group has nothing but the clothes on our backs and the Watcher Doll. "I'm not putting you in danger. Don't follow me," I tell them, my voice firm.

"Kacey, this is madness—we need to stick together." Maggot sniffs loudly, and she looks weak. *Weak.* "I'm leader of this group, not you. *I* make the decisions."

"A good leader listens," I say.

And then there's a figure stirring, behind Maggot. It's Shweta, standing up. She heads over to us and her eyes are soft under the moonlight. She lightly touches Maggot's shoulder, and she seems to know as she nods at me. "We have to let her go. Bad things happen if we don't." She squeezes Maggot's shoulder. "Go, Kacey. Go now. I'll keep Maggot back here." There's something deep in her eyes that I don't understand. But she sounds so earnest, so sincere.

"This is ridiculous." Smoke is practically coming out of Maggot's ears.

"Then humor me," I say. "You can't afford not to."

I turn and leave and partly expect to hear her footsteps following close. But I don't. When I flick my head back, a quick glance over my shoulder, Maggot and Shweta are standing stationary.

I walk off into the wilderness, and part of me expects something to happen. For some grand thing to happen—I don't know, the weather to change or a God or Goddess to appear. Or even a spirit.

Or the Enhanced, following me and not my group.

But nothing happens.

It's just me walking. With my Beast. Walking and

walking and walking.

Now we can start to save everyone, Kacey, the Beast says, and I feel him grinning because the grin is stretching across my face, too.

TWENTY-TWO

LONELINESS IS A CURSE. IT'S torture. It means I think of Kazem. I cannot stop thinking of him. I remember the way he laughs, the way he smells. I remember how he lightly touches my back, the shapes he traces over my skin. I remember our kisses.

I remember everything, and I scream.

The Beast has retreated inside me, and after a little while, the isolation that wraps around me reminds me of when I walked away from the dead clansmen. It's a shawl of darkness around me, and it's enough to make me think things I wouldn't normally think. Imagine things I never normally do.

I think about my mother, my father, the faceless parents whom I don't know. I wonder if, wherever they are—whether they got to the New World or not—they're somehow watching me. Have I got two stars up there keeping an eye on me? Are they soundlessly screaming at me now, for doing the wrong thing? Am I doing the wrong thing?

"Give me a sign, Mum, Dad," I say, and then I laugh. What am I doing? This is stupid. I don't even know them. I cannot picture them. There's just nothing in my memory where their faces should be.

I wished I'd asked Caia-Lu more about them, when we were at D'Elinous. I wonder if she looks like her brother: my dad. Maybe he's got the same build too. Sturdy, round. Keelie once said that Caia-Lu was built like a teddy-bear, and I remember thinking how I liked that image. It made Caia-Lu seem reassuring, familiar, good. Was my father like a teddy bear, too?

And my mother?

All I can do is look at myself, try to see how I could've come from two different people. But genetics are weird. I know that. Kazem always said he never looked much like his brother or parents, except for his skin tone and hair coloring. They had different shaped jaws and noses and eyes and builds.

Kazem. My chest tightens.

I find a cave and bed down for the rest of the night. There are probably only a few hours left until dawn, but it's cold. I'm shivering. I keep expecting to see Maggot or Shweta or Clive. To see they've followed me. But they haven't. They've let me go.

I'm alone.

I made the right decision, I know that. No sign of the Enhanced though, or the other Untamed. I think about the Watcher Doll. I wonder if Clive is still clutching hold of it. I hope it brings him comfort.

I close my eyes, and I pray that things will be better in the morning.

"What the hell do you mean they got away?" Abdi stares at me, the muscles in his jaw and temples pulsing.

I hold my hands up, frantic. The others aren't here yet. The bosses. I still can't believe I got away. It was only my power that saved me. "Look, it'll be okay." I try to give him a reassuring smile, but I am nervous. I need a shot of Confidence. But it will be fine, I know that. There is no way the bosses will find out, so long as Abdi doesn't tell..

Abdi shakes his head. "They are going to wonder why you came back empty-handed."

"Because my team didn't find her." It surprises me how easy it is to lie, but I know that sooner or later, Abdi is going to find out that my team of foot soldiers is dead.

"They're not going to believe that when you've already claimed that you can always find her."

I breathe out hard. Yes, I did claim that. And I want to kick myself now. My power can find hers. It is easy to track her. And I did boast about this.

"Well, I'll say it's harder than I thought." I look at him, imploringly. I need Abdi to back me up on this.

"But this is just like with Keelie."

Keelie. Just her name makes everything inside me tighten, like I am being squeezed by a cobra.

"It's nothing like with her." My words come out fast.

"It is. You're sympathizing." He tilts his head to one side and gives me a strong, stern look. "You're not converting them at the first opportunity. You're letting them suffer. Don't you see how cruel that is?"

My jaw tenses. "I'm not sympathizing."

"I have to report this." Abdi reaches for the radio in his belt.

"Please, no—I can't go through a level three again. Seriously, please."

Abdi's eyes seem to darken, but I know they can't have. They're still the mirrors, reflecting my appearance back at him. And I look pathetic. There's weakness written all over my face, and in the way I'm standing, slouching against the wall. My power may have saved me, but it still fucking hurts.

"I'm not talking about reconversion." There's a strange edge to Abdi's voice now, like he's just eaten something really bitter. "Raleigh put me in charge of you when you transferred over here. Me. And I am not letting him down. Reconversion hasn't worked for you, even after all these times. I don't know what it is because you yourself don't want to be Untamed, yet you're not as determined to save *others as you should be—"*

"I am—"

"And Raleigh said that if this happens, then we have no choice." Abdi moves closer to me. "You are a liability, Red. And we cannot have you undermining our work." He presses something cold against my neck and—

I choke as cold metal presses against my skin, my throat. Darkness around me, and I'm fighting and—

Red's alive, and he's here. My heart pounds too fast. He's somehow here. I scrabble about, trying to fight back, but I'm lying down and he's leaning over me. On me. I can feel his body, his weight, pinning me down.

"I'd say it's lovely to see you again, Kassandra, but it's not nice to see you at all."

The words creep over me, but it's not Red who speaks. It's a woman. A rich, dark, velvety voice. A strong accent.

The weapon at my neck bites my skin with a sharp, deadly edge. Just a tiny bite, a tiny cut. But everything inside me freezes. I know this voice. I *know* it.

No…

My core is ice.

No, it can't be *her*! She's dead, she's…

She's *here*.

"Did you miss me, Kassandra?" Ysabelle's voice is the most venomous snake, but she doesn't give me time to answer.

She drags the sharp blade across my throat.

The cut is swift, sudden. Hotness bursts over my skin. I let out a noise that sounds like a choked squawk, and then I see her as orange light floods the cave. She holds a torch in her other hand, and she's stepping off of my body now. I splutter, looking up at her, feel hot wetness gushing from my neck, spilling over me. So much of it and—

Time slows down.

I try to stop the bleeding. My hands are at my neck. I'm pressing and pressing, and the pain is wicked and…

She *cut* me.

She's slashed my neck.

And how the fuck is she here?

I stare up at Ysabelle, unable to speak. Her face is lined, older. She's an elderly woman now, but she's strong. She's just *slashed* my neck.

She stands there, a soft smile stretching her chapped, dry lips, the knife in her hand, its blade dripping onto me. Those haunting, bright eyes blink, and her flaming hair almost glows in the broken darkness. She's still got that amber-bead necklace—like a burning sunset, its amber and yellow and orange glass beads rest delicately over her prominent collarbones, trailing down her chest across the tops of her breasts and the dark fabric of her shirt.

Ysabelle of the clansmen. Ysabelle who died in the massacre. Ysabelle who the Beast killed.

The Beast! *Help me!*

But he doesn't; he does nothing, and I don't understand, and my life is flooding from me, drenching me, marking me, taking me…

I try to move, try to do anything—but I cannot. All I can do is lie here and choke, struggling to breathe as a cool fog fills my brain. My vision swirls, and *how* is Ysabelle here?

"How?" I try to speak, but there is no sound apart from raspiness and a high-pitched squealing and a heavy, raspy wheezing…

Ysabelle's face is the last thing I see.

TWENTY-THREE

I OPEN MY EYES TO the sounds of voices: low and murmuring. Darkness is a cushion around me. Soft, comforting. Yes, I am in the cave and—

I jolt.

Ysabelle. My neck! I reach for it, and my skin is smooth. My skin is *dry*. What? No blood, no gnash, no scar?

Was that a dream? Ysabelle and—

But, no. There are *blankets* over me. Blankets I have not got with me. What the hell?

My eyes widen, and I try to think. And then, I realize that in this darkness, someone is lying next to me. I can hear their breathing, slow and steady, sense the warmth of the body, hear the slight movement of the blanket as their chest rises and falls.

I bolt up, and Kazem's next to me.

Kazem. What? How?

"Kazem!" I grab him, jolting him awake, and then I'm crying, clinging onto him. My tears wet his face, and I'm kissing him, pressing his lips to mine, my hands on his head, his neck, his back. He's *here*. He's really here, and I can't hold onto him tightly enough.

"Wait, what?" His voice is sluggish as he pulls back from me.

My heart pounds. I look up, behind him. See the stone walls. The stone walls I've woken up to for the past six years. The tunnels. I am in the tunnels under New Zeralzi. A curling sensation fills my chest. My head feels too light. I'm back here? What the fuck? Is this the New World? Are we both dead?

But if we are, it's okay. We're together.

"Oh Gods," I cry.

"Kace?" Kazem's tone is urgent. He blinks. The early morning light, seeping through the small ventilation grid we put in the ceiling, emphasizes the mole just to the right of the end of his nose. "What's wrong?"

"I—I… I don't know." I haven't got the words. How do I even ask him how this is all possible? What if we *are* dead? I swallow too quickly, and a speck of saliva goes down the wrong way. I start coughing. The sound rouses Kazem enough to get up and then he's lit the candles in our quarters.

With more light in here—the soft candlelight flickering—I see *everything*, and it looks all the more real. Hell, it *feels* real, *smells* real. Body odor and mustiness and damp and the spearmint gum Kazem likes. Our room always smells of this, even when he's not chewing it. Even when it's nighttime and he's asleep.

I really am back here. My heart pounds way too fast and way too heavily for this not to be a dream. I reach out for Kazem again, catch onto his arm to steady myself. My fingers curl around his biceps. He's *real*.

"Did you have a bad dream?" he asks, and then he's wiping away my tears with his thumb.

"A bad dream?" I say. "A bad dream! This is… It can't be…"

"It's understandable," he says. "I had my reoccurring one again." His eyes meet mine.

Even though I don't understand how I am here, how this cannot be a dream that I am in right now, I know which dream he's talking about. One where he's alone in a house—a modern, Enhanced-style house—and there are no doors or windows. He can't get out, and no one can get in.

"But we're going to do it, aren't we?" He gives me a squeeze, and I find myself leaning into his warmth. "We're going to win today."

I can hardly concentrate on his words. There's still pain in my head, and I touch it—the bit where the lump was before. It's still there. The lump. Under my hair. Hot pain squeezes through me as I touch it again, more firmly.

A wave of dizziness pours over me.

Kazem gives me what I'm sure is supposed to be a reassuring squeeze of the shoulder, but all it does is make nausea rise in me. "We'll get the town today. We'll—oh." His tone drops.

"What?"

"Your hands are going to bleed at the slightest thing." He takes my hands in his and peers at them intently, then he gets one of the candles and brings it closer, using the light from it.

Voices sound nearby. Maggot's and Bhavesh's and Rohan's. I inhale sharply. It's the same voices I heard on the morning of our planned siege. Only it's darker now, isn't it? Things are happening earlier. I frown, then focus on what Kazem just said: *Your hands are going to bleed at the slightest thing*. He said that before, days ago.

My head spins. Is this the time loop Shweta mentioned?

Kazem stares at me, concern in his eyes. About my hands? I scramble to remember what I said, before.

"Just from the gravel…" I frown. Was that what I said? Do I have to say the same things? Oh Gods. Is this why things are already a little different, because I'm behaving differently?

"I think you should wear your gloves today," Kazem says. "Or you can borrow mine."

Borrow his? But, no, I can't—I didn't before. And this…

"Is this *real*?" I stare at him, then rub my head. The side of it's all itchy, and I scratch it hard, feel something collecting under my nails. "It can't be real. Can it?" I pull my hand through my hair, shoving it away from my forehead. "I... I need to find Shweta."

But I can't bring myself to do it, to go out and search for her and let go of Kazem. My Kazem. *My* man. Because what if this is the last time I see him? What if none of this is real, but this is the last chance we get to be together?

"What's going on, Kace?" Kazem asks.

Tears pierce my eyes, and I pull him close again, holding onto him. Holding onto him as tightly as I can. I'm crying properly now, but I know we can't stay like this. Something weird is happening.

"Just come with me," I say, and I hold onto his hand so tightly I think one of us might break.

Shweta is in the gathering room, handing out tools and helping Maggot with the last-minute preparations. She looks up as Kazem and I approach, and maybe it's the expression on my face or how fast I'm rushing toward her—and how I accidentally knock over a table with water bottles on—that grabs everyone's attention, because I realize it's not just Shweta staring at me. Everyone is.

And, shit. I'm changing things already. What effect is this going to have? And how did I even knock into that table? I'm not clumsy. My co-ordination is amazing. It always has been.

"You all right?" Maggot asks, and everyone is still looking at me.

I don't understand. I shouldn't be here. I should still be out there, in that cave. Or dead, at the hands of Ysabelle. Not here with all my Untamed group. Not here with Kazem.

Kazem.

I don't know what to say to Maggot, so I scuttle to pick up the bottles of water. Kazem helps me, making some joke I can't concentrate on. My hands are shaking. No, the whole of my body is shaking, trembling.

"I'm fine, sorry. Really. I am." I don't know why I'm not shouting to everyone about how none of this can be real—because yesterday and today can't both exist. Not like this. I try to meet Shweta's eye, but my head's swimming and I can't see properly. I try to assess my body, everything that I'm feeling. I try to name this differentness, this sensation, but all I can come up with is that my stomach feels full, like I ate a few hours ago.

"Okay," Maggot says a few moments later. "Everyone, take your weapons and assemble outside. We're runnin' late already."

Running late?

Somehow, those words make me panic, and I breathe deeper. Shweta turns away, starts to head out the tunnel. Kazem gives my hand a squeeze, then lets go of me and follows her.

Kazem! "No, wait!" I call after him.

Kazem doesn't stop, but Shweta does.

She turns. There are shadows over her face, and I see the lines there. The weariness in her expression. "Let me guess. You want me to keep an eye on Kazem?" She rolls her eyes.

"No. This has all happened before. You were right." My head pounds, and lighter shapes haloed in yellow are appearing over my vision. The shapes are moving, and it makes me feel sick.

Shweta inhales sharply—and that's enough. That's enough for me to feel some ounce of reassurance. I widen my eyes, can't bring myself to say the words because there are still so many other people here, and I don't know if they're listening to me and I don't want them thinking I'm weird or mad.

"What is it, Kacey?" Shweta's eyes narrow a little, but her voice is different now. There's meaning in it. "Do you need more ammunition? There's some in the store. You'll have to help me. I can't reach the shelves." She gives me a small nod. "We'd better go quickly now, together."

In the store, Shweta takes a deep breath and leans against the shelves. They're full of boxes and boxes of ammunition, all stacked neatly and according to Sian's system.

"You're saying you know this isn't the first time we've done this attack?" Shweta's posture slackens a little. Is that relief on her face?

"It's the second time." I swallow hard and place my hand on the wall to steady myself. "For me." I still don't feel right. Is that the effects of this *time-travel* or whatever it is? Or maybe the concussion? "What are my eyes like?" I ask. "I hit my head last time, and it's *still* killing me. Is that right? Evor said I was concussed? Wait, is Evor still alive?" I didn't see him out there, with everyone else. A bubbly sensation rises through me.

"He's alive. But you better not be playing with me here."

"Playing with you? No!" It's hot in here, and sweat drips down the back of my spine. "No. I'm not. I promise."

She tuts under her breath. "You've done it before."

"What?"

"A while ago," she says. "One of the first times this day began again. Back when I was desperate to get people to believe me. I tried to make Maggot understand about the time loop, and you and Kazem thought it would be funny to say you remembered the previous days too. You *humored* me." Even now—and how many days or weeks later is this, if they're even counted as days?—hurt curdles her words.

"We did?" I stare at her. An empty feeling carves its home in my chest.

Cold, heartless. See, that's the Beast!

I try to shove away the memory of Ysabelle's voice, but like with all the times when a fragment of memory emerges, it calls its friends. I close my eyes to the whisperings, feel the stirrings of the Beast.

No. I have to stay in control. I hug myself tighter. My legs feel too heavy, like my feet are filling with liquid concrete. I sway a little.

"Why should I believe you this time?" Shweta crosses her arms carefully, precisely.

"I… I don't know. But look—I remember the last few days, days which haven't happened yet this time around, if I understand this correctly?" She doesn't correct me, so I continue. "We started the plan, but the Enhanced knew about it. They caught us all. Most of us."

"And do you still think it was me who betrayed us—in that timeline?" Shweta eyes me carefully. "Or are you going to out me now, tell Maggot I've turned to the enemy?"

"No." I rub my face, drag my skin downward in a way that somehow irritates my right eye. That's the side of my head I injured mostly, wasn't it? "But I don't understand all of this. You said timelines? Shweta, what is going on?"

"I don't know," she says. "I've been trying to find out—but it's difficult when you can only live in the moment and I don't have my powers."

"But your powers came back two days before the siege, last time."

She nods. "I don't understand it, either. There are so many variants to this, and finding things out takes time. There's got to be a Seer who knows, especially one who was blessed by the Goddess of Time Streams, but finding such a Seer is tricky when I don't know how long this timeline will last for."

"How long it will last for?" My heart's still going like crazy, and I try to breathe deeply as Shweta talks, try to calm myself—only it doesn't work. "What do you mean?"

"Before this one stops," she explains, "and I get thrown back—sometimes to this day, sometimes two days ago. Sometimes two days ahead."

"Ahead?" I frown, pressing a hand to my chest, like I can physically slow my heart, but all it does is make me aware of how clammy my skin is. I stare at the rows and rows of ammunition, bewildered. The boxes blur out of focus. "Wait? How long has this been going on for?"

"A long time. I lost count at two hundred resets."

Everything in me stutters, and my vision dims. What if this is it now? What if Shweta and I are just going to be stuck in this loop, forever?

"Are you okay?" Shweta's hand leaps out at me and grabs me just as everything dims around me.

Then I'm on the floor, and my head hurts, and she's peering at me. She's speaking but her words are mangled in my ears. My head pounds even harder. And my heart, it's never been so fast. What's happening to me?

"You fainted?" Shweta crouches in front of me, pivoting a little on the balls of her feet. She reaches out like she's going to touch me, but then she stops. "Are you still concussed from last time?"

"I don't know..." I shake my head and absentmindedly brush some debris away from me. "This is just... How? This time stuff—how?"

Shweta shrugs. "Like I said, I haven't been able to find such a Seer who can help me understand it. And no one here ever believes me."

"I'm sorry," I say, looking across at her. "For not believing you before."

"Don't be." She smiles, only it's not a reassuring

smile. It doesn't reach her eyes. "I know it sounds unbelievable. But, hey, maybe now whatever has happened has claimed you too, it'll be my last reset? Maybe I'll get to *live* now."

My heart pounds, and I feel so small suddenly, and injured, wounded, and the thought of me going through all of this alone in the future terrifies me. Gods, Shweta must've been so scared. I reach out for her, and she lets me take her hands. She nods, giving me another smile. This one has a little more warmth in it.

"Just go with it," Shweta says. "And don't worry too much—worrying is the thing that makes it worse, because the day's going to go how the day's going to go. The times when I've worried or acted strangely have always been the worst for me. And when you get hurt in these timelines—physically and emotionally— it really *does* hurt, even if by the time it's reset, the injuries have mostly gone. Depends on their severity, really. But just go with it. That's the easiest way."

"But does it always start the same? As in, we never get the town? I know you said sometimes the starting day is different." I lean forward, and the movement flares up some pain in my left hip. I think of my fall from the roof of the pharmacy, how my leg was injured. I stretch it out, roll my trouser leg up. It's bruised, but I can't really feel pain.

Shweta nods. "Yeah, they always know about the plan. And I've not been able to find out who the real traitor is, by the way. Each time I think I know it and I stop that person the next time, it doesn't make a difference. Either it's the wrong person or they've already given the message to the Enhanced or it's a different traitor each time. I haven't found anything that stops the resets, so I just go with it."

"Go with it?" I shake my head, exhaling hard. I don't think I can do that. But it doesn't look like I've got a choice.

She nods again. "And don't freak out if the Enhanced get you. Sometimes, they do. Sometimes, they don't.

Some of our group gets away each time. You nearly always do—you're almost always in the escaping group. But now you're in the know, with me." She relaxes a little. "Maybe it will be different now. Just don't panic."

"What about Maggot and Evor?" I ask. "And Clive? Do they remember?"

Shweta shakes her head. "They've never said anything and like I said earlier, its's not something I can just ask them. Not if I want to be respected."

I take a deep breath and then try to stand up. Shweta steadies me for a moment, and then I hug her. I'm not a big hugger—normally, Kazem is the only person I like to hug—but I just do it.

Shweta holds onto me hesitantly at first, then tighter. "I'm glad you're here," she says.

I smile into her hair. "Me too." I pull back. "There has to be an explanation for why the day resets though."

"Ha, you think?"

"Are you nearly ready?" It's Sian, standing in the doorway—so suddenly.

I look at her, sharply. Did she see me and Shweta hug? I know it doesn't matter if she did, but it still makes me feel uneasy.

"Maggot's not happy," Sian says. "We're super late already. Have you got the ammo sorted?"

"We're ready," Shweta says. She pats her belt, where I see some clips of bullets. "Kacey was just getting a little stage fright."

Stage fright? Me? I roll my eyes and give Shweta a look. She just smiles back.

We follow Sian.

"Just have fun," Shweta murmurs into my ear as we get ready to separate into our teams a few moments later. Her voice is low, and the buzz of everyone's excitement and anticipation rises around us. "It's easier that way. Oh, and try not to get killed. Assuming you get reset, like I do, you *really* hurt for days after."

TWENTY-FOUR

I HAVE SO MANY QUESTIONS, but Shweta has disappeared. My head spins, and I can't think about where I'm supposed to be or what I'm supposed to be doing. Everything in me feels like it doesn't belong here, in this world—and I don't. Not in this timeline. This isn't mine.

I take a deep breath and try to remember the arrangements before. I was in a team with someone… but who? I look around. Most people have filed out of the tunnels by now, and I blink, stunned. Have I lost time? Does that happen now?

"You okay?"

I turn to find Evor behind me. His bald head looks strangely shiny in the candlelight, but I can't deny the relief that floods through me upon seeing him. He's here. He's alive.

No one is dead. Yet.

"Not like you to be nervous, eh?" He laughs.

I laugh too, but then I stop. "Something's wrong with me," I say, and I surprise myself, hadn't realized I was going to say that.

Evor stops, too. A frown tugs its way across his

head. "Wrong?"

"I don't feel well." My words are soft, and I feel a bit embarrassed. What if this is just what it feels like to be in a time loop? Yet I can't shake away the feeling that I am still a bit concussed.

"Kacey, it's probably just nerves," he says.

"No!" I shake my head so hard that pain reverberates through me. I focus back on him, but my vision does that blurry thing again. For a split second, he has three eyes. "Evor, please." I take a deep breath. "I banged my head, a little while ago. And my head still doesn't feel right."

He peers at me, his frown deepening.

"I... I don't know what's wrong exactly." I'm babbling, and again, this isn't like me. "But have you got your medicine bag? You need to have it." Because we will need it when it's just us out there. Now I know that some of us will get away and be on the run, we can plan ahead. And I can stop him being killed this time.

Evor shines a light into my eyes so suddenly I nearly jump a foot in the air—or at least I would if I had the energy.

But I haven't. My body's just slow and sluggish, and everything feels too heavy. And my heart—it won't stop pounding. Too fast. It's making me nauseous again.

"I think you're okay," he says, and he puts the little torchlight away in the top pocket of his shirt. "Your pupils are dilating as they should. Here, follow my finger."

I follow his finger with my eyes as he moves it from side to side. Then he asks to feel my head and neck.

"Hmmm, you do have a bump here," he says, finding the lump on my head. "But you seem okay. Are you all right to free-run this morning? How do you feel? Maybe we should tell Maggot."

Didn't I already say to him that I didn't feel well? But he's not taking this seriously.

"I... I'm fine." I take a deep breath. Shweta says I most often get away in each timeline, so I've got to be out there, with them all.

"After you," Evor says. "And you better put your mirrors in now."

Numbly, I do so, and then I move forward, and time blurs around me, moving faster than it should. Gray buildings rush past me, and trees and dark windows and lampposts. We're moving out and we're in the town, and then it's me and Bhavesh, heading away from the other teams. We run across the road and then we're weaving among more buildings, heading for the tower. Running doesn't feel good to me now—it's making me too hot, and I'm sweating, and my vision's still not right. My head's hurting, and I feel jarred, like part of me is moving at a slower rate, getting left behind.

There are no Enhanced Ones about. New Zeralzi may as well be deserted.

I falter a little, trip on a bit of loose gravel and skid. Bhavesh keeps going, doesn't even look back my way, but I slow even more, see a puddle on the road with a distorted reflection of buildings in it. A frown pulls its way across my eyebrows, and I'm not sure what it is about that which makes me think of what Shweta said—that every single time the Enhanced know of our plan—but I do. It fills my mind, those words.

Every single time, in every timeline, there's a traitor.

Yet she lets our people file out every time—lets us die? Get converted?

Is that what I'm just supposed to do too? I have stopped, and my lungs are burning. What if things aren't reset this time? Things are already happening differently, because I'm aware of the time loop now. So what if this is it? What if things this time stay as they are?

I look up at Bhavesh's retreating figure. I can't let him die. I can't let anyone die. And this—it's worth a try, isn't it?

"Stop!" I shout after him, my heart pounding. Immediately, I feel sicker. We're never supposed to yell when we're in an Enhanced Ones' town. That's just asking for trouble. But I shout the word again. Bhavesh looks so tiny—he's run so far in that time. How has he ran so far? And he's *still* running. He hasn't heard me. I try to shout louder. "The Enhanced know!"

Bhavesh turns back. He shouts something to me, but I can't make out his words. I just yell "Enhanced!" at him, and I try not to be sick. Because what the hell? Why is my stomach churning? Why is my heart beating so fast?

I watch as Bhavesh grabs his radio, and then he's speaking into it. My shoulders lighten a bit, and then I'm staggering backward. I feel *drunk*. Need to hold onto something. I grab at a nearby wall, but the rough surface just grates skin off my fingers. I wince at the sharp pain.

"Kace!" Bhavesh shouts.

My head jerks up, and he's running toward me and—

A lot of things happen at once.

I whirl around as I hear a sound—footsteps—and suddenly three men are racing toward me. Three Enhanced. One of them is Red. I recognize him instantly. He's here already, so quickly. For a moment, I think he's here because I shouted. Because I alerted them. But then I realize it's too quick. They were already waiting.

My legs start shaking—proper violent shakes. I try to move, but I can't. I try to grab the wall again, but my fingers are bleeding. There's a whistling in my head, and a series of snapshots close around me, one after another, each punctuated by a gunshot.

Time is speeding up, faster and faster, and I fall.

I hit the ground hard, wind myself.

I can't breathe.

Bang.

Bhavesh fires his gun. I see his face—the snapshot of his face, like someone's shoving a photograph of this moment in my face—but then he's falling. And there's blood. So much blood.

Bang.

"Oh, dear," Red says, and he's so near me. The sun glints off his mirror eyes, and my own eyes burn with it. He's right in front of me, but his voice is different as he tells me...

What is he telling me?

He's speaking, but I can't understand. I can't hear him.

I touch my ears, but they're wet. My fingers come away sticky with blood.

Bang.

An augmenter rolls toward me. I'm sitting in a puddle. Water. Not blood. A large clock tower looms over me, but I look back down at the vial in front of me. It's stopped by my feet. My bare feet. The augmenter is neon pink.

Angry words hang in the air above me, but I can't hear the words—I see them. And it doesn't make sense.

Bang.

"No!" I scream, and I taste the word—salty and bitter—and there are so many Enhanced Ones here. They are sinister and dangerous and bad and evil, and they are reaching for me.

I try to cover my head, try to do something to... to get away from this all. I don't understand this world I'm in now. Nothing makes sense.

Bang.

And nothing exists. There is only nothing.

TWENTY-FIVE

I OPEN MY EYES, STARE up at a ceiling. Buttercup yellow. It's the same ceiling. I remember this ceiling. I sit up—and nearly faint. *Shit*. What is wrong with me? I pull my legs up to my chest, feeling sick and weak. But I'm not tied up. I try to concentrate on that—then realize that someone has changed my clothes. I am wearing a flimsy purple gown, and my underwear is scratchy. I still have my shoes, though.

Red enters the room. His entrance is abrupt, quick. "Hello," he says, his eyes on me.

"Hello?" My voice is a wispy scratch against my face.

He locks the door—he didn't do that last time, but I was tied up then—then steps up to my bed. My bed is the only thing in this room. Is this like before? I struggle to think. He's peering at me intently, and though he's got mirrors, I can't detect any sign of recognition in him this time.

He doesn't know me this time? I frown. Doesn't recognize me? Did he say my name earlier, when we were outside? I can't remember. But maybe this is a different timeline. It's not just a replay. Of course it isn't. Things have already happened differently.

"Yes," Red says suddenly. "You'll do."

I'll do?

I blink, and my head's spinning, and my vision's so blurry, like I'm looking at everything underwater. But that's good—that means I'm definitely not Enhanced, right?

I take a deep breath, but my lungs don't feel right. Neither does my chest. I can't breathe deeply enough.

His hands go to his pockets, and I notice he's wearing a white lab coat this time. He produces an augmenter and an ID card. My mouth dries when I see the augmenter. But Red's still undercover, right?

No, he never was!

"This is you," he says, giving me the card.

I take it, my body numb. It takes a moment for my eyes to adjust and my vision to unwobble enough to read the name on the card. "Keelie Lin-Sykes?"

"That's you." His tone is sharper this time.

"No." I try to lean back away from him, but the wall is against my spine. "I'm Kacey."

Irritation flashes across his face. "But from now on you'll be Keelie. You'll be my best friend. My girlfriend. My fiancée."

I stare at him, feel sweat beading across my forehead. "What?"

"I loved her, and I lost her," he says, and his voice sounds weird. More robotic. "And I want to feel that love again—and I can, with this augmenter." He holds up the vial. It's so pink. Neon pink. "But I'll need a subject. And you look enough like Keelie. So you're going to be her. I need a replacement. We'll get married."

Lightheadedness pulls at me. What the hell? I stare at him. Wait for him to say something else. To laugh. To say that this is a joke.

"We're just waiting for the conversion rooms to free up," he says. "There were a lot of you. Then we'll convert you and head to the chapel."

"We're going straight there?" I ask. "Conversion?" I scratch my neck, then press my hand flat against the top of my chest. I don't know why I do that.

Red nods, all brisk and efficient. "Be easier for you if you don't put up a fight. Remember who you're dealing with here."

"But you're not giving *me* the augmenter now," I say, and my eyes are on it in his hand.

"Oh, I am. I know exactly what to do, and I will do it. You can have the taste before we go to the conversion room."

He tries to force my mouth open, his fingers pulling at my lips.

And *shit*—this is real.

This is *real*.

Electric shocks bolt through me, and I scream. Adrenaline pours through me and—

The door flies open, hits the wall. A cacophony of sound and—

"Shweta?" I cry, just as she lifts her gun and shoots Red.

He falls to the side, sliding off the edge of my bed. And blood—blood is on the floor. So much blood.

"Let's get out of there," she says, and then she grabs my hand, and I've never been so happy to see her.

But when I start running, my head gets heavier. Darkness fogs the edges of my vision, and my lungs seem to disappear.

I slow, wheezing, pain in my chest. We're in a corridor, somewhere, but I can't recognize it. Can hardly see.

"What is it?" Shweta demands.

All I can do is shake my head as my vision dims even more. Can't speak. Can't think. Can't—

"Stop them!" a voice cries, and then Shweta's pulling me along.

I pant, feeling sick. Feeling like my insides are too hot, they're burning me, trying to burn their way out of my body. I can't—can't breathe…. can't….

I'm losing track… Can't hear anything… My vision…

And there are voices, but I can't hear them…

And then there's nothing.

"Yes, she fainted in there," Shweta says, and I'm not exactly sure where she is or where I am. I'm trying to look at her, but I can't really see her. It's just dark. "She hit her head."

"How long ago?" Evor's voice.

"I don't know. She was mumbling about hitting it." Was I?

"And now she keeps fainting."

"Keeps? How many times?"

"This is the second that I've seen. But this Enhanced man had her, and he was—"

"Red," I say, interjecting. "It was Red." That seems important.

I can't see them, but there's a silence that makes me wonder if everyone here—whoever that comprises of—is staring at me, giving me odd looks.

"She didn't look right," Shweta says. "She still doesn't. She's too pale."

"How did I get out?" I whisper. "Where are we?" But as soon as I ask the question, I find I *can* see. Maybe I've been able to see all the time, and I just didn't realize? I'm with Shweta and Maggot and Evor. We're in the steppe, out by Dawn's Rock where I told Clive we'd meet before. Only… My body grows heavier. "Where's Clive?"

"Enhanced," Shweta says.

He's Enhanced? My eyes widen, and my stomach twists. He's Enhanced because I didn't go and get him? Or he's in that cupboard still, hiding.

"We have to go back," I say. "Clive's—"

"I saw his conversion," Shweta says, her eyes sharp and on me.

His conversion?

Of course. Things are happening differently this time.

"It's just the four of us," Maggot says.

I nod slowly, and then find that my head wants to keep nodding.

"Something's wrong with her," Shweta says to Evor, and I don't know why it takes me a moment to realize she's talking about me. "I think she hit her head pretty hard? I'm not sure when… but she's not right."

"I'll look her over again," Evor says, and he's got his medicine bag.

Yes! He's got his medicine bag! He listened!

He takes out his stethoscope. He stole it on a raid once, along with a book about the autonomic system, and was delighted with both those things, and the stethoscope is always with him.

Except it wasn't last time.

Evor presses the cold metal disc to my chest and tells me to breathe evenly. "Are you feeling faint now?"

My legs feel too hot pressed to the grassy ground. And there's so much grass and the grass strands are dry. Not damp. I press my hands into the grass, letting the blades flow over them. "No. But I'm sitting down. If I stand, I think I would."

He nods, his brow furrowing, and I see there's a cut on the top of his head. Then he's counting with that cold metal disc still pressed to my chest. "Okay, stand."

I don't want to get up. Everything tells me not to, but I do. Maggot's frowning, looking annoyed. Her face is all swollen again on one side. A brilliant bruise stretches over the swelling, purple and shiny.

"We need to work out how the Enhanced knew of our plan," she says to Shweta, who nods. "They knew everything…"

But then I can't pay attention to their words because a heaviness grows around the base of my skull, down my neck and across into my shoulders. There's a rough, abrasive sensation in my chest and a rushing sound in my chest.

"Her heart's beating too fast," Evor says, looking at them. "Especially when she stands. I'd say that's the cause of her fainting. If the heart gets too fast, blood pressure's going to drop in response. It's a type of dysautonomia. I'm sure of it."

"Can it be caused by a concussion?" Shweta asks.

"Could be—though I think I read that some people just develop it. It's relatively common in teenage girls."

"I'm not a teenager," I grit out, but I'm having to concentrate hard on not falling, not swaying because I'm still standing and I don't want to be standing because it's making my chest hurt and my legs feel too heavy . "I'm twenty-two." I frown. Aren't I? Or am I twenty-one? I only know roughly when my birthday is… I might be twenty-one. Or twenty-three.

"And women in their twenties," Evor adds. "It's postural. Kacey, sit back down."

"So every time she stands she's goin' to faint?" Maggot asks. She shakes her head, and I know exactly what she's thinking—that I'm a liability. Because of course I am. How the hell am I going to outrun the Enhanced if I faint every time I'm upright?

"We'll see if we can treat it," Evor says. "And if we can't, we'll adapt."

"Adapt?"

"There were plenty disabled folk at my old group, and they were Untamed. Never got caught."

Disabled?

I recoil at the word. I'm *not* disabled. This is just… This is temporary. It's my concussion. That's all.

"My free-running," I say. "How soon can I do that?" Right now, it feels a lifetime away, and just thinking about it makes me dizzy—but I also know it's who I am. I need to be able to do it. I need to prove that I am still strong.

"You can't until you're better," Evor says. "*If* you're better. But you can still do other things. Try not to be too down. If this *is* because you hit your head, it might just be temporary anyway."

Well, it is. It has to be. Because this can't be my new normal. It can't.

"Right, well we better set off," Evor says. "We need to get as far away from New Zeralzi as we can. Kacey, I can carry you if needed. But the movement of just walking might be enough to keep pumping your blood, keep it from pooling in your calves. I believe, in cases like this, it's standing stationary or running that are the worse. But, Kacey, you must let us know when you need to stop."

I nod, numb. How can this have happened?

How?

TWENTY-SIX

WE WALK FOR HOURS—WELL, what seems like hours. I keep having to stop. I catch Maggot looking annoyed. Evor doesn't seem annoyed though. Neither does Shweta.

I picture Clive, back in the conversion compound, with real mirror eyes. Or maybe he's in the store cupboard again, hiding, waiting for someone. Waiting for me.

My belly hurts, and then I think of Kazem, and I try not to focus on him. Try not to see him at all in my mind's eye. His beautiful eyes, his dark hair with the slight iridescent effect, his warm brown skin. What if this really is it? Kazem—and everyone else—gone, forever.

"You need to explain more to me," I say to Shweta when we stop again. I sink onto the ground, wincing. My legs are bruised and covered in cuts that I don't remember getting, and I wish I was wearing jeans or something. But all I've got is this stupid purple gown that the Enhanced Ones put me in and Evor's over-sized jumper that's scratchy around my neck. "Come on, you have to know more about this all? The time stuff."

She sits next to me. She looks tired and keeps rubbing

her earlobe. It looks a bit swollen, infected maybe. There's a small cut there. She sways a bit. We think we're going to rest here a while, and Maggot and Evor are just checking the area. We're in a sort of flattish area, and there's lots of vegetation and spiky plants.

"I don't," Shweta says softly. She lets out a long sigh, and then reaches to tie her hair back. The hair band she uses is old and it breaks as she's trying to secure it.

"You do—you've got experience. I haven't. I've got so many questions and you must have answers." And we need to talk now—before Maggot and Evor are back.

"Well, ask me then." She shrugs and then unties the jacket that's around her waist. She fidgets a little to pull the garment out from under her and then unzips one of the pockets. "But I don't know how much more I can tell you." From the pocket she produces a cereal bar, and she peels the wrapper back carefully then snaps the bar in half. She gives half to me. "I've got another in here for Evor and Maggot."

I take the bar slowly, and then bring it to my lips. I am hungry—of course I am—even if when I awoke this morning, I felt strangely full. I need food, but I also feel a little sick. I take a small bite, testing it. Testing myself. "Okay," I say after a moment of chewing. "So, like, things can happen differently—in these resets?"

She nods. "Sometimes, yeah. Other times not. Believe me, the repetitive ones are so boring."

In the scrubby trees a little way away, I see movement—then Maggot's figure as she looks around. "But do things happen differently because of stuff we're doing? Like, do we influence it?"

"Sometimes," she says. "Like, yeah, I can change things now, and it might change things later on—or it might not. I guess there are fixed points that have to happen. Other times, not. It's like there are no rules."

"Okay." I take another bite of the cereal bar. "But there is someone who can help us—that Seer you mentioned." A bit of the food gets stuck in my throat, feels all scratchy, and I swallow twice in quick succession to try and move it downward. "Look, you couldn't find them when it was just you, but if I'm searching too, then maybe we'll get somewhere? If we both leave, go in different directions—maybe one of us will find other Untamed, one with such a Seer."

"I've never managed to stay in a timeline for more than two weeks," she says. "And two weeks has never been long enough. I've tried walking in all sorts of directions. But this," she says, looking at me, "I think this timeline is more unstable with you here. We'll get days. It was a minute, once. Kacey, you have to accept that there might be no getting out of this time loop. Believe me, I've tried."

"Maybe you haven't tried hard enough."

She laughs, sarcastic. "You really think I haven't done anything in all the days I've been living in this nightmare? How arrogant are you, to think you can just fix this on your first day?" She screws up the wrapper of the cereal bar and zips it back into her jacket pocket. Then she drapes the jacket around her shoulders.

"Sorry—I didn't mean that, I just…" I tail off and find I've been picking at the hem of my borrowed jumper. A woolen thread is unravelling and I wrap it around my pointer finger as tightly as I can, watching as the tip of my finger turns purple, then I undo it.

It's a long time before either Shweta or I speak again, but at last she breaks the silence.

"I get it. You're desperate. But that doesn't mean you're this special person who'll just be able to solve this at a drop of a hat, when I've been trying for way too long. I don't know how this world works, but this world doesn't work like *that*." She sighs. "Just don't think too much about it—it's enough to drive anyone mad. Believe me, I know."

I nod, numb, as I watch Maggot. She's heading back toward us, and Evor's not far behind. I turn over Shweta's words in my head, and I don't know what it is that makes me look the other direction. Back toward New Zeralzi, the town just about visible on the horizon.

But I look there. And I see the ground we've already covered. The grass and the rocks and the trees and—

"People!" I spring up, and I nearly fall over, and there's dizziness washing over me, but it doesn't matter, because there *are* people. Two of them. Coming toward us. Maybe half a mile away. I let out a strangled-sounding cry, pointing, then try and get Maggot's and Evor's attention, as well as Shweta's. Because the Enhanced are coming, and they've found me already.

They're going to fight us, kill us.

I'm here, the Beast tells me, and a sinking feeling fills me.

"It's Kazem!" Shweta says, and her voice is so soft that I nearly miss her words. "And is that Celena?"

Kazem? I jolt, and turn back, and I try and focus my eyes and see past the pain in my head and... and it is him. It *is* him.

He's alive.

He's Untamed.

"Evor said you're not well now?" Kazem touches my face gently, and I can't stop staring at him. His eyes, his nose, his mouth, his hair, his chin with the stubble on. He's *here*. His thumbs brush over my lips. "What's wrong?"

I shake my head. "It's nothing. I'm fine." And I will be. I know that. My body's always been strong. It'll heal. "This is just temporary." We're sitting on the ground, and I wrap him in another hug, then pepper him in kisses, breathing in his scent: it's mainly sweat—I mean, we're all sweating—but there's the hint of mint too. Like from old gum. Was he chewing gum earlier, before we began this mission?

"But what is it?" he asks, his voice soft.

I don't want to be discussing this now. I want to be escaping somewhere with Kazem, so I can kiss him and hold him properly—away from everyone else.

Maggot and Celena and Evor and Shweta are still talking. Kazem and Celena joined us maybe half an hour ago. They said they could see us in the distance, were following us, but they had to walk slowly at times because Celena's foot was bitten by a snake.

Evor's already made some sort of poultice for her and bandaged it to her foot, and now they're all trying to work out where we'll go next. But Kazem's looking at me, waiting for an answer.

"Evor said it's my autonomic system. That's what he thinks. It's malfunctioning."

"That sounds serious." He takes hold of my hands and meets my gaze full on. That's one thing I've always liked about him: how to can maintain such steady eye contact.

"It's not." I swallow hard. It can't be. "I'll be back to normal soon. Be beating you at free-running." I give him a sly look, expecting him to laugh—but he doesn't.

He just stares at me, shakes his head softly. It's the same look in his eyes he has when he talks about his brother. Yusuf was twelve when he died. Kazem was just fifteen. It was years before I met Kazem. Yusuf died of natural causes. A bad case of flu, I think, though Kazem's never really told me much about it. What I do know about Yusuf's death comes from Maggot. But when Kazem talks of his late brother, it's usually about how he lost Yusuf's favorite pair of socks: a pair with cartoon yellow men and women on them. Kazem had them for three years after Yusuf died. Or Kazem will tell me about the time he ruined Yusuf's cuddly toy, ripping it open in a fit of anger when he was like eight years old or something, and how he feels really bad about that now. Those are the only things Kazem talks about to do with his brother—the things that make him feel sad or ashamed now. I don't know if he thinks about their happy memories, but he never talks about them.

"I'll be fine," I say, but we both know I'm trying to convince myself of it, too. Because this can't be my life now. It can't.

I turn and look away, because, suddenly, I feel like crying, but I don't want to seem weak. Can't seem weak. So I focus on my surroundings. The low sloping hills in the distance. I squint. And is that a body of water there? There's something bright, and the air is shimmering around it, and—

There's a person there, beside the water. A figure, hazy in the glimmering air, but, somehow, I see her hair. Flaming red.

I jolt, feel everything inside me tighten.

Ysabelle, she's alive, *of course*. And she is here. She's coming for me and—

I let out a strangled-sounding cry, trying to alert the others, but as I do, the air shimmers again and Ysabelle disappears completely. She's just…*gone*.

"Kacey? You okay?" Kazem's voice. I hear him move, hear the plastic bags he always keeps in his pockets rustle.

"What is it?" Suddenly, Shweta is by my side.

I gulp, looking between Kazem and Shweta and then back toward the water. It looks like a lake. The air is still now, crystal clear, definitely no woman there.

"I'm fine," I say to them, but my heart twists with the lie. I wait until he nods, and then I look at Shweta. I try to communicate with her, and she nods.

"Maggot's discussing doing a hunt," she tells Kazem. "They're thinking about going tonight. You should go and get the details."

Kazem looks a bit puzzled but he leaves, and the moment he's out of clear earshot, I whisper to Shweta that I thought I saw a woman. I don't give her any details. I don't say who it is, because I don't want to talk about Ysabelle and that she should be dead. Maggot's group has never known about my time with the clansmen. But I make it clear to Shweta that the woman I thought was there just disappeared after a second.

"Oh, that happens sometimes."

"It does?"

She nods again. "Especially when the timeline isn't stable. So far, every timeline I've been in has had some instability. Little things that don't make sense. But when people literally appear one moment and are gone the next, it usually means the timeline will end shortly. Within a day or two, at the most."

My mouth feels grainy, my tongue gritty. "And then everything will start again."

"Uh huh. You'll get used to it. And I sure hope to the Gods that this isn't a one-off, that you remember it all next time too."

Maggot, Evor, and Kazem go out on a hunt. They've seen tracks around and are confident they can get something. Celena and Shweta make some traps out of sticks and pieces of wire from our bras. I try and hide how sick I am feeling, but it's difficult. I feel lazy and floaty and heavy, like I'm not fully grounded in my body, which is ridiculous. I've got some rocks, and I'm supposed to be trying to make them into scrapers or handaxes. We need more weapons than what we've got. Just a couple of guns and a knife. Two lots of spare ammunition.

I sit with my back to a tree and breathe in and out, heavily. I tap, tap, tap the rocks but to be honest, I don't really know what I'm doing. It also reminds me of the stone tools of the clansmen, and a bad feeling sets into my bones.

Shweta sets the traps in among the bushes, and then a little while later, the others return, empty-handed except for some berries and stems which Evor says are edible. We end up regrouping here, and Maggot says we'll spend the night and then set out early the next morning, once we're all well rested.

Through extraordinarily heavy eyelids, I watch as Celena starts her evening routine. She does it out in the open, no worries about us all watching. She hasn't got her pink mat she usually sits on, but she folds herself onto her knees on the grassy ground, sits upright with her spine dead straight, and tosses her head back. Her blond hair falls in glossy, perfect waves over her shoulder.

"Please, Divine Gods and Goddesses of Life and Fertility and Hope and Renewal, please bless me with what I desire most."

I want to look away, but as always when I see her praying, I cannot. There's something enticing about it, about seeing her at apparently her most vulnerable, and I can't look away. Others, back in the tunnels, spoke of this too. Because sitting here, like this, you'd think Celena was *lovely*. And she is, but she also isn't. She's like one of those delicate flowers with the yellow petals that I know Sian likes. The type that looks fragile, like something to be protected, but is a nightmare to pick. Robust because of the razor-like thorns on its stems.

"Please know that I'd do anything you ask to have my own baby, and please know that I am not fussy. I have put my whole life into fulfilling my purpose to be a mother. Every decision I have made, though it may not be understood, is for this outcome, so please help me in my methods, guide me in my choices, and I will be eternally grateful."

Celena turns her head and looks directly at me. I turn my head, feel color rushing to my face. I clear my throat. I don't know why she prays. I can't see it making a difference. And if she wants to conceive out here, well she's only got the choice between Evor and Kazem.

I swallow hard and focus on Kazem a little way away. He's sorting out all of our resources and has everything spread out in front of him. The weapons—guns and ammo, a Swiss Army knife, a smaller pen-knife, and a slingshot—along with medicines, antiseptics, and bandages from Evor's bag. Next there are two boxes of matches, three pairs of mirror contact lenses, a container of Vaseline, Kasem's empty carrier bags, soap, and three little bottles of hand sanitizer. We have one rucksack, too. It looks empty, flattened on the ground with water bottles and water purification tablets atop it. I'm not sure whose bag it was, but we're not claiming things individually now. We have to pool everything. Kazem is methodical as he sorts through everything. I guess Maggot will decide who gets the guns later.

"Please, Gods and Goddesses," Celena continues, "make me a mother."

I blink and for a moment—just a split-second—as I watch Kazem, it's baby clothes that he's folding up. No. I shake my head, and my vision returns to normal.

I wonder if the two of us will ever have a baby, then I shudder. Not because I know we'd have to have sex—probably a lot of times—but because it would be a *baby*. A tiny, little human whom we'd be responsible for. Whom I'd be responsible for. Oh Gods. Why did I even think about the possibility of a baby? I can't have one when children remind me of all the ones I killed in the clansmen massacre. The baby.

I swallow hard and shove the thoughts out of my mind, glad that I'm not like Celena. That I haven't got a desperate yearning to be a mother. But I know Kazem wants to be a parent. He's mentioned it as something that will happen one time, in an unspecified future. I'd wondered before if it was my lack of sexual attraction that meant I didn't feel maternal or want children, but Kazem's feelings on children don't support that hypothesis.

I breathe out hard and tell myself not to think of it, not to worry about it. I've already lost countless evenings and nights worrying if there was something integral I am lacking—whether in my sexuality or makeup as a woman—and each of those times, I'd told myself firmly, after hours and hours, that we are all different. So that's what I tell myself now as I strike the rocks again, as I listen to Celena praying, as I look out to the hills, as I stare at that lake where Ysabelle momentarily was.

TWENTY-EIGHT

THE NEXT MORNING, WE MOVE with the first of the light. I feel better this time around, on the run, even though I know still that the Enhanced could be tracking me. I'm not well enough to strike out on my own and try to take down the enemy—I know that, and it does scare me. I wouldn't even make it to the next town or city, probably. Not on my own, so I have to stick with my group. And we're stronger now. We have more people in our group, more capable of people. Safety is in numbers. And I've got the Beast. I know what he can do. I know I can control him, and I tell myself that if the Enhanced come upon us, then I'll summon the Beast immediately.

But the most important thing, and the thing that reassures me the most, is that Kazem is here. My Kazem. This is better, this time, but I think of what Shweta said— how many different versions of this she's lived through. How many more are still to come—if that's how it's still working, with me too now?

"You don't look so good," Kazem says. He grips my hand tightly, like he's ready to propel me along again. With his other hand, he pushes his blue-black hair from his eyes.

I try to speak, but there's a weight in my chest that makes it difficult. The more I walk, the sicker I feel, and I have this bubbling sensation in my lower throat and keep tasting those last berries I ate this morning before we set off. They were so sharp, bitter. The traps had caught a few rodents and Evor had skinned them and cooked them, but I hate eating animals.

My pace is lagging, and there's pain in my upper back too now, and my shoulders. I feel weak—*weak*. Something I've never been in my entire life. In fact, I've despised those who were weak. I always judged Clive for being slow, and that makes me feel bad. Strange. Because I'm weaker than Clive now.

I'm *useless*.

I'm a *liability*.

No. I can't be!

But I am.

"I'm fine," I bite out, putting way too much energy into getting those two words loud enough. Gods, why is even *speaking* so hard?

"I think you need to rest," Kazem says, bringing my hand up to his mouth. Lightly, he kisses the back of it—an action that always makes me smile—except it doesn't this time. Because I am worrying. We're at the back of our group, and he says that he'll tell Maggot that we need to stop.

"No. I'm fine." I shake my head at him hard and try to ignore how much I am sweating. "I really am."

But Kazem knows I'm not. We're connected, and I see the worry in his eyes. How it's weighing him down.

I look away, focus on the others. They're way ahead of us now, thanks to my slow pace. Maggot's walking the fastest, and I think about how I should be at her side, as her second-in-command. Instead, Celena is there. Her hair is tied up with a purple ribbon and her ponytail swishes with every step.

I try to speed up. Pain squeezes through my chest.

"I can carry you," Kazem says.

I shake my head, patches of thick darkness hovering in front of me. I force myself to go faster and faster. Kazem matches my pace with ease, and I try to pretend that there isn't a thick humming sound in my ears, that my breaths aren't too fast and too ragged, that my legs don't feel like stone.

But I catch up with the others.

Maggot casts a look over her shoulder at me. "We we're just sayin' we need to get a vehicle, move much faster. We ain't gonna get far like this."

Because of me.

I swallow hard.

"And we have no food now," Maggot says. "Only one bottle o' water left now, too. We've got the purification tablets and can fill up from springs, but we need to raid for supplies."

"We should get salt," Evor says, looking at me. "That will help Kacey with the fast heart rate."

"It will?" I stare at him.

Celena mouths something at me that I suspect is *loser*.

Evor nods. "It was in the books I read. There are medications too—but I doubt we can get those. Salt will be easier. Salt and water are both very important."

"So, that's the plan," Maggot says. She brings a hand up to her eyes, shading them from the bright sun. "The next town should be New Krouz. Probably get there tomorrow. We can make plans tonight on how we'll raid it."

A raid. I breathe deeply. I love raids. I love the running.

And I'll be better by the morrow. I'll be my old self again. I'll be fine, and everything will be back to normal.

We walk and walk and walk, and then we stop at the bottom of a rugged mountainside. There are loads of outcrops of granite rocks, so many little tors. Kazem's eyes lit up as when he first saw them, and I can still detect the energy in his body—because it's the same energy in mine. It's adrenaline and it's pure and it's hope. It's everything I love, and my body's buzzing with it.

I want to run straight for those rocks. I know I can't, but I want to. I feel it like a need inside me. I want to run over there, climb, jump over rocks, leap. I want to reach that rocky outcrop up there that's like a cliff, and I can imagine myself scaling in, feeling the burn in my muscles as I climb, as I push myself to the limit.

You can't run there. And you won't be able to join the raid tomorrow.

I breathe in deeply, shifting my weight from foot to foot as I try to clear my head and ignore the Beast's voice. He's wrong anyway. I will be fine. This is just concussion—not that dysautonomia thing that Evor was talking about. It's concussion, and it'll clear.

It will clear by tomorrow. Tomorrow, I will climb those rocks.

The Beast starts to laugh.

"Hey," Kazem says softly. His gaze is still on the rocks as he touches my arm, and the touch that is normally so perfect makes me flinch. "What's wrong?"

I shake my head. "Nothing." I take his hand, but even that touch feels strange. It's like the nerves in my skin are too sensitive. It's almost painful. But this is Kazem. This is my boyfriend—alive. He's here.

I sit down, pulling him with me onto the soft ground. It's damp, but I ignore it. I lean my head against his shoulder, and his arm goes around me. He presses his lips to my forehead, kisses me ever so lightly. His fingers creep under the edge of my jumper and settle on my waist. Only the thin fabric of the gown is between his fingers and my skin. I smile. There's nothing better than sitting with him, so close.

To our right, Maggot and Evor are talking about

setting more traps for any rodents that might cross this way tonight. Shweta's a little way behind, meditating, trying to connect with her Seer powers.

"Doesn't this just look amazing?" Celena moves closer as she drops the rucksack on the ground. "Those rocks up there are mega." Her eyes are sharp, excited. "You coming?" Celena looks at me and Kazem—or maybe it's just him whom she's looking at. "That cliff-face looks great for climbing. And we need to keep practicing."

Kazem pulls away from me and starts to stand, but then he glances back down at me. "Ah, no. I'll stay here with you."

"Don't be silly," I say. "You want to run. So, run. Seriously."

After a long moment, he nods. His Adam's apple visibly bobs. "I'll be back here in no time. Promise."

There's usually something beautiful about watching Kazem free-run, watching him do what he loves, what he's so good at. But watching *him and Celena* free-running across the mountainside when I can't, when I'm stuck here, makes me angry. So angry.

And I don't want to be—it's jealousy, I know. It's not their fault that I got hurt. It's mine—I shouldn't have tried to jump from that roof. I should've known. I've got no one to blame but myself.

"It's okay." Shweta's voice makes me jump, and I turn my head, find she's standing just behind me. "It'll be okay. You'll get used to this time stuff."

"It's not that," I say, my voice steely. My eyes are on Kazem and Celena. Their figures are smaller now, higher up. They look so free, like spirits gliding on the mountains' energy as they almost fly from one rock to another.

I hear Celena's excited shrieks, and part of me suddenly wishes she'd misstep out there, misstep and fall. Then I realize what a horrible person that makes me. Maybe the thought comes from the Beast. Or maybe it's me. Maybe that's who I am and that's why the Beast chose me.

"This whole situation will be okay, too," Shweta says.

I turn my gaze on her. "How do you know that?"

"Because we've got time to make it okay," she says. "Time restarting is the one thing we know will happen. And now that there are two of us in this, I have hope again."

I nod. Of course she's not talking about the Beast.

Once Kazem and Celena are back, Maggot calls a meeting.

"I want to leave 'ere in the early hours, after we've got some kip," she says. "So we need to get to sleep shortly. We'll get to New Krouz at first light, before the town's properly wakin' up. Kazem, I want you with me. We're gettin' weapons and ammo, plus any food we can carry."

Kazem smiles. His face is flushed from the running—as is Celena's. The two of them look energized, and they're standing close together. Closer than I'd like. I am sitting down but I still have to calm my racing heart.

"Evor, you'll get medical supplies," Maggot says. "Celena and Shweta, you'll get the vehicle, and then food, too. Time's gonna be of the essence, so I suggest seein' if you can kill two birds with one stone and get one of their supermarket delivery vans, one already stocked up—and with water too. They've got the warehouse there, at the northern side of New Krouz. We'll target that rather than a supermarket. It'll be quieter. So you just wait until the Enhanced have packed up their delivery vans, and then you get one. Think you can do it?"

Celena grunts and ties her hair back into that

long ponytail she had it in yesterday. It makes her cheekbones look sharper, her wide face more defined. She's a tiny bit tanned too, from the sun. "Of course."

Shweta nods.

"Good," Maggot says. "That's sorted then."

There are nods all around.

"But what about me?" I ask, leaning forward. "You've missed me out."

"You're staying here," Maggot says. "We don't take the injured on raids. That's just asking for trouble."

See? They know you're a liability.

No! I am not.

I sit up straighter. "Maggot, I'm fine! I am." As if to prove it, I stand up. Dizziness tugs at my edges, but I remain standing. I don't think I even sway. I am stronger now. "I can do this, really." I make my voice as assertive as possible. "I *can*. Look, I can go with Shweta—and that will free Celena up for another role. Something easy."

Celena scowls at me, but I just couldn't help myself from saying it, but we all know what happened on a recent raid that Celena went on. It was only the quick-thinking actions of Winston and Mal that kept her Untamed.

"Or I can be with Celena getting the van and food.," I say as a second passes without Maggot saying anything. "And Shweta can—"

"I decide who's doin' what," Maggot says.

"But I'm fine to do this." I try to smile. "Trust me."

Everyone gives me a dubious look, including Kazem—and that hurts. That hurts more than I thought it would. But I swallow hard. I am strong. I don't need a man backing me.

"Look, I can drive the van." Driving will be easier, I decide. "I'll be sitting down. Not like I'll be fainting then. And if I get the van, then the other person with me, either Celena or Shweta could get extra fuel. Those cans. We're going to need fuel." I give Maggot a triumphant look because I've thought of something we need that she hasn't accounted for.

Maggot's eyes narrow. Her gaze pierces a hole through me. "Fine. In that case, Kacey, you're with Celena. You can decide between the two of you how you sort things, so long as you get the van, food, *and* fuel. Shweta, you go with Evor. Better that he's not on his own if we can help it." She gives him a look that I can't quite understand, but she doesn't say anything more.

And that appears to be it. The plan.

Are you sure you can do this? the Beast asks.

I nod. I can. I will.

TWENTY-NINE

IT'S DARK AND I'M GROGGY when we leave. I half expect for Maggot to change her mind on the plan. To say again that I have to stay behind. But she doesn't.

We walk and walk. The night sky is a swirl of stars and fog, and when we eventually get to New Krouz, I'm telling myself over and over again that I'm fine. Because I am.

New Krouz is a big place. More industrial than homely. Large red-brick buildings block out the area, lit by so many streetlights, and huge chimneys chug smoke into the sky. Everything smells fumy, even from the outskirts.

I rub my eyes. I've not got the mirror contacts in because we only had three sets, and each of our pairs has one set between them. For some reason, when Maggot divided them between us earlier, I mistakenly thought it meant that we'd each wear only one. Celena had snorted when I'd said that I thought that was a bad idea.

"No, idiot. Only one of us will wear them," she said, swiping the last set from Maggot's outstretched hand.

Still, I'm glad I haven't got to wear them. My head's

hurting enough already, and contacts often give me a headache. Not to mention that I don't think I could stand the scratchy sensation of them on my eyes, not when my vision keeps blurring.

Maggot and Kazem head off first, branching away from our group. Then Evor and Shweta. I glance at Celena. Her expression is determined, and her hand rests on the gun in her belt. Each pair has one gun, and Kazem and Maggot also have the slingshot, because they're both the most skilled at using it.

"You really are all right to drive?" Celena asks me, and I wait for her to say something mean or have a dig at me. But she doesn't.

I nod. "I'm absolutely fine."

She looks at me for a long moment, and I stare back at her, trying not to see myself reflected in her contacts. I think of how she and Kazem were free-running in the mountains yesterday. How I heard her excited shrieks. How both of them returned flushed. I know what free-running does to you, and I know how it can bond you to someone—because that's one of the things that bonded Kazem with me.

"I guess I have no choice but to get the fuel," Celena says.

I don't know why she says that because of course she has to get the fuel because she's the one who can literally pose as an Enhanced One.

"You just stay in the van once we've got it." Celena wrinkles her nose, then licks her lips and presses them together. "Hope there's some containers I can put it in. And a fuel station right by the food shop would be ideal."

Neither of us have been to this town before, though Maggot has. She gave us brief instructions on how to find the supermarket warehouse and where we'd find the vans. We follow those instructions, walking through the deserted, dim streets. There's only a sliver of dawn light at the moment—the rest is this artificial orange light from blinking streetlights, but there are even fewer of those in this part—and the air smells of gas and fumes.

My heart pounds—but it's not the usual energy I adore. It's something heavier now.

"You better not let us down, Kachler," Celena says, and her voice makes me jump. Her words seem too loud. "But if there's a chance of it, you tell me now. Is there?" She raises her eyebrows.

"No." I cross the road, forcing a spring into my step. "I'm fine. We'll do this fine."

I have to do this. It's not just about proving myself to the others, it's about proving to *myself* that I can still do this. That I can still be useful.

You could be useful in other ways.

I push away the Beast's voice. He shouldn't speak unless he's spoken to.

"Good." Celena catches me up and nods. Her ponytail bobs. She cracks her knuckles. "I'm gonna kick some butt then."

We navigate the last of the roads, the whole way keeping an eye out for Enhanced Ones. We only see one, and I pull my hair down over my eyes as he comes into view. A moment later, we've passed him.

"Okay," I say as I see the correct warehouse.

It's a huge building with a large car park in front of it. At least a dozen green-and-white delivery vans with a supermarket's logo are parked in front of it, their engines running. The side of each van has an image of an Enhanced One biting into a juicy pear, and it's eerie, seeing them all lined up like that.

There are two figures out there, too. One stands by the door of the van farthest to the left, checking some papers on a clipboard. The other is by the entrance to the warehouse, looking at some sort of device in his hands. We're too far away for me to see what it is. Both men are wearing high-vis jackets. Bright orange.

"Shame we've not got a nice orange jacket too," I mutter, but Celena ignores me. She doesn't even acknowledge I've spoken, just moves to the side of the car park, sticking to the shadows.

I follow her, watching as Celena looks around to the left, going up on her tiptoes. The Enhanced man by the van gets in, places the clipboard on the dashboard for a few moments before he removes it and then drives away.

"No sign of a fuel station here," Celena says in a low voice to me, turning back for a moment.

"Must be somewhere else." I strain my neck as I look around. Didn't Maggot say that it would be nearby?

"Right. Well, you get a van and drive it out," Celena says, pointing. "If you can manage that."

"Of course." I don't like her tone. "And you'll get the fuel?"

She nods. "I need containers, too. I'm going to go and ask that man where the fuel station is." She points at the one by the supermarket entrance, the one peering at his handheld device.

She's confident and there's something admirable abut that—even if I know that this is something I should be able to do. Just a week ago, and I'd have had the confidence to that when my lenses were in.

"When I'm talking to him, you get the van out," Celena instructs.

I nod. More adrenaline fills me. "I'm going to go for that one." I point to the van nearest to us. It's also the farthest away from the warehouse's entrance where the remaining Enhanced man is standing, still looking at that device.

Celena nods. "If you can, follow me. I'll be walking to wherever the nearest fuel station is. Don't make it obvious you're following me though." She gives me a look. "Not in case anyone's watching."

"When I see the fuel station, I'll just drive in there. Could even top up the van, or pretend to."

"And once I've got the fuel cans, pick me up and we'll be off. Simples."

I nod. The searching for the fuel station in the van though, once I've got it, will be risky. Enhanced Ones always know where they're going, and chances are the way Celena walks will be through narrow paths, not suitable for driving.

"Right," Celena says, then she's marching toward the Enhanced man by the entrance.

I start moving, keeping my head down and sticking to the shadows as much as I can. I urge myself to walk faster, faster, faster. My heart beats quickly, but there's a lightness to it, like it isn't beating deep enough. Like I'm not getting enough blood to my brain. Like I'm going to faint.

No!

I take a deep breath. I'm fine. Of course I am. I can do this. I will do this.

I hear Celena's voice. Light and airy. Distant. I move faster, reach my chosen van. My heart pounds and my breath fogs the window for a second as I reach for the door handle. Not locked. Good. And the keys are in the ignition, the engine already rumbling.

I pull myself in, see a high-vis jacket on the passenger seat. *Result.* I put it on. The material scratches my jaw as I pull it into position, zipping it up. I glance up at the rear-view mirror and discover I can see nothing of use. Plastic crates full of food block everything. The hum is loud in here. Maybe some are refrigerated items.

Celena's still talking to the Enhanced man. He's pointing to the right. I twist around, looking for the way out of the car park. Yes. There it is. To the left. Shit.

Celena's moving now—to the right. She's walking quickly, but she glances over toward me. Her mirror eyes flash, making me inhale. She's *not* an Enhanced. She's not real.

But the man is. He's really Enhanced.

And we're in an Enhanced town.

Suddenly, I'm shaking. So much adrenaline—but it's not doing what it normally does. It's not fueling me. It's making me feel like I'm collapsing. My thighs shake, and my legs feel insubstantial. Pins and needles fill my left foot.

"Come on," I mutter, wiping sweat from my forehead with the back of my hand. "Keep it together."

I look in Celena's direction again, but she's gone now.

Time for me to move? I can't think. My head's spinning too fast. The longer I wait, the longer Celena has to get fuel. But it could take me a while to navigate to the fuel station when I don't know where it is. I can't just ask someone when I've got no mirrors.

I take several deep breaths and—

The flash of mirrors catches my eyes. My head jolts. Two more Enhanced have stepped out of the warehouse. Both are wearing the same high-vis vests, and one is coming right for me.

Shit.

My fingers cramp as I reach for the keys—but, no, the engine's already on. So what do I do? My head's foggy, and I can't think. What do I do next to drive? I stare at the wheel. My breaths are a rushing sound in my ears. The gearstick? But that's not a manual gearstick. This is an automatic? I stare at the letters on the stick, and the letters are moving and my eyeballs feel too furry.

Just go!

It clicks all of a sudden, and I put the van into drive and pull away. As I drive away, the nearest newcomer stares at me. I lift a hand, giving a wave, but turn my head, angling it away. Is that enough? Did he see my eyes? He'll see the high vis jacket I'm wearing though. I pray it'll be enough to make him think that I'm one of them.

I swing the van out of the car park, putting my foot down. There are road signs here that I don't understand. I didn't learn to drive until I was with the Muskoxen group, and they had an old copy of some driving manual that they'd stolen on a raid, but the signs here aren't familiar at all.

Still, no other traffic is about. And no sign of Celena either. Great.

I head around a roundabout and take a right turn, keeping my eyes peeled for fuel station signs. They'll have them here, won't they?

Yes, there it is! But—oh Gods, there are people running. Celena's at the front of the group, being chased by a horde of Enhanced. She turns and sees me, and she screams something. And why the hell isn't she using her gun? That's what it's for!

I put my foot down, then swerve the vehicle toward her. Dizziness tugs at me, and my vision wobbles, but I manage to skid to a stop by her. I lean across, wrenching a muscle in my back as I throw open the door on the other side of the cab.

"Stop at once!" Enhanced voices cry out, all of them in unison.

"You can fuck right off!" Celena yells back as she pulls herself into the cab. She sticks her middle finger up at them. "I ain't joining you and I ain't popping my clogs just yet either!"

"Shut the door!" I growl, already pulling the delivery van away. The engine is sluggish though, and there's a low humming in my ears that somehow makes my skin crawl, like thousands of ants are running over me.

Celena slams the door shut. Hot air suddenly blows out of one of the air vents, blasting my face. My vision sparkles, and an alarm goes off. A red light flashes on the dashboard.

"That way," Celena says, shoving a pointing finger right under my nose.

I grip the wheel tightly as I turn it, but something isn't right. My arms are weak or the wheel is locking up, or we've got no power-steering. And the Enhanced are right there, suddenly so many more of them and—

My chest goes all fluttery. My heart's pounding too fast because that's all it ever seems to do now, and there's too much adrenaline and—

Shit.

I recognize the feeling.

No. No. No! This can't be happening.

"Celena," I say, but my word is whipped away by my fast breaths, and I don't know if I've actually spoken out loud. Can't work it out and my vision's tunnelling, too much darkness closing in on me. Rushing sounds fill my ears. "Celena, help me, I'm—"

Pain in my chest. A twisting sensation in my head. The last thing I see is her panicked face.

THIRTY

"YOU'RE NOT DRIVIN' AGAIN," MAGGOT yells, her eyes alight with fury. Her hands are on her hips, and the swollen side of her face is blotchy. I think it must be hurting her, to shout like this, but she keeps yelling. "Do you see how irresponsible that was? You put my daughter in danger, all because of your pride. Do you understand?"

I nod and hang my head, letting the wind whip my hair across my face. I've still got the high-vis jacket on, and it's so thick and padded, but I'm too hot. I'm sweating so much, yet my hands and feet are cold.

Out of the corner of my eye, I can see the delivery van. It's parked over by some trees, and I don't want to look at it, don't want to see it. Anger fills me. Anger at my body, for betraying me, letting me down again. For bloody fainting at the most important and crucial moment, like some weak person. And anger at myself—for letting me do that. For thinking that I could've driven away just fine. That I didn't even consider that that could've happened.

I can hardly even look at Celena, because every time I see her I think about how she could've died.

I could've killed her. Killed both of us. All because I was too proud to admit that there really is something wrong with me.

But there is. There really is. And I could've caused so much disaster.

It is a miracle we're both alive. Not dead or Enhanced.

When I came around, Celena was driving and I was lying askew across the front of the cab, one of my feet still down in the driver's footwell. She grunted and wiped sweat from her forehead as she looked down at me.

"You're awake then." Her tone was blunt. "What the fuck was that?"

I hadn't been able to answer. I was dazed and foggy, with so much heaviness in my head and pain dancing behind my eyes. We'd picked up the rest of them somewhere on the edge of the town. It was a tight squeeze, all of us in the cab, and Evor checked me over as best as he could after Celena filled them all in. He'd told them all more about the dysautonomia he reckons I have, and then when we'd driven for what felt like an age and were making a stop, far out in the wilderness, away from any Enhanced Ones' towns or cities, he tested my pulse when I was lying down, then seated, then standing. Standing had nearly made me faint again. I had wobbled, my vision dimming and blurring out of focus, and Shweta had grabbed hold of me to steady me, then helped me to sit down on the ground. And that was when Maggot had started yelling at me.

"It'll be okay," Kazem says now. He places his hand on the back of mine, and I look up at him. How long before he gets bored of me? We bonded because we were both athletic. Because we both loved free-running. That was how we spent our time together.

But not anymore.

I think again of how Kazem and Celena were free-running across the mountains yesterday. How I wanted to join in, but I realized I couldn't. I knew my limitation then—but not in the delivery van. Not when it really mattered.

I pull my hand out from under Kazem's and cover my face. But I can't stop my tears, and Gods, *everyone* is seeing me like this.

"Come on, then," Maggot says, her voice gruff. "Let's sort through the food Celena and Kacey"—she says my name in the most begrudging way, almost spitting it out—"managed to get. We will need to use the perishables first. I don't want to be runnin' the fridges in the back for much longer. They'll use more fuel."

Fuel that we haven't got a lot of. Celena didn't manage to get any more, so we've only got the half a tank that is already in the delivery van.

I hear them move away, chattering, but I stay on the ground, sort of crumpled, still hiding my face. After a moment, Kazem tells me he had better go and help too. I just nod and use the sturdy collar of the jacket to hide my face. I breathe onto the fabric, and my breaths rebound onto my face, making me even warmer.

Help. I don't even feel strong enough to do that. I am useless. I am actually useless.

"It's not the end of the world," Evor says to me sometime later, and I look up to see him standing in front of me. "Being ill or disabled doesn't make you any less."

I frown at him. "I'm not...*disabled*." I spit the word out. "This is temporary." That's all it is. That's all it can be.

"There's nothing wrong with being disabled," he says. "It isn't a bad word, you know."

"I know it isn't." I shrug, but the movement hurts my neck. "I'm not prejudiced."

He gives me a long look. "Then why are you so adamant that you won't be like this for long? As if it's a something so bad that you can't even admit you have it?"

"I'm not treating it like that," I say through gritted teeth.

"You are. And June was like it too."

"June?"

"My cousin's sister," he says. "Well, half-sister. She had this."

"But she's better now?" I ask.

He looks at the ground for a moment. "Dysautonomia is a long-term illness, Kacey. Some people get better from it. Others have it for their whole lives. I guess it depends what is causing it and whether that makes the changes permanent. And I don't know which you'll be—but it doesn't make you any less, whichever it turns out to be. You're still you."

I pick up a loose bit of gravel then toss it forward, skimming it along the ground. I watch the stones cascade over each other as they race forward. *It depends what is causing it...* This started when I fell off the pharmacy roof. When I hit my head. Does concussion cause permanent damage? Have I got brain damage; is that what this means?

I glance across at Evor. "But I'm a free-runner. I'm a climber. My body is so important to me—and I can't be me if I can't even run."

"You're more than just a runner," he says.

"Am I?" I snort. "I've dedicated the last eight years to free-running. It's part of me, part of who I am. Running has always been part of me. And now my body has betrayed me."

"You need to look at this from a different angle," he says. "I know it's difficult, but you need to accept that you have these limitations now, but that these limitations don't limit who *you* are. You're still the girl who wonders at the moon. You're the girl who's headstrong and defiant and who stands up for what she believes. You're the girl who can be a pain in the backside when she doesn't get her own way. You're still my friend, Shweta's friend, Maggot's second-in-command, and—"

"Not for much longer," I mutter. Because Maggot's going to choose someone else—that much is obvious.

And it will be Celena, I guess. Even though she's not leader material. But she is *here*. And Kazem has never wanted that authority. Shweta is our Seer, so I doubt she'd be the second. Evor's the only doctor we have now. So it will have to be Celena.

But Evor carries on, ignoring me. "And you're Kazem's girlfriend too. You're passionate about animal rights, so much so that you're vegetarian and even when we hunt you make sure we kill them in a humane way. You love music—and you're amazing at singing. And you're an artist. You're still the person that survived for years on her own. You're the person who's escaped the Enhanced unconverted—do you realize how rare that is? There are so many facets to your identity. You're still *all* these things. The illness doesn't change any of that."

"But I want to run," I say, and my voice wobbles. "That's the biggest part of me. It's everything I want to do." I drop my voice to a whisper. "It almost feels like all the other stuff isn't worth it if I can't run."

He gives me a long, sad look. "You have to see things differently, Kacey. We can't change what's happened, and if you're looking at it like this, it's going to make things harder for you. You've got to make the best of this situation."

The best of it? The best of fainting all the time, of being too weak to do anything? Of nearly getting Celena killed and ruining our whole mission because of my stupid body?

"But I want to run," I say again, and I know I sound like a petulant, whiny little child. I can't help it. My body has always been so, so important to me. I've always been able to push myself to my limits and be confident that my body would hold up,

And now I have no confidence. How can I?

"Maybe you will run again," Evor says, and he rubs the back of his neck. I think it's a bit sunburnt. Looks like it stings. "I don't know. Maybe we can find some sort of adaption that allows you to, once you've improved a bit. But you can't think of running as your only defining characteristic. You need to accept it."

"But I can't. I'm *weak* now." The word is bitter on my tongue.

"Disability does not equal weakness." Evor gives me a look.

"I was useless on the raid. No, I was *dangerous*." I shake my head. That's even worse. "How am I ever going to be able to help everyone? Maggot's already said I'll have to sit out the next raid." He goes to speak, but I cut him off. "I *can't* be a liability, Evor. You don't understand—I just can't."

"But you're not."

Anger pulls through me, and a fly buzzes around my head. I lash out at it, but miss because the high-vis jacket restricts my movements. The garment's so bulky. "You just don't get it!"

"I get it. My cousin's sister—"

"Yes, exactly! *You* don't get it because this happened to your cousin's sister. Not you! You haven't experienced this."

He's quiet for a moment, and I realize that the others are looking at us. I pointedly look away from them, down at my lap.

"Kacey, no amount of anger is going to change this. You've just got to accept it, no matter how difficult it is. It's the only way. Accept it, find the positives in it, and—"

"The positives?" I snort, rage uncurling through my bones. "How are there any positives?"

"June found plenty."

"Well good for her," I mutter. "I'm tired now." I sigh, shaking my head, feeling more and more darkness taking over me—and of course that makes the Beast stir inside me. That bloody Beast is still here.

"Kacey, we're *all* trying to help you," Evor says.

"I need to rest." My voice is blunt. "Can you go, please?"

He does go. Walks back to the delivery van. Maggot

is lifting crates out of the back and I hear her say we need to fashion seats inside it. Only two seats in the front, even if we can all cram in there. But I know that it means four of us will regularly be in the back of the van. And I'll be one of them, sitting in there in the dark. And I expect to feel anger at that—but I don't. Because it will dark, and suddenly the dark doesn't seem so bad.

So when they've all finished and Maggot yells for us all to get in, I head straight for the back door.

I pull myself up and into the space, ignoring the hand that Kazem offers me, and head to the farthest, darkest corner. Celena and Shweta sit next to Kazem on upturned crates near the doors. Kazem mutters something about he hopes he doesn't get travel sick, and I wonder why he's not in the front. Why he's chosen to come in here, because he must've—everyone knows how sick he gets.

I just sit on the floor—the worn, wooden boards. After a moment, I unzip the jacket and use it as a padded mat to sit on. It doesn't make it that much more comfortable though.

When the doors close and it's truly dark, I silently cry, and I know I'm just feeling sorry for myself, but I can't help it. I can't see how this will ever get better. How this *disability* could ever be a good thing, like Evor insists it can be. I mean, he's just looking at this from the outside—it's not something affecting him, so of course he can afford to be optimistic. And it's not like I'm even a Seer and can get visions to help my group. My strength is in my body.

I'm useless. The one thing I was good at is now something I can't do. I know I'm wallowing, but I can't help it. I *am* useless. If I can't run, I'm going to get caught. I can't expect the others to protect me. I really am a liability.

Maybe I should just join the Enhanced. Maybe…

No. I swallow hard, then nearly choke on my tears.

I'm not giving in. I think of my parents—my Untamed

parents—wherever they are up there, watching me. I feel their disgust that their daughter even thought about giving up. That I even contemplated it makes me feel sick, my stomach slimy.

No. I'm not doing that.

Not ever.

THIRTY-ONE

"THIS ONE IS DEFINITELY NOT going to go far," Shweta tells me when we stop for a break.

I've been wandering around outside aimlessly, kicking bits of gravel and debris, hating how weak and dizzy I feel. Hating how I feel like I desperately need to sit down and rest, or sleep, even though I've been resting the whole time Evor was driving.

"It is a dud for sure," Shweta says.

"What are you talking about?" I turn on her. A little way away, Kazem is peeing, and I look away. In the dark of the delivery van, we listened to him throwing up into his carrier bags. Evor's already emptied those bags out, and I think he's trying to find a stream or something to rinse out the carriers.

"The timeline we're on," Shweta says to me, like it's obvious. "We've met up with one of the firm pathways, I'm sure. Nothing new is going to happen now. Look, I've been thinking about it a lot, and it's all about pathways."

She stops and pulls me down to the ground with her. I try to shrug her off, but she makes me sit. It's not difficult to make me do anything now, with this body. I just wish we weren't in the mud. My legs are still bare, and I don't want the mud on them—but it is, and it's gone inside my shoes, too. I left the high-vis jacket on the floor of the van, and I wish I was wearing it now. I've still got Evor's jumper on that he let me borrow, but it's not doing much and now it's got mud on, as well.

I watch as Shweta draws a line in the mud. A short line. A bird caws in the sky as it soars, and the caw almost perfectly lines up with the moment when she draws.

"See this?" Shweta pushes her hair from her face with one hand, while tapping the line she's just drawn with the other. "This is where it started—with that day when we tried to take over the city. So this line here is the trunk of the tree, okay?" She then draws four different lines extending upward from the trunk. "And these are four of the pathways. These are of varying lengths. A few hours—see, that's the shortest one—to the longest, there, two weeks." The longest line—or, rather, branch—is the farthest to the right of the branches.

She then traces over the trunk of the tree. "So this is us, when we're living the day over and over." She draws fainter lines in the mud, smaller and thinner lines that wobble left and right. "Each day we relive is slightly different—but we cross over with one of the four main branches. These are the firm pathways— they have distinctive events."

"What are the events in these firm pathways?" I ask. I lean back a little.

"Well, it depends which of us makes it out of there. In pathway one, it's Maggot, Kazem, you, Evor, and me. Pathway two it's just me and Clive—that's the one that's only two hours."

"So I don't make it out of the town alive in that one?"

"No. But I don't know if you're actually dead. You could be Enhanced. Or maybe you're surviving, Untamed, but hiding in their city? Anyway, that's the only one where you don't escape. And pathway three is you, Maggot, Evor, Clive, and me getting out New Zeralzi."

"Like this time," I say.

"Nah, because we've also got Kazem and Celena with us, making it pathway number four."

"So, this is the one that lasts for two weeks?" I ask, looking at the marks in the mud.

"Usually, yes."

"Usually?"

"Like I said, I think we are in a dud. You saw that woman before who disappeared, right?"

I nod.

"And I've seen one too."

"What?" I ask, and my breaths come in short, sharp bursts.

But Shweta doesn't answer my question. She just carries on with, "So although this pathway has the potential to last for two weeks, I reckon it will cut short at any moment. And like I said earlier, we don't follow the exact same footsteps each time. Things are always different. But whenever we've made it the two weeks, it's been when it's you, me, Evor, Maggot, Kazem, and Celena."

I mull over this information for a moment. I want to ask why she didn't tell me this earlier, but instead I ask, "What happens at the two-week mark to stop it each time? Or at any of these times, any of the resets?"

Shweta pushes her hair back. The underarm part of her shirt is ripped, and I can see cuts on her revealed skin. "Sometimes, it's death."

That makes sense. Ysabelle killed me at the point of the last reset. And Red died, too—if that is what I saw in that memory. His death. And is death what happened to Maggot and Shweta and Clive the last time, at the same point in which Ysabelle slit my throat?

"Sometimes, it's not anything big or dramatic though," Shweta says. "Sometimes, I just get thrown back to the start."

I take a deep breath. "So at the most we've got two

weeks to find a Seer who can help us with this loop?"

"We're already onto the third day of the two weeks," she says. "But I don't think we're going to make it much farther, to be honest." She sighs. "This is a dud one, I'm sure. Too unstable. I'm telling you, we could get thrown back any second from now. It really is about living in the moment." She lets out a strange laugh that sounds forced.

I stare at the diagram in the mud. "So what other things always happen on this pathway?"

"We always travel."

"In a food delivery van?" I ask.

"More often than not," she says. "Previously it's mostly been you and I getting it. But of course things are going to have to change if you've got this condition now. And even if you remembering this reset is a fluke, I will remember—so I can stop you driving. But whatever the pathway is, we're always being chased by the Enhanced. Story of our lives, right? So why would the time loop be any different?"

I frown. I still can't shake the feeling that there's a tracker on me. I was in the compound again. They changed my clothes. I look down at the skirt of the purple gown sticking out from under Evor's oversized jumper. I've not taken the gown completely off, in all these days. What if there's a tracker on that?

Then I remember what Red said in that last memory-vision type thing. He can find my Beast. I look at Shweta. "You remember I've got this Beast thing in me, right?"

"You did mention that in the last timeline, yes."

"Do I mention it in others?"

"Sometimes. Not always." She frowns and looks at me. "I can't sense anything in you, so I don't really understand what this can be. It's not a Seer power."

"Because I'm not a Seer," I say. "But it's just this thing inside me." I take a deep breath. "Should I tell Maggot about it? Because I did kill all the Enhanced in that last timeline, didn't I?"

"You did," Shweta says. "But can you do it again? Is this 'Beast' in you right now? Could you do that again?"

I breathe out slowly and try to feel the Beast in me. He's there—of course he is—but he's not stirring. Although he's spoken to me in this timeline, he's not been as active, as forceful as before.

"Only tell Maggot if you're sure you can control it and use it to kill the enemy. Otherwise there's no point in telling her. You'd just be giving her false hope. And besides, this timeline's going to end soon, so you'd just end up telling her again and again, anyway."

THIRTY-TWO

"I WANT TO KNOW MORE about your cousin's sister," I tell Evor later that day. My voice is level, flat, no emotion. We're sitting in the back of the van, and there's something about the darkness and the fact that he, Celena, and Shweta cannot see me that makes me feel more confident. More like I can ask Evor about this all. "I want to know more about this disorder that I have, that she has."

The engine is a reassuring rumble, and we bump over ground and appear to hit almost every pothole. I wonder if it's Maggot or Kazem driving.

"We're assuming it is the same one." There are rustling sounds as Evor moves about a bit. "I'm pretty sure it is. But I can't be certain. Not without all the proper tests."

"Okay, but how did she cope with it?"

"June accepted it first of all," he says, and I think he clicks his tongue. It's hard to tell what sounds are, in this darkness. "She accepted that there were things she couldn't do, but she didn't let that rule her life. She helped look after the children, with my aunt. Even more so when her eyesight went as well. Not that that

207

was because of the condition. It wasn't. Just one of those things. But she loved looking after the children."

Well, there are no children here for me to look after. Not that I want to. I don't like children. Even if I hadn't had that whole massacre experience, I don't think I'd like them much. They're ill, like, *all the time.* Way too many gallons of bodily fluids to deal with.

I wrinkle my nose and hold on tighter to the crate in front of me. It's wedged in, between others, so it's pretty sturdy and provides a good handhold for the way the van is bouncing about.

"But how long did she have dysautonomia?" My words echo a little, and I shift my weight on the jacket, spread out on the wooden boards.

"Six years."

I lean forward closer to him, even though he won't see. "Six years? So, she got better?" Hope blossoms in me.

There is a pause and someone's shifting their weight a little, but it's not Evor. Maybe Celena? I think she's over there, to my left. But she's being remarkably quiet. Maybe she's not actually as bad as I've always thought.

"No, uh, June died."

"What?" I startle and hear Shweta gasp.

"Not because of the dysautonomia," Evor says quickly. She was in a car-wreck."

A car-wreck? My breath makes a squeaky sound. A car-wreck, just like how I could've killed Celena.

"They were being chased. By the Enhanced. June was in the back, with my aunt. Some of the men were driving. I was in the car ahead of them, and the Enhanced were shooting at both our vehicles. They shot the tires of the car June was in. There was this high-pitched popping sound. And I remember looking in the mirror and seeing their car spinning. Like it was completely out of control. It crashed. We managed to shoot back at the Enhanced from our vehicle, but when we ran over to the wreck..." He takes several deep breaths. "June and my aunt were dead."

"I'm sorry," I whisper. "I'm so sorry. I didn't know."

Evor says it's all right—but I know it's anything but all right.

"She was so full of life," he says. "She never once complained about the dysautonomia." *Not like you do.* He doesn't say the words, but I feel them. "It's just not fair."

After we've stopped to eat, and our bellies are full of rich, creamy foods, Kazem wants to go for a walk. Shweta says she'll go with him. I do, too, more to prove to myself that I can. We leave Evor, Celena, and Maggot behind. Evor's now weaving a mat of some sorts from strips of birch bark, Celena is sleeping, and Maggot's meditating, says she needs to ask the Gods and Goddesses for what we do next. It's obvious what we do next—find Untamed. We walk through long grassland, under a clear blue sky, and I'm panting and out of breath more than I care to admit. It's not that the terrain's difficult—in fact, it's pretty flat albeit stoney—but any exertion I'm finding challenging.

I huff and puff as we make our way through the knee-high grasses. They're a light flaxen color, swaying in the wind, and there's a pretty good view from here of the hills ahead. A thicket of trees stands to one side, leading into thick woodland, and in the very far distance, I can see mountains. Not like the one yesterday, though, because these ones are proper: huge, giant formations, looking hazy and kind of blue in the distance, snow on their peaks.

Kazem and Shweta are talking about the weather—if it's going to get colder or not—but I can't concentrate enough to take in their words fully, let alone join in. My breaths are so loud, kind of crackly in my ears, and

I hate how unfit this makes me look.

Suddenly, Kazem stops. I'm a step or so behind him and Shweta, and I nearly crash into him, but he turns to me, his eyes sparkling. "Deer." His voice is hushed. "Up ahead." turns toward us.

I look up, and on the slope of the hillside opposite us, I see a small herd. Red deer, probably. They're moving, have just come out of the woods. Several of them stop and look around, while others begin grazing.

"We can get fresh meat." Kazem's voice is a whisper.

"We shouldn't miss the opportunity," Shweta says, and her hand moves slowly to the hilt of her gun, tucked in her waistband. "Though we'd need to dry the meat. Can we do it out there? Maggot doesn't want us running the fridges in the van."

"We've got salt. Evor's good at preserving stuff. He can sort it." Out of the corner of his eye, Kazem looks at me. "Are you…okay to do this?"

Am I? I feel my heart judder. Normally, I don't like hunting because I don't like to see animals dead. But I would hunt every now and again, because I knew that our whole group couldn't survive with no meat, and I could only afford to be vegetarian if others weren't, else there simply wouldn't be enough non-meat produce to go around. And I was good at hunting, too. I had good aim. I prided myself on killing humanely, not letting the animals suffer.

But now everything feels different. It's not that I don't care about animal welfare now, more that I can't imagine myself being able to do *anything* properly now. Probably faint or something at the critical moment. Or I'll get nervous and it won't be a heart-kill if I'm taking the shot. I should just leave it all to Kazem and Shweta.

But I say, "Yes." Of course I do. I can't admit my weakness. And anyway, they're asking me. They're thinking I might be able to do this. They have faith in me.

And I can't let them down, not again.

"Let's do this." I give them both a grin that I hope is more convincing than I feel. "Have we got clear enough shots from here?" I watch the deer as they move about. There's ten of them, but I can't see any antlers.

"Let's just crouch down," Kazem says.

Slowly, so slowly, so as not to startle the herd, we inch to the ground. Stalks of dried grass stab my knees and arms, through the woolen jumper.

Kazem and Shweta both have guns, and Kazem hands me his. It's a small, semi-automatic pistol, and I hadn't expected to feel nerves bolting through me just from holding it, but that's what happens.

I check the safety's on and glance at the others. Kazem's got his slingshot out, and he searches among the grasses, then gathers up a handful of small rocks and pockets all but two. I hear the crinkling rustles of the plastic bags in his pocket as the stones move them. In soft voices, we talk strategy for a moment, confirming a plan and double-checking which way the wind's blowing and if there are any features of the land we can use to our advantage. Kazem reckons we won't need to get that much closer to them, because me and Shweta have good aims, but getting closer is always preferable, especially if one shot is off and you have to put a second bullet in an escaping but injured animal. We don't want to be too far away and lose one. The thought of a deer dying slowly and painfully from a wound makes my gut feel slimy.

We set off, each of us crawling and fanning out rather than trying to close the distance between us and our prey, stooping low to use the grasses as cover.

I can do this, I can do this, I can do this, I tell myself, just as I crawl through a large cobweb and what feels like a hundred insects on the silks drape over my face. I try to drag them off, revulsion running through me.

I'm heading toward the eastern side, closer to where the fir trees start. The ground becomes softer, and my breathing louder. The stooping makes my back hurt, and I keep an eye on where Kazem and Shweta are, and then tilt my head up a bit, checking on the herd. There are about ten or twelve deer. I can't see any antlers on any of them, but my vision also isn't great.

I reach my designated point, marked by a young fir tree growing several hundred yards away from the other trees, and I back myself against it as I get the gun out of my belt. To my left, I can just about see Shweta's head, just raised enough above the long grass to be visible. I can't see Kazem, but Shweta lifts her hand just above her head and makes a closed fist.

I ready my gun, clicking the safety off, and then wait for Shweta's signal. A moment or two passes, and then Shweta's fist disappears back into the grasses. The sign. Ten seconds.

I count under my breath. *Ten, nine, eight.* We've had a lot of practice at this counting, the speed at which to do it, because the majority of our hunts where we're trying to get more than one wild animal depend on this.

I line my aim up with the doe who's closest to me. *Seven, six, five.* Adrenaline rises in me, and I feel too warm. Both my hands are on the gun, but the metal's hot, too, like it's absorbing the sun's rays. Even though the sun isn't particularly strong.

My chosen deer starts to graze. *Four, three, two.* My hands shake. The gun's dancing about.

One.

I pull the trigger at the exact same moment Shweta does. The gun jumps in my hands, the recoil and the gunshot startling me in a way they never have before. The herd bolts back into the woods, and I try to focus, try to see if any of them are down or injured. I try to count them, but they're moving too quickly, and a wave of dizziness washes over me. There's no follow-up shot from Shweta, and I don't know if Kazem used his slingshot.

I stand slowly. Kazem and Shweta are already standing.

My legs shake, and I keep hearing a strange echo of the gunshots as I head to where the deer were. I scan the ground, but I don't think we got any.

"It's okay," Kazem says as he reaches me. We're checking the area, but I was right. None of our shots hit. No splashes of blood on the grass or anything.

"There aren't going to be any Enhanced in the area who heard our shots, are there?" I ask. My throat feels heavy, my ears too hot.

"Nah," Kazem says. "And if there are, they'll think it's just their own people shooting for sport." He sounds confident, but there's a sheen of sweat on his forehead that makes him look worried.

We search for a bit longer though. Shweta finds a ground nest with eight eggs in. The shells are a golden color with darker mottling over them in a pretty pattern, resting in moss. Willow Ptarmigan, I think.

We collect the eggs, carefully placing them in one of Kazem's carrier bags, and head back.

"You did well, Kace," Kazem says to me.

Well? I blink. "I didn't get the deer."

"Neither did we. But you did well, and I'm proud of you."

THIRTY-THREE

MAGGOT'S KEEN TO GET BACK on the road. She, Kazem, and I sit in the front of the van. I was going to get in the back, but Maggot asked for me upfront, said that the three of us can squeeze in. Everyone else is in the back, and I hadn't realized just how well I'd be able to hear them all. Celena's telling the others a story, and her voice is pretty clear. I guess the partition behind our seats isn't very dense.

It's hot in the cab, and the air smells of sweat and body odor twisting with the faint tangy echo of something sweet.

I wait for Maggot to say something, to reveal why she wanted me upfront, but she doesn't speak. She just drives across the bumpy terrain, and my head feels thick with thoughts that I don't quite understand yet.

After maybe an hour, Kazem falls asleep, his head lolling against the passenger window. I'm squeezed between the two of them, and Maggot hums under her breath. She's hunched over the wheel, and then she cricks her neck.

"You know," Maggot says at last, her voice all rough, "if I have one regret, it's that I'm so dedicated to being a leader."

The words are unexpected, out of nowhere, and I stare at her. My mouth opens, on its own accord, but no words come out. I don't know what to say.

Maggot laughs softly, under her breath, then glances across at me. The injury around her right eye looks darker, but the swelling is finally starting to reduce. "I never really talked to June much. It's only hearin' Evor and you talkin' 'bout her that I've realized it. How fucked up is that?" She steers the van to the right a little, avoiding a large dip in the rough terrain that might be a hole. It's hard to see with all the grass. "It does make me wonder if I had prejudices, though."

"Because she had this condition?" My fingers curl. I'm gripping the front edge of the seat too hard and it's sending pain through me, but there's not really a lot to hold on. There are only two seats in the front, and so I'm sitting across a two-inch gap where they both meet, and it's not the comfiest of seats.

"I don't know what it was," Maggot says. "Maybe. I just don't know. I... My father always said I was a natural leader 'cause I evaluate people well. I see their strengths, see how we'd all work together. He called it objectivity. I was objective. And I am. I still am." She clicks her tongue. "I look at people, and I know what they can offer me and my group, how they can aid our overall survival. It's important to be able to do that. And I'd never put people down, mind. But I don't think I ever said anythin' to June. Not to her face. But I... I didn't pay her much attention, then or now in my memories, not the way Evor does. I guess I just focus on the people who can offer what I need."

I stare at a grimy mark on the windshield. "And you don't think I can offer anything?"

"Hell, no. You can. You're clever. Intelligent. And I've been thinkin', like, I know this 'cause I know you. And I got to know you 'cause I saw the qualities you had that my group needed. I... I only seem to put time into knowin' the people who I think can benefit our group. I'm focused on it. That's how my dad trained me to be. So, I disregarded June, and it's only these last few days that I realized I shouldn't have. That I..." She frowns. "It's like with Celena."

"What do you mean?"

Maggot starts to speak, but then she stops. She shakes her head. "I could've been more...personal, with her. Recently, I looked at how Kate was with all her young'uns. And I'm not that person. But, sometimes, I wish I was. Maybe I'd be a better leader. Balance is important, Kacey. I've learnt that the hard way. It's too late for me now, but it's not too late for you."

I don't know what to say to that, so I just continue staring at the mark on the windshield, and Maggot continues.

"I think I was trainin' you in my own image, and inadvertently rejectin' Celena because she wasn't me. Because she never could be. Like, I still don't understand how she's so desperate to be a mother. She's so different to me. I never was the motherly type, and I know not all mothers create a bond with their children. Not like our circumstances gave us a chance to play happy families, though. But havin' Celena made my father change. He became softer, talked of my mother more, and I saw it as a weakness. She'd changed him, and people expected me to step down as leader—they had done since the moment I started showin'. But I didn't. Didn't want to. I had to prove I was still this hard person, you know? And sometimes, no matter what I did, people didn't change their perception, saw me only as a mother. So, I resented Celena, 'specially when she was a baby. She stopped me doin' all the things I wanted and stopped so many people respectin' me in the way they used to." She breathes out hard. "Did she tell you Rohan's late wife looked after her until she was seven?"

I shake my head. "No. I didn't know that."

"My dad did a bit. But he wasn't that well, so Rohan's wife took her a lot. Celena liked her." She presses a couple of buttons on the dashboard. "Once Celena got to that age, I saw value in her. Things she could offer the group as a whole, you know. She was faster than the other children, quicker. That's when I became interested in her. And I wish I wasn't like this, only seeing people in terms of their usefulness—or how useful I *think* they are—because it makes me a shitty person, doesn't it?"

"No," I say, but I still don't really know *what* to say. I look at Kazem, but he still seems to be asleep. His mouth is open slightly.

Maggot laughs. "You can tell me I've fucked up badly, because I have. And I don't know if I can change now. I'm set in my ways. But I wanted to tell you this, because I'm a cold person. And I think I've been makin' you into a cold person too—not as cold as me, 'cause you've found love and you relate *personally* to some. But I've been thinkin' part of the reason you're bein' so harsh on yourself about your illness is because of me, the way I've trained you to be. But it's not too late for you. You're young. You can adapt your way of thinkin'. You don't need to have the same regrets that I do."

She sniffs loudly. I stare straight ahead at the snow-capped mountains. The skin on the back of my neck crawls, and I try to rub it, scratch it, do anything because I don't like this sensation.

Maggot turns the van sharply to the right, slowing down. "A good leader sees the errors in her ways, in her thinkin', and a good leader—"

Everything flashes white—and it's so blindingly bright it imprints a film over my vision.

Maggot slams on the brakes, and my arms jerk out and I just about stop myself from hitting the dashboard. Kazem's body flies forward though, hitting it as he wakes with a strangled cry.

"Kaz?" I can hardly speak, and he turns to me with wide, startled eyes. "Are you okay?"

He mumbles, nods, rubbing his forehead.

"What the hell was that?" Maggot grunts, holding a hand to her eyes, blinking furiously. "At least I wasn't goin' fast when we had no seat belts on."

With three of us in the cab, we'd not been able to use them.

Maggot bangs her fist on the partition behind the seats. "Everyone all right, back there?"

There's a bit of mumbling but everyone seems to be, and then Maggot ducks a little in her seat, looking through the windshield. The bright light has gone, and I, too, peer at the sky. It's getting darker, night time drawing in—is it that late already? I can see the moon, a faint hazy disk.

"I... I don't know," I say. What *was* that? The air is humming, humming with energy, electricity.

We hear the sounds of the van's back doors opening, and then Celena and Evor are at Maggot's window. She winds the window down. The glass moves in a bit of a jolty way.

"A trap?" Maggot raises one eyebrow as she looks at them. "Or the spirits, the Turning? What are we thinking? Where is Shweta?"

Shweta and Kazem appear behind Evor.

"If it's a trap, we should all be in the van," I say, just as Shweta says, "Don't think it's spirits. I can't feel any." She's holding her Seer pendant carefully at the hollow of her neck.

"Me neither," Celena says, as if she can detect spirits like Shweta can, which she most definitely cannot. I almost want to laugh.

Celena and Maggot speculate how it might be the Enhanced., and I notice the strange way they're talking. Their words are like a volley between them, a challenge. They're both trying to prove themselves. Even Maggot, after everything she said to me in the van, isn't agreeing with *anything* Celena is saying. She's defensive, arguing. And before I probably would've seen it as Maggot dismissing Celena's stupid ideas— because I'd have followed Maggot's example and viewed Celena's ideas as stupid. But now I'm listening to Celena, and her suggestions aren't actually that bad. They make sense. They're logical.

"If it is the Enhanced we should keep going," I say, swallowing awkwardly. "No point being sitting ducks."

"Then I'll sit in the front," Celena says. "We need to have able-bodied people there." Her tone is curling, hiding amusement. "Kazem, you can of course stay here with me and Mum."

I glare at her and am about to protest when Shweta catches my eye. She shakes her head in the smallest of movements, but there's a sharp look in her eye.

"Uh, I'll go in the back with Kace," Kazem says.

Maggot just shrugs. "Well, quickly then. We better get movin'."

I follow Shweta into the back. Kazem and Evor join us, and the engine starts up again. We rumble along. There's a large torch on in the back now, and I don't know where they got it from, but it throws a haunted kind of light around.

"You all right, mate?" Evor asks Kazem. "There's an empty container there if you're going to be sick."

Kazem says he'll be fine—though that is debatable—and I look toward Shweta. She puts a finger to her lips. Her gaze on me is still charged. *Not yet*, she mouths, and then she's holding her Seer pendant again and closing her eyes. Is she doing some sort of Seer stuff? Have her powers returned?

As I wait for Shweta to talk, I listen for sounds—the hum of Celena and Maggot talking. Maybe we just can't get hear them the same way those in the cab can hear us. I wonder if Maggot will ever open up to her daughter the way she just opened up to me. Then I wonder if things were different, if somehow my mother was here, alive, whether *we'd* be close. Whether I'd be just like her. If we would open up to each other, trust each other enough—and ourselves— to show vulnerability. Because I think Maggot is right:

Kazem is the only person I allow myself to be fragile around. And even then, not completely. I've still not told him I'm scared that he'll discover one day he *does* want a sexual relationship. He's even assured me he won't, without me even having to say anything, but the worry is still more there. I don't want to lose him.

Maybe we do need to talk more. Maybe everyone does.

I look over toward him. He's pulled carrier bags out of his trouser pockets and is folding them up carefully, condensing them into small plastic squares and triangles. I think he's concentrating on that to try and distract himself from the nausea.

Evor is looking at a bit of paper, squinting, and then finally, Shweta scoots closer to me. She crashes into a crate of food and winces.

"This is it starting." Her voice is low.

"The reset?" I frown. It's happening *now*? Was that what that white flash of light was?

Giddiness fills me. Am I about to die? Or will this be a reset I experience without dying? My chest flutters. Is it going to hurt?

"I think it causes the flashes," she says. "Something to do with electrical disturbances. Something…" Her voice fades, then *she* fades. Her whole being gets fainter and fainter, letting more of the torchlight—a great beam of it—through her, until she's… gone.

I frown, turning, shifting my weight. Energy thrums through me, and I reach out to where she was. My fingertips graze the crate she was leaning against, but then that disappears too, and I turn to Kazem and Evor.

Neither man is there.

My pulse quickens. My lungs ache, and pain snakes through my head. All I can see is a bright red light. I frown, trying to work out where it's coming from— and then I realize. I look at my hand, at the way that rays of the crimson light is coming from it. And my legs, too.

I am emitting this light.

I turn, my throat drying, and cold eyes blaze in front of me. Another person is here. I start to move my hands—it's automatic—but the person smiles, and I see her hair. Amber, so bright.

No.

"Come here, Kassandra."

Hissing sounds fill my head. I want to scream, but I can't make a sound as I stare at Ysabelle. She's here, again. And she shouldn't be, but she is. I look around the back of the van, but I can't see any of the crates now, or the torchlight, or the walls. There's just nothing but Ysabelle.

Her face is all anger and frustration, and then I notice that she's not alone. She pulls a child onto her lap, and the child is glowing red too, just like I am.

I jolt.

"Kassandra!" Ysabelle yells, and her presence is like viscous honey, drenching to me, too sweet, too sticky. I cannot move. "Come here and—"

But her words get swallowed up, and she and the child seem to disintegrate. Everything is disintegrating; there's only dust around me. Dust swirling and swirling and swirling in the red light, clogging up my throat, my nose, my lungs.

I choke and—

And then there is nothing more.

THIRTY-FOUR

"KACEY, KACEY," A VOICE WHISPERS, *dripping like moonlight in the night. "Kacey, you need to do more to stop her."*

Stop her?

Caia-Lu's words float past me, and I don't know where I am. I am…nowhere. I see a field with the moon high in the inky sky, and I see the lush grass below. But I have no substance, and neither does Caia-Lu. Yet I hear her.

"Stop who?" I whisper.

"She is causing all of this. I can see it all more clearly now. I should've realized you were in the loop too, before. I should've told you of it, but I cannot see everything and I do not understand everything. I only saw him, and I thought he had the ability to end it. But he does not! It is you, Kacey! You must stop the time loop. You need to stop the resets, because you're not moving forward, and that's what she wants."

"Someone started this time loop on purpose?" My voice echoes a little, before my words are absorbed by the moonlight.

"You're in a pocket," Caia-Lu says. "Even when you die, you start over, while time outside continues. But you're

not moving forward—you're stuck—and you need to move forward. The war can't end without you."

"Without me?" I snort. "Don't tell me I'm some kind of savior. That's ridiculous."

I don't want to be a savior.

"You're not the savior. The Seventh One, a Seer of Death, will end the war—but for her to do so, you must keep the balance of Rijikarii as constant as you can, between your world and mine."

"The balance of what?" I ask.

Caia-Lu's look gets even more serious. "The energy inside you."

"The Beast?" And even just saying the words makes me feel sick, because he rises up inside me.

"Rijikarii," Caia-Lu insists. "If you find others with it, you can break the time loop. And you need to—she put it in place to trap you, but she does not know of your importance, of how the Death Seer needs a stable world to end the war. Rijikarii is intricate and more complex than almost anything else. Just the right amount of it must exist in just the right places at all times, but that amount can change. We've got it correct in the New World, but the time loop's messing it up in the mortal world, and if you don't sort it soon, the timelines will irreparably unravel—and the Seventh One will never be able to save us."

I OPEN MY EYES TO laughter, to music, to bright lights.

"All right there, Kace?" Maggot grins down at me. Her smile is garish, too much color in her cheeks. She's holding a glass of dark liquid, which sloshes over the rim and lands on me as she beams, swaying to the beat of the drums. "Having a little nap? Never could handle your drink, right!"

Then she moves off, swaying, still singing, dancing to the drums, melting into the night.

The *drums*.

I turn, my eyes widening. Evor's playing the drums about a hundred yards away. Kazem's dancing near him, doing his wild dance, arms thrashing, legs kicking. And there are people—so many people. It's *everyone*. Maggot's group and the Muskoxens. And this is…

No…. it can't be.

A fluttery feeling emanates from my heart, across my chest. This is… I remember this. I was dancing wildly *with him*.

"Kacey, there you are!" Shweta grabs me. Her eyes are wide. Her grip on my upper arm is strong, tight. She's shaking. "I don't know what's happening, how we're—"

"So far back in time?" I stare at her. My voice sounds strange, kind of echoey, getting lost in the beat of the drums. I look around, then back at Shweta. But her eyes gloss over as she looks behind me. Her mouth drops open.

I turn and look.

It's Hana. Shweta's Hana.

Hana's *alive*.

My mind whirs. We're at least four months back in time. *Four months*. Hana died just short of four months before we tried to takeover New Zeralzi.

I focus back on Shweta. My heart pounds because of course it does. I feel unsteady. "Why has this happened?" I ask Shweta. "Come on, you have to know."

Shweta's eyes look glazed. "I knew I'd see her again," is all she says. She lets go of me and moves toward Hana. Hana who's lifting her arms into the air, swaying to the music, eyes shut, long blond hair fluttering around her.

Shweta approaches her, gets right up to Hana before she opens her eyes. I find I am following Shweta. The two embrace, and then they're kissing. Kissing *a lot*, and Shweta's crying, tears glistening as they roll down her face.

"What's the matter, love?" Hana asks, her voice like a melody.

Shweta just cries and cries, and I turn away, feeling like an intruder. My heart won't stop pounding. This isn't... We're at least four months back in time. Way before the siege. Why? So, we can find out who the traitor is? Stop that happening? And stop the person setting the time loop?

The time loop! *Ysabelle*—Ysabelle set it. That's what Caia-Lu was telling me. That has to be! And I see Ysabelle's eyes as I blink. See the fire in them, the cunningness. See *her*. She's playing with me. She's playing with time. She and the Overlord Seer, it has to be them. You need a Seer to do this kind of work.

They survived my attack, somehow, and now they're playing with me.

And I've gone back four fucking months.

Clive runs past me, grinning wildly, manically. Everyone's dancing and drinking.

"Hey, Kacey," a voice shouts, only just audible above the pounding music. It's Sian, her red face beaming. Her blond hair's spiked, partly matted. "Come and dance with me."

And then she's here, taking my hand, leading me toward Evor, where Kazem and the others are still dancing. I feel myself starting to move, too. I'm swept along with it. My head feels lighter, strange, and my body's fluttery.

I stumble toward Kazem. The beat of the drums gets louder and louder, and I stare at one of the drums for a moment. The way the taut cowskin stretches with every beat of the deer's leg bone on it. How it rebounds and stretches. I imagine the cowskin breaking, snapping, a huge bang that stops…everything.

Kazem's face is blank, yet he's smiling at the same time. I try shouting to him, but he doesn't appear to hear my words. I shout louder, and I try Evor, but I can't even hear my own words. I don't know I'm actually shouting anything at all.

I take a deep breath, casting my mind back to the last Night Celebration. Was I drunk? I can't remember. Shit—of course I was. I'm always drunk at these. I drink, just like everyone else does. We all have fun. The only people that don't are—

"The guards!" I shout, but the word's swept away by the music.

But there will be sober people here. We always make sure there are, and the guards will be on our perimeter… Out at the stones… the rocks? What are they called? I frown.

I stumble to the right, following a small gravel path that I don't recognize. Of course I wouldn't. We always hold the celebrations far, far away from New Zeralzi in the no man's lands. The lands that we don't use a lot because of high spirit activity. But on the evenings of the Night Celebrations, the Seers encourage the spirits to move along a little, so it's safer for us.

The Seers…

More than one Seer… Not just Shweta. Others too…

Yes! We're near Muskoxen lands. Of course! The land even looks different. How didn't I recognize it? But it'll be their guards who are protecting us, it'll—

There's a figure far away, up on the hillside. A woman screaming at the sky. And above her, the sky is changing. A dark mist swirling. A spirit.

My eyes widen, my heart thrums. "Who's that?" I ask the nearest person.

It's Bhavesh, but he doesn't answer. He's high or something. His eyes are bulging, too round.

I look back to the person. The spirit's going for her. She's screaming, and it's almost like I can hear her screams now. Scared screams.

No one is helping her.

I pat my thighs—no weapons in my pockets. But I've got trousers on, finally! It's not that stupid purple gown any longer. I look around. There are no weapons here. A glance back shows me the woman has fallen down. The spirit's going for her—going to feed? Oh Gods.

I've got to go now, got to help her.

What, you're going to fight a spirit with your bare hands?

I don't think anymore. I just run.

Dizziness washes over me, and I stagger, head pounding. My heart squeezes as I try to catch my breath, try to blink away the dark dots in my vision, try to stop the colors swirling around me.

The woman screams. The spirit—it's definitely feeding on her.

Go!

I push myself. A fast walk. I start to run then slow down as the dizziness takes me again. I scream at myself, clench the muscles in my legs in the way Evor taught me to. Imagine my blood *not* pooling. Myself *not* fainting.

I can do this. I have to do this.

And I do—I leave the dancing and the singing and the drinking and the drumming behind, and I climb the hillside, knowing I'm going to be too late. But knowing I'm still trying.

Because that's what matters.

Or maybe you should've been smarter! Alerted someone else! There has to have been a guard about…

"Hey!" I scream, running at the spirit, surging forward, begging myself not to faint. My eyes flit around, trying not to settle on the seething dark misty creature. You must never look a spirit in the eye. That's one of the first things I was taught at D'Elinous. Few people live if they do…

The woman…. Maybe she's already dead? She's not moving. Icy pinpricks run over my body as the spirit whips toward me.

"Stop it! Leave her alone!" I yell, and the woman lifts her face. Blond hair, panicked eyes.

It's *Celena*.

Celena? What the hell is she doing out here? Why isn't she back down there, celebrating?

The spirit looks at me, and I look at it. A thousand glittering eyes in the dark, swirling mist. I jolt. I am looking a spirit dead in the eye. I am going to die. This is it.

But the spirit doesn't come toward me. It doesn't reveal gnashing teeth or whatever spirits like these have to eat people with. It just looks, and it hisses.

Oh Gods. The hiss grates through me, so much of it inside my head. I cover my head with my hands as best as I can and feel blood rushing through my ear canals. Feel wetness on my hands, sticky and hot. I'm bleeding. Shit. Blood's pouring out of me.

So much blood.

"What the hell are you doing here?" Celena screams at me. Her words are only just audible through my bleeding. But she's still alive, somehow, miraculously

I jolt, look up at her, my hands in front of my chest. Hands that are dripping blood. I feel more of it trickling down the sides of my neck, my shoulders, my chest.

"Saving you!" I mutter.

"No!" Celena staggers to her feet. She swears at the top of her voice, then looks at the sky. "Where are you going? Come back! We've got—"

A high-pitched screeching answers her. The spirit? Celena is literally talking to a spirit?

"What the hell is happening?" I stare at Celena. My heart's pounding hard again, and I can also feel my pulse in my thighs and my feet. I don't like it.

Celena glares at me. "You're ruining *everything*. He was only just getting started. It takes him a while to get it up."

I stare at her. My mouth drops open. My eyeballs begin to hurt because I realize I'm not blinking. But Celena was...

I take a step back. "Were you trying to have sex with...with that?" My head pounds, and I stare at her. "That's a fucking *spirit*," I hiss. My hands drip blood everywhere as I flick them about. I can't even comprehend this. Is this how she gets around the no-sex rule that Maggot set? By having sex with a bloody spirit? Is that... is she *that* desperate for sex, for a baby, much so that she'd sleep with one of the most dangerous entities?

"You know nothing!" Her eyes flash. "Just go! Leave me alone! It might not be too late."

"Go?" I echo her word. "You want to call that thing back? Are you actually that stupid? You can't make a deal with them. It'll kill you."

"And that proves how much you don't know." She gives me the strongest glare ever—and it is so strong that I stumble back. What the hell? She shouldn't be able to do that. I blink hard. Am I *that* drunk?

But I stumble again, and then I'm moving backward.

Shweta. I need to find Shweta. Shweta will sort all of

this out. She has to.

"I don't want to be away from her for long," Shweta tells me. Her gaze lingers back to where Hana is waiting.

The Night Celebration is still going strong, and Celena is presumably still on the hillside trying to get that spirit to come back, but my head's clearer now. Even if it is still pounding.

"Yes, I know," I say, "but just listen." I don't even know what to tell her first. "I saw Caia-Lu before the reset. And I know who did the time loop. Who set it up." *Ysabelle*. I don't want to say her name because I've spent so many years trying not to think about her, picture her, acknowledge her. But I have to. She is trying to hurt me, trap me. Revenge for killing her group? But I know what I have to do: I have to tell Shweta about the clansmen. About what I did.

I take a deep breath, and then it just pours out of me, and as I tell her I look toward the hillside where—oh Gods...

Celena's actually... *copulating* with the spirit. I look away quickly, my stomach twisting, heat rushing to my face. My eyes widen. Celena had that pregnancy test. Or rather, she will have one when we get to that part of the timeline.

She'll think she's pregnant. Can she even get pregnant by a freaking *spirit*?

"And you think he's alive, too?" Shweta rubs her eyes. She's peering at me intently. There's glitter in her dark hair—it only has a few threads of gray in it, not like what I've become used to—and her eyes look brighter.

It takes me a moment to realize she's talking about

the Overlord Seer. About what I just said about the clansmen. "Yes." I shake my head. "I need to find Ysabelle and the Overlord Seer."

We're farther back this time—that has to be for a reason. Caia-Lu somehow helping me? Because I need to find those two before they begin the time loop the first time. If it hasn't already happened—and it can't have, because it's always coincided with the rough starting day of the siege of New Zeralzi before. That's what Shweta said.

Shweta nods.

I meet her eyes. "We need to kill them, don't we?" *I need to kill them.*

Her gaze darkens, and a twisting feeling fills my heart. There's no need for her to say the word, but she says it anyway. "Yes."

This is exactly what I was made for, says the Beast. *Killing. Let's kill everyone.*

THIRTY-SIX

"SO, I'VE SEEN YSABELLE HERE and…there." I point at different parts of the map we've got stretched over the large granite rock. The map belongs to one of the Muskoxen men. When Shweta and I asked if we could see it, he gave us a look like he thought we were crazy wanting to study the land in the Night Celebration.

I breathe deeply and try to concentrate on the map, but my head's hurting. The Beast is still active in me, still whispering. Whispering about how he wants to kill *everyone*.

But that won't happen. It can't. Killing two people will be enough.

"So, Ysabelle and the Overlord could be anywhere in this area, then?" Shweta glances up at me, and I nod. "Or she's still traveling here. We've not seen any signs of other Untamed around here. I'll check with the Muskoxens, too. And look, New Zeralzi's over there. Could Ysabelle have been traveling toward us, from this direction?" She waves at a large portion of the map. "We're four months ago now though, so she could be even farther that way. If she's not already here, then I don't know how we're going to find her."

I grit my teeth. There has to be a way. "What about the Overlord Seer? Seer contact?"

"I can't do that, not personally," Shweta says. "Seer powers are always quite individual, even though there are some things that we can all do. But from what I understand, contact usually works best if the two people are related."

My head spins. "So, it won't work?"

"We can ask the Seers here," Shweta says. "It might be possible. But I wouldn't hold my breath."

The Muskoxen group has two seers. A middle-aged white man named Aaron who has a very narrow face and a pointy moustache which is currently covered in glitter, and an elderly mixed-race woman named Emma who has the most powerful, echoing voice I've ever heard when she introduces herself.

"So you want to find your friend," Emma says. She was sitting on the edge of all the celebrations and came quite eagerly with us when Shweta said we needed her Seer powers. I don't think Emma's had much to drink. "But you don't have anything to go on, location-wise."

"Well, we think she's that way." I gesture vaguely. *And she's not my friend.* I don't even know why Shweta said that to these two. I look at Aaron. He's definitely had quite a bit to drink.

"And you also don't know anything about what she wants?" Emma asks.

"Wants?" I frown.

"I can sense people who desire something—or someone—strongly," Emma says. "Do you know what Ysabelle or this other Seer want?"

"Uh, *me*?" I look at Shweta and she gives an encouraging smile.

Aaron starts to laugh. I try and ignore him. He's sitting kind of in the shadows anyway. We're in a large cave now, and it wasn't easy to lure him away from all the celebrations.

"You?" Emma raises her eyebrows. There's a thin scar that divides one of them, and the candlelight in here catches onto that silvery scar, makes it glisten. "Love, is it?"

About as opposite of that as you can get, I'm about to say, but Shweta says, "Yes."

I look at her. Her eyes flash, a shock that seems to go right through me. *Go with it.*

So I do. I let Shweta do the talking. Listen to the incredible story she spins, how she says it all so earnestly, sincerely. If I didn't know better, I might even start to believe that Ysabelle really is my long-lost love.

"She'd do anything to see her again," Shweta finishes and looks at me.

There's a lump in my throat, and I get the feeling that I'd better say something, too. "Oh, uh, yeah." My voice squeaks and my attention's caught by a tiny amount of movement in the shadows. A spider of some sorts, under the hanging body of a hare.

"Then we'd better begin," Emma says. "Allow us to go and gather our materials. Aaron, come with me."

The two Seers leave, ambling along, out of the little cave.

"Materials?" I say to Shweta, but my eyes are on the spider. I think it's a tarantula, and that doesn't make me feel any better. "Uh, can we get out of this cave too?"

"No," Shweta says. "The ritual will take place here, once Emma and Aaron have got their crystals."

"Right." I shake my head a little. The shadows where the tarantula is seem to dance. "And why have you made it sound like Ysabelle and I are together? It doesn't even make sense. They know I've been with

Maggot's group for years, so they're hardly going to believe that."

"I had to say something that would make them want to help. And who's to say this isn't a special friend from before you even came to us?"

"Well, what about the truth?" I counter. I want to sit down, but I also don't want anything crawling over me from the ground. "Like, finding Ysabelle is pretty important when the whole of the tunnels group is either dead, Enhanced, or stuck in a time loop."

"They won't want to try and find a Seer who wants to harm you all," Shweta says in a low voice. "Muskoxen aren't going to want any trouble here. They'd want to keep a distance. Remember, they're defenders, not attackers. There's a reason they didn't come to the tunnels with us."

"Well, there won't be any trouble for them." I shrug. We're here anyway, and as soon as Ysabelle and the Overlord Seer are in sights, we're going to kill them. My fingers buzz a little as I think about that—the Beast stirring, pulling on the nerves in my fingertips, my palms.

"We have to play them," Shweta says. "Trust me."

I nod, and the Muskoxen Seers return. They're each holding various implements—keys, chains, crystals, and what looks like some animal hair. My stomach roils at the thought that it's bison hair, and I swallow quickly then nearly choke as a bit of saliva goes the wrong way. I take several deep breaths and by the time my eyes have stopped watering, the man and woman have arranged the objects by our feet. We're standing in a circle, and the moon's behind the elderly woman so she's silhouetted in front of me.

"Gods and Goddesses of Searching," Emma murmurs, and even her murmurs echo, have a strange throaty quality to them. "We call upon you today."

"Join hands with us," Aaron instructs, and then he's guiding me, his hands either side of my shoulders. He moves me to a worn out spot on the ground, a slight groove. He positions Shweta opposite me, and then the Muskoxen Seers are either side of me.

We join hands. Emma's hands are hot, Aaron's cold. I keep my gaze firmly on Shweta—hers is on mine, too, her eyes wide, waiting.

The man begins to chant. A slow, monotonous chant. I can't pick the words out.

"Ysabelle of the Clansmen," Emma murmurs. "We are looking for you. Kacey, picture her now. Think about her desire for you and yours for her."

If I wasn't so nervous and desperate to find Ysabelle and the Overlord Seer, I'd laugh. or I'd squirm or something. But I don't do anything. My body's stock still, and I'm so aware of every movement. My rapid breaths. The way my chest rises and falls so quickly.

"Ysabelle, we are searching for you."

Aaron's chanting rises in volume, and then Emma joins in. Their words somehow get both louder and quieter at the same time. It's like I'm being submerged underwater, and I grip their hands harder and harder. The woman's touch is burning now and the man's freezing. I can't let go from either.

I glance at their faces, but they're expressionless, giving nothing away. Shweta's eyes are still wide, still full of worry.

I wait for something to happen. Wait and wait. I hear the sounds outside. The other Muskoxen residents, still dancing, celebrating. Minutes pass. The candlelight flickers. The Seers are still chanting. And still nothing.

I catch Shweta's eye again.

"Is anything happening?" I keep my voice low, but the other two Seers don't even act like they hear me. They continue chanting.

Oh Gods. This is useless. We're just wasting time, I'm sure of it. I'm—

Shweta's eyes widen.

"What is it?" I ask.

But before she can answer, she falls forward—straight

toward me. Her body sags against mine, and I stumble back under her weight, my arms reflexively wrapping around her. The two Muskoxen Seers call out something, and then Shweta's weight had pulled me to the ground, and then before I can do anything, Emma crashes down next to us. Aaron falls too, onto the implements, and they make clanging sounds.

And all three Seers are unconscious.

"Um…?" I stare at them, feel a strange pressure building up inside me. This is… this can't be happening… This…

I look around, but there's no one else here. The candlelight flickers, and the cave's walls appear to dance. I tap Shweta on the shoulder, but she doesn't react. She's still breathing though. They all are. I pull at her arm, tell her to wake up. My words get louder and louder, and I feel it—panic, inside me, rising up.

The Beast laughs, but it's not his normal laugh. This is different too, nervous.

"What the hell is happening?" Sweat drips down the back of my neck. I turn and look toward the entrance of the cave. Do I go and get help? Do I—

"They're in the Dream Land!" Shweta screams suddenly.

I jolt, turning back to her—but somehow she's still unconscious. Quiet now, just lying there. Breaths shuddering. And they're in the Dream Land—is that what she's telling me?

The Dream Land: the place Seers go to get warnings of Enhanced Ones' attacks upon us.

"Warn them, please," Emma murmurs, and it's so freaky, seeing her speak while she's not *here*.

I jump up, stumble to the cave's entrance. Pain snakes through me as I move, forcing myself to go faster and faster. I ignore the dizziness that pulls through me, how my legs suddenly feel like they're made of stone.

People are milling about a little way away.

"Maggot!" I yell, seeing her. Relief pounds through me.

Her face is still flushed from the drinking and the dancing, but she sees me, and hurries forward, only swaying a little.

"The Seers!" I scream. "Shweta, Emma, and Aaron have just been summoned…to the Dream Land and…and they're all there and I don't know if this means the Enhanced are coming!" Or is it just that they've gone there to find where Ysabelle is? "I don't know what's happening, and I…"

I can't finish my words, bending over, hands on my knees to brace myself as the world twists in a kaleidoscope of colors. Then a cool hand is on my shoulder.

"Kace, breathe." Kazem's scent washes over me, and I realize everyone's moving now. Moving around me. "Do you need to sit? Come on, let's sit you down."

I shake my head, fast. "No. Not time…" I force myself to move back toward the Muskoxen Seers' cave. Kazem supports me, and I'm sure without his strong arms, I'd be on the floor. I'm so weak—I shouldn't be weak!

Bodies press inside the cave, but I fight my way to the middle of the room. I drop down beside Shweta. Is she still breathing? I touch her wrist, her wrist that suddenly seems fragile. So thin. Her brown skin looks almost translucent in places, the color drained so I can see the pulsing blue veins.

"What's goin' on?" Maggot pushes me away from Shweta as she bends over her. The smell of alcohol wafts over me. "Why ain't they wakin' up?"

"I don't know!" My hands brush Shweta's neck. Yes. She's got her pendant. It's right there, falling toward her left shoulder on an old piece of discolored string.

Someone shouts for Evor and the other doctors, and then they're here too, squeezing among people.

"Kace, we should wait outside," Kazem says. "There's not room for all of us in there." But just as he says the words Shweta's closed eyelids flicker slightly.

I gasp, pointing to her, trying to get words out but

everything inside me feels stuck, stuck with all the nausea in me. Everything combining and swirling in a viscous mess.

But Shweta's eyelids flicker again, and then she opens them. She looks directly at me, and I jolt, feel the power in her gaze. Feel the importance of it. The Beast moves in response.

"It's *gone*." Shweta's words are hollow. Next to her, Emma and Aaron are stirring. "The Enhanced. They got in there."

"Where?" Maggot asks, her tone sharp. "How close are they?"

Suddenly, everyone around is drawing weapons. Several people elbow me and someone stands on my foot, but I barely notice.

"No," Shweta says. "Not… not *here*." She looks terrible. Huge bags hang under her eyes, and she's shaking. "There. The Dream Land."

"Oh the Gods protects us," Emma wails, but I lose sight of her as people step between us.

"The Dream Land?" I whisper. "Ysabelle and the Overlord Seer? But where are they in the mortal world?"

But my questions get lost amid the sudden cacophony of voices, because several people are asking questions all at once, and the Seers are trying to answer, trying to speak. I can't concentrate. There are just so many words, so many voices competing, wrapping around each other. Yet when Shweta speaks again, somehow, it's her words I focus on. Her words that I hear loud and clear.

"The *Enhanced* got in the Dream Land. They tore it apart. And it's gone. The Dream Land's *gone*."

THIRTY-SEVEN

FOR A LONG MOMENT, THERE'S silence. Everything inside me tightens, and a delicate kind of pain twists around my neck. This isn't to do with Ysabelle and the Overlord Seer? I don't understand. The Enhanced were in the Dream Land? I look up at Kazem. The stubble on his chin grazes the side of my forehead. He's got his arm around me protectively, and I lean into his embrace, feeling myself getting weaker and weaker.

Then Aaron and Emma and Shweta talk. They tell us that the Enhanced Ones were in the one place that's sacred to the Untamed, sacred to our survival.

"The Seventh One was also there," Shweta says, her voice shaking. She reaches out and her hand's almost skeletal. Hana's by her side in an instant, supporting her. Shweta's shoulders tremble. "I saw her, the Seventh One. She was there. I don't know if she summoned us to fight, or if it was the Dream Land pulling all Untamed Seers there because—" She breaks off, choking. Her eyes bulge, watering.

"It's okay, it's okay," Hana says softly.

Maggot and Traci and others all start asking questions, but I can't keep up. Kazem's grip on me tightens, and

I lean into him more. His warmth and reassurance. If all the Untamed Seers were there, then that means the Overlord Seer would be. Did Shweta find him? But she doesn't know what he looks like. Not properly. I can't remember if I described him to her.

"It can't be." Emma shakes her head. I can see her again now, and her eyes are so wide, haunted. Her voice, for once, barely has any oomph to it—it's so quiet I don't know how I hear her words, but I do. "A nightmare. That's all it can…"

"It was so hot, burning everywhere." Shweta's voice is small. She looks at me. Her face is flushed. "The Enhanced were there. Not just their Seers," she clarifies. "But all of them. Ordinary ones."

"What?" I jolt. But no, that can't be right. Only Seers can get to the Dream Land. And Enhanced Seers have broken in, but bringing their non-Seers with them?

"There were so many of them—the Enhanced," Shweta says. "One of their Seers, this powerful man, was bringing them all there. He's too powerful.."

"And the Gods and Goddesses were furious about it," Aaron says. "They were there too."

"I've never seen so many," Emma whispers, a tear trickling down her cheek.

"*So* many of them." Aaron looks down, and shadows fall over his face. "So many *dead* now."

I stare at them, looking from one to another. "Dead?" The Gods and Goddesses can't die. They can't be dead. I want to laugh—because this has to be some sort of elaborate joke.

But no one is laughing. There is just a hushed silence around the Seers' words now.

"The Enhanced were ripping the place apart. The whole Dream Land," Shweta says. "They killed several of the Gods and Goddesses. And us. Some of us are dead. There was this black hole, sucking people up, and… We couldn't… We…" She gulps. "They were killing us, and we were trying to fight. All of us."

"And trying to get out," Emma says. "It was all we

could do. We've lost so many."

"But you got out," I say, and part of me wants to reach forward and hug Shweta. Even though I'm not a hugger. But she needs the comfort. They all do. But Shweta's got Hana at her side, and I know she'd much rather have her girlfriend there than me.

Shweta gulps. "I think the Seventh One threw us out of there. Saved us. I don't know how she did it."

"Or if she got out," Aaron says, and there's a strange metallic taste in my mouth. "She was still there, and I was one of the last to get out. It was all…all *burning*. The whole place."

Maggot frowns. "The Seventh One might not have got out? Am I understandin' this correctly? The Seventh One might be dead?" Her voice is sharp.

"If that's true, the augury won't hold," another voice says. It's Evor. He rubs his bald head, and he looks distinctly green. "The war would never end."

Maggot holds up her hand. She looks at Traci, who's standing next to her. "We need a council meeting. Your council and mine."

Traci nods. "The councils and our Seers."

Maggot claps her hand. "Everyone, spread the word. If we've lost our Savior and the Dream Land, we need to work out what we're doin' next."

Everyone starts to clear out of the cave. Kazem and I move to go too, but then Shweta pulls on my hand.

"Wait back here a moment," she says.

And I do.

Once everyone has cleared out of the Muskoxen Seers' cave, into the dark of the night, she starts talking. "We're going to have to tell them about the time loop."

"Will they believe us?" I run a hand through my hair. I don't fancy being labeled as insane, now of all times.

"We have to *make* them. The overall timeline isn't right." Shweta's voice trembles.

I think of what Caia-Lu told me. If we don't sort

this out, get rid of the time loop, the timelines will irreparably unravel—and then the Seventh One can't save any of us. If she's even still alive.

"The time loop's getting bigger," Shweta says. "It's affecting Muskoxen now."

"Was it not before?" I ask her.

"I don't know. I don't think so, I just have that feeling. But the time loop problem is getting bigger. We got out of it just now."

"What?" I frown. "Out of what?"

"The time loop," Shweta says, like it's obvious. "Emma, Aaron, and I—we broke out of the time loop—and we were called to the Dream Land in its *current* state. Or what was its current state. Which is our future—as we've not got there yet. With the exception of some of the Enhanced who were also called there from the time loop, I reckon everyone else present was from the future."

"So time is definitely continuing as normal?" I ask. "For everyone else... so we're missing out on things that are happening." My mind spins. There could be all sorts of new developments in the War of Humanity that we just don't know about.

"And now I'm back here in the time loop again." Shweta tucks a stray strand of hair behind her ear. "And in the real present time, the Dream Land's gone. But in *our* now, it might not have been destroyed too. I don't know. There's a chance it is still here, for us, this older version of it."

"So you could get visions?" I ask, but I feel like we're just grasping at straws here. "Actual warnings."

Shweta nods. "And we're far back enough that I've still got my Seer powers. I haven't lost them yet." She swallows hard.

Yes. I nod. Hana's still alive. Shweta has no grief to cloud them.

"But we need everyone here on the same page as us," Shweta says. "We're going to have to see if we can convince everyone that the time loop is happening. We need everyone to understand, and we need everyone to be on the lookout for Ysabelle and the Overlord. It's too dangerous to keep anyone in the dark."

I nod. "And this isn't going to be easy, right?" I raise my eyebrows, and a part of me hopes that she'll say it will be easy. That persuading everyone that we're in a time loop won't be a problem at all.

"You took the words right out of my mouth."

It's been about two years since I've been in the Muskoxen group's council meeting space. It's a long barn, with chopped slices of tree-trunk for seats. Maggot, Sian, Markus, Winston, Shweta, Evor, Rohan, Bhavesh, and I sit on one side of the room. Celena is here as well, even though she's not part of the tunnel group's council. But she followed us in, only stumbling a little—I guess that's the cost of having sex with a spirit. Maggot saw her enter the council space but didn't stop her. Opposite us are the Muskoxen council members: Traci, Clawton, Emma, Aaron, Franya, Michael, Jesse, and two men I don't recognize. Several of them look a little worse for wear, after the celebrations. Many of them are yawning.

And everyone is staring at Shweta and I, their gazes ranging from disbelief to fear to incredulity. The light isn't great in here. A few lanterns are rigged up, and some more torches, but the light is flickering, sending lots of shadows across people's faces.

"We need to focus on what's happened to the Seventh One, whether she's alive or not," Celena says. She casts a scorn-filled look at me. "Not listen to this load of bullshit."

"It's not bullshit," I say, folding my arms. I look at Evor. "I've got dysautonomia now. The same condition your cousin's half-sister had. *You* diagnosed me—I got injured in one of the loops, but that's stayed with me in both restarts I've had."

Before he can answer, Celena throws her arms up in the air. "This is ridiculous! We need to work out what we're doing about the end of the war if the Savior's been killed."

"We can only do that if we're in the same part of the timeline as everyone else," Shweta says.

Maggot nods, her face a picture of calm. She raises one arm, a glare on her face, just as Celena appears about to interrupt again. Maggot clears her throat. "If there is a time loop, how do we stop it?"

"We kill the people who cast this on us all," Shweta says. "An individual named Ysabelle who is most likely working with a very powerful Seer known as the Overlord."

I glance at Emma and Aaron for their reactions. Emma looks a bit annoyed and her eyes narrow on me, but Aaron's expression doesn't change. He's just sitting there.

"Untamed?" Maggot asks.

I nod.

"Why would Untamed try to hurt us?" Traci asks. "We're on the same side."

"They hate me," I say. "I hurt them… before."

I take a deep breath, and I tell them a condensed version. Shweta gives me encouraging looks and fills in any parts that I miss out, parts she must deem to be important. I hate saying all the words. I hate it so much, bringing to life this part of me that I thought I could just leave behind. But I can't hide who I am. I can't pretend that I didn't live through all of that. I can't pretend there isn't this monster inside me.

There are hushed gasps as I finish.

Celena's rolling her eyes. "That is the biggest load of tosh I've ever heard."

"The Beast inside Kacey isn't really a Beast," Shweta says, ignoring her. She looks toward Maggot, and then at the Muskoxen council. "It's *energy*. Energy that will be crucial for ending the war—energy that the Seventh One will use."

If she's alive, I think, swallowing a lump in my throat. Because what if she's not? What if I've got this energy and the Seventh One's gone, and now *I'm* supposed to be the one using it, saving everyone? What if I'm now the Savior?

I don't want to be a savior. Tears fill my eyes. I never wanted any of this. Shweta squeezes my arm, reassuringly.

And then the council starts talking. Everyone gets a chance to speak, to voice their thoughts, and we go around the room, starting with Emma.

"I believe it," she says. Her eyes narrow even more on me. "But don't deceive me again."

Shame fills my body. I give her a small nod.

"You believe we're in a time loop?" Celena exclaims. "This is madness."

"I tell you what else is madness," I say. "You sle—"

"Be quiet, both of you," Maggot hisses, standing up. "Or you're going to 'ave to leave. Council is a place of order."

I swallow hard and apologize. Celena doesn't. She just scowls at me. The council members all talk, each taking turns to ask Shweta more questions—and Shweta answers all of them, and none of them really want to ask me anything. I'm glad. Very glad.

My left foot twitches as I wait and wait. Maggot asks me if I need to step out for a moment. I shake my head. Shweta touches my foot with her own.

"They're believing us," she whispers to me, "they're actually believing us. They never believed me before."

"But two of us," I say quietly. "Maybe that makes all the difference."

That and in this timeline, Shweta hasn't yet had that period of altered behavior and thoughts, due to grief.

"Maybe," Shweta says, and the meeting goes on and on and on.

"Okay," Maggot finally says, and I sit up a little straighter as she claps her hands once for attention. "So, to sum up, we've got an action plan. First step is to find this Ysabelle and her Seer. She's somewhere in this region, but could be weeks' travel away?" Maggot glances at me and I nod—because I have to hope that Ysabelle is somewhere in this area. That she's not even farther away. "Then we're goin' to split up. We're goin' to find her. I'll rally the troops, and Kacey, you'll give everyone a detailed description of this couple. We'll get our best artists to draw it. Franya, you've still got art supplies?"

"Of course I have," Franya says.

Outside, a Eurasian Eagle Owl calls, a low, humming *hewwww* that sends shivers through me.

"Then we will go out in teams, each armed with a drawin'. If we find Ysabelle and her Seer, we'll question them. Make sure it is them. And then we'll kill them." Maggot's gaze crosses back to Shweta and me. "And then this time loop will stop, and we'll all wake up in the actual time, along with all the other Untamed. Then we can unite with them, find out if the Seventh Seer is alive, and what we're going to do next."

"Best plan we've had in years," one of the men mumbles. "We're actually doing something."

Maggot divides us into groups while some of the others pore over the map, trying to work out the most likely places that Ysabelle and the Overlord Seer will be. I really hope that Shweta and I are right, assuming Ysabelle will also be in the area, given we're now four months before when she was last seen in these lands. I want to be on the same team as Shweta, but Maggot says I've got the value of a Seer, with my Beast power. She wants all the Seers leading separate teams, me leading my own team, and all the other council members and best fighters leading their own ones. We'll be departing as soon as the drink's out of most people's systems.

Franya's artists are hard at work, drawing pictures under candlelight and lanterns of Ysabelle and the Overlord Seer while I provide visual clues.

"They've both got fire-like hair. And he always wears a mask. Or at least he did. I've never seen what his face looks like. But they dress differently to us. Like, knotted rags. Animal skins. Furs. That kind of thing. They don't raid from the Enhanced. So no jeans or hoodies."

"Unless they've found some on the way and decided to use them," Kazem murmurs. "If they're cold and find a hoodie, would make sense for them to take it, regardless of what their beliefs are."

"Beliefs can be important though," Shweta says.

We continue preparing. On my team is Clive— again—and three of the Muskoxen women.

"I'm so glad we'll be out there with you," Clive tells me. We're in one of the huts now, and he just keeps grinning at me. Somehow, he looks a lot younger, even though it's only been four months. "You've got the Beast. You can protect us."

I swallow hard. Let's hope I can. I give him a smile. For him, it might be the first time I've ever smiled at him. It might be for me, too.

"Right," Maggot calls, maybe half an hour later, when we're outside. The sun's early rays are beginning to light up the land in a hazy gray. "We—"

But a voice shrieks instead. A voice that drowns out her words. A voice that utters one word, over and over, in the most anguish-filled cry:

"*Enhanced!*"

THIRTY-EIGHT

WE MOVE IN A BLUR, arms and legs pumping. Dizziness pulls over me and—

And they're *here*. Enhanced Ones. Suddenly, so many of them. Their mirror eyes flash in the grayness of the early morning. They're making a circle around the Muskoxen settlement.

"Try that way!" Kazem yells, and I don't know who he's talking to, but he grabs my hand and pulls me sharply to the right. My elbow and shoulder sear with pain, and I stumble after him, skidding on damp grass and—

More Enhanced rise, right in front of us. Guns. They've got guns, again.

We're trapped.

We're actually trapped. They are a circle around us.

"The Beast, Kacey!" Maggot yells at me—but I can't use the Beast now. Doesn't she know that the Beast doesn't always discriminate between Untamed and Enhanced? No, maybe I didn't tell her that. I can't remember, and I can't remember before how I made sure it didn't kill Untamed. But Evor still died.

My head pounds, and Maggot's shouting at me

again and again. *Everyone* is shouting.

And Red is here. Red is right in front of me, dressed in a pristine, fitted suit. Navy blue. It makes his black hair look glossier.

He grins. "Hello, Kacey."

"The Beast!" Maggot screams.

Red's holding a gun, and he lifts it up and points it at me, and all around, I can hear gunshots. So many gunshots. But we're… we're not holding guns. We haven't sorted out our weapons. We are not armed. But they are. And there are gunshots. They're shooting us. Killing us. What? Not trying to convert us? Not—

"Kill them, Kachler!" Celena yells, and I see a streak of her blond hair as she moves to me. She sounds scared. I've never heard her sound like that.

Red jerks his gun, moving it away and then back to me, and my attention zeroes in on him. He smiles, and Celena's tugging at my sleeve, and so is Bhavesh. Kazem's shouting at me, his words breaking, his tone raw. Maggot's screaming too, and the gun in my face— the gun held by Red—is exactly three inches from my head. I am staring down the barrel. I don't know what to do. I don't know!

I tremble and shake, and I'm dizzy. I'm so dizzy. I'm going to fall. I can't do this. I'm not strong. I can't do this!

Red pulls the trigger.

And

the gunshot swallows the silence

and

no one moves

and

everyone moves

and

no.

Nothing happens and everything happens.

And…

There's blood and screaming. And we've been hit.

We've been *hit*.

"Kacey? Kacey, come here." Maggot's voice echoes in my ears, and she's pulling at me, trying to move me from the ground.

The *ground*.

I'm on the ground. I'm screaming. My hands are slippery and red, and—

Shweta gurgles.

Shweta

More gunshots. Evor's gun—I see it in his hand now. He's got a gun now, too. And so has Celena. They're firing, charging at the Enhanced, shooting them. A pathway out of the circle of Enhanced Ones is opening up. The Untamed are running. A mass of us trying to get out, even while we're still being picked off.

Picked off.

I stumble, and I see her. Her dark hair. Her arm, reaching out, on the ground. She's on the ground. Shweta. She's not moving.

I scream her name, and then I'm fighting someone who's trying to pull me back, and I get away, and adrenaline drives me, and I'm at her side, and I'm cradling her small, fragile body in my arms, and my tears fall on her face, mixing with blood and dirt, and she doesn't move because her chest is a mess of red flesh and blood, and the blood's spurting out, and there's so much of it, and she's not moving. She's not fucking moving.

"Kacey! Come on! Leave her," Maggot commands. Her voice is fire, licking me, burning me.

"No! I can't!"

"We have to go *now*!"

Hands grab me. Hands attached to strong arms and a warm body, and Kazem's voice in my ear. I scream and fight, and the Beast is stirring—the Beast is stirring!

No! He's going to—

I try to shove him down, but he's so strong, and he's surging, and…

I can't stop him. I can't—

Something hard hits me across the back of my head. A bright white light flashes in front of my eyes, and then there's nothing.

SHWETA IS DEAD. THAT'S ALL I can concentrate on as we drive away in one of the Muskoxen group's trucks. Not Emma's apologies for knocking me unconscious when she sensed I was struggling to contain the great power inside me and she got a flash vision of me killing them all, Untamed included. Not Evor's instructions as he tries to work out if I'm concussed. Or more concussed than I already was. Not Kazem's soft touch as he holds me, as he tries to tell me things will be okay, while he's also trying not to throw up.

Just Shweta. Only Shweta. Shweta being dead. That's all I focus on.

We left her. We left her body there.

And they're going to have her now. The Enhanced. We left her there, and we didn't send her body off.

Will they take her with them? Do they take our bodies when they kill us? Would they send her off? Do they have the same beliefs, or do the augmenters and their lifestyle change that?

I feel sick as wind whips across my face. I see the other trucks behind us, too. I don't know how many of us got away. I just woke up, and we were driving.

But this can't be happening. Shweta cannot be dead. I look at Kazem, and I think of the intense grief I felt when he was dead. But he's here. He's got a paper bag clamped to his mouth now.

My eyes widen.

"We can reset it," I say. The truck goes over a rough bit of ground, and I grab hold of the side of the wall.

Kazem frowns.

"The time loop," I say. "It has to restart. It has to. We won't be trapped in this particular nightmare much longer. We just have to make this timeline stop, and then…then, somehow, we make it start again and then Shweta will be alive, and then we can sort it out." My words get faster. "Maybe the loop will restart again at the Night Celebration. Or—or I know! We continue as we are now, until we know where Ysabelle and the Overlord Seer are. We find them, and then I'll know where we are, and we'll reset the time loop. Then Shweta and everyone"—because others have died too—"will be alive, and we'll know about this ambush so we can avoid that. We can just get away, redo all of this, and we'll have time to travel to where Ysabelle is, and we can kill her and the Overlord Seer then." My words tumble out too quickly, crashing, merging into each other. "We'll get Shweta back, and everything will be all right."

Kazem's face pales. He squeezes my hand. "How do you restart the time loop?"

The muscles in face slacken. I… I don't know. I can't even utter those words. I…*can't*. "It'll just happen." I try to muster as much confidence into my voice as I can. The confidence of someone who knows what they're doing. Not someone whose life is unraveling, strands fraying and falling apart. "It will happen soon. It—" I frown, my eyes focusing on something in the distance. Some*one* in the distance. No. More than one person. Fire-red hair and—

It's Ysabelle.

My mouth dries. She's there. She's right fucking there. And the Overlord Seer—a bulking man with an ivory mask over his whole face. It has to be him. And that child—the child Ysabelle had last time. They're all there, dressed in gold like they're some sort of freaking prize.

I let out a strangled laugh.

"Oh Gods." Kazem jumps. A glance at him tells me he's seen them too. "Kacey? Kace, that's them, isn't it?"

But I don't answer. I can't answer. There's something wrong with me, my body, my brain. Not just the dizziness and lightheadedness, and the way my heart pounds too fast so often now, but it's like I can't move. Like I'm not connected to my body. Like there's another *me* inside my body—me, not the Beast—and I've just stepped out of sync with my physicality. Only a fraction. But I can't control my arms, my legs. I'm hovering, powerless, trapped in the ether.

"Maggot!" Kazem yells, and then he's banging on the back of the cab.

I... I...

Maggot turns. Her eyes light up and the corners of her mouth twist into a delicious smile. "Kill her!" she yells, and her voice is so loud, and she's got a radio in the cab. A radio connecting to the other trucks. The other trucks that are driving—driving straight for the figures.

Everyone's seen Ysabelle now. I know it. I feel it. Everyone's looking toward her. They're hanging over the sides of the open-back trucks, holding on with one hand as they line up shots.

Some Muskoxen men grab spears, slingshots, knives. Kazem's shouting something at me—he hasn't moved, and he's so close, and I should be deafened by his words because he's shouting that loudly, but I'm not. They just float over me, through me, as I look around. Everyone's doing something. Except me. I'm just watching. Watching as our vehicles charge toward Ysabelle and the Overlord Seer and the child.

They are going to kill her, the Beast whispers. I can feel his pride, but there's something else too. A sense of loss.

Loss?

I jolt.

"No!" I scream, and I nearly fall from the truck, but someone grabs me. Killing Ysabelle breaks the time loop—permanently. I need it to *reset*. I need to get Shweta back.

I pound on the back of the cab. "Stop! Stop!"

But Maggot's not listening. No one is. They're going to kill Ysabelle and the Overlord Seer, and maybe the child too. They're going to kill them, and the time loop will stop and—

Shweta: gone, forever. Permanently.

"You have to stop them!" I turn to Kazem—the only person, other than myself, who hasn't moved. He's still crouching in the bed of the truck, looking queasy. He's not grabbed a weapon.

But I see it, behind him. I see it everywhere. I see the bullets released by sudden, cacophonous gunshots. Bullets I shouldn't be able to *see* fly through the air, as if everything's slowed down. And I see the spears soar. Three of them. Sent by the Muskoxen group's best spearmen.

The Beast and I flinch, our bodies collapsing, hitting the floor of the truck bed, just as Ysabelle and the Overlord Seer and the child do. I see it happen even though I'm not looking, even though there's the metal of the truck's side between us and so much land. But I feel it happen. I don't understand, but all of us are on the floor. My head pounds, too much blood roaring through me. Too much anger and—

Death.

Ysabelle. Her head to one side. A spear in her chest, a bullet in her skull, another in her pelvis. The land around her bleeds.

And it's over.

It's finally over.

I wait for things to happen. Things to change. The time loop to stop. For us to be in the future—whatever that means. Wait for something, anything. Because Ysabelle's dead and the Overlord Seer's dead and the clansman child is dead, because somehow I can see their bodies in my mind, and the world should go back to normal now.

But it doesn't.

Nothing happens.

I don't know what the hell is going on. Confusion pulls through me, and I sit up. I'm groggy.

"Kacey?" Kazem crouches in front of me, and then he's wiping something from my head. His fingers come back red. Blood.

I frown, touching my face. I'm bleeding. How am I bleeding? I wasn't hit.

"Did she faint and hit her head in the excitement?" a sickly-sweet voice says.

Before Celena can say another word, I tell her to go away—except in more unpleasant language than I've ever used before. Celena melts back into the scenery, into the people talking and whispering, into Kazem who's still talking to me, still crouched in front of me. Our truck has stopped. I'm not sure when that happened.

I look at my hands, the left one still slick with my blood. A shadow falls over Kazem and I. It's Emma. I never realized just how small she is, but she looks tiny now. Or maybe it's my vision. My head. I touch the back of my skull, feeling a bump there.

"The time loop hasn't stopped." Her eyes are wide, frightened. "I can *feel* it stronger. We are still in it. We haven't broken out."

I take several deep, shuddering breaths. It didn't work. Well, that's good because we need it to reset. We need Shweta back to sort all this out.

"And I'll get her back," I whisper, watching as Maggot and the others inspect Ysabelle's and the Overlord Seer's and the child's bodies. The clansmen are dead. Finally. "Shweta, I'm not giving up on you."

Time goes on, but the loop doesn't reset. I'm not sure how many days have passed since Ysabelle and the Overlord Seer and the clansmen child were killed. How many days have begun and ended since Shweta was killed. But *time* has passed. The sky's lightened and darkened several times. Maggot, on several occasions, has told me to get some rest, and Kazem has held me while I pretended to sleep.

But I couldn't sleep, and I can't sleep now. I'm awake, and I can't ever *not* be awake. I can't close my eyes to the destruction around us.

It's dark out, and there's too much pent up energy inside me. It's a hundred thousand termites crawling inside my veins, their footsteps getting faster and faster, spiraling, torpedoing through me, trying to escape. But they can't. There's no release.

No release from any of this.

I push the covers back. Kazem and I are sharing several old, moth-eaten blankets. We're in a Muskoxen hut. He's breathing deeply, asleep, and I crawl out from under his muscular arm. He doesn't stir. Always a heavy sleeper.

My chest aches something fierce as I open the hut door, step outside. The night sky looks down me, and I nod at the moon. At Caia-Lu—because that's what it feels like I'm doing. As if she's up there, looking down, even though I know the New World isn't in the moon. That's just silly. A child's imagination.

I'm barefoot, but I'm walking—and I only realize it when I'm on the edge of the Muskoxen settlement. Walking feels good. It's movement, it's doing something.

Run!

The need comes to me, storming my body. The ants in my veins urge me to. Yes, if I run fast enough, I can get rid of them. I just have to move faster than they are.

So I do it—I fight the fatigue and dizziness, and I push myself. My thighs pump and adrenaline propels me forward. I leap over branches and rocks, skid on the dried ground, on gravel, small loose stones, shrubbery, low-creeping foliage.

I am flying.

"See! This body's not broken!" I scream into the sky—and then I keep screaming and screaming, even though I'm stumbling. Fall heavily, hit my knee. Pain shocks through me, but I scramble up. My heart's beating so fast it feels like it's going to explode, and I can hardly see anything, not just because it's dark but my vision's wavering, blackening still, only to be interrupted by bright white pinpricks of light. Lights that zoom around and around, trying to chase me, catch me.

Sweat drips down my forehead, stinging my eyes when it reaches them, and then I nearly end up in the river. Don't know how—it's just suddenly there. The water. But I veer to the left, running with the river, following it, pushing myself faster and faster and I can't breathe.

I cannot breathe.

I cannot think.

I cannot do anything but force myself to run faster, ignore the pain lassoing my chest, the way my heart's squeezing like a rope's wrapped around it, being yanked tighter and tighter.

I just have to run.

And somehow, I scramble to a stop as I reach the edge of the land, where everything drops away. The sounds of crashing water roar in my ears. I look down at the waterfall, at the water crashing over the rocks below. I shouldn't stand so close to the edge. I know that. It would be certain death.

Death.

I take in a shuddery breath. My death reset the time loop before. When Ysabelle killed me. When—
I don't think.
I just jump.

"WHAT THE HELL ARE YOU doing?" Caia-Lu demands. She's in a hut, a hut like she had at D'Elinous. No, we are in it. I'm here too. I lift my hand and stare at my skin—and it's not glowing red. It's normal and—

"Kacey, are you even listening to me?" Caia-Lu snaps, her face an angry red. She grabs me by the shoulders. Her touch is hot. "I had to save you and…"

But I can't focus on her words. They're too fast, and there's more pressing things. Like how I'm in this hut now. And how it doesn't feel right.

"Is… is this the New World?" My eyes widen, and my breaths come too quickly. The reset. It didn't work.

I've died. I've actually died.

Oh Gods.

I blink. The New World. It's got to be bigger than one hut. Is it exactly like our world—or exactly like it would've been if the Enhanced hadn't developed, if no augmenters had ever been created over four hundred years ago? Because this is a land just for Untamed. And maybe this is D'Elinous. An alternate version of it. An alternate reality. Is that what happens when we die and the Untamed send us off to the New World? We cross to an alternate reality?

"I had to pull you here, and I wasn't ready—it's got to be the right time for that, Kacey! Do you have any idea what you've done? You're in the New World. And you shouldn't be. Your Rijikarii needs to stay in the mortal world longer than this! You need to stop the time loop! I told you this." Caia-Lu shakes me. "There must be no time loop before you come here,, else how can the Seventh One win the war for us?"

"She's alive still, the Seventh One?" I look up at my aunt.

"Yes, and she needs you alive. She needs the mortal world stable. Not you killing yourself."

"I wasn't trying to die," I whisper, and I think I'm telling the truth. The truth as I know it. "I was trying to reset the time loop. But I don't know what I'm doing! And Shweta— Is she here? Oh Gods, we didn't send her off. I told Maggot that we—"

"Shweta is not here," Caia-Lu confirms. "But she is not dead. The Enhanced have her, and you need to get her back."

My mouth dries. "Not dead?" My words hang heavy.

And we left her.

No. Maggot left her. Everyone else left her.

"So, I can go back?" I whisper. My heart pounds. A rescue mission, that's what we need to do.

"Yes," Caia-Lu says. "Go back before the God of Death has realized what you've done. And for the Gods' sake, stop the loop before it stretches and traps any more people in it. Because you've only got a small timeframe now, Kacey. Once it's too big, there's no going back. The Seventh One can only save the Untamed if the balance of Rijikarii is exactly right and if there is no time loop! Don't let the world unravel!"

FORTY-ONE

I SPLUTTER BACK TO LIFE, on the bank, dripping wet. Something hot and warm over my mouth. Air is forced through me, and I jolt, lungs burning. Everything burning. Someone helps me sit up, and I vomit up water once, twice, three times. Pain wracks through me.

Kazem holds me up. Evor's here too, talking. So is Emma. And Maggot. Some others too, sort of appearing out of the darkness. Torchlights whip around, and they hurt my eyes.

"She's… She's okay?"

"I think so. We'll need to watch for secondary drowning though."

"Secondary drowning?"

"Water could still be in her lungs. It's good she's been sick, but she's not in the clear."

They talk more and more, to each other, then Kazem turns to me. There is fire and anguish and pain in his eyes. But he kisses me. It's fast and urgent, and he doesn't like public displays of affection, but he's kissing me, in front of people.

Then he pulls back. "What the hell were you doing?"

His hair's sopping wet, sending droplets down his strong nose. I watch those droplets fall—onto my hand. "Kacey, do you have any idea what that was like? Watching you do that?"

"I…" The word rasps against my throat, feels like a nail-file—like the one Maggot got on a raid once— being dragged against my tender insides. Above me, the moon seems to get brighter. "I wasn't…"

"Weren't what?" he demands, anger in his voice now. "Trying to kill yourself?"

"Trying to… reset the time loop." My voice is weak. I can't even tell if he hears my answer, if I managed to get the words out at a suitable volume. "Trying to… get Shweta… back."

"Well, it didn't work, did it?" he snaps. "She's not here, and you practically drowned."

"I know what we need to do though," I whisper. I turn. "Where's Maggot? Get Maggot."

Kazem shakes his head in clear bewilderment and annoyance, but he calls over Maggot. She crouches next to me, holding a torch, balancing on the balls of her feet. She's wet too, her clothes soaked, stuck to her sturdy form. How many people went in the water to get me out?

"Shweta's not dead," I tell her, trying not to look directly at the bright light. "She was still alive, and the Enhanced took her. I was just in the New World—"

"So, you *did* die," Kazem mutters, and then his arms are around me and he's holding me close. I feel him shaking, his whole body wracking with emotion.

"Caia-Lu told me the Enhanced have Shweta. She said we need to break the time loop sooner than ever. We need Shweta to do that. We need to do a rescue mission."

Maggot tilts her head to one side, looking at me. There's a cut on her face, I now notice, and her skin's turning a bluish-gray color, even despite the yellow of the torch beams all around. She nods once and then looks toward Evor. "Rally the troops."

"No, you're not going," Kazem says, placing a strong hand on my arm as I try to grab one of the survival kits.

The Muskoxen group were surprisingly quick at getting preparations together. It's only been an hour or so since I told Maggot that the Enhanced have Shweta, and we've got vehicles ready to go, loaded with supplies. The only things left in the council barn are the survival kits for each member of the rescue mission. That's Maggot, Bhavesh, Winston, Sian, Celena, Kazem, *and* me.

"Of course I'm going," I say. "I have to."

He shakes his head. "You're staying right here. I am not having you there, distracting me—"

"I'm not going to distract you!"

"Yeah?" he challenges. "You really think that? You really think after you've just thrown yourself off a cliff and drowned that I'm not going to think you might do something stupid there? Might freak out about the Enhanced or get converted, or even kill yourself there if you get into a situation you can't get out of?"

Anger seethes in me. "I wouldn't!"

"Nah, you're not thinking straight. You're not thinking *at all*. And, anyway, Evor says medically you're not well enough. You're not going, Kace."

"I have to!" I cry. Why can't he see that I must?

"You don't," he says, his tone firm, voice low. "You are not."

"I'm the one who knows the most about what is going on here. I have to get Shweta back."

"No," he says. "You're too close to Shweta. You're practically best friends all of a sudden, and you know the rescue rules."

I do know rules. You can't be on a rescue team for your immediate family or close friends. Not when it'd be more personal. Not when you're going to be more emotional. More likely to make mistakes. Or at least that's what Maggot says. But I think that's stupid. I think having that connection, that emotional closeness, will make you fight stronger.

I take Kazem's hand. "Please," I whisper. "I have to go."

He shakes his head. "It's not just up to me," he says. "Maggot decided. Just… just stay safe here. Okay? Evor's going to be looking after you."

"I don't need looking after."

"Then prove me wrong," he says, and he picks up his survival bag, gives me a quick hug, then leaves.

I don't follow him out of the hut. I just stand here, watch him. Watch him go and do another thing that I'm no longer allowed to.

FORTY-TWO

WHEN THE RESCUE TEAM IS away, Evor does his best to cheer me up, but I'm just mean to him. I know I am. I'm barely replying when he talks, ignoring most of his questions, and not laughing at the seriously bad jokes he tells. I just want to be on my own, but Evor's not one to break his word, and he watches me like a hawk, just as he apparently promised Kazem he would.

Everyone else at Muskoxen is busy sorting out food, ropes, and stuff, but Evor and I just sit outside a hut. It's later in the day now, and I'm watching the horizon, looking for the first sign of the trucks coming back. The group left in two of the Muskoxen trucks. Franya reckons they'd have taken Shweta to New Zeralzi.

"She's going to be *really* Enhanced now," a small girl says to her mother. The child's eyes are wide.

"Yes, most likely," her mother says. "But that's what the ropes are for."

Restraints. That's what a lot of them are making. Because Shweta is going to have to be tied up until she runs lean—if she *can* run lean enough that we can untie her. My heart squeezes. It's impossible for someone to be Untamed fully again, once they've been converted.

Shweta's going to fight us on everything, and I can't help but wonder how easy it's going to be to break the time loop now without her help. Especially when I don't know how to do it. Killing Ysabelle didn't work. So, Ysabelle didn't set it—someone else must have, and we still don't know who.

"Hey, Kacey, you should be listening to this," Evor says, and he's standing now. I didn't notice him get up, but he beckons for me and him to join a group of Muskoxens, a little way away.

It takes me a few moments to realize that they're just talking about strategy for how to contain Shweta. Hardly a new topic. And listening to them talk about her, like she's the enemy, or a wild animal, not even human, just angers me.

This is Shweta!

But they're not even calling her *Shweta* now. They refer to her as 'freshly Enhanced' or 'the converted one'—like she doesn't even deserve her name now. Anger prickles under my skin. It's not like she chose for this to happen. No, this was done to her.

Maggot did this to her, leaving her there. Not even checking if she was actually dead.

I want to scream at them, but I don't. I just watch, sullen, my mood darkening more and more. It's so dark that I feel the Beast stirring. He's a parasite who's stronger than his host, and he's letting me know this. I am a vessel, an empty husk waiting to be filled, to be used by him and his power. And that scares me.

I need to stop him. I must stop him. If the Gods and Goddesses won't purge the Beast from me, then I have to make myself stronger. I can't be a vessel, an empty husk waiting for him to take over, to fill me, control me. This is my freaking body. *Mine.*

"And you're not welcome," I hiss, my voice low— just about low enough that I don't think any of the Muskoxen group or Evor hears me.

The Beast hisses back, and he's angry—and that makes me angrier, makes me stronger. He's not going to take my body away from me. It's *mine*. I need to make sure he can never take me over again.

I can do that. I must be able to do that.

Sure, I've tried to do this before—tried to build walls every time I squash him back down, but I always thought of that as a temporary measurement until the Gods and Goddesses removed him. But now I know it'll have to be permanent. I'll have to put more energy, more fervor into it.

And I can do it. I can build walls, unbreakable walls that no one—not even me—will be able to tear down. But first, he needs to be locked away, so I push him down, farther and farther, deeper inside me, as far as he will go. And then I picture walls—huge granite blocks rising around him—and I've no idea if this is right. If I'm doing this correctly, if this is how I build stronger walls. Permanent walls. Do I imagine it into being or do I need a Seer to help?

The Beast growls—and I know it's doing something.

So, I keep building. My hands shake with the effort, so I clench them, press them against the sides of my thighs. Sweat beads on my brow, the back of my neck, the top of my back. My knees weaken, and I'm trembling. My whole body wracks with tremors.

"You've gone white."

Several of the Muskoxens are looking at me.

"I'm fine," I mutter. They can't distract me, they—

The Beast pushes back: a sharp tug inside me. Granite blocks crumble, and he laughs, pushing and pulling at my mind, his fingers in my soul.

Dark shapes form in front of my eyes, but when I blink they clear—and I see the Untamed staring at me—until the dark shapes rematerialize. The Beast, taking over my eyes.

"No!" I cry, but the shapes get stronger, building together to create something. A figure, a person.

Let me show you something, the Beast says.

I am powerless to stop him.

"This is it," Caia-Lu says. "This is our new start, and you see now why you're all so important, don't you?"

I am standing amid a group of people. I recognize faces: Keelie and Elf—from the photos and videos that Red had—and others. Men and women, all around about the same age as me, give or take a few years. There are thirty, forty of us. Maybe a few more. I turn and look, and they're turning and looking too. Snatches of eye contact as we rotate, moving.

And I feel it. The power within us all. We all have Beasts, but the Beasts are good, I know that. I can feel it—my Beast is warmth, honey, and reassurance. And all of us are to be protected, because we are their vessels, and Caia-Lu is our leader. These Beasts are bigger than we ever knew, and they were planted in us, because we are their protectors.

"We can manage this," Caia-Lu says. "We will work together, and we will keep the New World safe."

"Kacey?" Evor's face hovers over mine. Cool fingers—his fingers, presumably—are against my forehead, and then he's yelling for someone to get me water. "You're all right, Kacey. Just fainted. Went down with quite a thump though."

My breaths rush out of me all in one go. I didn't faint! I... the Beast did that. Took complete control of me. Gave me a vision. I frown. *Keep the New World safe?* So, I'm going to die after soon?

I feel the Beast sinking back down inside me. *It's not time yet,* he says. *But it will be soon. It's coming.*

My death is coming? *Brilliant.* I breathe out hard,

feeling waves of heaviness crash over me. I mean, everyone dies I know that, but I'm going to die soon? And why the hell is the Beast showing me this?

Because you need to be prepared.

There's something about his tone that's dark, that I instinctively don't like. Yet it makes me think of how I sensed the Beast was good in that vision. How I could feel it. He showed me that to make me trust him.

Yes. Don't fight me, Kacey. I am of the power that your aunt unleashed in the world many moons ago. I can feel your restraints going up, but you mustn't fight me.

"You kill people," I mutter, then realize I've spoken aloud and more of the Muskoxen group are crowding into my vision.

"Kacey, you're just confused," Evor says. "I need to have a look at your head. The back of it. I think you're bleeding…"

Kacey, concentrate on me! the Beast shouts in my mind, shoving Evor's words away. *You must not fight me for the next part—for our destiny—to happen.*

"But you kill people!" I yell.

Evor flinches. All the Muskoxen men and women do—and then they're talking fast, and I hear the words *severe concussion* and *aggression* and *what do we do?* before I force them out of my mind and focus solely on the Beast.

Yes, he says, *I do kill people—for I need energy for what we are all about to accomplish, when we become the Guardians. And you and I—the Grand Guardian—will be the greatest of them all. So, you mustn't fight me, Kacey. You must trust me. You must let me rest, let me sleep now so I am ready. Don't build up the restraints. I need to be able to blossom when it's time.*

Blossom? I nearly snort.

Trust your aunt, and everything will be as it's supposed to. Your aunt realizes this now. We've shown her.

"We?" I don't even care that I'm speaking aloud. Everyone obviously thinks I'm insane now. This isn't going to change that.

Yes, we—

An anguished shout cuts the Beast off, and I feel him fall inside me. Like he's dropped from a great height, plunging into my depths. I flinch, turning, and see the trucks. The trucks are back, and our people are back, and everyone's shouting.

"Get them now!"

"I can't!"

"We need them!"

"Hey, pack the trucks!"

"Evor, help! Sian's hurt."

I turn to where the shouts are coming from and see Maggot and several others running toward us. They're shouting, looking scared. And the rest of our group is behind them—except... except people are missing.

My heart drops. Have we lost more?

"Get the restraints! And we need more guns!" Bhavesh yells. "Get them in the trucks! We need to go!"

Go? I falter.

"Guns? Are... are the Enhanced coming after you?" someone shouts from behind me.

And I try to ask if Kazem's okay, but my words are breathy, and they're not loud enough. No one hears them.

I jump into action. The weapons store is nearby, and I race to it, grab two handguns and several rounds of ammunition. Dizziness tugs at me as I head back, and nausea's gripping my throat. I stop, head pounding, eyes smarting as I dry-retch, dropping the guns and ammunition. A sour taste fills my mouth, but there's no substance.

My eyes sting, and my head throbs, pain shooting between my ears. My chest tightens, and I clap a hand to it, feel my heart flutter.

Anger pulls through me—this is pathetic! Having an episode at a time like this! A time when we're under attack! A time when I need to be helping and—

A hand touches me. I look into Maggot's face.

"You got more magazines?" she asks, but then she

must see where I've dropped them, because she's picking those up.

"Did you get her?" I cry. "Did you get Shweta?"

Maggot looks at me, and I stare at the way blood has splattered across her fair skin, how it's dried. It's the right side of her face again, the same place that was all bruised and swollen in the other loops. "Yes."

"And the Enhanced are coming after her, after us?" I ask. "And… and is Kazem okay?"

"Tell the others to get the vehicles moving," Maggot says. "We need to go now, but we've got another problem."

"What?" My blood makes rushing sounds in my ears.

"Shweta had augmenters in her pockets. We didn't check—didn't think to. So fucking stupid of us. Now we've got two to run lean."

"Who?" I whisper. My chest squeezes. "Who's the other?"

"Just get everyone ready to go. We've got a head-start on the Enhanced—their trucks are still in the distance. But they saw us come here. And they're following."

"Who is it?" I yell. "Who else is Enhanced?"

The muscles in her face tighten. "Kazem. But we'll get him back, Kacey. We'll get them both Untamed again."

FORTY-THREE

KAZEM. *MY KAZEM.* I CAN'T breathe. I… I can't… He's… he's *Enhanced.*

Once it's done, you're never the same. I had faith that Shweta would be able to fight it, return to us, but Kazem? He's not a Seer. He's… he's my sweet and kind and fun boyfriend. My partner. My everything.

And he's gone. His humanity just… *gone.*

Maggot moves back, runs to the trucks. Everyone's running. Jumping into the vehicles. And I can't move. I'm sitting on the grass. When did I sit down? I don't know. I dig my hands into the ground, trying to feel something, anything, how the dirt gouges its way under my nails. I try to feel the hardness of it.

"Kacey, come on!" Clive calls as he runs into view. "We have to go now."

But I don't move.

I can't move.

Clive runs up to me, and then somehow, he's strong enough to move me. It doesn't make sense, but he's pulling me along—maybe I'm just going with it, I don't know. But we're running and the door of a silver truck is open, and people pull me in. Winston and SJ and two Muskoxen women. Clive climbs in after me. The door slams shut. Six of us in in the back.

"Kacey, swap places with me." Evor's voice.

In a daze, I see he's in the front of the truck's cabin, next to Celena who's driving.

"Help her," Evor says. "I want her in the front where she's got more room. She's concussed."

"Again?" Celena snorts.

There's a small panel between the cab and the truck bed that's moveable. I watch as it slides away, as if by itself. Hands and arms move me, voices instruct me. My knee thwacks into the middle console as I climb over it, as I'm pushed over it, as I slide past Evor's body. Then I'm in the passenger seat. Huh. Left-hand drive. Not been in one of these before.

My head hits the window—the truck's bouncing over uneven ground.

Celena's driving fast, keeping up with two trucks ahead of us. There's another a few hundred meters to our right, keeping parallel with us, driving across the steppe. And I can see more in the wing-mirror. Are these all of us, these trucks?

I turn, frowning. "Are the Enhanced behind us?"

"Ask Maggot on the radio," Celena says, thrusting a hand-held radio into my lap. "I can't do that at the same time as driving. Not if I'm trying to avoid blowing a tire."

"Blowing a tire?" From the back, Clive sounds worried. The panel still hasn't been put back and when I twist my neck, I see his little face.

"There are so many ditches," Celena pants. "It's not even a road."

"We didn't adjust the tire pressure for offroad driving," one of the Muskoxen women says. "Didn't have time. But it's more likely to cut a tire. Not blow a tire."

"Suspension's more likely to break. Damage to the alloys, et cetera," the other Muskoxen woman says.

"Just ask Maggot if the Enhanced are still chasing us all," Celena says. "Kachler!"

I lift the radio, but it's unfamiliar. Should it be? I don't know how to use it. I turn to the people in the back, and Clive takes it from me. He speaks into it. I hear Maggot's voice, but I can't make out her words. I look out of my window, see Sian's face in the driver's seat of the truck that's parallel to us on our right. Sian. Was she injured? I can't remember. I touch my forehead. All I remember is Kazem… Kazem and Shweta and…

I knock Celena with my arm as I try to turn, try to see into the other trucks, on the other side of our vehicle. "Where are they? Kazem and Shweta."

"Just sit down!" Celena shoves me back into the passenger seat. "Put your goddam seat belt on."

"I want to see them!" I yell. "I need to see—"

Excruciating pain fills me. Every ounce of me. My body, my soul.

"What—" Celena shrieks, and the world lights up in a white flash—a flash that sears and burns everything I can see onto the insides of my eyelids. I scream, reaching out for something, anything—but my hand brushes nothing.

There's nothing here.

Nothing at all. Everything's gone and…

…and I open my eyes to singing and dancing and music. Darkness, moonlight, candles.

"All right, Kacey?" It's Maggot, Maggot laughing as she sloshes a drink about. The earthy smell of the bitter liquid wafts over me.

I'm back here. Back at the Night Celebration.

Except it's not… the music is different. No drums. And this land is different, and I look up at the dark sky. The moon is the tiniest of crescents. This is a Moon Worship. And we're not far from the main entrance to our tunnels. We're not at the Muskoxen group.

I frown as I see Celena. She's just behind Maggot, not up on a hillside, and her arm's in a sling. A *sling*. She sprained her elbow two weeks before we attempted to take over New Zeralzi. She had the sling on until the day we did the raid. The day she stole that pregnancy test from a chemist, the day before the siege. And the only Moon Worship we had when she was wearing a sling was the night before we raided New Bere for weapons ready for the takeover of New Zeralzi.

The reset has happened again, but it's thrown us closer to the day of the siege.

Maggot is frowning at me. "I…" Her frown deepens. She's not smiling now. She looks sad. "I didn't mean to make her this way," she says.

"What?" I stare at her.

"My daughter… it's hard, being a mother and a leader. And I just… I feel like I've let her down."

I stare at her, because I don't know what to say.

Tears glaze Maggot's eyes. "I've never really been a mother to her," she says, slurring. "So focused on this." She waves her arm vaguely and her drink sloshes over the side of the cup. "All of this." She looks down at her drink, at her hand. She's shaking, really properly trembling. "Something's… *wrong*."

My heart pounds. "You remember?" Is that what's happening? It's not just Shweta and I who remember now? It's extending—because the pocket's getting bigger, just like Caia-Lu warned? More people are remembering.

"Remember what?" Maggot asks, frowning.

"The time loop."

Maggot stares at me. "I think we've both had too much to drink." She frowns, sadness overtaking her countenance. "I should speak to my daughter."

She stumbles off, moving slowly, so slowly, after Celena, who's walking away. Maggot's feet drag, her whole body's dragging. The distorted eyes of the tiger tattoo on her back, just visible above her low-backed purple Cami top, watch me.

I shudder.

"Oh, Kacey, thank goodness. There you are!" a low and beautiful voice cries.

I turn and see her. Shweta. Untamed eyes. Alive.

I breathe out hard, and then we're rushing toward each other. My arms spring around her, hers around me, and we hold each other close. I'm shaking, or she's shaking, or we both are and—

"A different start," she says. "Hana's not here." Her face crumples. "A different pathway."

"At least you're not Enhanced," I say, because I don't know what else to say.

But Shweta doesn't look like she cares about that. Her eyes are heavy, and she is shaking.

"Where's Kazem?" I ask. More and more people are dancing around us, to the music—but I notice some of them are stopping now, frowning in just the way Maggot was. The way she still is.

"I think they can sense something's wrong," Shweta says. "Maybe a feeling of déjà vu, but they can't quite remember."

I nod. "The time loop's got bigger."

"Well, as we know, killing Ysabelle didn't stop it," Shweta says. "And that's useful info because"—she points behind me—"I believe she's right there."

FORTY-FOUR

I DON'T REMEMBER TURNING AROUND. I'm just suddenly facing the opposite way. Facing Ysabelle. She's here. *Again.*

She's close to me, three feet away. The moonlight bathes her, and she looks like danger. The same sharp gaze, pasty white skin. But her hair is a little different. It's still flaming red, but now I'm up close I can see the silver hairs in it, how it makes parts look a little more strawberry blond, like Sian's hair. And it's dry too, so dry. Frizzy. Nothing like the glossy, voluminous waves it used to be. It looks frazzled, burnt. Was her hair like this when she slit my throat? I can't think, can't remember. But she looks older, too, Ysabelle. Maybe even older than last time. Grooves dig deep around her eyes and join the corners of her mouth. Her eyes are still burning amber.

The child is with her. I suddenly notice her. She's about four or five years old. A child I don't know. A child who must have been born after the massacre. But Ysabelle would've been too old to give birth again, right?

"Hello, Kassandra." Ysabelle's voice booms, loud and rich and dark and velvety, and it wraps around me and clings to me, just as it did back then, always. It's just the two of them, her and this child. No sign of the Overlord Seer.

The hairs on the back of my neck rise. I want to run. Every part of me is screaming this, or to grab a weapon because she's going to hurt me, going to kill me, but I don't move. I can't move. My legs are stone. I just stare at her.

"That's her, isn't it?" Maggot's voice is low. "I... I remember something... She's bad."

More Untamed are crowding around. Sian and Bhavesh and Kate. Some still carry drinks and some are singing, dancing, but they all gradually stop and stare at us.

"So, Kassandra," Ysabelle says, and she gives me a devilish look that makes me shake so much that Shweta grabs hold of my arm. "We need to *end* the time loop."

"You know about the time loop?" My heart does a jumpy thing, and my voice doesn't even sound like me. Hell, I sound scared. Actually scared. I feel like I'm either going to be sick or pass out or both. Ysabelle hasn't made any move to hurt me, but I feel like my brain's in overdrive, trying to work out her next move.

"Unfortunately for me, Kassandra I've been caught in it, too." Ysabelle tilts her head to one side, and then the child is murmuring something. She bends down to listen to her for a moment, and tells her that it's going to be okay. When she stands again and looks at me, her eyes are softer. It's a softness that's not right in her gaze. Ysabelle is a serpent, she's vicious. She's *pretending right now*, and that's got to be more dangerous.

"What *is* going on?" Maggot demands, and then Bhavesh is stepping closer. He's got a knife out, and he points it at Ysabelle. More people crowd around, and I see Maggot signaling to them.

The beat of the music dies down.

Ysabelle casts a lazy glance to me. "You want to call him off?" She glares at Bhavesh. "I'm not threatening you, Kassandra, and this really isn't good manners. I'd have expected better of you, really."

Suddenly, there's loads of shouting all at once—Maggot and Bhavesh and everyone, and then even more of our group is here. We're crowding around Ysabelle, in a way that I think would be intimidating, but Ysabelle doesn't look intimidated at all. If anything, she's reveling in this.

"Think carefully whether you want my help, Kassandra," Ysabelle says, that lazy smile on her face once more. There's something almost demonic about her look and the way the moonlight is falling on her face. "Because I can just as easily *not* help you sort out all of this."

My face flashes hot then cold. Ysabelle can help? Or is this just a trick? She definitely didn't help me before. "You expect me to believe you're going to help? You tried to kill me. You *did* kill me."

"Right, that's it," Maggot snarls. "Leave now or we are usin' our weapons on you."

Ysabelle ignores her, her gaze solely on me. "Did I?" She shrugs. "Did it really happen? You're right here, Kassandra. Well, that's the beauty of the time loop, I guess. Has its perks, even if it's annoying as hell."

"I said *back off*." Maggot's voice is a bit slurred as she steps closer to Ysabelle, a knife in her hand too now. She touches the point of the knife to Ysabelle's clothes. Some sort of animal hide.

Ysabelle doesn't even flinch, but the girl lets out a scared cry, and I look down at her, see how much she's shaking. My heart pounds. No child should be scared. But she is—and now the guns are coming out. I see them in the hands of our group, and the child looks absolutely petrified.

"So, you didn't set it?" Shweta asks. She steps forward. "The time loop?"

"No," Ysabelle says, nonchalantly, but her eyes are on the knife blade at her chest. She looks mildly disgusted. "I did not." She flicks her fingers at Maggot, then Bhavesh. "Kassandra, call off your dogs, will you? I'd rather have a more *sophisticated* chat."

"Uh, just stand down a moment," I say, the words rushing out of me. Maggot looks to me, a hundred questions on her face, but I just nod again, and then my gaze is unfocused. I just see the darkness of the night on our edges, and then all the torch beams are pointing at us, held by my people. The lights are disorientating.

"Are you armed?" Shweta asks Ysabelle.

Ysabelle shakes her head. "Can we go somewhere more private? It's only really the two of you I want to talk to." She points—almost delicately—at Shweta and me.

I swallow hard. "How are you here? I killed you— before. Years ago." I don't know why I say the words, when it's been apparent for so long now that she didn't die.

"Kace, what's goin' on?" Maggot asks, her voice gruff.

"Give me a gun." I hold my hand out vaguely behind me, to any of my people. And then one's in my hand. I grip it tightly.

"Uh, Kassandra, is that really wise?" Ysabelle says, her voice slow, like it's dripping with venom.

"It is," I say. "Because you killed me."

"And you killed me." Her nostrils flare, and her upper lip twitches. I see she's missing a tooth, and seeing that—this imperfection—makes me feel stronger, better, like I've somehow got more power. "You left me dying, Kassandra. But here's a tip. Make sure those you kill are actually dead before you flee."

My breaths shudder across my whole body. A cold wind descends.

"Now, are we going to go somewhere private to talk, or what? Because this is my last offer of helping you."

"Let us search you," I say, "and then we'll go somewhere more private. Just the three of us." I glance back at Maggot. "I'll explain everything to you after, but just trust me on this."

We take Ysabelle into the tunnels. Me and Shweta. The girl comes too, because she won't let go of Ysabelle's hand. Maggot's not happy about any of this, but Shweta and I are both armed. And Ysabelle isn't.

"How do we stop the time loop then?" My voice is steely. We're in a small section of the tunnels, a room that's at the end of a corridor. Shweta and I block Ysabelle's exit, and there's nothing in this room apart from a lantern hanging from the ceiling. Nothing that Ysabelle can use as a weapon.

Ysabelle clicks her tongue. "Really? Just getting straight to business?"

"That's why you're here, is it not?" Shweta asks.

"True, but there's nothing wrong with a bit of chit-chat."

Rage burns through me, and the gun jerks in my hand. "Why would I want to have *chit-chat* with you? You killed me."

Ysabelle rolls her eyes. "We're even on that count, now, Kassandra. But perhaps we should start there— when you did end my life."

I swallow uncomfortably. "So you *did* die." She was lying earlier, when she said I left her not quite dead. And anyway, I know she died. I *felt* the clansmen's deaths. "How did you survive?"

"Made a deal with a spirit in my final second," she says. "Good job there was one around. I died and the spirit brought me back. It could only save two of us though."

Two of us.

"The Overlord Seer?" I turn my head, looking around, as if expecting to see him standing right behind me. But he's not. "Is he here, too?" Could he be above ground, watching our people?

Ysabelle makes a considering noise at the back of her throat. "About half the time, when time is resetting."

"So he's not here *now*?" I breathe out hard and glance at Shweta. Her gaze is intent, focused on Ysabelle.

"He got killed. Half the time, in this repetition of life, we see a lynx and it always goes for him. Leaving us, me and our baby."

Baby.

My stomach recoils, and I look at the girl. This child is the offspring of Ysabelle and the Overlord Seer? A sibling for Iralda. Iralda who's dead. Whom I killed. Whom the Beast killed. Whom the spirit that Ysabelle consulted with couldn't save.

"What did you exchange with the spirit?" I ask. "For saving you and the Overlord Seer?"

For a moment, I don't think Ysabelle is going to answer. She frowns and glares at me, giving me such a pointed look that practically says *know your place*. She never did like me asking questions. But then she sighs.

"The birth of a future child." She glances down at the child. "Not this one. They said they'd claim the right one when he or she was born. And it was a week ago— well, no, it might be longer. I've been stuck in this time loop for months. It was a day before time went wrong, when he was born. The moment he was born, the spirits claimed him. Tore him apart." She breathes out heavily, and then glances up—looks right at the light of the lantern. She blinks. "I still hear his screams."

My mind spins. A baby, torn apart by the spirits? A slimy sensation rolls around the pit of my stomach. And how the hell is Ysabelle still able to give birth? She must be nearly seventy!

Shweta's frowning. "You made a deal with the spirits and when you fulfilled the deal, giving them your newborn, the time loop started?"

"I am not *anything* to do with the time loop," Ysabelle says. "You understand? Someone else has done that."

"And we need to find out who—and kill them," I say.

"There is another way though," Ysabelle says.

"What is it?" Shweta asks.

"Sorry, but who actually are you? I do keep seeing you in these loops, in the distance, but we've never had the good fortune of meeting."

"My name is Shweta," Shweta says. "And I've been in the time loop for months. Now, are you a Seer? You know how to break it?"

"I'm not a Seer," Ysabelle says slowly.

"But the Overlord Seer is," I say. "And he's dead in this reset?" I let out a shaky breath. "Do we need to wait for another loop to start then, when he's alive?"

"No," Ysabelle says. "Because he's already told me what to do. A way of ending the loop even if we do not know who started it. He consulted Marta's Lore."

"Marta's Lore?" I ask.

"It's Seer knowledge, deep knowledge," Ysabelle says. "A Seer called Marta put together an archive that contains information, knowledge, secrets, and power. There, we found that a huge amount of dark, dangerous energy can overthrow a time loop and get rid of it. And that's why we've been looking for you."

I frown. "You're talking about my Beast." I wince, wishing I hadn't said that. Being under Ysabelle's steely gaze makes me want to distance myself from the creature inside me. To show that it's not me. That I'm not it.

Ysabelle nods slowly, but her gaze isn't on me. It's slightly behind me. "It makes sense now, how you were able to get away from us. The world knew you'd be needed for this. You and the others."

"The others?" I ask. Then I frown. "Wait—if I'm so important, why did you kill me?"

"Oh that was just for fun, really," Ysabelle says. She laughs, and the sound buries under my skin. "Well, the first time I *really* wanted to, and we didn't yet understand. But after that, well either the Overlord knew that we were in a timeline that wasn't going to be the one or we lost Lani." Her voice catches a bit—but only for a moment. And then her slyness in back. "And who can blame me for indulging in my fantasies?"

I take a small step back, and I grip the gun harder. "Remember who's in charge here." My voice is dry.

"What others are there?" Shweta asks. "You said Kacey and others are needed?"

Ysabelle pushes the child—her child—in front of her. The toddler. "I've taught Lani how to conceal her Beast. She's pretty good at it, given the Gods and Goddesses also chose her as a Seer. Not that there was any question of her power, given her parentage." Her tone is haughty.

My eyebrows shoot up. "You have a child who has the Beast?" I stare at the girl with the fire-red hair and try to send a Beast in her too. I cannot.

Ysabelle's eyes darken. "*All* my children have Beasts. We taught them well, ensured they knew how to hide them."

I inhale quickly. Iralda had a Beast, too? Iralda who painted my face with bison blood, to sacrifice me? To kill my Beast? And she had one herself. Anger ripples under my skin.

"I didn't understand it then," Ysabelle said. "I was scared. But I know now that it was for this moment. To get us out of this time loop." She looks around. "Where's your child?"

I stare at her. "I haven't got a child."

"But… but then we have a problem," Ysabelle says. "The Overlord Seer says—or rather *said*, as it were this time—we need three Beasts to break the time loop. That's why we had to find you. We had to bring you Lani, because he said there were two of you here. We assumed it was your child. You're old enough to have one now."

Yes. I'm twenty-two. Quite a few Untamed have children by this age—in the clansmen, it was encouraged as soon as the girl was able to sustain a pregnancy. They really focused on making their population viable, making it continue.

"We assumed the other Beast would be your child. That it runs in blood."

"But it doesn't with you," I say. "You've given birth to two with Beasts, if what you say is true, yet you yourself have not got a Beast."

Ysabelle's shoulders drop. Her gaze becomes sharper, more dangerous, and the shadows on her face change. "I assumed it would be your child."

Shweta takes a deep breath. "Okay, so we need three Beasts. And now we've got two. So we just need to search for a third one, then we're all set?"

Ysabelle nods, but there's something in her eyes that I just can't trust.

"Well," I say. "We don't need to search for a third one. I know where he is. We can just get him to work with us. Well, force him to work with us."

"Who is it?" Shweta looks at me. Her eyes are dark. "I don't like the idea of forcing someone to do something. That's what the Enhanced do."

"Then he's used to it," I say. "Because he is Enhanced. His name is Red."

MAGGOT LOOKS FIRST TO SHWETA then to me, then finally to Ysabelle. We're all above ground again now, and we've told Maggot everything. Everything that's happened, everything that's going on now, and everything we need to do next.

"You've seen that takin' over New Zeralzi doesn't work?" Maggot frowns.

Shweta shakes her head. "It never works. And we need to break this time loop as soon as possible, which means we need to get the Enhanced man that Kacey knows has this power too."

Maggot sits on an upturned crate. She rests her elbows on her knees for a moment, then looks up at the three of us. "You're sure about this?"

The three of us nod.

"I've been searching for Kassandra for weeks upon weeks," Ysabelle says. "I was shown that she has one of the powers in her that we need."

Maggot squints at me. "And you ain't a Seer, too?"

"No, she's not," Shweta says. "But we need to do this quickly. Time is unravelling." She glances at me, and I know what she's worried about—because

I'm worried about this too now: this is the first time, in any replay or pathway, that Ysabelle has been working *with* us. And time could reset at any moment and undo our progress, drop us into a loop where Ysabelle's nowhere nearby or where Lani gets injured, dies? There could be hundreds of resets until we'd be in a pathway where we find each other again.

Maggot breathes out hard then rubs her eyes. They're a little bloodshot, probably from the drink she had. "So we need to plan an infiltration *and* rescue mission?"

I nod. "Just like we do for Untamed." Just like they did for Shweta, when we were in that other pathway.

Maggot nods once then stands. She holds her hand out to Ysabelle, ready to shake. "Yes, we will help you."

Maggot and Ysabelle shake hands, and it's the most bizarre thing. I blink several times, as if expecting none of this to be true. But it is.

"When do you want to do this extraction?" Maggot asks.

"Right away," Shweta says. "We've still got a few hours before sunrise. We need to use that to our advantage."

Maggot nods. "Then we have a lot of planning to do. Kacey, call a group meeting. Make sure everyone's briefed on the new plan and ready to follow these orders."

"Isn't that going to delay things?" Shweta says.

"We can't run straight into an infiltration and extraction without a proper plan," Maggot says, and I nod and grit my teeth.

We can't risk anyone getting converted. I let out a shaky breath and try not to picture Kazem with mirror eyes.

"Kacey, you're in charge of this," Maggot says.

I nod. Her confidence in me makes me smile—even if my smile is wiped away by the look on Ysabelle's face. Because she's staring right at me, and something tells me that as soon as the time loop is solved and we're out of it, she's going to be coming for me.

"I think you should tell someone about your dysautonomia," Shweta says in a low voice as we wait for the meeting room to fill up. "And I don't think you should take an active part in this mission."

"I'm fine to be an active part in this mission. I'm in charge!" I push my hair back from my face and angle myself toward Shweta. Ysabelle's fairly close by—in conversation with Celena and some of the council members—and being watched carefully by Bhavesh, but I don't want her finding out about this weakness of mine. "I have to be on this mission. I'm the only one who knows what Red looks like."

"I might be able to sense the Beast in him," Shweta says. "Or Ysabelle can?"

"Look, I'm going, okay. No arguments." I expect her to fight me on this, and I kind of know her concerns are valid, but I also need to do this. I can't explain it, and there also isn't time to try. The council meeting used up so much time, and we need to get into New Zeralzi as soon as possible. The sky's going to be lightening soon, and we need all the advantages we can get.

But Shweta just nods. "Well, I guess this is it." She hands me a radio. "Have you got enough ammo?"

"Yes. Two clips."

Not that I should be using the gun at all. The hope is that I'll get to Red's apartment undetected, and I'll knock on his door. When he opens it, I'll punch him. A quick strike, and I should be able to render him unconscious. Kate has shown me exactly where to punch him. I'll radio through to the extraction team who'll be waiting nearby. Getting him out of New Zeralzi without any trouble from the Enhanced is going to be the tricky part. But we've got our free-runners as a distraction team, if needed. They can put on a display.

"Just keep a level head," Shweta says to me.

A few minutes later, everyone who's involved in this mission has gathered in the chamber before the entrance of our tunnels, as well as several people who are staying behind. Ysabelle and Lani are both staying behind with Bhavesh and Maggot keeping an eye on them. I told Maggot that I don't fully trust Ysabelle, but I trust that they of all people can keep her contained. I don't want Ysabelle in the town, her menace a distraction for me.

Now, I look at everyone who's here. Kazem makes his way to my side. His eyes brim with warmth and love, and he presses a quick kiss to my forehead.

"I'm so proud of you," he whispers.

I want to lean into him. I want to hold him tight, but I know this isn't the time. We've got to get going.

"Urgh," Celena says loudly, and I turn on her, expecting a mean comment or something, but she's not even looking at me and Kazem. Her face is very pink, and her good hand is clutching her stomach, the other in the sling. After a moment, she looks up at me. "Just as well I'm too injured to come along. I feel peaky, too."

"Peaky?" I raise my eyebrows.

"Yeah, I had a lot to drink at the Moon Party," Celena says. "More than I should've."

Yeah, a lot of people have. In fact, some of our best fighters are too intoxicated to come with us. But I look at the people I have got: Winston and SJ for the extraction; Sian and Kazem for a distraction, if needed; and finally Shweta and Tammy as backup for each team.

I think we've got enough. And I think we can do this. "Let's get our mirrors in."

Just as I'm about to step forward to receive my pair from Kate, Kazem catches my hand.

"You'll be careful, won't you?" His eyes hold worry. But they don't hold fear that I can't do it—not like they did in the last loop, when he stopped me going on Shweta's rescue mission. He doesn't know that I'm unwell still, that I'm fighting to keep consciousness, and I want to keep it this way.

"Of course," I say, giving his hand a squeeze. "I always am."

FORTY-SIX

MY HEART POUNDS AS WE squeeze through the gap in the wall into New Zeralzi, and then we're walking through the town, past the offices and factories, weaving among buildings. Adrenaline hurtles through me, and I walk faster and faster. I rub at my eyes a little. The lenses are irritating them. But I look at my group. The seven of us look like Enhanced Ones.

"Are you sure you're okay to do this?" Shweta murmurs to me for what feels like the hundredth time since we left the tunnels.

I wait for some Enhanced Ones to pass us before I reply with, "Of course," and I give her a sharp look. She better not say anything to Kazem.

Shweta nods. "I want regular radio contact."

"When it's safe, yes." I pat my pocket absentmindedly. The hair pins click together. If he doesn't answer the door—if he's a heavy sleeper or he's not in—then I can pick the lock and get inside, either render him unconscious there or wait for him to return to his apartment from wherever he's been.

I look up at the buildings I know so well. The walls I've climbed, the rooftops I've run along. I try not

293

to look at the pharmacy building. I just keep going. Kazem walks a little faster, so that he's by my side.

"I love you." His voice is a whisper.

"I love you, too."

We kiss once—a quick kiss—and he touches my face. Then he and Sian—our distraction team—and Tammy head off. Kazem and Sian are going to the other side of the leisure center. It's far from Red's apartment building, and it provides a good place for them to pull a whole group of Enhanced Ones to if needed. Tammy will wait nearby, watching them, in case they need help. All three have guns.

The warmth on my cheek, from Kazem's hand, lingers as I walk on. It almost feels like his hand is still there.

Winston, SJ, Shweta, and I reach the apartment block about ten minutes later. It's a huge white building. Each apartment has a balcony that looks out on either the town or a small lake with flowers around it, around the other side of the building.

There are cellars beneath the apartment block, too. That's where Winston, SJ, and Shweta will wait. We decided that the group of us all heading up to Red's apartment might raise suspicions if any Enhanced Ones see us. One person that they don't recognize might be plausible. They might not know the odd person who lives here. But a whole group of us? Too risky.

This is it, I think, as I watch them go. Shweta's got tears in her eyes, and she looks so nervous, and I try not to let that unsettle me. I can do this. I will.

I'm on my own now, and I breathe deeply, clenching my fists. Before, I relished being on my own in Enhanced Ones' towns and cities. Relished knowing that I was strong enough to face whatever challenge I was up against alone. I was confident in my abilities.

I swallow, trying to dislodge the lump in my throat. I can still manage alone. I can.

My heart hammers as I let myself into the building. That door isn't locked. Maybe Red's won't be at all?

The Enhanced think they're the perfect society. They have no crime, apparently. The only times I've seen them lock doors were when I was being kept captive—and even then, Red didn't lock the door that first time, when he left his apartment. When I escaped. He trusted me. Or he really was trying to make me trust him, make me believe he was undercover.

I climb the stairs. Red's apartment is three floors up, and with every step, I take a deep breath. I'm sweating so much, and my clothes are sticking to me. Lightheadedness pulls at me again—and this is silly! I shouldn't be dizzy from just going up the stairs. I shouldn't!

It's just nerves, I tell myself.

Once I get to the second floor, with only one more flight to go, I spot some Enhanced Ones. They open a door and step into the stairwell. As I approach, I give what I hope is a respectful smile and a nod. I hold my breath, part of me waiting for them to realize the deception. To realize what I am.

"Good day to you," one of them says. "I heard Malik's got some more Tranquility in today. Isn't that wonderful?"

"Very wonderful." My voice comes out thick, like wool.

They descend the stairs, and I keep going up, using the banister heavily until I reach Red's floor. A dull pain spreads around my chest as I leave the stairwell. Yes, this is the corridor. My legs ache and my arms. And yes, there's Red's apartment. Number 18.

I take a deep breath and knock. *Come on, Kace. Confidence.*

I hear footsteps. *I can do this. I will do this.*

I don't know whether it's because I know he's got the Beast too, that he's powerful, but I feel his Beast pushing toward mine as he opens the door. It's a tidal wave sweeping over me, energy released in a tsunami that floods the corridor. And the energy surges through me.

My feet are firmly planted, and I aim for his jaw, a swift uppercut. My punch lands, but it doesn't do the job. *Shit.*

He grabs me.

I pull back, and the Beast is shouting inside me, making my head so full and busy, and I don't know what to do.

"Oh, hello," he whispers, holding me close in an iron grip. He's strong. Too strong. It's his Beast.

He shoves me, and I crash onto the floor, the hard marble flooring. I twist, trying to reach for my gun, but my vision darkens, waves of even darker lines moving across, from my peripheral vision. I gasp, pain in my chest.

Red stares down at me—his face seems to loom, too big, too garish. Just like one of those nightmares I used to have of the Overlord Seer. I blink rapidly.

"What's wrong with you?" he snarls, and his power radiates over me.

Wrong with *me*? "Nothing!" I yell, and yes, maybe I'm being too noisy—maybe I'm going to attract the attention of his neighbors—but my Beast surges again, and this time, I don't fight the takeover at all. I welcome it.

I rise up, and power ripples through me. I am the power, and the power is me. My hand clenches into a fist, and I punch Red again. This time, it does the job. He lets out a startled noise, and then he falls backward, into his apartment. There's a loud bang as his head hits the floor.

The Beast in me smiles viciously, and I stare down at Red. Blood pools rapidly around him.

Blood. I jolt. And the Beast wants to hurt him again, but I fight to regain control.

I squash the Beast down, and I look at Red. Oh Gods. I can't have killed him. If he's dead, the time loop can't be destroyed.

I shut the apartment door quickly, pulling my radio out from my back pocket. The outer-casing is cracked from my fall, but I turn the dial and it works.

"Kacey, here. Winston, SJ, get up here now. Over."

Winston's reply is fuzzy, but I'm not really concentrating, because as I lean over Red, getting his blood all over me, I cannot find a pulse.

"HE'S ALIVE," WINSTON SAYS IN a low voice, his voice quick and urgent. His mirror eyes flash, and I remind myself they're just contacts. That's all. "But I don't know how long he'll stay unconscious for." He glances at SJ. "We need to get him out now. Tie him up now."

My hands are shaking. Hell, I'm shaking so much, I can't help as they tie him up and gag him. SJ pulls a large muslin bag over Red's face and then Duct-tapes it around his neck. Shweta watches on. The three of us are in Red's apartment, and I just watch.

"Not too tight," I say.

"I know what I'm doing."

Winston heaves Red over his shoulder, and Shweta radios through to Kazem, Sian, and Tammy, letting them know that we're about to leave.

"Be ready for our signal," she tells them, but I expect they already are. Then Shweta opens the door of Red's apartment and sticks her face out. "It's clear."

SJ goes first, and then Shweta. They each go different ways. The idea is that SJ will lead our team, and if he encounters any Enhanced, he'll redirect them. If he can't, he'll shoot, and then Shweta or I—hearing the gunshot—will alert our distraction team. But if all goes to plan, we should just be able to walk out. SJ first, then Winston carrying Red, and then me, with Shweta a few paces behind us. She'll be there to stall anyone else who might come along from the opposite direction. We don't want an Enhanced sneaking up behind us.

Every step is tense. I have one hand on my gun, the other on my radio. My mouth is too dry, and I'm struggling to swallow. But we make it outside with no trouble. We see no one. I breathe out a huge sigh of relief.

It's lighter now, morning rays creeping in. Some of the streetlights are flickering, others turning off. I gulp in the fresh air, tell myself it'll help me feel better. I just need air. That's all it is. It was too stuffy in the apartment block. Couldn't breathe. But out here I can.

We walk a longer way around the town now, sticking to the darker areas that are full of shadows. SJ's in the lead again, and I keep an eye on his figure, his signals to us that all is clear ahead, with every turn he makes.

Shweta walks behind us all, still. When we near the leisure center, I radio through for the others, and moments later, Tammy's here. Even with her contacts in, her eyes seem to sparkle.

"You did it then?" She grins.

"Yes," I say. "We did it."

We're abducting an Enhanced One.

"What bad luck would it be if everything were to reset right now?" Shweta mutters.

"Yep," I say, but I'm focused on Kazem. He's tying Red up more securely.

We're in the tunnels now, and Kazem and several

others are securing Red to manacles and chains—all things we'd brought from the Muskoxen group in here in case we ever had to rescue one of our own and make them run lean.

Red is still unconscious—something that is worrying Evor.

"I don't know what internal damage has been done," he says, getting out his pocket torch again. Once more, he directs someone to pull open Red's eyes—this time it's Sian who does it—and he shines the light into each. Not that he can see anything; the light just reflects off the mirrors and bounces back, making rays of light dance on the rough rock around us.

Evor continues examining Red, and Kate and Shweta help. Behind us, some of the others are standing with guns. Just in case the Enhanced man wakes up and somehow has superhuman strength and rips through the bindings.

Kazem finishes typing up Red and turns to me. He lets out a shaky breath, then his arms go around me. I hold onto him, breathing in his scent, his warmth, his reassurance.

"He could be out for quite a while," Evor finally says. "May as well do something else with your time now. He's secure now. There don't need to be six of us guarding him. Two will do. You lot should probably get something to eat."

Shweta nods, says how hungry she is, and then Kazem and I are also moving. But we don't go to the kitchen area. We find ourselves in our room, instead.

"You okay?" Kazem asks me.

I nod.

"Good." He pushes my hair back from my face, and then his hands touch my waist, lightly, in the way he knows I like.

I lean into the embrace, and we sink onto the bed, my head flopping over his shoulder. My arms are around him, and I hug him, cling to him. He rubs my back, his touch firm, certain, reassuring. I cling to him tighter.

"It'll be okay, you know." He breathes the words into my hair.

I straighten up a little, though still holding onto him, and lean back just enough so that I can see his face, so my eyes can focus on him. I stare at the hard lines of his countenance, feel myself getting a bit overwhelmed with how masculine and attractive he looks. I could stare at him all day.

"I know." I find his hands and squeeze them.

He brings his face closer to mine, and we kiss, lightly at first. Then harder, with more certainty. Kissing Kazem always makes me smile, makes me feel better. He grounds me, and I feel complete when I'm with him.

And then a crawling sensation tickles over the back of my neck, and I startle. I pull away from Kazem, and look around.

Ysabelle's daughter, Lani, is in the doorway. Her eyes are wide, almost haunted. She doesn't say anything, just watches me and Kazem, her bottom lip sticking slightly out.

Heat flushes through me. "You okay?" I ask.

"All right?" Kazem says. "Lani, isn't it?"

Her gaze is on me—directly on me—and I know she's seeing me, but she doesn't answer me, nor Kazem. Doesn't move. She's gripping something tightly in her hands—what looks like a scrap of fabric. I edge nearer and before I realize what I'm doing, I encourage my Beast forward, encourage him to sense out Lani's Beast. He obliges.

It's a strange thing, knowing there's another person with a Beast here. Because Lani's is different to Red's. Red's is all about power and magnificence and making sure that the viewer knows his is powerful. Lani's is quieter. I have to actively search for it, really listen hard, get in tune with it to know that it is there. But once I find it, it's like it unravels. More and more threads and spirals and dimensions, all of them revealing themselves to show the whole tapestry.

Lani's powerful, that's for sure.

"Well, uh, I'm supposed to go and check in with Maggot," Kazem says. "She wants to discuss strategy for after we've got this time loop sorted, whether a siege on the town is now out of the question." He stands and heads toward the door. Still, Lani doesn't move, so he edges around her. "See you later, Kace."

In a flash, he's gone, and the room gets colder under Lani's gaze.

Awkwardly, I head toward her. What am I supposed to do? I don't know how to interact with her. Well, with any children in general. I wasn't great with Clive—or aren't great, given he's alive again now—but with Lani, things feel even harder. More challenging, more difficult.

"You ever used your Beast?" My voice is thick. Maybe it's her age, why her Beast is so hidden away. Mine hid from me when I was a child. Hid from Ysabelle for a while, too.

Lani shakes her head. She doesn't speak. The corners of her mouth are turned down and she clenches her scrap of fabric so tightly her knuckles whiten, look like bright pearls.

"You don't need to be scared," I tell her, even though I don't know what her Beast will do. The first time I used my Beast—or rather, he used me—I caused the clansmen massacre. But telling the girl she doesn't need to be scared seems to be the right thing to do. And anyway, if her Beast does try and cause that, maybe I can stop it.

No. It wouldn't happen that way, anyway. I can't use what happened to me as a guide. I was under attack—literally—when the massacre happened. No one is going to attack Lani. And Ysabelle wouldn't let anyone hurt or attack Lani. She protected Iralda for all those years, after all.

"Ah, Kassandra. I see you've met Lani properly, then."

I look up to find Ysabelle heading toward us.

"She's a great conversationalist, as you can tell," Ysabelle says, and Lani looks at the floor, then adjusts the scrap of fabric in her hands. "She won't ever let go of that," Ysabelle tells me.

I feel the hairs on the back of my neck rising as I realize that no one else is in this section of the tunnels. It's just me, Lani, and Ysabelle. A woman who definitely hates me.

Ysabelle yawns. "The most Lani ever spoke to me was the day the Overlord and I took that away from her. And then it was a banshee shriek. Didn't stop for days. Just wasn't worth it. And we had to go and look for where we'd thrown it."

I don't know what to say to that, so I don't say anything. Conversing with Ysabelle feels like it's a challenge, a game I don't understand. Every time I look at her, I remember what she did to me. What she did to Jaqueline. What she did to all those with Beasts. And all along she was protecting Iralda. The hypocrite.

"So, are we going to talk about it?" There's a hard edge to Ysabelle's voice that reminds me of a segment of quartz the Overlord Seer would carry round. It had the sharpest edge and he'd cut anything with it that he needed to—vegetation, food, skin.

I look at Ysabelle properly now. She's dressed in her usual attire, but she has shoes on. Not handmade ones but proper ones. Khaki army boots. They look like Celena's. I wonder if Celena knows Ysabelle's got them.

"Talk about what?" Sweat beads across my upper back, and I take several deep breaths.

Ysabelle closes the distance between us, slowly, carefully, each movement precise and planned. Always a hunter. "We both know what." Before I can do anything, her hand snakes out. She grabs my left wrist, encasing it in her long, slender fingers. Her grasp is firm, unrelenting. "You're not forgiven, Kassandra. Did you really think you were? Did you think that I'd made peace with what you did to my people?"

My heart hammers. I lift my chin higher, even though I feel like I'm about to faint. "I wouldn't be so stupid as to think you'd forget."

"Good," she says. "Because, at the moment, I need your help with all this." She waves her other hand around vaguely. "I don't want Lani growing up in a time loop, and she needs you and another Beast to stop this. Which you will do." She's looking at me sharply so I nod. "But the moment we're back in the real time, it's *on*."

Just as I thought. I don't look away from her.

"On like it's never been on before." She picks up Lani and then turns away, just as footsteps echo in the tunnel nearby.

I sink down to the ground, feeling sicker and sicker. I knew that she was going to do this, come for me, later—I *knew* it because the way she looked at me before promised me that—but it doesn't make me feel any less panicky now.

I try to breathe slowly, try to calm myself, but then I hear footsteps. I force myself to stand up. She's coming back.

But it's not Ysabelle who appears. It's Clive. His face lights up when he sees me.

"It's Red," he says. "He's awake."

FORTY-EIGHT

WITHIN WHAT SEEMS LIKE SECONDS, I'm back in our newly-appointed prisoners' area of the tunnels. Red is sitting up on his own now, not trying to escape, but he looks pissed off. Not that I can blame him.

Shweta arrives a second later, along with Bhavesh, Winston, and Rohan. The four of them are armed, adding to the two armed guards already here.

"Is Ysabelle on her way with Lani?" Shweta asks me.

"I don't know."

"I'll go and get her now," Clive says, and I hadn't realized he'd followed me back here.

I focus on Red, the way he's scowling, and then suddenly Ysabelle and Lani are here. Did Clive go and get them that quickly? I blink and he's back here, too. Ysabelle walks right past me. She's holding her daughter, but she still manages somehow to shove her elbow into my side as she passes. I don't give her the satisfaction of a reaction.

Bhavesh looks down at Red. "You try anything but what these women say, then we will kill you in an instant."

Red looks up at her slowly. "Please. Just let me go."

His voice is strange, lighter than I'd expected it to be. "Return me to the—"

"*After*," Bhavesh says, and I shoot her a sharp look. *Are* we returning him? "But you've got to do this first."

"Do what?"

Bhavesh nods at me, so I approach our prisoner. It means I'm closer to Ysabelle, but I ignore her. She's still unarmed and there are a lot of people here who'd defend me if she tried anything. Right now, I just need to focus on Red.

I eye up his restraints and ropes, and then crouch three feet from him—a distance I'm confident he won't be able to get me at.

Red blinks hazily, and I feel his Beast awaken at the presence of mine. A slow grin lifts up his features. "Nice to see you again, Kacey."

So he does know me, still. "And you." I keep my voice steely. "We need to use your Beast."

His eyebrows shoot up. "I beg your pardon. You need to use my *what?*"

"The Beast. The energy inside you. The…" Damn, what did my aunt call it? And him too… "Riji-something."

A knowing look passes over his face—something I didn't think would be possible to recognize with nothing but the mirrors in his eyes. They have only faded a little. "And why would you need *my* energy?" He looks behind me. "There's two of you blessed with the gift."

"Cut to the chase," Ysabelle snaps, and then she's pushing past me, a blaze of auburn hair. Lani is no longer in her arms, and Ysabelle pokes Red squarely in the chest. "We need three Beasts. We're stuck in a time loop. Marta's Lore says three Beasts will have enough energy to override it."

He makes a clucking sound deep in his throat. "The question still stands as to *why* I would help you."

"Because," Ysabelle says, "you're stuck in the time loop, too—I don't know if you've noticed yet, or felt off. You've clearly not been aware of it all of the time. But the whole of your town is trapped in it, too. And when you're stuck in the time loop, the war won't end, and the Enhanced won't win. It'll just go on and on. More blood will be shed."

Red sits up a little straighter. I glance at Shweta. Her gaze is intent on Red. Nearby, Bhavesh shifts his weight from foot to foot.

"Your superiors will commend you for ensuring you win the war." Ysabelle nods eagerly. "Because you will. You help us, and you will win. You'll go down in history, Red."

Red frowns. "Why would *you* want me to help you, if it means you lose the war?" His tone is careful. "You're bluffing."

"I'm a fucking Seer," Ysabelle hisses. "And so is she." She jabs a finger back toward Shweta. "We've seen who wins. We all know who wins. There's a fucking augury about it."

I lean away a little, but her anger radiates out— so sudden, so strong. I know what happens when Ysabelle gets angry. And I know what my Beast does. He's quiet at the moment, but I need to be on guard.

"Yes." Red tilts his head to one side, slowly. "Seven Sarr, the Seventh One. But she is Untamed right this second. Whichever side she's on when the war ends will be victorious. We cannot win without converting her."

Shweta moves forward. She moves like liquid, so graceful, fluid. "We know where she is." Her voice is soft. "We will deliver you to her."

I glance at her. She's bluffing. Of course she is. They both are. If we want to use Red, we have to play this game.

"I don't believe you," Red says.

"We will *definitely* take you to the Seventh One," Ysabelle says. "Because there's a second augury. An augury that says no Untamed will survive the war in the mortal realm. It means *only* the Enhanced can win."

Red frowns a little. "A *second* augury? You're lying."

"It was given to my husband. A precious secondary augury. He worshipped his God and his God rewarded him. We know that no Untamed survive the war's end. We cannot win. We are all going to die. It has already been written that way. And only *we* know." She clears her throat, pointing among herself, Shweta, and me. "And I want to live, and I don't want to live in fear. I don't want this war to go on. So we are going to break the time loop. You're going to help us do that. And then we are going to take you to the Seventh One. We'll help you convert her, and then you'll convert us."

"You?" He laughs. "Do you really expect me to believe you're going to switch sides? After what you've just done to me?"

"We had to kidnap you," Ysabelle says simply, "because it's the only way we can stop the time loop. Are you not listening? We want the war to stop. There's no point in *all* of humanity dying. Someone needs to survive."

"You could've converted yourselves, and then come to me."

"We couldn't," I say. "Time loops can only be broken if the majority of those with Rijikarii are Untamed. Do you not know that? Did Caia-Lu not tell you?"

Ysabelle gives me a small smile.

Red presses his mouth into a thin line until his lips pale a few shades. I think he's making eye contact with Ysabelle, but it's hard to tell. Although his mirrors are fading, and I can just see the outlines around his pupils about irises, there's a murky quality there. Like he's still hidden, guarded.

"We haven't got much time," Ysabelle says. "This timeline is running out fast, and there's only a small window in which the time loop can be broken. We've got everyone together now. So, you'll help?"

"You bloody *will*," Bhavesh says, pointing the gun at Red. "Do this or you won't leave—at all."

Shweta sends a sharp look toward Bhavesh.

I give a dramatic sigh, looking at Red. "Just do it,

okay? We're working on the same side, but we've no qualms hurting you, too. And you don't want to suffer unnecessarily, do you?"

"Fine," Red says.

And, apparently, it's as easy as that. Winston and Rohan adjust Red's chains so his arms are freer. The others still point guns at Red, and then Shweta asks if I have a weapon.

"We don't want him getting hold of any," she adds, casting a look at Red, but I show her I am unarmed.

"Join hands," Ysabelle instructs, looking first at Red, then Lani, then me. "Marta's Lore says you need a physical connection as you call your Beasts up."

"Uh, shouldn't we wait for Maggot?" I ask, because surely our leader wants to be here for this?

"There's no time," Ysabelle snaps. "Now join hands."

"And then what?" I ask, moving into place. Lani takes my right hand. Her grip is limp. Nothing like her mother's. But her hand is still gentle, fragile, small. Something to be looked after, protected.

Just like all the children I've killed were beings I should've protected.

Ysabelle clears her throat. "I haven't got all day. Chop chop."

I don't want to touch Red, and he looks like he doesn't want to touch me. I have to steel myself to put my hand in his. But the moment the three of us are touching, I feel something. I feel energy. Energy billowing within all of us. And my skin. I'm glowing— I'm glowing so suddenly. A crimson glow, and the glow is brighter, stronger and—

They're glowing too.

Our glows light up everything. The whole tunnel's filled with crimson.

"Oh Gods," Bhavesh says.

Red does a double-take, blinking widely. Lani's got her eyes closed now, and she's breathing deeply. The scrap of fabric is draped over her lap. Maybe it's a security blanket or something.

"Then you all ask the Beasts to break the time loop," Ysabelle instructs.

"Just like that," I mutter. Like, how do we even accomplish that?

"*Just like that*," Ysabelle repeats, but her voice booms. "The Lore says that a time loop has a big energy field, and energies are attracted to others of roughly equal sizes. When three Beasts come together, they should have the same energy mass. Unless the time loop's energy field has grown as it's extended. But your Beasts should gravitate toward it."

"And how do we destroy it?"

Ysabelle laughs. "You don't even need to *ask* that. Destroying things is what the Beasts do best."

That appears to be all the guidance we're going to get, because Ysabelle goes quiet.

"It'll be okay," Shweta says, placing a hand on my shoulder. She gives me a quick squeeze. "You can do this. I know you can."

I take a deep breath. My gaze connects with Red's. He nods. I look at Lani. Her eyes are still shut. Her lips are moving slightly, quivering. I squeeze her hand and—

We release the Beasts. It happens, just like that.

Lightness and energy soar through me, up my torso, to my head. Lightness and dizziness, and I look up as my mouth is forced open, and I expel light. White light that *explodes*—blinding, burning, searing.

Smoke, everywhere. Skin frying, singing—the pungent smell of it fills my nostrils, fills everything. I hear Shweta and Bhavesh shouting, but I can't see them. The air is too thick and white. The smoke and the light.

And in the smoke and the light, there's a shape, a…

A silhouetted woman lifts her arms above her head, her face upturned.

A spirit hovers above her.

The spirit is speaking in the eerie way that spirits speak: And you also want me to trap Kassandra Kachler?

"I want her never to realize," *the woman shouts.* "I want no one to realize!"

Seers may see through it, *the spirit says.* Especially any who are in the area or close to Kassandra.

"I don't care," *the woman says.* "Shweta Basu is crazy anyway. No one will believe her."

Things may not work exactly as you wish, *the spirit warns.* And others may start to realize too, as the trap goes on. Non-Seers, those who are metaphysically linked to Kassandra. It could prove a problem.

"I don't care! So long as she is trapped and I get what I want—that's the important thing."

I can do that, *the spirit says.* But it will require regular further exchanges from you. You are asking a lot from me.

"I'm giving you a lot for it!" *The woman speaks quickly.*

The spirit appears to smile. And how difficult do you want it to be to break our work?

"Very difficult," *the woman says.* "I want breaking it to kill others. If there's one thing I now know about Kassandra Kachler, it's that she'll do anything *to avoid killing others."*

Very well, *the spirit says.* From the powers bestowed in me, I have called upon the timestreams, taking the energy freely given forth by this woman, and I have trapped Kassandra Kachler.

I jolt as the vision is snatched from me. Not a vision. The past. Was that how the time loop was created? Who was the woman? But I couldn't see well enough.

Couldn't—

Something snaps around me.

Thwack. My head.

I scream, see darkness around me. Rushing sounds in my ears, and something wet sliding, slipping over me.

And I feel it, I feel the last of the time loop energy expanding, flying out—but this is different, I am this energy too. The Beasts are the energy. We are all this energy, and we are searching. We are hungry.

We *want* to kill.

No!

And there he is—

"No!" I scream, out loud this time.

Red screams.

Lani screams.

We all scream, and we all know.

We jolt, the Beasts slinking back inside us and—

"Oh Gods," Shweta murmurs. "You did it, you've broken the time loop. You've—"

She sees the body at the same moment I do.

Clive lies broken on the ground, his head bent back at an angle that can only mean one thing.

I CANNOT MOVE. I PHYSICALLY cannot move. All I can do is stare at Clive. His body. Dead. Because of us. Because of me. My Beast. Another child, dead, killed, murdered.

Winston screams and shouts, and he's pulling Clive toward him. He's shaking him, screaming at him. Footsteps, more of them. Evor and Kate. More shrieking.

"What the hell happened?" Kate turns on me, eyes suddenly bloodshot and bulging.

I recoil. My foot catches on something, and I half-fall against the wall, grazing my arm. Her eyes are still on me, eyeballs too big, and she's shouting that same question over and over.

I can't answer her.

Bile rises in my throat, and I clap a hand to my mouth, trying to swallow it down. I don't succeed, just end up spluttering and choking, eyes watering. Pain lassoes my chest.

They're carrying his body away. Clive's body. Taking him away. Removing him.

He's gone…

Another child. Another child dead because of me. No!

I want to run after him. He can't be dead. They're going to save him. That's what they're going to do. They have to.

But I don't move.

"Come on, then," Red says, directing my attention to him. His breaths comes fast and heavy. He looks a mess. Sweat's stained rivulets down his face, and his short hair's sticking up at ridiculous angles. "Unchain me. Let's go to the Seventh One."

Ysabelle laughs—a rough, coarse sound. She hasn't moved, yet it's like she suddenly appears again, growing out of the wall, just springing up. Her red hair is a halo of fire. Her eyes hold a wicked light. "Oh, poor baby, you're so gullible."

"None of that was true?" Red stands—the chains are just long enough to allow him to, though they clang terribly.

Ysabelle flicks something off her thigh, then brushes her clothes down. "Bits and pieces." Her tone is bored—she's bored?

Bored? She didn't even look at Clive or react to Kate's screams.

Red screams at Ysabelle, suddenly, and he's trying to get to her. Some of our group step in, to protect her, but he can't get to her anyway.

My eyes glaze over. "Clive's *dead*." It's all I can say, as I stare up at them, them both standing. That's when I realize I've completely collapsed on the stone floor. I feel like I am disintegrating.

"Let's just calm down." Shweta's voice echoes from somewhere behind me. She's here too…she hasn't left me. "Uh, Kacey, I think you need to get some air."

Some air. Yes. Air. That sounds like a good idea.

I choke, and then Shweta's by my side. She helps me stand, and she leads me past Ysabelle who's now laughing at Red. His voice is getting more and more high-pitched, until it doesn't even sound like him as he screams at her. I glance back at them, just as I'm in the doorway, and Ysabelle meets my gaze.

It's on, she mouths the reminder. She laughs loudly—almost theatrically—and then she leaves, pushing in front of me and Shweta. Her walk is over-exaggerated, swaying her hips. Bhavesh is here—I don't know if he was here the whole time or if he left and came back—but I notice the way his gaze lingers on Ysabelle as she exits. Because she's powerful and still so beautiful, and I suddenly realize that's clearly the most dangerous combination of them all. Ysabelle always makes sure everyone notices her and she makes sure everyone continues thinking about her long after she's out of sight. She's always been like that.

"Come on," Shweta says, a hand on my back guiding me.

"What about Lani?" I whisper, because the girl's still back there. Ysabelle just left her.

"They'll look after her," Shweta says.

But I can't tell who she's referring to. I screw my eyes tightly shut for a moment, then allow Shweta to take me away.

The screams haunt me as we walk, and I can't tell if it's my mind echoing Winston's and Kate's cries, or if more people are shrieking now as well. But I hear his name: Clive's. Over and over again. And the worst part is I can still feel the echo of my Beast's joy, feel how he wanted to kill. But the Beast is me.

I'm the Beast.

I choke, again. Wracking coughs and gulps. Eyes watering. Lungs burning. Snatches of faces in my vision. Faces looming around me, narrowed eyes, accusatory whispers.

She did this.

It's her.

She's bad.

Kill her.

Shweta is pulling me faster and faster through the tunnels—we never stop moving. She's whisking me past Untamed face after Untamed face. But then she stops. I crash into her. She lets out a strangled cry, her eyes focused on something ahead.

I look ahead.

And I see…see *her*, ahead.

Another body.

My heart drops. My mouth dries.

No.

I see the tattoos on her creamy arms, the curves of her body, the shirt, the cropped hair.

No.

No.

No!

I try to move, try to turn, try to do anything that means I'm not looking at her. But my body is stone. I didn't just kill Clive.

I killed Maggot as well.

FIFTY

"WHO THE FUCK DID THIS?" Ada yells, and so many of our group are here now, swarming. Shweta's cry must've alerted them.

Shweta is still stock-still. So am I. My lungs are burning, trying to get air, but I can't breathe. My throat tightens, my chest squeezes. Saliva pools in my mouth, under my tongue.

Maggot is dead.

Someone shouts Maggot's name—I can't tell who—then I hear snatched words.

"It's just like Clive".

"The three of them did that. Killed them both."

"Kacey, come on." Shweta—again. She's pulling me back. And—and Kazem's here.

He grabs my hand. "I know you didn't do this, but we have got to go now."

"You *know*?" I stare at him, feel something twisting inside me. He thinks I didn't… but I did. My Beast did.

He nods. "Come on."

Shweta and Kazem pull me along, forcing me to run.

"Don't let her go," someone shouts.

But we get out. We get out so quickly, and we're

moving fast, through light rain—the kind that clings to you, dotting your hair with an almost-sparkly confetti—and my head is pounding and none of this makes any sense.

"You didn't kill Maggot," Kazem says, his voice low, labored. He's panting hard. He's still pulling me along. They both are. "Someone else did. When you were breaking the time loop."

"But... Clive..." I hear my breaths in my ears, too loud, and I nearly trip on an uneven bit of ground, but they both stop me falling. "I killed him," I say, because I did.

There are shouts behind us, and I try to turn my head, but Kazem barks, "No!" at me. "Just run."

I run and run, and I don't think I can run any faster. "Are they going to shoot at us?" I pant.

"I've got a gun," Kazem says.

"And me," Shweta adds. "We're not unarmed."

The rain gets heavier, and my muscles feel too tight, like they're locking up. I look down at my legs, at how they're moving, how I'm running, even though I don't think I can move. But it's like it's not my body, and this body just runs. This body wants to get me as far away as possible. Maybe it's the Beast doing it.

"That way," Shweta says, and she's pulling me to the right. I blink, trying to see where we're going, but the air's all hazy. The sky's white with clouds, and the clouds have fallen down onto us, too.

Kazem slips a bit, nearly falls, but somehow doesn't. Ghostly outlines of trees hover on the edge of my vision, and we splash through some lying water.

"I think we've lost them," he says, sometime later.

I don't know how long we've been running. I think I zoned out. But we're slowing to a brisk, fast walk. Everything in my body pounds.

"Are you okay?" Kazem asks me.

I nod, and he asks Shweta if she is, too.

My teeth begin to chatter. My lips feel numb. "Maggot's dead." I don't know why I say it, so loudly.

Maybe I'm wanting them to argue, contradict me. But they don't.

"It wasn't you, though," Kazem says.

I shake my head. "My Beast—it was me!"

"Look, I don't know about Clive," he says. "But Evor already found Maggot's body. It was knife wounds. In her back. She was probably killed somewhere else, he thinks. When you and Lani and Red were breaking the time loop. And then she was moved here. The wounds were hidden the way she'd been laid out."

I step over some scratchy vegetation but I misjudge my step, and thorns drag across my ankle. I wince. Maggot was murdered—by someone else? The wind picks up around us.

"Who did it?" Shweta asks. She lets go of my hand then presses both of her hands to her chest. She gulps.

"We don't know," Kazem says. "Evor was trying to find out but then we heard about Clive. We realized they were going to see this as the same thing. Blame you." His eyes are dark, but he squeezes my hand. "It's okay though. We've got your back."

"Yeah, we have," Shweta says. "Although whoever the murderer is, they must've known breaking the time loop would cost someone their life. It's the perfect cover up."

"It's a woman," I say. And I try to remember her words, and I try to tell them. But what was it that the Beast showed me? The spirit saying that breaking the time loop would kill people?

Oh Gods. And it was Clive. Only Clive, or are there others dead too whom we've not discovered? Because I feel sick at the idea of someone choosing to kill Clive, a child, picking him out of everyone.

"But you don't know who this woman is?" Shweta asks me.

I shake my head. Exhaustion pulls through me. "I couldn't see her clearly enough. She was silhouetted. Where are we going?"

"Evor told us to get far away, today. We'll double

back tomorrow and meet him at Crier's Rock."

Tomorrow. Tomorrow seems like so far away. My vision blurs, and my head pounds.

"Wait, who's that?" Kazem halts, stepping in front of me, and I nearly crash into him.

I peer through the rain and the fog. A flash of gold.

"Shit, it's a spirit," Shweta says. "Is it the Turning?"

But I'm squinting, frowning, trying not to look at the spirit—but there is another shape too. "There's someone up there, too."

"I think it's Celena," Kazem says.

"Oh," I say. "She's doing that again." I frown. "Or still." My headache gets sharper.

"What?" Shweta shoots me a sharp look.

I explain about before, in the last loop, when Celena appeared to be trying to get a spirit to sleep with her. "I think it's the same spirit, too."

Kazem frowns. "We need to help her. It's not safe for her. She must be under some kind of delusion from them. Can they do that, cast spells on people?" He looks at Shweta.

Shweta purses her lips for a moment. "Spirits can do all sorts, if it's part of a deal." She glances at me. "He's right. We have to help. What's the best way?"

Kazem shrugs and produces his gun. "Shoot it?"

"No," Shweta says. "That would anger it. It might attack us." She holds a hand up to her eyes, trying to shield them from more rain. "How long has she been out here? Shit—she won't know about Maggot."

I react like I've been punched. I don't know why, why I feel it like a sharp pain in my gut. But Shweta is right: Maggot's dead, and Celena doesn't know. My heart squeezes. As much as I don't like Celena, I wouldn't wish this on anyone.

"Let's just see if we can pull her away from the spirit," Kazem says. "Remember not to look directly at it."

As if we need reminding. Huh.

I feel weird as we rush toward Celena and the spirit, like I'm both overthinking this too much and not taking the situation seriously. Like this is all happening around me, and I'm not really involved.

Shweta and Kazem talk in low voices. Shweta says she and I should try and scare off the spirit while Kazem pulls Celena away.

"Wrap your arms right around her," she tells him.

Kazem nods.

We get closer and closer. There are ethereal tendrils linking Celena to the spirit, but she's not unconscious. She's sitting up, her blond hair a mess around her shoulders. Her chest is rising and falling with loud sobs, and there's anger in her eyes.

"You have to do it this time," Celena is saying, looking directly at the spirit. It's hovering a few feet from her, still connected with her. It doesn't look at us either. I don't even know if it's aware we're here. Or if Celena is.

We're ten feet away, eight, six…

"Uh, Celena," Kazem says, waving a hand, but Celena's still crying at the spirit.

We're right in front of her, now, and I force myself to look at her and not the spirit, even though it's tempting to just glance that way. But I can't.

Celena's eyes are glassy, and the strap of her Cami top has fallen right down her arm, exposing her left breast completely. Her skin is flushed, and she's growling at the spirit.

"I gave you exactly what you wanted before, and you didn't—"

No, you didn't feed me enough. The spirit's voice sends shivers through me. *I set the trap for you, but if you truly wanted a baby as well, you should've given me extra.*

"I fed you all I could!" she yells.

And it was enough for the time trap. But you were greedy, wanting two things, and yet you only gave me one.

My breaths make a raspy sound in my throat. *The time trap.* My mouth is too dry. Celena? I stare at her, then look at Kazem and Shweta. They have both frozen. But it *was* Celena. Celena did this. To hurt me.

And she's pretended, this whole time, to be oblivious to the loops.

"You agreed to the deal! And I gave you *my body*! Is that not enough?" Celena cries. Her words echo through the air, sailing on the light breeze. "I even killed my own mother for you!"

I flush hot, then cold. Celena killed Maggot, her own mother. I feel sick.

I never asked you to do that! The spirit moves suddenly, and I freeze.

"You wanted more energy," Celena cries. "Energy like mine. That's what you said! I did that for you! Now give me my baby!"

I open my mouth. I don't know what I'm about to say, but Shweta grabs my arm and shakes her head. Kazem gestures for us to crouch down with him, so we're in the grass. And why the hell are we hiding? We're right by them, and we know it's her!

I glare across at Shweta—I'm not really meaning to glare at her, but I can't help it, can't stop it. "We need to confront her," I hiss.

The wind picks up, and Celena's still shouting at the spirit.

"Quiet," Shweta hisses at me. She's still trying to watch the interaction.

Kazem shakes his head at me a fraction, eyes wide. A warning. He grabs my hand and then tugs me backward, farther away from Celena. Shweta moves with us, too, until we're several feet away, in the wet grass.

"Just stop it!" Celena screams, and her voice seems to break with the emotion. I look up and her face is so red, so angry, and her tears so heavy. "Stop it, all right! Give me a baby *please*. You owe me a baby!"

I owe you nothing. You were asking for too much, thinking a baby would be part of it as well.

"I'll feed you now," she says. "I'll do whatever you want." She starts to lift the hem of her top up. "Come on, take what you want!"

That's when Celena turns and I see the change in

her eyes. She looks down, and she sees us. Her eyes widen, and she inhales. Her gaze settles on me.

The spirit flickers, then it shoots into the sky. The movement makes me blink, jump back. I feel slightly jarred.

"No, come back!" Celena yells, looking at the sky.

It doesn't.

"Celena," Kazem says, rising slowly. His voice is low, cautious, careful. "What the hell have you done?"

I stand up. My back creaks. "You killed your own mother."

Celena's face pinches in and she's putting her top right, covering herself. "No…" she says. "That wasn't me."

"You just admitted it!" I cry, flinging my arms out. There's so much pent-up energy inside me that wants out. "You killed Maggot."

Celena shakes her head vigorously. "That wasn't me!"

I stare at her. I can't believe her. "Are you seriously denying this? You actually have the audacity to deny it?" I feel sick as I stare at her, and I'm sure the churning contents of my stomach are going to make an appearance.

"We know you set the time loop." Somehow, Shweta's voice is calm, controlled, measured. She's the picture of calm in fact, standing there so stoically. "There's no denying that."

Celena takes a step back, and she looks so small now. Small and defeated. "I'm sorry. I… I'm not a bad person. I just wanted a baby badly, and for my mum to notice me and—"

"But what have you been giving to that spirit?" Shweta asks. "This is important, Celena. You need to answer honestly. Tell me everything, because deals with spirits, they're unpredictable. They affect more than you think, more than you expect."

Celena looks at her feet. "Just sex." She runs a hand through her hair, then pulls out several fine strands. They drift to the ground. "Just sex for the baby and to…to get rid of you. And… and some knowledge." Her face reddens.

"Knowledge?" Shweta asks, just as Kazem says, "What?"

"He wanted to know our plans—the siege at New Zeralzi. I told him. He said he wouldn't tell the Enhanced, but I think he did. I've been in this time loop, too. I know what happens." She shakes her head. "I don't know why he'd tell them though. He's on our side."

"Uh, he's a fucking spirit," I say. "You can't trust them! Gods, he could've made deal with the Enhanced, too. Or even just wanted entertainment, seeing us all fail—and it happening over and over in the loop." I run a hand through my hair and turn to Kazem. "We should just kill her."

Then I freeze as I realize what I've said. How easily I've said it.

No. The Beast kills people. Not me.

"The council will deal with her," Shweta says. "But until we see Evor, tomorrow, she stays with us."

Tomorrow. Tomorrow seems so far away—almost far enough, that it'll never come.

The moment I've thought that, the Beast stirs. He rises in me, and he's different.

Because you're going to die before tomorrow, he says.

I squash him down.

"You got any weapons on you?" Kazem asks Celena. She shakes her head.

"Really, you came out here with nothing?" I ask.

"I didn't think I'd need anything." Her voice is sulky. "But why are you out here?"

"You're not in any position to ask questions," I mutter. "Just be quiet, do as we say, and be glad we're letting you live."

FIFTY-ONE

WE WALK UNTIL I CANNOT walk anymore. The rain has stopped, but the ground's sopping. We're near an outcrop of rocks, and there's a small cave in there. Not really enough for the four of us to shelter in, but we squeeze in, shoulder to shoulder.

We lapse into silence, and I find myself watching insects flitting about in the damp air. Every now and again, one gets too close to me, and I try to bat it away. But even doing that—the movement—hurts my shoulder, sends pain through my back.

I want to lie down. I need to. Celena also looks like she needs to. Her face is terrible. Did she feed that spirit today, too? But there is no space in this cave for anyone to lie down, not unless the others are kicked out.

"So we just wait until tomorrow?" I ask. I rest my head on Kazem's shoulder.

He nods. "Evor will sort things. We have to trust him."

"What things?" Celena asks, but we don't answer her.

I just stare straight ahead. The day is still hazy, but I reckon night might be falling soon. My stomach gurgles a bit, aching.

"*Shit*," Shweta suddenly says. "People."

I jolt, and so does Kazem. "What? You can see them?" My breathing is off, and pain jabs at my ribs as I try to see. There's just the haze, and I can't see anyone, but I trust Shweta. "Are they coming after me?"

Of course they're coming after me. I click my fingers. Kazem and Shweta both pull out their guns.

"We'll protect you," Kazem says.

"What is going on?" Celena asks.

"Shut up," Shweta tells her. Then, "We should all lie down in the grass."

She pulls me down flat, onto my front. Dampness spreads across my stomach, my legs, seeping through the fabric of my clothes.

I lift my head slightly to get a better look. Two figures emerge from the fog. An adult and a child. Ysabelle and Lani.

My breaths chill me even more. I feel Kazem's hand lightly on the small of my back.

Ysabelle and Lani are closer than I expected, but they're heading at an angle that's slightly to our right. Following one of the deer-paths through the grasslands? I crane my neck and then see that Ysabelle and Lani have both stopped. They're bending down, dragging something out from under foliage. Something large and bulky, with flies buzzing thickly around them.

"Oh Gods." My stomach roils, and Celena makes a startled noise. "That's a body."

Shweta pales and claps a hand to her mouth.

Another body. Another dead person. Oh Gods. And somehow I smell the body. The stench of death carries on the wind toward us, over us, around us.

Then Ysabelle and Lani lift their arms toward the sky. Ysabelle's are long and slender, and they almost seem to elongate as we watch. Just as I'm about to think this is some kind of weird yoga pose, the sky darkens and there's movement. Something deep purple and orange.

"Shit, the Turning." My heart pounds. "We need

to get back in the cave." We need cover. You can't be outside during the Turning. The spirits will kill you. Tear you apart—like Ysabelle's baby.

"No." Shweta's voice is low. "It's just *one* spirit."

"My spirit!" Celena whispers, and then she's trying to get up. Kazem slams her back down, and then Shweta's crawling to Celena, holding her down, too.

Just one spirit? But it is, and I see the spirit, and I blink fast, knowing it's not safe to look at a spirit for long, as if my blinking will somehow prevent the direct eye contact that is dangerous, if not deadly.

But the spirit isn't looking at me. It's changing its form, getting more silvery and long, like a snake. *No, don't look!*

But I find myself mesmerized. The spirit is a snake with invisible wings, directly above Ysabelle and Lani and—

Ah, how I have missed you, the spirit croons. And then it's saying more to Ysabelle and Lani, but I can't make out the words. All I can do is soak in the melting tone of its voice, feel it wrapping around me.

"Shit," Shweta says. "Shit, shit, shit."

"What?" I look at her.

She's still holding Celena down, but her eyes are focused on Ysabelle and Lani and the spirit. "She's bringing him back to life. I don't understand—this doesn't make sense. The spirit shouldn't have that much power, but maybe it's the time loop. If the man died in the time loop—that *is* the Overlord that Ysabelle kept talking about, yes?"

I squint, trying to get a good look at the body. The Overlord Seer always wore a mask—yet I can see this man's face. White, pasty skin. A face that's bloated. Skin that's almost iridescence as it stretches over his stomach—wait, he's... *naked.*

I blink, feel heat rushing to my face. I look back at Shweta.

"Well, is it him?" She looks at me expectantly.

"It could be." I make a considering noise—mainly

to try and trick myself. Make myself believe my uncertainty. Even though I know the man down there is the Overlord Seer. Of course it's *him*. I feel it. But I don't want to say those words, don't want to acknowledge that certainty. I need time to process this. Hell, I need time to process *everything*. Too many things are happening around me, to me.

Shweta makes a growling sound, deep in her throat. "Yes." She sucks in air so quickly there's a slight whistling sound. "You know, I didn't get it." She casts her eyes over at Ysabelle.

"Didn't get what?"

"Why she didn't want another reset of the time loop before ending it. I thought she'd want to make sure her husband would be here." Shweta grimaces. "But she already had this plan. She must've given the spirit a hell of a something for the spirit to *give* life in return." She glances at Celena. "Just feeding isn't enough." She breathes hard. "We need to find out what that was."

"We do?" My voice wobbles, and then—oh Gods.

The body of the Overlord Seer moves. Just an arm at first, twitching, then a leg. Then a tremor wracks through his whole body—and I feel it, somehow I feel life flooding inside him, even with the distance between us, and I don't know how I can feel it. Because it's me feeling it, not the Beast.

The Beast who's quiet. So quiet.

I dig inside myself, searching. He's not there.

What?

"This could affect all of us," Shweta says in an urgent and low tone. "Not just us, but *everyone*. I can't even think what Ysabelle must have promised or given a spirit to do this work. This is beyond everything—this changes everything. Don't you see?" She's speaking so fast her words seem to take flight around us.

But I don't see—not in the way she wants me to.

But I see something else. Something that does change everything.

People don't need to stay dead.

The corners of my lips twitch. There's warmth inside me, growing from my core. The spirits can bring people back. Clive and Maggot, they don't need to stay dead.

"What do we do?" Kazem asks.

"We need to warn Evor," Shweta says.

"We're seeing Evor tomorrow," I say.

Shweta shakes her head. "Tomorrow might be too late."

Tomorrow, you're going to die.

I swallow hard. Our groups wants me dead. I can't just go back. "Shouldn't we keep a watch on them?" I flick a hand toward Ysabelle and Lani and the Overlord Seer. "We need to know what they're—"

A deep rumbling laughter cuts me off just as a shadow falls in front of me.

I twist my head to find Ysabelle, Lani, and the Overlord Seer right in front of me. How the hell have they moved so quickly? But I can't think. All I can do is stare.

The Overlord Seer looks older—that's the first thing I think. The second is how naked he is, because he *is*. He wears absolutely nothing, but there's not a single hair on his body either. No red cloud of hair, no bristly auburn beard that would poke out from under a mask if he wore one. No…nothing. It's like he's been *plucked*.

His stomach is bulging, so round, and his skin has an iridescent quality, accentuated somehow by the evening light, exaggerated, and it's like his skin's stretched so thin, almost to breaking point, swollen around the contents of his belly.

"Do not look at me," the Overlord Seer says. He sounds the same. Voice a deep rumble of thunder. I recoil—it's instinct—backing against Shweta. "Do not *ever* look upon me."

"Then don't stand over me," I hiss.

"Uh, what do we do?" Kazem asks me.

I can hear Celena's sobs, and Shweta's saying something to her, trying to calm her.

Ysabelle barks out a snide laugh. I glance across at her, but then my gaze goes back to the Overlord Seer. He's here…he's actually here. Alive, again.

"No!" he screams. "You are not worthy to look upon my face." He lifts his hands, shielding the one part of him that he claimed lore said was to be hidden at all times. But he's the only Seer I know who follows that rule, just as he appears to be the only Seer who refers to themselves as an *Overlord* Seer. I think he made it up.

The spirit's behind him—suddenly, I see it again, noticing the way it shimmers in the air, fogging the surroundings—and then it rises above the Overlord Seer. It's still in a semi-humanoid form—a long, elongated body, four limbs that are growing thinner and look sticky—and a protruding head on a long, long neck.

I clock its eyes on me, feel its gaze penetrate my skull.

Shivers run down my spine, and I stare back at the spirit—doing the one thing we're all warned never to do. But I can't look away. There's something familiar about the spirit. Something I don't understand about… *Her*.

This spirit is *female*. I feel that so suddenly, so powerfully.

I inhale sharply.

Iralda's eyes stare back at me from the spirit's head. My head pounds. I don't understand. Iralda's dead.

Yet even as I look at the spirit, the snake-like mass, it changes. She changes. Looks a little more human. Wispy strands wind together to create mass and solidness. Building the image, bit by bit. Until it really is Iralda glaring at me.

It really is you, she says, her voice like a black hole. *I'm glad we found you.*

She does not sound *glad* in a good way. She says it in a way that says she wants to kill me.

Ysabelle laughs. It is a ground-shaking bark that shudders through me. "Finally, the time has finally come."

Kazem tries to pull me backward, away from them. Because this is bad, very bad, we can all feel it. The air is alive with badness.

"I don't think so," Ysabelle says. "You're staying here. All of you."

"Yes," the Overlord Seer says. "The transaction is not complete."

"Transaction?" I say, just as Shweta swears loudly—the worst word I've ever heard come from her mouth. She looks at me, and I see the fear in her eyes.

Then I get it. The spirit is still here. The spirit who is still looking right at me. The *transaction*.

"*Run!*" Shweta and I scream, and then I'm pulling Kazem up as I jump to my feet. I see a flash of Celena's hair as she stumbles, but she's up too, and then we're grappling at each other's arms, trying to move.

Our feet pound the ground. My head's hazy, heavy, thick, and I'm going as fast as I can. Kazem's grip on my wrist burns, and I turn my head to him just in time to see him lift the gun up, pointing it back behind us.

Gunshots sound, like holes in the world. I hear shouts, but not screams. I twist my head, trying to see if he hit any of them, but my vision's just all streaks of color.

My foot catches something. I stumble, start to fall. Someone saves me. Kazem? I don't know.

Celena screams, and I turn to her, and—

Something hits my back, right between my shoulder blades. I scream as I fall, hit the ground hard. Knees crack. I turn, roll, taste blood at the back of my mouth as I look at the sky and the spirit. Iralda. She is right above me.

Ysabelle and the Overlord Seer are shouting, their voices fogging me, but I can't work out their words. All I can do is stare at the spirit.

"Kacey!" Kazem screams. But I can't look away from Iralda.

The spirit's arms are getting longer and longer, thinner, and thinner, stretching until they're barely anything more than stringy sinewy tendrils. Stringy sinewy tendrils reaching right for me.

No!

Energy surges through me, and, somehow, I stand again, lunge to my right. I crash into someone and try to shove them away, then realize it's Shweta and—

We're not quick enough, with moving—if that's what we were going to do. Iralda's *tentacles* wrap around me and Shweta, forcing us together, bindings tightening, tightening, tightening. I catch sight of Kazem with the gun, trying to line it up, but then Ysabelle has a gun too, and she's pointing it at him.

"Kazem!" I yell. "Watch out—"

My words disintegrate into a gut-wrenching scream as my ribs are crushed. The tendrils get tighter and tighter around my torso, digging in. My hands pull at them, and I try to get my fingers under the tentacles, try to pry them off. But I can't—they're too tight. Digging in so sharply. Air is forced out of my lungs. I try to turn, but end up with Shweta's bony hip jabbing into my side.

"Stop it, please, just... stop," Shweta is begging. "Please."

But Iralda doesn't stop, and the light's fading rapidly around us. I try to inhale, need air, oxygen, but my lungs... I can't move them... too tight... need to fight... need to...

Beast!

And I can feel him now. He is still here, but I feel his exhaustion, feel how he's weighed down, worn out by everything.

I can't do a thing but look up into the faces of the clansmen. The Overlord Seer who's laughing, his garish smile visible in streaks through swollen fingers. Ysabelle whose eyes are ablaze. Lani who's standing behind her mother, her dark eyes boring straight into me. And Iralda—Iralda whose face is three feet above me, while her tentacle-arms are squeezing the life out of me.

For the second time, the clansmen are sentencing me

to death.
    And this time, they're going to win.
    This is their revenge.

FIFTY-TWO

I RUN AS FAST AS I can.

Can't breathe.

Head hurts.

Panting.

Running lean. Pain and—

Augmenters. I need augmenters. Need to stop this, stop all the bad stuff.

Feet slap ground. Just more darkness, walls. My arm hits something, instant bruising pain.

Where's the way out?

Voices, loud, angry, abrasive like they're cutting my skin, fly at me.

"Get back!"

"He's out!"

"Stop him!"

"Grab him!"

Hands try to reach for me, stop me, but I am fueled by desperation. I need to get back. Need to—

No, you should be trying to convert these poor Untamed too, *a voice says.* These poor, misguided people.

And I'm not. I'm not trying to do that.

The instinct for self-preservation is just too strong.

So I run, running faster and faster.

I cannot smell her. Kacey. I cannot smell her at all. She's not here? But I don't know why that's important, why I'm noticing. It doesn't matter!

I scream and then, then I see light ahead—bright light. Daylight.

I run for it, drop down to my hands and knees to crawl, and then have to slither on my belly to get out of the last bit. But I make it.

Out in the open, I gulp air, but it doesn't stop the pain.

The moon grins a ghostly, vague smile above me, hazy amid the blue sky.

The moon.

The power in me rises, takes over, steers me—and it's drinking it up, drinking the moon. Shudders run through me, delicious shudders, and the power grows. My pain ebbs away, not fully, just a little. And it's doing it, it's doing exactly what I heard Caia-Lu promise to Kacey that it would—that promise, so long ago. Lunar energy regenerates our powers.

So I let it fill me, and I am running, and I am moving so fast. Faster than I ever thought I could move. Faster even than the augmenters could let me.

I am moving still, moving toward the outline of New Zeralzi. I am near the town—so soon!

The buildings seem to have lives of their own, energies, they're coming to me.

And I know it's going to be okay now.

I can hear the augmenters calling to me. And—

The air shimmers. There's, there's a woman. A gray haired, rounded woman, old. Long hair tied back in a swishing ponytail.

"That way," she shouts, and she shimmers. She's not here. She can't be. "Kacey's that way. She needs your help!"

Kacey. I freeze.

Cara-Lu. The woman. That's her... that's...

But then the woman disappears, and I know I'm hallucinating. That's how much I'm running lean.

New Zeralzi. Augmenters. Yes. That's what I've got to

focus on.

I still can't breathe, and it's too warm, in here, too much darkness, and Red! Red running… He's got out the tunnels… but he's… he's going to help me, isn't he? But as I think, the vision is slipping. The ending whipped away from me, and I can't recall it, and—and the moon!

The moon!

I need the moon, the energy. The energy can help me, will help me… lunar energy regenerates power…I need to do that. I need to do it until Red gets here.

But there's no moon, here… It's not dark enough to see it. And there's only heavy cloud, obscuring… no nothing, and—

"Ease off a little." The Overlord Seer's voice breaks through my haze. "We need her conscious if she's going to suffer."

Dimly, I'm aware of my body. Of the tentacles loosening a little, then a little more. Pain wracks through me, and I gulp in air, hear ragged, gasping sounds that might be me, might be Shweta. I can't tell.

"Kazem?" I cry. But I can't see him. Or Celena.

But I *can* see… I blink as my vision clears, until I see Shweta here, on the ground, collapsed against me. No, we're still bound together by Iralda's tentacles.

But that family has eased off me now, and that's good. That gives Red time to get here, until… until I can harness lunar energy, recharge my Beast.

"Shweta?" I try to pull her upward, try to get her to move, try to…

Oh Gods, what if she's…

But Shweta isn't dead. She's stirring now. Crying and shaking. Her tears are wet against my face.

I look up, and then I see the figures of Ysabelle, the Overlord Seer, and Lani. Iralda still hovers above. She grins at me, and the tentacle-bindings tighten.

Nausea pulls through me. "What have you done with Kazem?" I yell. "Where is he?"

Ysabelle laughs.

I scream again, but then the Overlord Seer is saying something. He's pointing at Iralda.

"Where *are* they?" he asks. "I thought you said they'd come back?"

Come back? I taste blood at the back of my mouth. Kazem's coming back? And Celena, too?

Lani whimpers. I look across at her. Her eyes are large, and there's rugged fear in them.

Then the tentacles binding Shweta and me pulse. It's an electric jolt caging my body, jagged and hard. I gasp, the air squeezed out of me in rhythmic pulses.

They're coming now, Iralda whispers.

"Please," Shweta begs.

"Kazem!" I cry.

Pain spirals down my spine as I look at Ysabelle's eyes. Look at how the glint in them gets brighter. She steps closer to me and Shweta, then she's leaning over me, so close I can see the pores in her skin, smell the sour tang of her breath.

"Kassandra Kachler," she says, and I hate the way she calls me Kassandra. I am *not* Kassandra. "You are finally going to get what you deserve." She cackles and claps her hands. The sound is sudden, makes me wince. "*Now!*"

Iralda shrieks an ear-piercing shriek. I feel the pain inside me intensify, somehow mingling with Iralda's shrieks. It's her pain, maybe, wracking through my body in waves. I fall forward. My face hits the ground. My nose cracks. Warmth and wetness spurt over my face.

I let out a cry, and I try to move, but there's something holding me down—no, not holding me. It's Shweta. I've pulled her back down with me. She's a heavy weight on my back—unconscious now? I don't know.

Air whips past me, and rushing sounds fill my ears, too heavy and warm and gloopy. Light flashes, and then the tentacles are whipped away, sharp like glass, edges slicing my skin. Blood bubbles down, across the ground—so much blood, everywhere—and I look up as another flash of light cleaves the sky.

Suddenly, the tendrils move. They move fast as Iralda yanks them away. I scream, my body spinning with the momentum. I try to grab hold of Shweta, protect her, but I can't get a grip.

I land in mud, face-up, staring at swirling darkness above. The wind picks up. Something roars. I fight to see the moon. Need to see it, but I can't.

Lani and the Overlord Seer raise their arms to the sky, palms upturned. Ysabelle's in between them, a hand on each of their shoulders—and there is light radiating from her hands. Light I don't understand— unless she's a Seer now, too.

Is she? Has she been all this time?

And I—I can't move. I look down at my body, but all I see is an ink-black sea of blood.

"Are you ready, Kassandra Kachler?" Ysabelle asks, her voice booming, echoing.

The sky moves.

The earth moves, rumbles. The ground shakes.

My head pounds, and I try to move, try to drag Shweta to the side even though I can't get my hands to work—but I have to get her away, somewhere, don't know where. We both just have to get away. We have to find Kazem and Celena, and we have to—

The chasm above the Overlord Seer, the inky hole in the sky, widens with a deafening reverberation. Lani shrieks, and then something swoops down. Something pale and misty and it grabs her, lifts her up.

Ysabelle doesn't do anything as her daughter is snatched into the rift above her. Another child taken, when perhaps the only one she wanted was Iralda.

The transaction has completed. Iralda's voice crawls through the night.

Completed? I gulp, and Lani's gone. And that was it—what Ysabelle wanted? Her people in exchange for her daughter? And she got her eldest daughter, in spirit form, to implement it.

But it was Lani—and she was a *child*.

I gulp, feeling her loss, feel it inside me, gnawing at flesh, and—

"Kacey! It's almost time!"

Caia-Lu's voice. I jolt, look up and—

I see it happen in slow motion. Shapes, plummeting. Figures. Not human. Spirits… but humanoid enough. Falling around me, hitting the ground with thuds, and then picking themselves up, laughing and cackling.

Arms and legs unfolding. Pale skin and dark tatters of clothes.

My mouth dries.

Every single clansman I murdered in the massacre is here, now.

They're all spirits. Spirits advancing toward me. Several of them lock gazes on me, and I *feel* their gazes. Feel the way they're tugging at my soul, trying to rip me apart.

I tear my gaze away, looking around. Red still isn't here. But he's coming, isn't he? He's going to help me.

We are hungry, the clansmen say.

I grapple at Shweta again, but she's not moving. Dead? I can't tell. My hands are too slick with blood, and they slip when I try to feel for a pulse. But the spirits aren't interested in her. Just me.

They're never interested in the dead.

Move!

I pull myself back, eyes streaming, every part of my body and soul screaming. I call on the Beast again, but there's nothing but his waves of exhaustion, and—

I said we are hungry! the spirits yell.

"Then feed," Ysabelle says. Her voice echoes around me. I cannot see her. "There's a whole batch of warm-blooded humans for you to feed on, too, hidden under the earth, only a few miles from here. They're

Kassandra's gift for you all. Her way of saying sorry."

My mouth dries "No!" I yell. "You can't…"

"I think you'll find we can do exactly as we want," Ysabelle says. "And we will—right after we've had our starter."

Our starter.

"Run, Kacey!" Caia-Lu screams.

But I cannot run. And I know it now. Red is not coming, and I cannot move as fifty-four sets of silver eyes turn to me. As fifty-four blood-red tongues flicker from gaping spirit-flesh. As fifty-four spirits feast their eyes on what their teeth are about to have.

Me.

FIFTY-THREE

THEY DESCEND LIKE CROWS. I scream, lift my arms above my head, look around. Cover. I need cover. But there's only low-lying grass.

"Please, no! don't hurt me!"

Don't hurt me, one of the spirits mocks, and somehow its voice tears chunks from my upper arms.

I run. Something tears across my back—muscle, clawed away. Cold water sprays over me, and I turn, see a spirit with its mouth gaping open, revealing thousands of gleaming teeth. I recoil—and as I do so, a jet of saliva flies from the spirit's mouth. Hits me across the face, stings. Stings and—

Oh Gods. The *pain.*

I clap my hands to my face, trying to rub the substance off. But it gets on my fingers—blisters welt up, bubbling, simmering. I scream, turning, more pain lassoing me, and Ysabelle yanks me to the left by the fingers of my hand. I fall, heavily, and spirits shriek. I try to pull my hand from Ysabelle's grip, but she's strong. Too strong.

"Feast, brave ones!" she yells.

More and more spirits. Clansmen.

Something large and heavy hits the side of my face. I taste blood and ash, and my nose—bleeding more, and—

Ysabelle grins as she cracks my fingers backward. I scream as they break, and her smile twists, more and more garish.

Something lands on my feet, crushing them and my ankles, and then a spirit's over my face, and I feel it feeding again—draining me, my soul lifting up toward it.

They are going to kill me.

I know it. I feel it.

"Beast!" I yell.

And my Beast stirs, he tries—he does, I feel him try. Feel the energy ripple away from him. He needs to recharge. He needs energy to do that, the lunar energy and—

Someone presses their nails into my eyes. Searing pain. White-hot. I shriek, trying to pull away, but whoever it is has a grip like a vise around my head, the rest of her fingers splayed.

"You're getting what you deserve." The Overlord Seer's voice. Harsh and raspy, and I feel more hands on my body. His?

But I can't concentrate on that. The nails in my eyes, they're digging deeper. A squelching sound, something slippery. Pain twisting inside me, behind my eyes. Something tearing. Hotness slipping over me.

"Kacey, for the Gods' sake, run!"

It's Caia-Lu's voice, again She's… still here? No, she can't be. She…

"Run!"

But I can't run. I can't feel my body. Is this what dying is like? Is this…

"No," a snarling voice says. Something cold hits my face. "You don't get out of it this easily."

My lungs burn, and everything is on fire. I can't breathe, my chest is heaving, and the world is spinning as I try to look—but there's a dark haze everywhere.

It's my vision. I bring my hands up to my eyes. The fingers with the sharp nails have gone.

I blink, but the dark haze doesn't go. Blood? Panic rises, and I wipe at my eyes, but the action's not doing anything. I can't see. I can't fucking see.

Just murky shapes. Light and dark and—

How am I going to see the moon, when it's there? When—

Pressure in my eyeballs. So much pressure, it—

I shriek as something bites my upper arm, feel gnashing teeth. I can't see the spirits. I can't see Ysabelle or the Overlord Seer.

Something opens up inside me—a sharp tug, and then there's something crashing. I don't know what it is, what—

Red screams, collapses, his eyes still in that murky transition between Enhanced and Untamed, and he's by buildings, concrete, limestone buildings—and I feel his Beast leaving. Far away, two women slumping against tree-trunks as others fuss around them; Elf—Keelie's brother!— moaning, head in his hands, feet thrashing.

"Hold on, Kacey," Caia-Lu shouts. "Hold on just a bit longer!"

Someone or something rips the skin off my right arm—and I know now that it's over. Because I'm not feeling the pain. I just feel it for what it is, my skin peeling back, like a banana skin being removed. The air feels cold against whatever rawness is under my skin. More blood, muscle, flesh? I don't know.

But I'm not in my body now. Not properly. The pain's mellowing.

I'm not breathing.

Cackles fill the air, the smell of burning. Fire and ash. I can taste blood, but I don't have a mouth or a tongue. I've got…nothing.

No one.

Red's not coming to help me. He's back at the town now, and—

—and I'm on my own.

Properly, truly.

I'm going to die.

My shoulders and chest slump.

"Let her go," a voice suddenly bellows.

My heart lifts—I still have a heart and it's lifting because he's here. *He* found me. Of course he would. He'd never leave me! All along there was only ever one man who'd help me. Who'd save me. I blink, trying to see him, but I can't. There's just haziness, or maybe I don't have eyes right now. Maybe…

"Well, well, well." Ysabelle's voice is deadly.

"Run!" I try to yell at Kazem, and then I'm turning my head—only I'm not. I don't have a body, and I don't think I'm actually making a noise.

"Let her go," Kazem screams. "Call off these spirits and let Kacey go."

"Or what?" Ysabelle is smirking; I can tell by the lilt in her voice.

"Or we'll kill you all," Kazem says.

"We? Boy, it's just you out here."

"Nah," Kazem says. "We're all here. We've got guns on you. All of you."

He's bluffing. He has to be. That's all I can think as I'm trying to find my way back to my body, wading through so much stickiness in the air. Haziness and blood and—

Too much.

It's all too much.

"Call off the spirits now!" Kazem's voice shakes. "Or we will kill."

"He's bluffing," the Overlord Seer says.

"He sure as hell ain't," says another voice, sickly sweet. Celena.

"Sort them out," Ysabelle says.

A flurry of movement—something swarming to my right. And I move that way too, to where Kazem has to be.

"Go!" I'm yelling at him, but I can't hear my words. Can't hear a thing, can't—

Kazem screams, a blood curdling sound that rips through me. And I see him, I hear him. Choking sounds, a gurgling.

"Kazem?" My voice echoes, and something warm and wet splashes over me. "Kazem, what's happening?" My heart pounds.

I scrabble forward, reaching for him. I slip on something, and my shoulder hits the ground and—

My hand, on him. Warm body shaking, trembling.

"Kacey!"

"Kazem! Kazem, what's happening?" I can't see again—it's the blood. It's in my eyes. It's stinging. "Are you okay? Are—"

Too much blood. I wipe at my eyes, and then above, something glimmers. My Beast senses it, and he's stirring. It's the moon. Visible? And—

Kazem's screams stop.

There is only silence. A sudden, heavy silence.

"Kazem?" My voice shakes.

Something falls onto my lap. Something heavy. My fingers wrap around it. Wet, slippery. This round thing… My nail catches something softer, and—and there's hair, soft, short hair.

My stomach twists, and I realize…realize what I am holding.

It's…

No.

The scream claws out of me.

My Beast surges up, furious.

But it is too late.

All I can do is cradle Kazem's decapitated head.

# FIFTY-FOUR

KAZEM IS DEAD.
Dead.
Dead.
Dead.
I scream, and the weight above me lightens, and I fight through the cloud. I send it away, and I find what I need, and I take.

I take and I take and I take, and I'm cradling him, and I am screaming and. I cannot let go. Cannot let *him* go.

My Kazem. *Gone.*

Iralda laughs, and I turn to her in a flash. I cannot see her, but she is there. She's right there, and it was her.

Her.

I rage, and my Beast rises, and moonlight shines down, and power, so much power floods me. I am screaming as the Beast erupts from me, as blood splatters, drenching all of us.

The clansmen spirits scream. Ysabelle shrieks.

I feel their pain, a wall of it pummeling toward me. A wall that my Beast and I vault over. A wall we destroy.

The moon fuels me, fuels us, fuels us all—all of us

with Beasts, I feel us *all*. We are connected. We are the same. Me and Elf and Red and Inga—Inga! From D'Elinous! I see her, see her with a beautiful dark-skinned Seer, another woman who wields a Beast. I see them all in my mind. I feel them.

I feel the power that we have, collectively. So, so many of us. So many of us with Beasts, waiting. Waiting for a moment—a moment that's coming. And I feel it. Feel it starting, the power shifting.

We are the Dangerous Ones. We are the ones people should fear, because the Beasts are something else entirely. Something that doesn't belong in this world. And I *feel* it, feel the displacement, and how my own Beast is calling for more—more power.

Power. It surges through me.

'Stop!" Ysabelle screams. "Stop, Kassandra, stop!"

Something sizzling, hissing. The acrid smell of burning flesh fills my nostrils, heat beats against me....

The Beast pours out of me, the invisible rope between him and me stretching, and I see their bodies burning, blood boiling as it bursts from eye sockets and noses and gurgling out of throats.

A clansman spirit collapses. Another is ripped apart. Screams and screams and more screams, and I am holding Kazem's head—but it's not his head. It's his *skull*. Flesh has dripping away, melting, a puddle of him on the ground.

An eye.

His eyeball. Looking at me. Detached and wrong and lost.

I scream in a way I've never screamed before. A way where I join with the Beast—and he's not a Beast, because he's a gift from my aunt—and I become him, and he is me. And there is no separation.

I roar, and Kazem's skull falls from my hands.

I snatch Ysabelle; my fingers are claws around her throat. Her skin is hot, wilting, peeling away in shreds. She is lighter than I thought she'd be. I slam her to the ground. I lean over her.

"Please, Kassandra, please." Her voice is little, a whisper. "We can stop this, we can—"

I laugh, the sound raucous. "Why would I want to stop this?" I squeeze her neck, and I watch how her eyeballs bulge. It reminds me of Kazem's lone one on the floor, and it just makes me angrier.

Makes me rage even more.

I squeeze, and I feel it. I feel the moment her soul leaves. A light fluttery sensation, followed by stillness. A bubble amid the raging world.

And then there's something stretching inside me, thinning, more and more—

Snap.

The sound, the feeling echoes through me, and I can no longer see—the Beast is inside me again, and my eyes… There's only pain where they should be, pain and pressure and something raw throbbing. My forehead, pain. My whole skull.

The Beast makes a strangled sound.

I scream and…

There's nothing…

I open one eye, but I cannot see. No pain though. I'm lying on my side. Something hard and rough, uncomfortable, beneath me. My hip hurts. I taste rust in my mouth.

It's dark, and I think time has passed.

I don't know where I am and I don't know if it's dark, or if I still have no vision. I blink, feel my lashes against my skin, sticky.

I squint and sit up—only I don't think I move.

I can't move.

I inhale, but there's a rasping sound. Something low and gritty. Something in my airway. My heart pounds, and everything in me tightens as I try to take another breath. As I try to move or do something. Anything.

But I cannot.

Is that a shape in the darkness? I squint. I don't know. I don't know if my eyes are working now. I can hear sounds, small sounds. A light whirring. A ticking, but then it is quiet. The spirits, gone?

They are all dead, the Beast says, *and that is enough.*

Yes. I nod. That is enough.

It's enough, it's enough. It's enough.

My head gets heavier.

Fear rises. *I'm* dying. This is what dying feels like, and it comes at me with certainty. There's nothing inside me that argues. The Beast is here, active but trapped, immobile. He doesn't say anything.

He doesn't need to.

I struggle again to breathe. The rasping sound grates my ears again, and I feel the pain there specifically, in my ears. Like a long, thin needle has been forced through my ear canals, connecting them together, piercing my brain.

I am speared.

We both are, me and the Beast. And I am scared. Terror ramps through me. There's no one to say the Spirit Releasing Words. No one who knows I'm dying.

I'm going to get stuck. I'm going to be a spirit, like the clansmen. Lost. Caught here. Trapped in worlds, in pain—and I feel it, the pain they felt, echoes of it carved into this world, being absorbed by my body, my soul.

I feel it all, because it's a promise. Never-ending pain. Just what Ysabelle wanted for me.

Sobs wrack up inside me, but I can't get them out. I cannot move. Cannot blink.

I'm stuck here… stuck here and…

It's okay. Kazem's voice.

I jolt. I feel his warmth, warmth that radiates toward me.

He's here, and I *feel* him, I sense him, and I'm reaching

for him—reaching and I'm free, not in my body, not in
this prison of pain, held back, but I'm *free*.
   I rise with him and I feel his arms in mind.
   It's not far, he says. *Come on. We'll go together.*

SOMEONE IS BRUSHING MY HAIR. Long sweeps, gentle. Soft. Silk sweeps over me. Delicate touches.

"It's okay, neshama sheli. It's all okay now."

I'm drifting, but every stroke on my hair feels better, stronger, and I focus on that. Feeling starts to come back, and I'm getting more solid. Flesh filling in, bones and muscles. I feel it, feel it like my body is constructing, building up.

"Don't worry, my dear. It's all okay now."

The voice is louder.

It's a voice I know. I open my mouth, and I feel my tongue and my lips and my teeth. I have a mouth and tongue and lips and teeth. And a throat and lungs, and I'm breathing—I'm breathing.

"Caia-Lu?" My voice wobbles, and I don't think I'm speaking properly—the sounds are distorted and not right, but it's my voice and I am speaking

"It's okay. I am here." Her voice doesn't echo or shimmer or sound distorted. It's… it's normal. "Kacey, neshama sheli, I am so very proud of you, girl."

I feel arms around me, a softness. Reassurance. I smell something light and floral but spicy.

"Your job is over now. You did so well."

I try to look up at her, and I feel my eyes. I know I have eyes, and I'm opening them. Eyelids moving, lashes moving. But I still can't see. There's nothing. Just… grayness.

"I'm so proud of you," Caria-Lu whispers. Her voice chokes. "So, so proud."

I have hands, and I move them. Her hand is suddenly in my left, and I think I'm trying to sit up, but dizziness pulls at me. And with my right, I'm touching my face, my eyes. My skin feels too smooth, shiny, but it doesn't feel like skin.

And I press at my eye, and I think I'm touching my eyeball, but I can't feel it like I should be able to.

"Why can't I see?" I whisper.

"Oh, duvshanit. Sometimes, the journey takes longer for everything to settle. But you are here, and you transferred here at the exact moment we needed your Rijikarii, to stabilize *this* world with the mortal world. This was the moment I have been waiting for. Our Rijikarii is setting everything up as it should be. You did so well."

I'm… I'm dead?

I'm actually dead.

"Where's Kazem?" I ask. "He died and…" I choke. "Then I was with him. We were together and… Did he get here?"

What if he's trapped? What if he's become a spirit— if that's what happens to the Untamed who don't make it here? All the clansmen…

"He is still on his way," Caia-Lu says. "Your Rijikarii made your journey quicker, but your souls are connected. He's following your trail. And his brother is guiding him, too. One of our Seers, also. He'll get here. Don't worry. Come, there are so many people waiting to see you."

"People?"

"Your mother and father. Keelie, Shweta, Clive, a very nice girl called Jaqueline…"

Caia-Lu names more and more people, but all I can concentrate on are my mother and father. The parents I can't remember. I wonder if they'll recognize me, if maybe part of me—my heart, my soul—will recognize them.

If I'll feel anything. And part of me is scared that I won't. Scared the Beast and everything I went through has carved out all feeling. I'm an empty husk.

"Shall we go and see them?" Caia-Lu asks.

"Is...is this it then?" I ask. "My...life?" I'm really *dead*. I can still feel the Beast inside me. Feel him in a different way now though.

"Oh, neshama sheli. Life is never over. It changes and transitions. Your life is here now, with us."

"But the..." My voice cracks. "The real world—"

"This is as much a real world as the mortal world. We are just in a different dimension."

I breathe out hard. "So, we're safe? There's no war happening here—no Enhanced?"

She covers my hand with her own. "There's no war against the Enhanced here, my darling. There's nothing more you have to do in that fight."

"It doesn't feel right," I say. "Being here now. No way back. Just..."

"We can watch it play out," Caia-Lu says.

"But observing it..." I shrug. "That just feels *flat*."

"It always feels like that to those who aren't taking part in any events or actions," she says. "But this is what it's like for many of us, after we have done our jobs. And you did yours. You kept the Rijikarii levels balanced, when they needed to be. You ended the time loop. You've stabilized the mortal world so the Seventh One can win the war."

"And she will?" I ask.

"The Seventh One has everything she needs to play her part." Her voice tightens a little. "Your part is done. You arrived here exactly when you were supposed to."

I nod, but there's a lump in my throat. I don't know

if I'm close to crying. I just can't tell. Everything seems so detached from me, even my body.

"You've done enough. Now it's your time to rest. Come on, yikiri, let's join the others."

Caia-Lu leads me out of the room, through a creaking door, and into a bright outside space—the change in light sparks through my eyelids. Caia-Lu narrates as we go, describing the garden we are in, the dark green bushes with red buds that line the path, the small huts that are visible from here.

We walk over small, hard stones, and then across something softer, warmer. Sand.

"There's a step here," Caia-Lu guides, and then we're going inside a hut. Inside, there's a lot that hits me all at once. Voices—so many, rugged and dark and light and sweet and young and old. A baby crying and a child whining. So many smells brush over me—something sweet, and the tangy smell of spices, and the richness of cooking meat.

"We think it's going to happen, yes," a woman is saying.

"What is this, Katya?" Caia-Lu asks. Hearing her voice makes me feel better, and I stand close to her, her arm still in mine.

The woman—Katya—has a soft voice. "I can feel the end is coming," she says. "The end of the war. Everything is as it should be, leading to this change. But the Seers will lose their powers. That is what we are discussing."

"I feel it too," another voice says. "But Amos does not. Do you?"

I hear Caia-Lu's intake of breath, and then she says, "I sense a time is coming of great change, but it will be Seven Sarr who saves us all."

"But what about your powers as a Seer?" Katya asks. "Do you feel it too? Like there is an end in sight for them? Mine are not renewing as quickly as they did."

Caia-Lu pauses, and I get the distinct feeling she's looking at me.

"If our powers are to cease, it is the way of the worlds. And, yes, I do sense it."

"We will be defenseless," someone says.

"Not defenseless. We can still fight." I think that's Keelie. I think I recognize her voice.

Caia-Lu clears her throat. "If we lose Seer powers, then it is because there are no Enhanced Ones. It is a good sign. But we will not lose our Rijikarii. Our energies are not like Seer powers that are bestowed upon individuals. These energies become part of us, and they grow in our souls, often from before birth. Great Guardians cannot be divided into energy and human. We work as one. Our Rijikarii will always remain with us. Seers may not be needed after the end of the war, but Guardians will be. Rijikarii is there to protect."

"And kill." Keelie, again.

There's a low grumbling voice. "So, there is still going to be a danger. A reason it's needed?"

"When there is mankind, there is the potential for danger. We are our own downfall. We create tension, conflict, war. We always have done, we always will." Caia-Lu breathes deeply and then hums. "Now, Kacey, neshama sheli, we will see your parents."

Caia-Lu guides me forward.

The crying baby gets louder, and I'm blinking, trying to see, when Caia-Lu stops.

"She still has no sight," Caia-Lu says, but then I'm engulfed.

Warm arms, and comfort. Soft touches to my face, firm embraces. Hands smoothing my hair back. Shaking figures. Soft sobs and cries, heavier breaths.

"My baby, my baby," a woman's voice. My mother—I feel it. Feel her voice, the connection to me.

A firmer hand on my arm, then I'm pulled in for a hug by my father—I know it is him and—

He's holding a baby. I freeze. A baby. An actual baby.

"Kacey, my darling. My precious… oh, I can't believe it, I… We're altogether, reunited and—"

"Meet your sister."

Sister.

"Eight days old and…"

Their words whizz over me, but I stumble, finding myself stepping back.

"It's okay," Caia-Lu says, her voice warmth, grounding. "This is a miracle," she says to me. "The first baby born here. And it is proof."

"It means things are getting better," the woman—my mother—says. "It means this world is adapting for life."

"Shortly, here," Caia-Lu says, "we will be living again. It will be different, not as we know it." She lets out a sigh. "Oh, I thought for so long that Rijikarii was a curse—a curse I unleashed on the world. But it's not a curse. It's an adaption, a protective mechanism. And I believe it formed ready for what will come."

"Well, what will come?" I ask. I let out a long breath. My lungs feel funny. The Beast stirs a little, but he's mine—I feel it. He's part of me. Inseparable.

"A new world," Caia-Lu says. "*This* New World. New possibilities. And those who wield Rijikarii will be the protectors."

"Causing more deaths?" Keelie asks.

"No. We'll be the Guardians."

"He's here now," a male voice says. It's a voice that sounds like Kazem's, but different. His…his brother, Yusef.

I turn, and everything stops.

I do not see Kazem, but I sense him.

And I feel complete, feel the last parts of me filling in.

Mumbled sounds filter through to me, but my heart's pounding. I hear rustling, like carrier bags, and then we're embracing.

My Kazem. I breathe him in. And I know. It'll be okay. Even if I can't see for a while, or at all, I'll be okay. Because we're safe now, and we're together.

THE END

AUTHOR NOTE

The Threat of the Hunt is one of the hardest books I've ever written. I struggled and struggled with this one—not only was I writing through numerous lockdowns, illness, and difficult circumstances, but I also had this huge question pounding through my brain at all times: how do you write the last book in a trilogy of loosely connecting standalones, which is also the last book set in a world you've been writing in for the last twelve years, giving everything you need to give to this story, while also keeping the door open in case you want to write more? I don't like goodbyes, and I don't like to say never.

I don't know if I will write more, that's the truth. At least, not for Kacey. Her story is over. Just as Keelie's and Inga's are. And if you've read the original four Untamed books, you'll also know how Seven's story also finishes. You'll see how their stories all interconnect and inform each other. And leaving the world at this point, where Kacey has solved the problem of the time-loop, unraveled mysteries, and finally met her parents again seems like a good place to leave, even though in Kacey's timeline, the war's end is still about to happen. I thought about coinciding the end of Kacey's story with the end of the war, but it didn't feel right. When I tried to do it, it felt forced. I was stretching Kacey's story on to reach this point that didn't inform her story arc. And I've always prioritized being true to my characters and their own individual stories.

I've always been fascinated by the New World in these books, and so this is why I've also chosen to leave the story at this point. The end of Kacey's story ties into the end of Seven's, and readers of those books will know the significance that the New World has (and will have for Kacey, in just a few weeks, when the War of Humanity ends). And so this is where I'm leaving the story for now—but we know that Kacey and Inga and Keelie (along with all the other Dangerous Ones) will have a very important role, after the war, as the Guardians of the New World.

So, it's not a permanent goodbye that I'm saying to this universe. More of a "I might see you again." Because exciting and dangerous shenanigans could very well happen in the New World too—but that would be a whole other interconnected series that I'd need to write…

We'll just have to wait and see.

ACKNOWLEDGEMENTS

There are so many people to thank with this book. Firstly, to Shara Cooper and Paul Fisher, who read an early draft of the prologue so many years ago, thank you for your feedback. Back then, I thought this story would turn out so differently, and for the most part, it has—but the prologue stood the test of time and largely remained unchanged, even when so many other things did.

Equally—but more recently—a big thank-you goes to Lisa Amowitz for helping greatly with shaping the first four chapters and helping me think critically about the whole book's structure.

To my beta-readers: Maria Sinclair, Sarah Anderson, and Kitty Ann Cavill, thank you so much.

Michelle Dunbar, I can't believe how many books you've been my editor for now. Thank you so much for all your work—and all your patience with this one when I kept telling you I was rewriting the ending yet again and needed more time to do it! I appreciate you so much. You're amazing.

Molly Phipps, once again you've blown me away with the amazing cover and design work. Your work is just phenomenal.

To my family: Mum, Dad, Sam, and Gill, and to my husband Michael: thank you for everything. I can't thank you enough.

And, to my readers: whether this is your first book from me you've read, or the twentieth (I had to count them all then!), thank you for sharing this journey with me.

ABOUT THE AUTHOR

MADELINE DYER (she/her) is a novelist, anthologist, poet, and literary academic, drawn to dark and monstrous stories. Her debut anthology *Being Ace* (Page Street YA, 2023) received a starred review from *School Library Journal* and was named a 2024 Lammy Award Finalist at the Lambda Literary Awards, commemorating "outstanding LGBTQ+ literature from 2023." Her debut novel *Untamed* (Prizm Books, 2015) also won the 2015 SIBA award for Best Dystopian Novel.

Madeline also writes romance and light-hearted contemporary fiction as Elin Annalise.

She is the author of twenty-two books.